BALLAD'S END

Cover Design by Lesia T.

Map by Thiago Liuth

ISBN (paperback): 979-8-9895166-6-7

ISBN (ebook): 979-8-9895166-5-0

I dedicate this book to the many friends and family who have supported me on this journey. Sami, Kira, Atlas, Francisco, Moona, Dylan, Ori, Terry, and everyone else who has touched my life since I began writing—You are living proof that friends are truly the family one chooses in life.

N
E
S
W
Misport
Shivershill
Faith Hollow
Hommire
Shineford
Runegarde
Whistlevale
Thorncrest
Galemore
Ballad's End
Granide
Featherbrook
Duskmarsh
Glimmerdale
Havenfall
Everstill

Chapter I

Nervousness was an emotion that brought with it a slew of uncomfortable sensations. A spine-tingling chill digging into the very marrow of one's bones. Palpitations that made it feel as though a person's chest would explode outward as their heart scrambled desperately to escape. The tingle of tiny pinpricks making their way down the limbs until festering in the tips of one's fingers and toes. It was a wholly awkward and irritating emotion, able to bring even the most certain and confident individuals to their knees.

It was also an emotion Kai Travaldi found himself experiencing more than he ever wished to over the past year. Even the mane of ebony fur covering his chest did little to block the frigid chill of unease crackling through his body. His fingers fiddled with the thin yellow ribbon tied around his right wrist. The soft lace gave him a measure of peace, giving him a focus as he took slow, deep breaths.

Considering the multiple scars lining his body, one would assume his nervousness stemmed from the recent trauma of battle he and his friends experienced over the course of the Faumen War, as many were calling it. However, that assumption would be incorrect. It wasn't a fear of war leaving both his cat-like tails stiffer than iron ingots or his triangular ears pressed flat against his scalp.

No, he was terrified of what awaited through the door in front of him and his two companions. It was a simplistic door compared to others found within Livoria's Royal Palace, but it contained a battle more daunting than any he'd faced so far.

Slender fingers wrapped around his hand, grasping it tight. "After all we've been through," the young, bronze-skinned woman at his side said, "you're afraid of an old man?"

A brief chuckle escaped his lips. "It's not the old man that scares me, Ora," he replied. "It's…the uncertainty. I know we've got a good chance at getting the approval we need to make everything official, but with everything that's happened, I can't help but wonder what our next steps will be if things go sideways."

Orelia raised a single eyebrow, her ocean blue eyes pinning him in place with an amused glance. Her long, fin-like ears fluttered. "This isn't like you. Are you saying you'd roll over if we somehow don't get approval from the church for your crazy plan?" She smoothed out the wrinkles in her temple vestments, a garment worn only by ordained clerics of the Windbringer church, with her free hand.

"Now I never said that," Kai answered with a smug grin. "I've already got a backup plan in place. Fusette agreed to perform the official ceremony herself if this meeting doesn't turn out like we expect."

A muffled snicker came from the woman on Kai's other side, an Aerivolk woman dressed in a brown homespun vest with brilliant yellow feathers making up the wings sprouting from her arms. A red lace ribbon like Kai's was tied around her left wrist. "Would she even be allowed to do officiate a marriage ceremony?" she asked.

"Maple, she's the Grand Duchess. Unless the Livorian Codex expressly forbids it, I reckon Fusette can do whatever she damn well pleases."

"Fair point."

"As much as I enjoy bantering with you both," said Orelia, "we do have something important we need approved. Focus."

A surge of warmth filled Kai's chest as he thought about the Vesikoi priestess. He couldn't help but admire the confidence she exuded; it was one of her finer qualities he adored. "Of course. Guess it's time." Raising his hand to the door in a sedate, controlled manner, Kai rapped his knuckles against the wood three times.

"Come in," a withered voice answered from within.

Clenching his jaw, Kai pulled the door open and allowed the two ladies to enter first. His eyes darted to both sides, verifying the hall's emptiness before ducking inside and easing the door shut behind him.

The room itself was warm and inviting. The stone tiles were freshly cleaned and sparkled in the summer sun peeking through the windows. Three large, plush chairs sat in a line, facing a large sturdy desk made of black oak. The desk was littered with many documents and trinkets. A small stone statuette of Vadako the Maiden, the Wind Saint of Generosity, stood at the left corner, turned so the figure's eyes faced both the chairs in front of the desk and the one behind it.

Sitting in the latter chair was a distinguished older human in intricate vestments, along with a scarlet stole encircling his neck which was a near match for the deep red of Kai's apothecary robes. A pair of round spectacles lay perched on his nose and his brown eyes were full of vigor that belied the deep wrinkles in his face.

Taking his place in front of the center chair, Kai helped the girls sit first before bowing. "A pleasant morning to you, Archbishop Jovanni. We appreciate you taking time from your duties to meet with us."

The old priest chuckled. "I always have time to spare for any children of the winds who seek help and guidance. You know this, Kai. Or shall I call you Gravebane?"

Kai shivered at the mention of his *other* name. "Kai is fine, Your Excellency. This meeting has nothing to do with my official Exarch duties, as I'm sure you're aware."

"Of course. Though I'll admit the idea of trying to pass off marriage as an 'official duty' is as amusing as it is ridiculous, even for this old goat."

Jovanni's comment produced titters from the women. "We're still grateful for your time," said Maple, "but perhaps we should get down to business. The longer we take, the more likely we are to be discovered by meddlers."

"Indeed. I can obviously see, Lady Maple, that Kai and you are already wed. Am I correct in assuming Sister Orelia was the one to officiate your vows?"

Orelia's bronze cheeks flushed a dusky sienna. "Yes, Your Excellency."

The priest emitted a loud burst of laughter. "Now, now. No need to be ashamed. I'm quite proud of you for sticking to your beliefs, even if those duffers in the Quorum would disagree with your decision. But then again, we're not here for that. We're here to discuss *your* situation."

Kai kept his mouth shut, though his eyes couldn't help but seek out Orelia on his left side. He gave her a gentle smile, his hand reaching out to grasp hers with a firm squeeze. Her palm was slick with sweat, prompting him to run his fingertips along the skin in a circular motion.

"You youngsters never fail to impress me," said Jovanni. The trio's eyes turned to see the bishop staring back with a wide, toothy grin. "This is proof not everything is black and white when it comes to concepts like love and faith. There is grey and color everywhere we look. Seeing the three of you fills this old heart with hope for the future."

"Thank you, Your Excellency," Kai replied.

"Regarding the official nonsense, I must confess the four most moderate members of the Quorum were made aware of your request and have still made a right stink about it, as you can imagine. Therefore, to soothe their fragile egos and keep the knowledge of your situation from the Quorum's more *traditional* members, I'm afraid concessions must be made on your side for us to provide a sort of legitimacy to your situation."

An irritated rumble came from Kai's chest. "I already suspected this would be the case. What concessions are they seeking? Am I to relinquish my Brand?" The idea of giving up his Exarch membership was vexing, as it gave him protections most Norzen could only dream of having.

But if he needed to do so in order to enjoy a peaceful life with Maple and Orelia at his side, he'd gladly rip the watch signifying his status from his robe pocket and pitch it into the Great Ardei River without a second thought.

"By the winds, no! I'll confess, it *was* their initial demand, until Her Grace put paid to that. I believe her exact words were, 'The next one to suggest such a fool idea will find themselves tied to a wiroch by their baubles and dragged over the Coliseum arena.'"

The trio erupted into laughter at Jovanni's words, the women leaning on Kai's shoulders as tears poured from their eyes. If there was one thing the Grand Duchess could be counted on, it was speaking her mind, no matter the situation.

"However," the Archbishop continued, causing the three to compose themselves, "it doesn't change the requirement for something to be given. After much deliberation, it was decided that, to separate yourselves from the church as much as possible short of full excommunication, Sister Orelia must surrender her priestess ordination."

Kai's breath hitched while Maple's hands flew to her mouth.

"In addition, it is likely none of you will be permitted to attend services unless changes are made to the church's core bylaws regarding intertribal relations. I know this is a difficult decision to consid—"

A sharp clang pierced Kai's ears, drawing his scrutiny to Jovanni's desk. Orelia's hand was splayed out on top, rising to reveal the lace choker from her neck and the circular brass emblem identifying her as a priestess which had been clasped to her vestment. They were soon covered by the gold stole Orelia wore when she officiated his marriage to Maple.

The Archbishop's eyes lifted and met Orelia's piercing stare. "You are that certain in your decision?" Jovanni inquired.

"With all due respect, Your Excellency, I have never been surer of anything in my life," Orelia answered. Her gaze was unwavering as she returned to her seat and clutched Kai's hand in a firm grip. "If I'm being honest, my primary reason for joining the clergy was only to defy my father's overbearing wishes. I am grateful for everything I learned while serving as a sister of the winds, but I refuse to give up what I have with these two for anything. Just like the other ladies in our party, Maple is my sister in all but blood, and Kai is the man I love beyond a shadow of a doubt."

Leaning back in his chair, Jovanni steepled his fingers together and regarded Orelia with an unblinking stare.

Kai's muscles tensed, wondering how the older man would respond to his partner's admission. He knew Orelia's relationship with her father was strained, but her statement made him wonder how their meeting with the Galstan admiral would go if the two got into a heated confrontation.

What he wasn't expecting was for Jovanni to burst into a full-bellied laugh. The bishop's head was pitched back with eyes closed as he crowed with mirth. The trio shared uneasy glances as they waited for Jovanni to calm down.

"I suppose this answers many of my remaining questions, though I still have one. Kai," said the priest as his breathing calmed, eyes swiveling to land on the Norzen, "are you prepared for the questions that will no doubt follow you? No faumen of your rank or reputation has taken an intertribal spouse in all of Livorian history. Not only have you done this, but you now plan to take a *second* wife not of your tribe. How do you intend to respond to the vitriol that will obviously accompany your decision?"

Rising to his feet, Kai slammed both palms on the desk and gave Jovanni a hardened gaze. "Archbishop, I have allowed fear and doubt to control me for much of my life. Even before the war started, I was afraid to speak my mind and did my best to avoid serious confrontation. No more. This war is driven by hatred and distrust, which I intend to fight with all I have. These two have given me love where I believed I didn't deserve it, and I will be forever grateful to them for it. Should anyone threaten their safety or happiness, I'll gladly charge the five voids of Nulyma to protect them."

The two men stared at each other without blinking. The tension in Kai's body eased up as he felt his partners' hands resting on his shoulders in silent support.

The Archbishop gave a short chuckle and nodded. "Then I've heard all I need to. The affection you all share is as clear as a summer day. With the evidence Lady Fusette presented regarding intertribal mixbloods like Ambroz, I see no reason to deny your request. As leader of the Order of the Windbringers, I shall permit you, Kai Travaldi, to take Orelia Basner as your bride."

Emitting a gleeful squeal, Orelia threw her hands around Kai's waist and buried her face in his mane. "Oh, thank you, Your Excellency!" she cried.

"As I said, seeing you three fills me with hope that love such as yours can overcome the hatred preached by the Liberators and their allies. In fact, I shall officiate your hand fasting myself once we have finished the necessary preparations."

Kai clapped his hands together and bowed low. The women followed suit with wide grins adorning their faces. "Many thanks, Archbishop. We won't take up any more of your time. We have other people to meet and our own preparations to attend."

"I can imagine. May the winds bless your path, young ones."

After leaving the Archbishop's office, the trio wandered the palace halls in search of the rest of their crew, among several others.

Since the party's return scant days ago after the disastrous Battle of Havenfall, the fields outside Whistlevale's walls bustled with activity. In addition to the Hunter Corps, driven out of Havenfall by the Liberation Army, the fields also hosted the allied fleet from Galstein's Holy Navy.

It would take some time to organize the Royalist response, a fact which stuck in the Grand Duchess' craw. Until then, the fields would be dotted with pinpricks of light from the groups' campfires.

"There you are!" a melodious voice rang out from down the hall. Kai's eyes flickered up to see Fusette marching towards them at a hurried pace.

The young duchess kept a regal demeanor, despite the obvious wrinkles of concern at the edges of her eyes. Her chartreuse robes billowed behind her, a silver shawl and veil covering her head. It was easy to see the toll the war was taking on her, as lines of grey were beginning to show in the ebony hair poking from beneath her shawl. However, Kai would be the first to admit she handled the monarchy's burden with a quiet dignity he would be hard pressed to match.

"Is everything alright, Fusette?" Kai asked, offering a quick bow. Maple and Orelia copied the gesture before rushing forward and embracing the monarch.

"I knew your interview with Jovanni was today, but I forgot the time! I'm so sorry I missed it. Did everything go as we hoped?"

Kai's lips curved into a grin as he nodded, sending Fusette into cheers as she returned the girls' hug. "We escaped in better shape than I was expecting. Orelia had to surrender her ordination and we're not welcome in services any longer, but the Archbishop offered to officiate the ceremony when we're ready."

Fusette rolled her eyes and thumped Kai behind the head. "Oh pish, you'll always be welcome at service here in the palace. Anyone who says otherwise shall answer to me." Turning to the girls, she glanced around the hallway before removing her shawl to reveal a pair of triangular ears identical to Kai's. "By the winds, I hate wearing this thing in the heat! I trust you two can keep my little cousin in line? He can be a bit of a dipwit, as I'm sure you know," Fusette inquired, waggling her eyebrows.

Clamping a hand over her mouth, Maple snickered while nodding. "I think we can handle Kai," she replied.

"He may be a dipwit," Orelia added, "but he's *our* dipwit."

"Oi! I'm standing right here, you know," Kai complained. His cheeks flushed red as his partners pressed themselves against his sides and gave him a pair of saucy smiles.

"We know," Maple whispered, "but you love us anyway."

Tilting his head back to stare at the ivory ceiling, Kai's chest rumbled with a deep purr while holding them close. "Of course. I don't know how I got so lucky."

"I hope you three don't plan on rutting in the middle of my hallway," Fusette teased. "Especially since we'll be receiving some important guests in the near future."

"Guests?" Kai asked.

"While you were in Havenfall, I sent out a call convening the Five Realms Council to discuss the ramifications of this war and Corlati's potential involvement. All four leaders accepted and are on their way to Whistlevale as we speak. Not that President Harmod has much choice in the matter, given the allegations facing him."

Kai paled. If his memories were correct, the last time the Council came together was back in AR 954, during the rule of Nessa Ardei, Fusette's great-grandmother. That meeting was infamous for the resulting riot which sparked the Fifty-Years War between Galstein and Corlati. It wasn't until Orelia's father, Fleet Admiral Ottoten Basner—who was a young commander at the time—achieved a series of decisive victories deep in Corlati territory that a peace treaty was finally forged in 1004.

"The Five Realms Council? How long until they arrive?"

"I believe they will be here sometime in early Regemond. Until then, we simply must contain the Liberation Army and prevent them from ransacking any more cities. Admiral Larimanz has assured me he and the Royal Navy are up to the task now with their recent preparations to deal with the enemy's advanced weaponry, though he admits the Liberators have proven themselves a slippery lot to track down."

Fusette's words filled Kai with a sense of ease. After what happened at Havenfall, he knew Larimanz, a fellow Exarch known by his Brand Waveweaver, would be chomping at the bit to pay the Liberators back ten-fold for the devastation they caused.

Orelia raised a hesitant hand. "Milady, I hope you warned them about what we heard back at Havenfall," she said.

"Not to worry, Orelia. The moment you lot told me of Hakan's plan to take advantage of the chaos, I sent the hawks out to warn them. Everyone has assured me they're prepared for any potential uprisings."

Kai released a heavy sigh. "That's a relief. Is there anything you need us to do while we await the Council's arrival?"

"As much as it pains me to say it, Kai, you and your party will need to train hard. Once the Council convenes, there will be changes coming, and I suspect elements within the government will try to prevent them by any means necessary."

The apothecary's eyes hardened, a hand twitching towards the flanged mace tied to his hip. "I've already lost one member of my family to this senseless war," he declared. "I won't lose another."

His body tensed when Fusette pulled him into a tender embrace. "I know, Kai. We may not have learned about our relation until recently but just knowing I'm not alone has given me strength. And what's better, our family is growing." The duchess' eyes spun towards Maple and Orelia, glistening with tears.

The two ladies nodded. "We're behind you every step of the way," said Maple.

"Thank you. Now, let us focus on happier thoughts. After all, we've got a handfasting to plan!"

Kai bit back a groan as Fusette dragged his giggling partners down the hall, likely towards her personal chambers. Whatever those three had planned for the ceremony, he knew it would be impressive.

Now he just had to avoid Orelia's father until Kai could face him with the former priestess at his side. He wasn't afraid to admit the grizzled admiral cut an imposing figure but Ottoten Basner, for all his accolades, had nothing on his feisty daughter.

Orelia was downright terrifying when she had her mind set on something.

Chapter II

A tremor of unease wracked Kai's body while wandering the gardens on the palace rooftop. The past few days since his talk with the Archbishop had been exhausting. In his desire to follow Fusette's orders, Kai spoke with each of his friends alone to discuss their preparation for the upcoming Five Realms Council.

In the almost three hundred years since Livoria's formation, the Council had only been convened four times before now. What's more, this would be the first meeting to take place in Livoria itself. Kai already knew the pomp and ceremony involved in such an occasion was going to give him a headache. At least training would be a productive use of time to avoid having to help with the preparations, and he already knew what he needed to focus on.

Kai bit back a swear the moment the thought crossed his mind. He really needed to stop hanging out with Morgan at the meadhouse during his off time. The sellsword's lackadaisical attitude was beginning to rub off on him.

"Gravebane!" a deep, commanding voice rang out from behind him. Kai winced, recognizing the voice from yesterday's strategy meeting Fusette insisted he attend. While he knew this confrontation was coming, he didn't like the idea of facing it alone.

Guess I don't have much choice, he thought while turning around.

Stomping towards him in full military regalia and brandishing a steel-headed spear was Ottoten Basner. Despite seeing the older man waving a weapon on the palace grounds, Kai refused to reach for his mace; Saredi, the Lord Chamberlain, would throttle him if he did.

"Good morning, Admiral," the apothecary greeted, offering a contrite bow of respect. Ottoten's spearhead glinted in the sunlight, forcing Kai to contract his pupils. "Is everything alright? You seem rather distressed."

"You know damn well what the problem is," Ottoten snapped, his piercing eyes narrowed. "It was concerning enough to hear from Lady Fusette about my daughter's attachment to you. But after seeing the proof of it myself yesterday, I can't hold my tongue any longer. What's more, I heard you're planning to take Orelia's hand in marriage. Give me one good reason why I shouldn't skewer you where you stand!"

Shifting his gaze back and forth and seeing no one else in the garden, Kai straightened his posture and met the officer's glare with unrelenting determination. "With all due respect, sir, I can think of several good reasons why that would be a bad idea. However, it was never my intent to disrespect you in asking Orelia to marry me."

Ottoten's eyes locked onto the ribbon on Kai's wrist. "It's not just the disrespect, boy. You've already spat on the church's precepts in taking an Aerivolk for a wife, knowing it's forbidden. I don't care how fond Her Grace is of you; what matters is the scandal of my half-Vesikoi daughter marrying a Norzen. I won't allow it!"

"Have you bothered asking Orelia her feelings on the matter?"

"Her rebellious nature has gone on long enough!" Ottoten roared. "It doesn't matter a lick what she feels, it's forbidden for a reason and I won't have my only daughter tie herself down to someone who can't possibly love her the way she needs."

A faint red haze shimmered around the edges of Kai's vision. His eyes pinched together as he stepped toward the admiral with a growl. "Sir, you may insult me however you wish," he whispered. "I've put up with it my entire life and I doubt it will much change. However, don't you fucking *dare* make assumptions about my feelings. Orelia is one of the kindest, most honorable people I've ever known. I'll be honest, I don't fully feel worthy of your daughter with how amazing she is. It doesn't change the fact I love her and want to give her the happy, peaceful life she deserves."

Ottoten snarled and pressed the tip of his spear against Kai's cheek, hard enough to draw a thin line of blood. "How can you possibly give her a peaceful life when you two being together is a scandal worthy of the newsletters? No, Orelia is better off returning with me after the war where she can be matched to someone more appropriate."

"You can't possibly think she'll agree to such an idea. Isn't that heavy-handed approach why she left Galstein in the first place?"

A loud thwack rang out when Ottoten slammed a meaty fist into Kai's mouth, sending him sprawling back. "It's not up for debate. I'm her father and by the winds, she will do as she's told for once in her life!"

Spitting a glob of blood and saliva onto the ground, Kai eased himself into a kneeling position. Looking up, he felt his lips curve into a smirk. "I wonder if you know Orelia as much as you think you do. So you plan to drag her back to Galstein, no matter if she wants to stay?"

"Yes, even if I have to carry her back kicking and screaming the entire way."

"Good. You can tell her yourself, then, because she's right behind you and looks a bit brassed off." It took every ounce of will Kai had to not laugh at the sunken expression on Ottoten's face.

"Wait, what...?"

Before the admiral could turn, a brown blur flew at him from the side, followed by the audible crack of a wooden staff smashing into his jaw. Kai flinched back with a hiss, seeing Ottoten taken off his feet by the force of the blow.

Pushing himself back up, Kai felt the familiar chill of Orelia's skin as she cradled his cheek with one hand as the other stroked his mane. His eyes swept over her figure, widening at the sight of her new attire.

Instead of the cream vestment he was so used to, Orelia now wore a sleeveless yellow shirt drawn snug against her slender frame. He noticed a pair of oval holes cut into the sides to expose her gills. Gone was the flowing skirt that rippled like water as she walked, replaced by leather trousers with a wide green sash around her waist. A pair of heavy steel bracers lined with fur covered her forearms, their upper sides extending to the knuckles.

"Are you hurt, sweetheart?" she asked in a soothing murmur. A finger wiped away the blood from the corner of his mouth, her eyes searching for other injuries.

Kai winced when her finger prodded his bruised lip. "I'll be fine, Ora. You know I've taken worse hits."

The Vesikoi's eyes furrowed. "That doesn't mean you have to take it." Turning her head, Orelia glowered at her father as he stumbled to his feet. She marched forward and grabbed the admiral by his cropped hair, hauling him up. Once he was standing, she shoved him backwards, the force of which almost put him on his backside again.

"Dammit, child, what in bloody Nulyma was that for?" Ottoten exclaimed.

"With how you're acting, Father, you have no grounds to call me a child. I always knew there would be a reckoning when Lady Fusette told us you were the one leading the Galstan fleet to aid Livoria. Still, I'm disgusted you would think striking my intended is acceptable."

"That boy is not your intended." Ottoten rubbed his swelling cheek and met his daughter's scowl with an equally furious one. "You're coming home with me when this is over and nothing you say will change my mind about it!"

"Piss off."

The admiral blanched, clearly unable to process the young woman's declaration. "What did you just say to me?!"

"Did I stutter? You're acting like a petulant toddler denied a treat, old man, and I won't have it! You haven't learned a blessed thing since I left, have you?"

His gaze shifting between the two, Kai wondered if he might have to hold Orelia back. She looked enraged enough to slip into a Frenzy Haze, despite the berserker state being almost unheard of in mixbloods.

"*You* won't have it? Orelia Basner, my job as your father is to make sure you're provided for and can have a stable life. The only reason I didn't have you dragged back when you ran off to join the clergy in the first place is because I thought maybe you'd learn just how harsh the world is and come back on your own. Now you're preparing to commit one of the church's greatest sins!"

"I suppose it's good I'm no longer a priestess, then."

Ottoten's tirade came to a sputtering stop. "Huh, what do you mean?"

"I surrendered my ordination and crest to Archbishop Jovanni. It was a required stipulation in order to get his approval for our handfasting."

"W-why would you give up your ordination? This isn't making any sense."

"You have *no idea* why I ran off to join the clergy in the first place, do you?"

Biting his lip, Kai did his best to maintain his composure at the admiral's befuddled expression. Laughing at this point would only draw Orelia's ire to him, and he preferred not taking lumps from his partners he didn't have to.

Orelia gave an exasperated sigh. "Father, I didn't leave because I wanted to be a priestess. I left because you refused to let me have any freedom to make my own choices. I enjoyed working in the temple and with the children, but what really made me happy was being free to live my life and help people in a way I decided for myself."

"You could've easily helped people if you enlisted in the Navy. At least then, your brothers would've been able to look out for you."

"But you never gave me a choice, did you, Father? You never gave any of us a choice! You simply decided 'This is what you will do!' and that was it, as far as you cared. I understand you want me to have a safe and stable life, and I appreciate the concern, but you need to ask yourself: Would the stability be worth spending the rest of my life miserable?"

Orelia's words seemed to have stunned her father far more than being struck with her staff did. Kai saw the conflicting emotions tugging at each other in his eyes.

"But..." Ottoten stammered. "Do you expect me to believe you'd be happy being gawked at for marrying a man from a tribe everyone reviles? What could Gravebane possibly offer to make you happy?"

Kai stiffened when he felt Orelia's arms around his elbow as she curled her body against him. "Changes are coming, Father. The Norzen won't be hated forever, of that I'm certain. And don't try to blame this on Kai being a Norzen; I know for a fact Lady Fusette's father was a good friend of yours before he passed. People like to talk in the Galstan court, after all. It's obvious you're letting the idea of public scandal drive your reaction. I'm marrying Kai because he's a good man who will treat me with respect and love. If you bothered to get to know him, you'd see what I do.

"When Adalbard murdered the children I looked after for over two years, my heart was in a dark place. Kai was the one who comforted me. He showed me there was still hope in the darkness. If it wasn't for him, I might not be standing here today. I want you to be in my life, father, but that can't happen unless you let go of this needless desire for control. Why do you think Octavo and Osmund volunteered for the border guard? Your own sons couldn't handle being under your thumb any longer!"

Throughout Orelia's tirade, her father stepped backwards until falling onto a stone bench. Kai could empathize with Ottoten to an extent; like any parent, he only wanted his child to be safe, even if he took it to an unnecessary extreme. Still, that punch hurt, so he was willing to sit back and let his partner verbally strip the man bare.

He wasn't expecting Ottoten's gaze to shift to him. "What do you think of this, Gravebane?" the admiral asked. "Do you agree with her? That I'm too controlling?"

Taking a deep breath, Kai focused on the scents of the garden to center himself. "What I see is a man who only wants the best for his children. I can't exactly fault you for such thinking. Maybe I'm a fool, but I think you've been in a position of military command for so long, it's bled into your family life. Expecting obedience from children when they're young is one thing, sir, but as you can see, Orelia is a grown woman."

"Then am I supposed to just let her do as she pleases?"

"Isn't that part of being an adult? Going out into the world and learning to stand on your own two feet. I'll be the first to admit I'm not perfect. I lived with my own parents after obtaining my Hunter's crest, partly because I wanted to save money for emergencies, and partly to look after my little sister. I've made mistakes which have caused me no end of trouble and there are many who will say my choice in who to marry is an affront to the church.

"However, we've learned the faumen were once human in the days before the Rebirth." Ottoten's eyes bulged at the revelation. "That means somewhere deep in our bodies, there's something tying us all together, proof we're not as different as those in power would have us believe. I may not be perfect, but I try to improve myself every day in the hope of being someone truly worthy of your daughter's love."

It was clear much of Ottoten's anger was dissipated. His shoulders sagged and he stared at the ground looking as though he'd lost a major military campaign. "Then can I ask you one question, Gravebane: Will you promise to look after my little girl, make her happy, and protect her with everything you have?"

Snapping his legs together, Kai thumped his right fist against his chest in a formal salute. "You have my word, Admiral. My greatest hope is for Orelia and Maple to live their lives in peace with joy and laughter. I'll love them equally and protect them with my very life if need be."

The grizzled officer gave an uneasy chuckle. "This may be odd to hear, but you remind me a bit of Vonlo." Kai and Orelia shared a confused look. "He was never sure of himself in his royal duties, always second-guessing his decisions. But there was no hesitation when it came to his family. He would've charged the gates of Nulyma to protect Lady Fusette and he'd do it with a grin on his face."

Orelia smiled, running her fingers along Kai's arm. "That certainly sounds like Kai. Father, I hope you realize this man isn't going anywhere if I have anything to say about it. Yes, our family will be rather unusual, but we already knew to expect that and have every intention of supporting each other no matter what comes. You used to say when I found love, I needed to grab it with both hands and not let go. Well, I refuse to let go of the man I love."

"Then I suppose there's no use in trying to fight it any longer. Damn it, I should've guessed you'd use my own words against me! Hanblum likes to tell me you're every bit as stubborn as I am, but I refused to see it until now. I'll give you my blessing for this match. Just...at least try to come home on occasion. This old man worries and I'm sure your mother would—"

Ottoten was cut off when Orelia threw her arms around his neck, nearly pitching the older man back. "Thank you, Father!" she cried out, tears streaming down her face.

"Cut it out. A young lady shouldn't cry so close to her wedding day." Ottoten turned to Kai and nodded. "And I owe you an apology. I'm sorry I struck you earlier."

"Apology accepted, sir. What matters most is seeing Orelia happy."

"I suppose that really is the most important thing, isn't it? I was so hung up on keeping my children safe from any sort of danger or scandal, I forgot a parent's most sacred duty is to give their children the tools to find their own happiness. If Orelia believes her happiness lies with you, I doubt I could stop her even if I wanted to."

Giving her father a peck on the cheek, Orelia rushed off emitting happy giggles. The two men watched her leave before Ottoten jabbed an elbow into Kai's ribs.

"So when's the happy day?" he asked.

Kai cast a nervous grin towards the admiral. "In two days. We're keeping the ceremony small to avoid causing a disturbance."

"Smart move. Her Grace certainly works fast."

"She had to, in this case. I hope we'll see you there."

"You think I'm going to miss my only daughter's wedding? Gravebane, not even a stampede of raging bison could keep me away."

Kai tugged at his shirt, using his other hand to wipe away the beads of sweat trailing down his cheeks. For the second time in a moon, he stood in front of a Windbringer cleric to get married, only this time it was Jovanni standing before him with two ribbons and a braided cord in hand. Kai himself carried two items: a small wristlet made of blue and yellow irises, and a silver necklace with a pendant made of soft blue glass encircled by gold plating cut into a pattern of swirling waves.

Just as he told Ottoten, the ceremony was kept small and being held in a tiny chapel at the rear of the palace grounds where the servants attended service. The building had minimal decorations, though bundles of bright flowers in various hues from the palace gardens gave it a splash of color. Lit torches lined the walls, illuminating the chapel against the backdrop of the evening shadows visible through the windows.

Among the main attendees were Saredi, the Lord Chamberlain, and Fusette sitting in the front pew to Kai's left. Next to them were the rest of Kai's family and friends.

Maple, as Kai's first wife, took the first spot on Fusette's other side. Next to her was the tavern maid Ione, her long brown hair pulled up in a tousled bun. To Ione's left was Teos, the party's Soltauri smuggler and helmsman. His rounded hat sat in his lap as he gave Kai a cocky smirk. The sellsword Morgan, who Kai noted was surprisingly sober, sat on Teos' other side. Rounding out the group was the prickly scholar Lucretia, a small tome tucked under one arm and a rare smile on her lips.

On the other side of the aisle, Ottoten took the aisle seat with Kai's adoptive family sitting next to him. His mother Verona, despite being a Hunter and housewife, looked resplendent in a puffy red silk dress common among noble women. On the other hand, his sister Serafina tugged and fiddled with the lace ruffles of her own blue dress. Verona swatted her daughter's hands with a stern gaze. Taking up the final spot was Tuvi, a blonde Norzen orphan Orelia raised during her tenure at Stahl Granz Temple.

At the back of the room in one corner was a small group of musicians, each carrying a wooden vessela flute. Shaped like a potato with mouthpieces jutting from the wide ends, the instruments were small and easy to carry but produced a melodious sound.

They also happened to be Orelia's favorite instrument, so Kai spent time since their talk with Ottoten rounding up musicians who knew how to play them specifically for the ceremony.

In the rear corner opposite the musicians were three individuals wearing grey robes and hoods drawn up over their heads, each leaning against the wall with arms crossed over their chests. One was clearly a Soltauri judging by their height, while the second looked to be about Morgan's height and the last was just a bit shorter than Maple. Scattered throughout the chapel were a dozen men and women wearing the distinct emerald chainmail armor of Fusette's personal guard.

Kai faced Jovanni with a wide smile. His heart pounded against his chest, hoping everything went smoothly. His ears twitched when the musicians started up with a wedding ballad. Gulping down the ball of nervousness in his throat, Kai turned his head and felt his breath catch.

Orelia entered the room, walking towards him in a form-fitting honey-yellow dress that hugged her curves, an ivory veil covering the lower face and neck. Her vermillion hair was braided into two ponytails, each resting over one shoulder, with both hands clasped over her stomach.

Each step she took towards him filled Kai with nervous energy. His body quivered in excitement as she came to a stop across from him, her brilliant smile visible through the veil.

"Friends. Family," Jovanni began as everyone settled into a quiet tension. "We are here this evening to celebrate the joining of Kai Travaldi and Orelia Basner in wedded bliss. As a servant of the holy winds, it is my honor to officiate their bonding.

"Love is one of the most powerful emotions to exist. From my experience, it's also the vastest and, like the winds, a dynamic, ever flowing force which can overcome even the darkest of trials. I've seen with my own eyes the love these two share and have every confidence their match is a portent of changes that will shape our world for the better."

Kai saw his mother and sister wiping tears from their eyes at the edge of his vision and smiled. Even knowing the challenges ahead, his family was willing to support his choices, a blessing he thanked the Saints for every day.

The Archbishop brought him and Orelia closer together and joined their hands. After tying the iris wristlet around her left arm, Kai held his hands out, palms up, as Orelia rested hers on top. He reveled in the cool sensation of her touch as Jovanni tied a thin, sky-blue silk ribbon around his left wrist, just behind the yellow ribbon signifying his bond to Maple. Likewise, the priest tied a red ribbon identical to Maple's around Orelia's right wrist. He then wrapped the braided cord around their joined arms and tied it in a loose knot underneath.

"We will now commence with the sharing of vows. I invite each partner to speak freely and share their innermost thoughts entering this union. Kai, you will go first."

Gazing into Orelia's bright blue eyes, Kai felt an anchor in his chest. Her fingers encircled his own and squeezed gently, giving him a sudden burst of courage.

"Orelia," he murmured, "every day that goes by, I thank the winds for bringing you into my life. From the day we met, it was easy to see the traits that make you such an amazing woman. Your kindness and devotion. Your sense of justice and wisdom. But what I appreciate most of all is that determination to always do what's right instead of what's easy. Even if it means popping me in the head when I'm feeling down about my mistakes."

A wave of muffled laughter rose from the audience. Kai chuckled before continuing, "You've shown me how, even though love may not be simple, it still doesn't have to be hard and should always be grabbed with both hands when it's found. Thank you for being my guiding light, and like these irises represent, I have complete faith in you and my devotion to your heart will never waver."

His breath hitched when Orelia brushed a lone tearaway before staring at him with eyes full of unabashed love.

"Maybe you're not quite the Ironskull I thought you were back on our trip to Havenfall." More titters rose from the crowd. "I know you've been told this before, Kai, but you have a soothing presence. One that serves as a beacon of hope for those who feel all is lost. After what happened in Faith Hollow, you were the one to keep me grounded and bring back the hope I thought was gone.

"I may not have been the first to capture your heart, but I'm grateful to you and Maple for your willingness to accept me anyways. My path may not be as clear, since I'm no longer a priestess, but I have more faith in you than anyone else to be there by my side and light my way. I love you, Kai, and I'm looking forward to walking the journey of life with you in my arms."

Gentle applause filled the chapel as Jovanni rested his hands on Kai and Orelia's shoulders.

"Such beautiful vows. I hope you both remember them in your hearts as you nurture the love you share. Never lose sight of your affections and share in each other's joys and sorrows. Tend to one another in times of sickness. Cleave together to be your family's sword and shield. I have high hopes for you both. You are the proof that love truly can defeat any darkness. By the authority granted me as leader of the Windbringer Order's Livorian branch, I hereby pronounce you as husband and wife."

Jovanni removed the cord from around their arms and turned the pair to face the crowd with a joyous smile on his face.

"It is my honor to present to you all Kai and Orelia Travaldi!"

Once again, Kai watched an audience burst into cheerful applause while the musicians switched to a cheerful fast-tempo melody. He muttered a quiet prayer of thanks the crowd this time was much smaller; getting married to Maple in front of the villagers of Havenfall nearly burst his ears.

Turning Orelia back towards him, Kai removed the veil and rested his arms on her waist. He gave a nervous smile at the mischievous expression on her face as she cupped his cheeks in hand and pulled him into a passionate kiss.

Kai's ears flattened at the teasing jeers he heard from Teos and Morgan. He raised a hand and waggled his pinky at where he assumed to two older men were, refusing to pull away from the woman in his arms.

Taking his new wife's hand, he led her down from the altar and braced himself as Tuvi threw herself against him. Taking the young girl by her single hand, Kai smiled and led her into a simplistic twirl while Tuvi squealed in delight.

"Thank you for inviting me, Mr. Kai. Sister Orelia," Tuvi said. Her cheeks dimpled when Kai spun her into the waiting Orelia's arms, the former priestess cradling the orphan in a loving hug.

"Of course, Tuvi," Orelia replied. "We couldn't imagine you not being here to help celebrate our special day. Fusette told us you're doing wonderfully with your studies. I'm so proud of you."

Tuvi's eyes shed fresh tears, her face buried in Orelia's stomach. The two newlyweds ruffled her hair while the rest of the wedding party looked on with broad smiles. As Tuvi rushed off towards Fusette, she was immediately replaced by Serafina launching herself towards her brother in a bone-crushing embrace.

Orelia peeled the younger girl off him and whispered a few words into her ear. The teen's face turned a sickly white before she bolted and hid behind her mother. Kai bit his lip to hold back his laughter.

"What did you just say to my sister?"

"I simply warned her if she broke any part of you before I got to enjoy my wedding night, there would be severe consequences."

"...You are one scary woman, my love. Brilliant and beautiful, but scary."

"Damn straight. Now let's go. You owe me the first *real* dance, my husband. Your little frolic with Tuvi doesn't count."

Chapter III

As the festivities winded down and everyone was beginning to show signs of fatigue, Fusette gathered the crowd and wrangled them outside, with Kai's group bringing up the rear. Once everyone was in the courtyard leading towards the palace, Fusette raised her hands and clapped, causing the group's eyes to spin towards the grinning monarch.

"I just want to thank everyone for coming to share in this wonderful occasion. As we prepare to tuck in, it is my fervent hope weddings such as this, that share in so much unrestrained adoration, will become the norm in our realm. We face many trials going forward, but I refuse to believe anything short of victory awaits us!"

The crowd burst into vociferous applause. Stepping closer to the front, with both his wives nestled under his arms, Kai gave his cousin a pleased smile.

"Now then, I think we've had enough fun for one evening," Fusette continued, "so perhaps we should take our—"

The doors of the palace flew open in a deafening bang as a flood of three dozen people stormed into the courtyard. Half of them wore the vivid indigo robes of Parliament nobles, while a full dozen were bedecked in the cream vestments and white mitre caps of Windbringer bishops. The remainder comprised a small contingent of guards.

"There they are!" one of the nobles cried out as the group advanced towards Kai's wedding party, many with looks of fury on their faces.

Nostrils flared, Fusette and Saredi both marched forward to meet the intruders halfway. The duchess held her hand up, palm facing out, and commanded them to halt.

"What is the meaning of this!?" Fusette demanded.

"Is it true, Your Grace?" a bishop on the far left asked. His hands were clenched into tight fists. "Have you really permitted a faumen to trample on our order's most forbidden taboo not once, but twice? And not just any faumen; a damned peltneck!"

The sound of singing steel rang out as Saredi drew his sword, pointing it at the offending bishop. "You dare use that slur here?" the Vesikoi noble snapped. "I think perhaps it's best you all leave before Her Grace and I become unpleasant."

"Shut yer mouth, Saredi," a tall, dark-skinned noble at the front of the crowd retorted in a grassland's brogue. "We aren't going anywhere until we deal with this pressing situation. As it stands, many members of Parliament have begun wondering if Her Grace is losing her faculties, given her recent questionable decisions."

Kai was stunned by the accusation, though Saredi looked even more so; the Chamberlain's pale face turned a ghastly shade of yellow. From the corner of one eye, he saw the three figures in grey robes spreading out around their group.

"What in bloody Nulyma are you talking about? Where's Remigo?" Saredi asked.

"You can't be that blind, Lord Chamberlain," a voice sprung up from the back. The crowd parted to reveal a lanky man in indigo with a crooked nose and square face; Lord Remigo, the Prime Minister. "We were prevented from providing aid to Lord Kendela due to Lady Fusette's ridiculous decree. Now the man is dead, his fortune seized to line the royal coffers, and Her Grace refuses to bring the murderer to justice!"

Fusette gave an unamused laugh. "Do not blame me for Kendela's stupidity. You know as well as anyone attempting to murder an Exarch Knight is a capital offense, and the fool tried stabbing Gravebane from behind in front of hundreds of witnesses. No, Kendela was dead the moment he drew that sword."

"Then perhaps we should remove that pesky protection from Gravebane before he can cause any more trouble."

"You mistake your place, Remigo!" Fusette shouted, her eyes contracted in fury. "Only I or the Exarch in question can renounce a Brand. Parliament has no authority over matters concerning the Knights, and no amount of politicking will change that."

"With all due respect, Your Grace," a Vesikoi bishop spoke up, his eyes half-lidded and a leery smile on his lips, "you have the entire Quorum of Bishops and half of Parliament standing here in opposition, though it's obvious some of our number were aiding you in direct conflict to church precepts." Kai noticed four of the bishops near the crowd's rear wincing. "You can't possibly think you can ignore our demands."

"Watch your tongue," Kai warned, placing himself at Fusette's side with eyes narrowed. "Your words reek of treason."

"You have no authority in this matter, Gravebane," the priest hissed. "Our voices will not be pushed aside any longer! Lady Fusette, we are giving you two options: You can either abdicate the throne and leave peacefully, or we will depose you here and have you locked in the palace gaol until we suppress the Liberator uprising."

To everyone's surprise, the bishop's demand sparked Fusette to erupt into peals of unrestrained hysterics. Bent at the waist, her laughter had the mass of indigo and cream robes staring at each other in confusion.

"Are you absolutely sure that's what you want?" Fusette finally wheezed out. "I don't think you'd much like me abdicating to the one next in line for the throne."

Remigo snarled, "What are you talking about? You have no siblings or children, so next in line to assume control of Livoria would be me as Prime Minister."

"Ah, but that's where you're wrong, *milord,*" the duchess purred, drawing out the last word in obvious sarcasm. "It turns out I do have family left in this world on my father's side. A distant cousin, in fact, who I discovered during my trip to Runegard."

The nobles shared uneasy glances, none wanting to ask the question clearly on their minds. Remigo scoffed. "Really? And who is this long-lost relative, Your Grace?"

To everyone's shock, Fusette raised her hands and peeled back her shawl, revealing her feline ears and grey eyes. Then, to the opposition's horror, she lifted a thin finger, pointing to Kai.

"He is. Now, are you *certain* you wish for me to abdicate, because I can assure you Sir Gravebane would be less forgiving than I've been with your foolishness."

Kai fought to keep himself from cackling at the variety of colors Remigo's face shifted through at Fusette's revelation. From white, to porridge grey, to purple, and finally to crimson. The man went through a rainbow's worth of color before their very eyes. He had no desire to take Fusette's place, but even he could admit the unexpected show was amusing.

The rest of the nobles stumbled back in terror. Many were stammering amongst themselves, each demanding the others if they knew Fusette was a Norzen. The bishops were equally repulsed, gazing at the Grand Duchess with undisguised loathing.

"You can't be serious!" one of the priests shouted.

"Throw them all in the gaol," another exclaimed, "and put those pelt-necks to the gallows."

A booming voice thundered over the tumult. "Not so fast!" one of the robed figures ordered, removing the grey garment in one swoop. The other two followed suit, revealing two men, a middle-aged Soltauri with chestnut fur and a blonde human, and an Aerivolk woman in her forties. All three wore cavalry chainmail armor with steel breastplates engraved with the seal of House Ardei.

Their most shocking ornaments, however, were the matching crystalline brass watches dangling from their necks. Watches identical to the one in Kai's pocket.

"What is this treachery?" Remigo demanded.

The Soltauri stepped forward, drawing a one-handed axe from his belt. "The only treachery I see is from you. The Exarch Knights are sworn protectors of the royal family," he explained. "Our duty changes not a whit simply because they have revealed themselves to be faumen. If you wish to harm Her Grace, you will contend with us."

"Many thanks for the assistance, Dewthorn," said Fusette, offering the taller faumen a short bow which he immediately reciprocated. She then copied the motion for the human and Aerivolk in turn. "The same goes for you as well, Swiftlock. Burnsong."

The amassed nobles began shouting in unison, accusing the three of treason. The Aerivolk, Burnsong, drew a pair of metal throwing arrows and twirled them like batons as her crimson feathers glimmered in the lantern light. "You dare accuse us of treason when you stand there demanding the Grand Duchess' abdication? I always knew you nobles were petty and hungry for power, but I didn't think you were brainless as well."

Kai's gaze swept over the opposing crowd. Many of the guards were bearing their weapons, pointing them at Fusette. His vision became rimmed in a pale red. He gave a sharp whistle and held out his hand. In moments, one of Fusette's guards slipped next to him and pushed the Norzen's mace into his hand. Behind him, the rest of the party twisted their heads as they watched the volley of arguments in front of them.

"I hope you lot understand the implications of your actions here tonight," Fusette said, fiddling with the sleeve of her robe. "You have all committed high treason, and by law could be executed where you stand."

"We have you outnumbered and outclassed," the Vesikoi bishop snapped.

Fusette snorted. "Outclassed? You truly believe those men stand a chance against *four* of my most experienced Exarchs? Dewthorn is Admiral Larimanz's second for a reason, while Swiftlock and Burnsong have proven themselves in the field assisting the Third Eastern Fleet against our enemy. And if you believe Gravebane is weak simply because of his profession, then it's obvious you're a bigger imbecile than I imagined."

The guards surrounding the opposition group lost much of their courage at the monarch's words, many of them inching backwards. Several dropped their weapons once Fusette's guards lined up in front of the wedding party and drew their swords in a single, united motion.

"Guards," Fusette commanded, "arrest them all and lead them to the gaol. I won't execute them, though the idea is quite tempting."

The nobles regarded the duchess with hesitant confusion. "Do you intend to starve us to death in that hovel of a gaol?" one of them asked.

"Also tempting, but no. I'm invoking Chapter 12 of the Livorian Codex and assuming full wartime authority. My first decree, while not what I desire, has been a long time coming. I officially declare Parliament disbanded until a special session can be held to reactivate it. Furthermore, each of you among the nobility can now consider your land and titles *stripped.*"

The nobles erupted into a furor. "You can't do that!" the dark-skinned noble bellowed.

"I've warned Parliament repeatedly; while you have some level of veto power, *I* am still the reigning monarch of Livoria. It may not have been your original intention, but it's obvious you decided to use this war as a chance to assume control for your own purposes. I won't have everything my family has fought to protect for almost three hundred years be thrown away in the name of petty power squabbles!"

"And what do you intend to do with us?" asked a woman bishop, her eyes cast downward in shame.

Jovanni stepped forward and gave her a disappointed shake of the head. "I am most concerned the Quorum believed it had any right to get involved in such a disgusting act. The Wind Saints would be ashamed to see how far we have fallen."

"Silence, Jovanni!" Remigo snapped. "You're nothing but a beast lover like the rest of them."

"That sounds like something a Liberator would say," Fusette replied in the Archbishop's place, her voice flat and dark. "Certain elements of the church leadership seem to have decided they have more authority than is true. I hereby decree the Order of the Windbringers shall now and forevermore be separated from the administrative affairs of the government. It shall be written into the Livorian Codex as official law going forward. While church members may hold government office, ordained clergy are forbidden to do so unless they agree to surrender their ordination. Also, clergy will not be permitted to stand as official advisors to any court officer with the exception of the Archbishop solely for matters pertaining to the church."

The bishops' faces sank at the woman's words. Whatever display of blazing power the group had hoped to accomplish was left a smoking pile of ash on the courtyard floor. Fusette snapped her fingers and ordered the group to be taken away. With the three Exarchs leading the way, the guards put the entire opposition in manacles and herded them back into the palace.

"Full wartime authority?" Kai repeated, a single eyebrow raised in amusement.

"In my defense, it has never once been used before now," said Fusette, "but Chapter 12 remains a legitimate power granted to the monarchy in times of dire need. I can't have half my government plotting to overthrow me, but at the same time, killing them will only exacerbate the situation and make me look like a tyrant."

"What do you plan to do?" asked Maple. "I reckon *someone's* gonna notice half the Parliament just up and vanished."

"I'm afraid I may have to finally tell the people the truth about me." Everyone gasped. Until now, Fusette had always been hesitant about revealing her heritage to the realm, despite a clear desire to do so.

Teos returned his hat to his head and scratched the base of his horn. "You sure about that? It'll stir up a hell of a hornet's nest."

"Your Grace," Jovanni interrupted, "perhaps I can assist you with preparations. I believe I may have a plan."

The entire group turned to face the Archbishop in surprise. The old man chuckled and tapped his own temple with a wry smirk. Fusette's face bloomed with glee as she agreed and grabbed both Jovanni and Saredi by the arms before dragging them away. She shouted a hurried goodbye to the others as she led them through the doors and out of sight.

"Well...that was interesting," Ione quipped, emitting a nervous chuckle.

"Indeed," added Lucretia, pushing her spectacles further up the bridge of her nose. "Whatever the Archbishop has planned, I am confident in saying it will be quite the performance, given his history."

Orelia and Maple whispered hurriedly amongst themselves, causing Kai's ears to twitch and a tremor of unease to prickle down the length of his tails.

The Aerivolk merchant raised her arm and called everyone's attention to her. "We'll have plenty of time to worry about tonight's events in the morning. For now, let's get some shut eye. I don't know about the rest of you, but this whole mess wore me out and all I did was watch!"

Muttering in agreement, the others entered the palace and made their way back to their assigned chambers. Maple leaned in and gave Kai a quick peck on the cheek. Brushing her feathers against his chest, she winked at him and skipped away, her talons clacking on the stone tiles.

Before Kai could ask where she was going, he felt a pair of hands grab his shirt and pull him down. His vision became overwhelmed by blue as Orelia smashed her lips against his. After taking a moment to regain his balance, Kai deepened the kiss. As he pulled back, he gave the Vesikoi a goofy grin.

"I'm not complaining or anything, but that was sudden."

A shiver wracked his body when Orelia's fingers clutched at his mane, a look of unrepentant desire filling her eyes.

"After all we've been through the past few days, I think I've earned my wedding night. You. Me. Bed. *Now!*"

Chapter IV

The crackle of the fire filled the cavern with sound as Hakan and his crew sat around the pit. Each eyed the others in hesitation. The remains of their meal, a pair of giant mallards, lay scattered about the cavern.

Behind their group, hidden among the shadows, lay a huge black mass shifting up and down every few seconds. As if it were breathing...

Directly across from Hakan sat the shortest member of the group: Hemlocke, an Aerivolk migrant with white feathers marred by layers of dust and wearing a ratty tunic and trousers.

"So explain this again," said Hemlocke. "Why exactly are we hiding in a cave while that pissant Agosti is scrambling around like a headless wiroch?"

Hakan released a heavy sigh and eyed the stein of cheap ale in his hand. During their most recent excursion to a nearby town, they'd taken time to pilfer a bevy of supplies from the locals. Sadly, little of their plunder was of the same high quality he was used to back in Corlati.

"I will confess I underestimated the Liberation Army's similarities to the Livorian Parliament," the forge master admitted, "including Doulterre's impressive skill at diverting their power-grabbing antics to more useful endeavors. Without him, Agosti appears unable to maintain a firm hold on the army."

On Hakan's right, the Soltauri monk Duarte eyed his master with concern. "Didn't many of their conscripts flee following the Battle of Havenfall? Also, I noticed their armor was in serious disrepair. Didn't you agree to provide them with equipment as part of your deal with the Conclave?" he asked.

"Indeed. I hoped putting Agosti in charge would bring results due to the man's unrestrained hatred for faumen making him an easy pawn to move as we needed. Instead, his harsh manner of command has sent most of his soldiers fleeing into the night and surrendering to the Royalists. As for their weapons and armor, I had to provide them the junk and less pristine items from my inventory. It was the only way to slip everything across the border without the Federation discovering my intent. The shipping manifests all read that the equipment was sold to Livoria to melt as scrap."

Mirabell, the young black-haired assassin on Hakan's other side, took a slow sip from her own stein. "That makes sense. The Senate would not be happy if they knew the true purpose of those weapons, if only because they weren't getting a slice of the profits for themselves. One thing still puzzles me, though. Why would the defectors surrender? Would that not result in them being imprisoned for being party to a rebellion?"

"You have to remember, the Liberation Army consists mostly of those pressed into service by the Conclave. I'd wager most of them were young scamps who'd never held a weapon until the Liberators forced them to." Hakan gave a dark, mirthless chuckle as he took another drink. Casting his eyes over the group, his face settled into a grim smile. "We shouldn't be surprised they would flee the moment an opportunity presented itself. Besides, with Havenfall's destruction, I have little doubt the ones who ran are hoping for mercy from the Royalists rather than risk being cut down as traitors to the realm."

Hemlocke snorted, pulling a long, yellow feather from the folds of his tunic and twirling it in his hand. While keeping his eyes locked on the feather, he asked Hakan how the plan was going to work with the Liberation Army now a broken mess.

"They still have enough men to make a legitimate strike on Whistlevale once we combine our scattered forces. One of the reasons we're here is to procure the new, improved Shatterstar I ordered Fedrin to produce. Once we deliver it, Agosti will have the means to wipe the Livorian capital off the map."

A slow whistle sounded from the figure on Hemlocke's left. Short and stocky with a fox-like tail and ears covered in grey fur, Obram was a Risbado sellsword from the northern continent. Despite his misgivings about the mercenary, Hakan would admit Obram was among his most efficient enforcers.

"Is it really so important to wipe out the capital?" Obram asked. "Seems like a bloody chore to deal with one piddling woman."

"Of course it is, you oaf!" Hakan snapped back. "Removing the duchess and her entire city in one swoop will send a message, not so much to the other realms, but to the continent's Norzen. Livoria has long been considered both my tribe's pride and stain. Pride that a Norzen sits on a seat of power in a legitimate realm outside our ancestral stronghold of Hilderic, even if hidden, yet also stained because of continued persecution across the world due to Cacovis' actions."

The sellsword snickered. "So you want to give them a cause to rally around. Remove the ones who allowed the persecution to continue while offering them another option. Not a bad plan, assuming you can pull it off."

Raising her hand, Mirabell questioned how Hakan planned to direct the Liberators towards the capital.

"Agosti knows there's no going back for him and those committed to the Liberators' crusade. Once we deliver the new Shatterstar, all it will take are a few honeyed words to have Agosti marching his army to Whistlevale as fast as he can."

"And what about the sellswords you convinced to join this mad plan?" Obram pressed. "I've worked with some of the companies you've drawn in and none of them are cheap. Or merciful to anyone who tries to cheat them."

"I have no intention of paying those vagabonds from my own funds," Hakan answered, "especially since I may have coaxed their cooperation by promising them the bulk of the Livorian treasury once the city has been taken."

The silence in the cave was deafening.

"Boss," said Obram, "didn't you say our plan was to blow the city up?"

"Correct."

"Then how will you pay them if the entire plan is to destroy Whistlevale, and I assume the treasury along with it?"

"That will be Agosti's problem to figure out once the fighting is over, won't it?"

None dared to speak, though Hemlocke broke into a trilling cackle. "Oh, this is perfect!" he screeched. "This is the kind of chaos I live for. Pitting your allies against each other while you get away unscathed; it sounds like poetry in real life!"

"I wouldn't exactly say 'unscathed.' I still owe that damned brat for getting in our way at Havenfall," Hakan said, lifting a finger to trace a thin scar on his cheek.

"You worry too much about him," Hemlocke assured the forge master. "Nulla and I can handle the whelp. His luck can't last forever."

"I warned you about underestimating Kaigo," Duarte reminded Hemlocke. "Did he not turn you into a chicken skewer during the battle?" A heavy growl came from the dark mass behind the Aerivolk, drawing inquisitive gazes from the rest of the cave's inhabitants.

Hemlocke growled, his lavender eyes narrowing. "You don't get to talk; not only did he beat you like a rawhide drum, but you couldn't even defeat that scholar."

"Enough!" Hakan bellowed, drawing the group's eyes to him. "We're not here to bicker among ourselves. Duarte, Mirabell. Once we finish up with the new Shatterstar, you'll be joining me on my trip to Duskmarsh."

"Duskmarsh?" asked Mirabell. The young maid's face scrunched up into a scowl. "Why do we need to go there, Master?"

"If my plan is to succeed, we'll need the Norzen of Livoria on our side. Thanks to years of scheming and shadow deals through my intermediaries in the realm, those fools in Parliament have done a fine job preventing the Grand Duchess from visiting Duskmarsh since her ascension."

"Why is that a good thing?" asked Obram. "Also, didn't Doulterre send an expeditionary force to Duskmarsh a while back?"

"Because Duskmarsh, for all the hate it receives, is how the Ardei family has remained in power so long. The reigning monarch selects a partner from the city to bring forth the next heir to the throne under complete secrecy. In return, the city provides the monarchy guardians in times of need. With Parliament's power struggles keeping Lady Fusette from the city, the Norzen are likely feeling ignored and furious with the current situation." Hakan emitted a grim chuckle. "As for Doulterre's expeditionary force, Duskmarsh wiped them out rather easily. If anything, the attack will make things easier as the Norzen were likely hoping for assistance from the capital in dealing with the attackers."

"Ah, now it makes sense. With them being brassed off at the duchess over everything, it'll make 'em easy pickings to swoop in and sway them to your way."

"Exactly," Hakan confirmed with a sly grin on his lips. "You picked my intentions up rather quick, Obram. I'm impressed."

"Boss, I consider myself a specialist in backstabbing techniques. The moment you explained the foundation, figuring your end plan out was simple."

The forge master eyed Obram with a look of respect. He knew his plans were often difficult for others to comprehend, considering their complexity, so having someone able to match his wiles was refreshing.

"So if you're taking these two with ya, what am I and Featherbrain over here supposed to do?" Obram ignored the pinched glare from Hemlocke, who whittled away at a piece of wood while his eyes flickered between the forge master and sellsword.

"I'd like the two of you to take Nulla and cause some chaos on the path between Duskmarsh and Whistlevale. If my guess is correct, the Grand Duchess will soon leave Parliament to themselves so she can plea for assistance from Duskmarsh. Your job is to cause enough trouble they'll hesitate to travel the main roads. Any way of slowing them down will help our cause."

The Aerivolk emitted a malicious chuckle. "Consider it done. Chaos is what I do best, after all."

The scent of burning wood filled the meadow as numerous campfires illuminated the area. Masses of men and women huddled around the fires, doing their best to eat the gruel filling their well-used bowls in silence. Their shoddy, piecemeal armor was covered in rust and dirt, and roughly half carried weapons that were chipped or dull.

From his command tent on the army's fringes, General Valdis Agosti studied the maps littering the desk at the tent's center with a look of vexation. He had little knowledge of cartography, and those among the senior officers who could explain things to him seemed more content to watch him bumble about in confusion, wearing smug grins. More than once, Agosti had to bite his tongue and remind himself he needed them to keep the mass of cowards making up their army in line.

It didn't mean the former pirate couldn't dream of slitting their throats, though.

"If you stare at those maps any harder, Agosti, they'll burst into flame," said an older man sitting in the corner, wearing grungy clerical vestments with a spike-headed staff leaning against the wall next to him.

Grumbling under his breath, Agosti grabbed a stale sweet roll from his plate and flung it at the chuckling elder. "Shut your gob, Adalbard, before I do it for you. I swear, if I knew things were going to go this pear-shaped following a major victory, I'd have let the damn Royalists kill me." While the disgraced former bishop was handy at keeping the troops' morale up, Agosti was rigid in his belief that Adalbard was too cowardly to be of any practical combat use. Still, the old priest was his staunchest ally, whose silver tongue had deflected at least two mutiny attempts since Havenfall.

Several among the surrounding officers snickered. "You know that's a bald-faced lie, Agosti," the shortest of the men crowed, a commander judging by the leaves on his epaulets. He was dumpy and rotund, with a bushy mustache and carrying a thin goblet of wine in one hand. "You'd sooner lie with a peltneck than let those Royalist bastards finish you off."

"Say that again," Agosti growled, his eyes locking on the corpulent officer, "and I'll hack your baubles off myself."

"Remind us again why our benefactor put *you* in charge," another officer, this one a vice general named Medoro, inquired.

"I've no bloody idea," Agosti confessed, "but the fact is we still need the bastard's weapons, grungy as they are, to replenish what we lost when the deserters fled. So it's best we do as he wants until we finish the Royalists and can deal with him. He sent me a hawk saying we'd be getting a new shipment within the next day or so. We're also receiving a replacement for the cannon he used to turn Havenfall into a crater."

"Do we really need such a horrid weapon to win?" the rotund commander asked.

Agosti eyed him in disbelief. "Have you seen our army?" he answered, jerking a thumb back towards the tent door. "We'd be lucky to put up a mediocre defense against even the smallest Royalist fleets with the rabble we have. The only reason we haven't been run to ground is because the Royalists are busy chasing those damned sellswords!"

Clicking his tongue, Adalbard reminded them their troops were exhausted, being driven on little food and less rest. "We need to restock our supplies if we wish to continue marching. An army can't dine on steel, after all."

"I'm aware, you foppish priest!" Agosti snapped. "But how in Nulyma are we supposed to support so many? Even when you remove the deserters, we still have roughly three thousand mouths to feed."

Medoro raised a confident hand. "Perhaps we should ransack the nearby villages. They should provide enough supplies to get our troops' strength back up before making a play for Whistlevale. As much as it pains me to say, we must end this war quickly if we are to have any hope of victory. The Royalists, while currently disjointed by the events at Havenfall, are more than capable of starving us out."

A sharp rap came from the corner, drawing the group's eyes to Adalbard. "I may have an idea to deal with one of those issues," the priest said.

"What kind of idea?" Medoro pressed.

"With everything that has happened, should we really be concerned with sending the faumen prisoners to the camps as Razarr requested? We have enough to worry about, after all."

Curling his lips back in a snarl, Agosti demanded to know what Adalbard was suggesting. "I certainly hope you aren't saying we should add them to our forces," he sneered. "Or, worse yet, release them."

"Oh sweet Finyt, no, but I think we all agree the faumen are beasts, correct?"

"Obviously."

"Well, what do you normally do with a beast when it can no longer serve its intended purpose?"

One by one, the men's faces bloomed in understanding as the bishop's intention became clear. Soon the tent was filled with the glinting toothy smiles of the assembled officers. Even Agosti had an unnerving grin on his lips.

"I knew there was a reason I kept you around, priest. Gather the prisoners, gentlemen. It's about time we got *some* use out of those damnable faumen."

"So what's your plan?" Obram asked as he and Hemlocke rode on top of Grimghast's back through the thick forest. A plate of bone carved to fit the beast's head was nestled over its lower jaw. Grimghast itself made little noise other than the panting huffs it emitted with every step.

Hemlocke snickered. He enjoyed the sellsword's curiosity, but he had no appreciation for a well-laid plot! "Patience, Obram. The boss wanted us to spread some chaos, so I intend to deliver. First, we'll need a proper foundation to accomplish our goal. It's why I asked for some soldiers and carts from the labor camp."

Obram gave a short huff. "You have no idea what you're doing, do you?"

"For your information, I know *exactly* what my end goal is. See, I've spent most of my life in pain due to this wretched affliction I was born with. Because of it, I've been treated as less than worthless by strangers. Or worse, they pity me!"

"Didn't that stupid boy heal you, though?"

"Not completely. If anything, Kai's elixir only stalled it. I can already feel the fatigue returning in waves. For some reason, I've also been feeling this burning sensation in my mouth since Havenfall and it's driving me crazy. I suspect it has to do with that vine he stabbed me with during the battle. I kept enough elixir in reserve to keep me alive, but there's only a half dozen sips left. I intend to keep those in reserve until I can finish him."

Obram stroked his chin as his tail twirled behind him. "So why go to all this trouble when all we need do is let your little pet run wild around the trail? That would stir up enough chaos for the boss to be happy."

"Remember the tonic I had you drink after we left?"

"You mean the horrible green gunk you shoved down my throat?" Obram's face twisted in disgust, as if smelling a putrid odor. "Don't ever make me drink that again. It tasted like what I can only assume was ass."

Hemlocke's face darkened into a malicious grin. "You'll thank me later, my friend. That gunk as you call it will protect you from this," he said, pulling two objects from his pack: the first, a small vial filled with a thick, black liquid. The other was a glass jar filled with hundreds of tiny insects hopping about.

"What in bloody hell are you planning to do with those?" Obram asked, peering at the jars with disdain.

"These are the instruments of our enemies' destruction. The fluid in this vial is a poison that's rather devastating and difficult to stop once it takes root. The ticks are nothing more than our method of spreading it. I want this realm to know what suffering truly is, Obram. I may not survive to see the fruits of my labor, but the entire continent will writhe in agony from my influence, one way or another."

CHAPTER V

Standing just inside the exit to the balcony overseeing the Royal Palace's entry plaza, Kai couldn't shake the anchor of unease lodged in his chest. The plaza was overrun with several thousand people. At the crowd's forefront nearest the balcony, bearing sheafs of parchment, Kai could make out a crowd of scriveners from newsletters across the realm.

Whatever story they were expecting, Kai doubted it would come close to measuring up to what they were about to hear.

The rest of the party lined up beside him, dressed in freshly cleaned clothes and each wearing a brass emblem on their right shoulders with the seal of the royal family. Across from him, Fusette fiddled with her robes, their brilliant chartreuse hue making her easy to spot even in the entry foyer's dimmed lantern light. Saredi, as always, stood at her side in a dark suit that made his pale face stand out beneath his slicked back ebony hair.

"Are you sure you wish to go through with this, Your Grace?" the Vesikoi noble asked, leaning over to let his eyes roam over the massive crowd below them.

Fusette released a long sigh while ensuring her shawl was loosely in place. "For the last time, Saredi, yes! I know you worry for my safety, and I appreciate it with every fiber of my soul, but this must be done. Rumors are already abound concerning the Quorum and Parliament. If we are to have any chance of defeating the Liberation Army, there cannot be any more secrets concerning my family. I only hope the people are willing to listen."

On the opposite side of the room, near the door leading into the hall, the three Exarchs who assisted them at the wedding party stood ready in full armor. Dewthorn clapped a hand to his chest and promised that they would be ready to defend Fusette's life from any who would do her harm.

A tremor rumbled down Kai's tails. His head turned to spot Swiftlock staring at him in a mixture of confusion and amusement. "Are you not going to wear your Exarch armor, Gravebane?" the blonde asked while stroking the tiny stubble on his chin. "You are on official duty."

"I haven't worn that armor since I received it following my Branding," Kai confessed. "It stifles my mane like you wouldn't believe. Besides, I consider my duties as an apothecary more important in most cases. Today is no exception."

Burnsong gave a lilting trill of laughter. "Gravebane, I think you might be the only Exarch who seems to be ashamed of your inclusion!"

Fighting back a blush as his friends joined in the redheaded Aerivolk's mirth, Kai cleared his throat. "I wouldn't say I'm ashamed, but I'll admit I often feel unworthy of the honor. Regardless, I'd much rather be known for my skill at saving lives as opposed to taking them."

"That's a fair argument, I suppose. It does sound like a much more pleasant way to be remembered." Before they could continue the conversation further, Fusette's voice cut through in a commanding tone.

"It's time."

Sharing a nod with his friends, Kai lined up behind Fusette and Saredi as they led the group out onto the balcony.

The crowd burst into thunderous applause once Fusette reached the balcony railing, causing Kai to flatten his ears. He could see her hands clench the alabaster stone hard, her fingers curling into hooks. He couldn't blame her; the last time she had stood here was the day the Faumen War began.

The day Gerhardt Falber was murdered by Hemlocke on Hakan's order.

Below them, the mass of people waved their arms in cheer, many swinging green ribbons in a circular motion as a visible show of support. Even those who couldn't fit into the plaza, forced to watch from the nearby rooftops and streets running parallel to the plaza itself, did their best to shout and whoop while waving their own ribbons.

Standing on the balcony, staring down at the vociferous crowd, Kai couldn't help being impressed. Fusette raised her arms palms out and lowered them at a sedate pace. In response, the crowd quieted to a level Kai found much easier to bear.

"My fellow Livorians," she exclaimed, "I apologize for taking so long to call you all here. This assembly has been a long time coming, and I confess I wasn't quite sure what to say to you all. However, I can stay silent no longer.

"Ever since that horrific day when Minister Falber was shot down in cold blood, I have hoped we would somehow be able to come together and discuss the problems which allowed such a travesty to occur. However, it pains me to say that hatred runs deep in the hearts of our enemies and having to label *any* Livorian as an enemy is like an arrow in my heart."

The crowd's silence was a stark contrast from the raucous tumult they exhibited moments ago. Fusette had them in a quiet stupor, everyone focusing on the young monarch's voice.

"But the fact remains the Liberation Army has made it clear; they *are* our enemies and are fully intent on exploiting our beautiful realm for their own twisted means. Thanks to the efforts and research of Exarch Gravebane's party, we've discovered evidence the Liberators were, in fact, enticed to rebel by a rogue faction within the Corlati Federation."

The crowd erupted into a clamor at her statement. Swiveling his ears, Kai could hear many calling for judgment against Corlati. His eyes twitched to his sides, where Maple and Orelia each rested a hand on his arms. He gazed back down and was surprised to see several within the crowd watching him with curious expressions.

Strange, Kai thought, *some of those faces look familiar.*

"I am here to inform you I refuse to allow such an act to go unpunished! I have summoned the Five Realms Council to present our evidence to the other rulers of Alezon. They have all consented to meet and are on their way to Whistlevale as we speak. It will take some time for all four to arrive, but I implore everyone here to treat our guests with the honor and respect you'd give any other foreign dignitary."

Several bellows of rage rang out. "What about the Corlatian President?" a male voice begged from among the throng of scriveners below. "If what you say is true, then why should he be given respect?" A chorus of agreement followed the question.

"I understand your anger," Fusette replied, giving the crowd a soothing smile. "However, the purpose of this Council summons is to present our evidence and hear President Harmod's defense before any action is agreed upon. Livoria remains a realm of honor and we will allow the accused to present their side. However, this is not the only reason I've called you here today, nor is it even the most important."

Murmurs of confusion spread throughout the mass of people. It was easy to see heads turning, questioning those next to them what other possible reason Fusette would have to call for an assembly.

"It hurts to admit, but this is something which has given me much worry ever since my ascension to the throne nine years ago. I have seen reports of the goings on in this war. The senseless bloodshed, the horrors our people have seen. What bothers me has been the stark increase in violence against faumen in the years leading up to this, and especially the Norzen. I know many of you here today are refugees from towns effected by the fighting, and so I pose a simple question:

"For those who have had the pleasure to meet him, what are your thoughts of Exarch Gravebane, and of the Norzen tribe to which he belongs?"

The crowd's mumbling grew louder at Fusette's words, and Kai's gaze snapped to her in confusion. Why was *he* suddenly being brought into the conversation? A quick glance told him the rest of his friends were just as befuddled. Even Saredi was sending a questioning look towards the duchess.

What worried Kai more than anything was her blunt request for the crowd's opinion on Norzen. As he expected, more than a few voices could be heard condemning his tribe. Many fingers were pointed towards him, their accompanying faces full of anger. Then, to his shock, a single stern voice roared above the din.

"Enough!"

Kai's eyes narrowed as he sought out the owner of the voice. It sounded familiar, though he couldn't place it.

The heavy clomp of boots on wood drew the party's attention to a single human sailor, clambering to the top of the platform used for Aerivolk and standing tall in the center of the feathered faumen, though it was clear he was favoring his right side. The man's commander's rank glinted in the sunlight, and his youthful face sent a spark of recognition through Kai's mane.

"Is that...Poretti?"

Orelia's eyes widened. "Wait, the battalion commander from Faith Hollow? I'd heard he was shot during the battle. What is he doing here?"

The party eyed the Royalist officer with interest. It was clear he had something to say. The real question was: what kind of message would he send?

"I'll be the first to admit I once thought the same way many of you folks do," said Poretti. "That the Norzen are a bunch of damned mongrels who don't deserve the freedoms they have. But let me tell you something; I wouldn't be standing here today if not for Gravebane! Many of you see his face and call him a peltneck, or a hellcat, but I'll tell you what he really is: A hero!"

A rumble echoed from Kai's chest as warmth spread throughout his body. The feel of the girls' arms wrapping around him in joy was almost an afterthought. His initial meeting with Poretti was combative and almost came to blows, so to hear the officer's praise filled him with relief.

Several voices cried out, demanding to know what Poretti meant.

"Without him, the entire city of Faith Hollow would be a smoking ruin like Thorncrest," the officer continued. "My name is Cassio Poretti, son of the lord of Faith Hollow, Count Argo Poretti, and I was commander of the Navy battalion defending the city during that battle with the Libbies outnumbering us four to one. Looking back, I fully admit my initial plan was complete foolishness. It was Gravebane's defensive tactics which saved the city and kept our casualties to a minimum. He saved thousands of lives that day. The more I think about it, the more I realize the Norzen are just like any other group of people. They have their good and rotten eggs just like any other tribe and even humans. But if we let our hatred blind us to those who are good people, we're no better than the Libbies."

"The commander is right!" another pair of voices rang out from the horde. Everyone's attention shifted to a couple near the edge of the crowd. Kai's eyes bulged when he recognized one of the couples they met in Grantide during their travels to Havenfall. The young blonde mother was carrying their child in her arms while her husband climbed atop a merchant's cart.

"We met Sir Gravebane during the Spring Festival back in Grantide. We didn't know it at the time, but a corrupt apothecary was using the festival as a cover to poison dozens of children so he could sell his overpriced concoctions." A wave of horrified gasps came from the crowd. "Gravebane had no reason to extend anyone kindness or compassion with how we looked upon him with fear and distrust, yet he still fought for us! Not only did he stop the apothecary, he also crafted the medicine which saved our daughter's life and only charged the people of Grantide a single copper per family for his treatment!"

Kai swayed in place, struggling to remain standing. It was only Maple and Orelia staying by his side that kept him from collapsing to the stone floor in shock. His ears twitched as more people from the crowd rose to his defense.

He heard the voice of Celio, a Vesikoi fisherman they met in Glimmerdale, testifying of the party's help in cleansing the town's underground spring and saving them from deadly illness. An unfamiliar voice chirped afterwards, causing Kai and the others to spot an Aerivolk couple standing with two young, red-feathered girls. Eyes watering, Kai recognized the children as their parents spoke of how the party gave their daughters money and food while in Glimmerdale for no other reason than kindness.

Dozens of familiar voices joined in as the Hunter Corps pledged their support. Peering over the edge, he watched his sister push past the guards blocking the stairs to the palace and rush halfway up before turning to face the crowd.

"You lot can say what you want about the Norzen, but that sailor is right!" Serafina shouted. All eyes swiveled to the teen as she pointed at the balcony above. "Not all Norzen are evil, and there's at least one perfect example standing before you. To many of you, he's Gravebane of the Exarch Knights, but to me, he's just Kai.

"He gets nervous like anyone else. I've seen the fear in his eyes when those he cares about are in danger. I've heard the love and devotion in his voice when he talks about those who mean more to him than anything. So what if he looks different, or if Cacovis or any other Norzen did something terrible in the past? That's all behind us, and if we're going to beat those Libbie bastards, we need to all stand and face the future together. No more of this human against faumen nonsense. We're *all* proud Livorians, no matter what tribe we hail from. He may be a dipwit at times, but Kai has proven time and again his loyalty to this realm and to life itself, and I for one am proud to call him by a title that means more than anything else: *my big brother!*"

The crowd erupted into booming applause at the end of Serafina's speech. Even those who criticized the Norzen moments ago were clapping in polite recognition. Sweeping his gaze over the balcony, Kai felt tears streaming down his cheeks as Fusette regarded him with a warm smile. A moment later, realization dawned on him as he swallowed back a gasp.

"Thank you, everyone," said Fusette while casting her eyes over the crowd, "for showing such understanding. This may come as a shock, but there's another secret I can no longer hide behind..." Her voice trailed off as she reached up to peel back her shawl.

A wave of gasps echoed through the plaza as Fusette allowed her ears and tails to flutter in the open air. She gave a choked sob as she spread her arms wide and faced the crowd with quiet tension.

"All I can say is the decision to keep this truth from the people was made generations before I was born, but I reveal it to you now: The Ardei family has been Norzen since our realm's founding. A wise man I know told me two things." Her gaze flickered to Kai as the confidence in her smile returned. "First, secrets hold more power the longer they're kept in the darkness, feeding off our fear of being discovered, and only the light of truth can dispel such fear. Second, the circumstances of one's heritage hold no power over their future. A person's identity and legacy are determined only by the paths and choices they make in life.

"I refuse to allow this secret to be hidden any longer. Yes, I am Norzen, and knowledge has been exposed revealing the early leaders of our realm and church, either through ignorance or subterfuge, warped and hid the true history of Livoria's founding. Many denounce Cacovis as a heretic and a monster, but the discovery of her personal journal taught me of a woman who fought for things we as Livorians hold dear. She fought for freedom, and for her family—"

A booming voice interrupted the duchess' speech, drawing Kai's attention to a heavily muscled man covered in soot and dressed in a blacksmith's apron. The man waved his hands in the air while screaming vehement curses. Mothers covered their children's ears as he called for Fusette's immediate execution. The man denounced the monarch as a liar and demanded to know why anyone would follow her.

Kai felt a tremor in his tails as he noticed several in the crowd pausing to visibly consider the man's words.

"I know you're frustrated," Fusette answered, refusing to back down, "but let me ask everyone here, and especially those who are parents: How many of you would go to any lengths to protect your family? Would you be willing to *kill* to save your children or siblings if someone threatened them?"

Stepping next to his cousin, Kai raised his hand without a hint of hesitation. Maple and Orelia copied the gesture moments later, followed by the rest of the party. In a wave of agreement, hundreds upon hundreds of hands rose into the air. The man growled but lowered his head and blended back into the crowd.

Nodding her head, Fusette pressed forward, "I know this must be shocking to you all, but Miss Serafina is right when she says we must look towards our future rather than cling to the past. We can only do this if we are willing to stand together. Despite her actions during the Desolation, Cacovis was still considered a Wind Saint by her comrades for a reason. They even looked to her as a leader in the same vein as Master Galen. It was church leadership, not the Saints themselves, who labeled her a heretic. She made the ultimate sacrifice to protect what was precious to her; the same sacrifice I am prepared to make in defense of everyone here. I asked what you thought of Norzen because I want it to be clear: we are not the enemy. *Hatred* is our true enemy.

"If it is the will of the people, I will quietly step down as Grand Duchess. However, I beg you to at least allow me to lead you back towards peace, in honor of my family's service to this realm for almost three hundred years. Once the Liberation Army has been defeated, I'll allow the people to decide my fate. Is this a fair compromise?"

Confused murmurs rippled through the crowd. Kai fought to urge to ask Fusette what she was thinking. He couldn't imagine anyone else sitting on the throne. While he had grown up during Duke Vonlo's reign, his entire adulthood was associated with serving the strong-willed, yet kind, woman in front of him.

"Her Grace is truly a shrewd woman," Saredi muttered from behind him. Kai turned to the Vesikoi with a befuddled expression. "You provided her the perfect argument to prevent a riot from breaking out. By showing you as an example of how the Norzen can be kind and honorable, she took the sting out of revealing her own heritage."

Kai chuckled. He couldn't refute the man's statement given the evidence below. Even now, Fusette was successfully soothing the mass of people with gentle words. "Not exactly how I would've planned it, but I'm happy the crowd is taking this better than expected. I shudder at how it would look if the guards had to quell a riot."

"Indeed. I should offer you my dearest thanks, Gravebane." Kai's eyes swelled. He was unused to Saredi expressing any sort of gratitude. "Discovering her link to you has given Lady Fusette a joy I haven't seen since her father passed. When Duke Vonlo succumbed to illness, many of us worried if Her Grace would die of a broken heart. It was enough of a miracle she avoided contracting the plague herself, as so many others in Whistlevale did."

"I remember reading about it in the newsletters. Duke Vonlo died of the Black Tear Blight, didn't he?"

Saredi nodded. "Correct. Such a vile disease. His Grace was in such pain during his final days, and we couldn't offer him any comfort without risking infection ourselves. To this day, we still know very little about the Blight or how it spreads so quickly. It was only by isolating the infected at once that we culled it as fast as we did. And even then, thousands lost their lives."

A sharp tingle spread through Kai's mane. He'd heard stories of the Blight, just as any other apothecary. His master, Geraldo, once told Kai he was lucky for having never faced it, as the disease was often known by a second name: The Realmbreaker, for its ability to bring entire nations to ruin. His mind raced over everything he'd learned about it during his studies.

The Blight was a plague-like disease capable of spreading rapidly and infamous for the festering boils of black pus it produced on its victims' bodies. Upon bursting, the boils' contents would ooze down the victim's body, giving the appearance of black tear stains which gave the affliction its common name.

Threading his fingers through his fur, Kai felt a sense of dread pooling in his chest. Something about Saredi's story set him on edge. "Lord Chamberlain," he whispered, drawing the noble's gaze to him. "Would you happen to know where I might find the historical and medical reports relating to the Blight outbreak nine years ago?"

"I do, but why in Nixtral would you ever want to read those?" The look on Saredi's face was one of undisguised horror.

"Consider it professional curiosity. I'll need something to occupy my time when I'm not training or spending time with Maple and Orelia."

"Very well, I will show you after Her Grace releases the assembly. However, I don't want to hear any complaints if those documents give you nightmares. The Royal Apothecaries refuse to even talk about the outbreak for a reason."

CHAPTER VI

In the two moons following Fusette's decision to reveal her heritage, Whistlevale experienced a torrent of changes. Many of those expressing disgust with the Grand Duchess fled the city and the realm in an exodus. Every day brought new bands of people flowing in and out of the capital.

News of Fusette's identity spread across Livoria like wildfire, prompting a wave of Norzen to take up residence in the fields on the western side of the city walls, away from the Hunters and Galstans. The majority claimed to be refugees from thieving bands seeking asylum, which led to Fusette assigning them an area outside the city until she had time to review their cases more thoroughly. To the shock of many, the Norzen proved to be quiet and amicable with any who crossed their path.

Kai and his party were among the busiest individuals in the Royal Palace after Fusette and Saredi, much of their time being spent preparing for the upcoming Council.

Upset with her performance against Mirabell in Havenfall, Ione threw herself into training with the Royal Navy's Shieldbearer Corps. The tavern maid traded her pan for a lightweight heater shield and her dagger for a sea officer's cutlass, learning how to properly fight in close quarters. While watching her train one day, Kai noticed her wearing a glove on the right hand with an odd button at the center of the palm, connected to a cord that disappeared beneath her sleeve. However, when he asked Ione what the contraption was, the tavern maid only gave him a cheeky grin. Ione even asked for assistance from Burnsong, asking the Exarch to help hone her reflexes and counter techniques.

Burnsong was quick to find herself with a second student once Maple begged the other Aerivolk to teach her how to use the metal uchine arrows she displayed against Parliament. Kai noticed Burnsong looking positively giddy at the chance to teach the two women everything she could. When he questioned Dewthorn about it, the Soltauri explained to his shock that, prior to joining the Navy, Burnsong had been a dancing teacher and performer.

She earned her Brand during an attack by a Corlatian thieving band on her hometown, Galemore. Despite having no formal combat training, the woman combined her dancing skills with a pair of daggers to cut down a third of the raiders single handed, saving hundreds of lives. After her Branding ceremony, she joined the Royal Navy and rose through the ranks with an elegant efficiency.

As it stood, Burnsong proved a capable instructor. Maple and Ione both gushed about their lessons, though Kai would often have to provide his wife a massage to work the tension out of her knotted muscles. Of course, he often benefited from this as well, considering Maple's amorous appreciation of the apothecary's ministrations.

Speaking of Dewthorn, the Soltauri Exarch was putting Morgan and Teos through their paces in building up their fighting skills. Kai knew from experience both men were exceptional warriors due to their history, so seeing them get tossed ass over kettle repeatedly was both amusing and humbling. Still, the 'training' was showing results, as every day showed his friends lasting longer with each spar and, even once, putting the crafty Dewthorn on his knees.

The last of Fusette's current Exarch guard, Swiftlock, took the initiative to train Lucretia; a smart move considering both preferred the rapier as a weapon. A shiver ran through Kai's tail whenever he watched the blonde teaching Lucretia how to use the environment to her advantage in the middle of a fight. Considering the scholar's sharp mind, Kai knew the training would make her an even more formidable opponent.

Orelia was an odd one out in preferring to train with her father and the Holy Navy's equivalent to the Marine Cavalry: the wiroch-mounted

Dragoon Brigade. The former priestess proved a quick study in learning new ways to use her staff in close quarters while also receiving instruction in marksmanship. After scoring a close win against him in a spar, Ottoten gifted his daughter a custom pistol crafted from black walnut, the words 'justice' and 'service' emblazoned on the grip.

For his own preparations, Kai took meticulous care in exploring the strange powers he discovered in Havenfall. Using small cuts capable of healing quickly, Kai learned his blood could induce rapid growth in any plant matter it touched. The sensation of a powerful pulse within his core accompanied any use of his Origin. At first, it took intense focus to generate a noticeable change in the plants he used.

He also discovered he could sow seeds inside his own body and assimilate some of their physical traits, something he realized after ruminating over his use of a wisteria vine against Hemlocke at Havenfall. His first attempt with the ability after reaching the capital was sowing midnight amaranth in his upper arms. The plant had potent health benefits and he wondered if binding it to his own body would produce any noticeable effects.

Needless to say, he was flabbergasted upon discovering the amaranth allowed him to spew clouds of fragrant pollen the plant was known for from the pores of his skin. He had a similar reaction once he acquired some rare torpothorn seeds from Hanblum and sowed them in his wrists. Within days, he figured out how to extend and launch the plant's needle-like thorns from between his knuckles.

However, after Orelia caught him in the middle of an experiment, his wives 'convinced' him to work on the ability only when at least one of them was with him. It didn't take long afterwards to learn that, while visualizing the effect he wanted was important, he got faster results when he allowed the pulse of energy in his body to flow naturally rather than trying to force it.

Soon enough, letters arrived announcing the imminent arrival of the other realm leaders. Fusette called the party to the throne room in order to discuss the event. Upon their arrival, they noticed the duchess flanked on both sides with Saredi on her right and a round-faced human woman in her forties on the left. She wore a long-sleeved noble dress in deep charcoal with her black hair trussed up in a tight bun. Her nose was short and pointed, and her upturned hazel eyes scanned the party in amusement.

Kai immediately recognized her as Lady Bidelga, the Minister of State and the one responsible for ensuring the party was trained in proper etiquette for the upcoming Council meeting.

"I know this is asking a lot," Fusette started, "but so far, you seven have proven yourselves as my most loyal, stalwart friends outside of my advisors. The Council shall convene in the Parliament chambers on the first floor. I'd like you all to keep an eye out for any suspicious activity or characters who may be skulking about. I refuse to have another incident like what happened with Minister Falber."

The party snapped off a crisp salute while declaring their understanding. They knew Saredi would expect nothing but proper conduct during this meeting.

"Thank you. Now for assignments, most of you will be allowed to wander the palace as you normally would. All I ask is you keep your heads down and immerse yourselves with the palace staff. The main exceptions...shall be you three," Fusette continued, her eyes locking on Kai, Maple, and Orelia.

Kai quirked an eyebrow. He already suspected he would be tasked with a more difficult duty, but having his partners included was a surprise. "And what will be our task, milady?" he asked while bowing at the waist.

"You three shall be serving two primary roles. Your main job, Gravebane, is to stand as my personal bodyguard in Saredi's place, with your ladies as support. He will be matched with Lady Bidelga for this event." Kai fought back a chuckle. He suspected Saredi wasn't pleased with the reassignment. "At the same time, you three will be ambassadors of a sort. News of your recent nuptials is beginning to spread, and I think it best to get everything out in the open regarding Livoria's official support of it."

"I can't imagine the Corlati faction will stand for it," said Maple.

"They're on Livorian soil, so their opinion is as pointless as teats on a buck; they won't have room to complain anyhow considering the accusations facing Harmod. Besides, Lady Maple, I doubt your husband will accept any insults directed your way."

Indeed, Kai's jaw clenched at the thought of a visiting dignitary hurling vitriol at either of the two women at his side. "Absolutely not," he growled. His body relaxed at the sensation of Maple and Orelia stroking his mane as they leaned against him.

"Must you three do that here?" grumbled Lucretia, pushing her spectacles further up the bridge of her nose. "You have a perfectly good bedroom for those activities."

The scholar visibly trembled at the smug grin Orelia cast her way. "Was that permission to leave, Madam Dineri?" the young Vesikoi asked.

"Save it for after I dismiss you," Fusette snickered. "If I let you leave now, I'm certain I wouldn't see the three of you again until tomorrow morning."

"Damn," Kai muttered, snapping his fingers and sending the rest of the group into peals of laughter. Except Saredi, of course, which made Kai wonder if the stern Vesikoi knew what a joke even was.

"Do we know when the leaders are expected to arrive?" Teos asked, tipping his hat in respect.

It was Bidelga who answered him, her clarion voice sharp and articulated. "We expect them to arrive at the palace early tomorrow afternoon. The Lord Chamberlain and I shall greet them in the grand hall before leading them to the Parliament chambers. This gives you all ample time to prepare yourselves."

Kai took his wives' hands, rubbing his fingers over their palms in a circular motion. "With all due respect, Lady Bidelga," he said, "I suggest you impress upon our visitors the importance of courtesy during this Council. While my family and I are willing to serve as an example of our...unique circumstances, I will not brook any disrespect from *anyone* towards my wives."

"I sympathize with you, Sir Gravebane," Bidelga replied, "but you must take care not to bring disrepute to Her Grace's name. Remember, you are representing her just as much as your family."

A thin, tilted grin formed along Kai's lips. "Perhaps I didn't make myself clear. Let it be known if any of our visitors do something to make either of these ladies on my arms cry, I will make them *bleed*, and I assure you I won't be gentle about it."

"But—"

"I agree with him, Bidelga," Fusette interrupted, causing the minister to turn towards her with wide eyes. "Regardless of the distance of relation, Kai is still my cousin, thus he and those ladies are technically members of my family via blood and marriage. If anyone dares to disrespect them, he has my full support in rebuking their behavior."

Unable to form a coherent sentence, Bidelga stammered in confusion as Saredi stared at Kai with a flat expression. "I hope you know what you're doing, Your Grace," she finally muttered. "I shudder to think of how this will go if you cannot control him."

"Bidelga, my friend, the only two people on Nixtral capable of controlling the man are right there. I think you'll be pleasantly surprised, even if our visitors prove unable to keep any unflattering opinions to themselves."

Waking up bright and early the next day, Kai was tempted to lay in bed until it was time to greet their foreign visitors. Maple and Orelia, however, had other plans and convinced him to spend their waking moments cuddling instead, thanks to an excessive application of kisses to his lips and face.

The apothecary made it a point to ignore Morgan's snickering during breakfast at the obvious grin stuck to his face. He refused to let the mischievous sellsword ruin his good mood. After finishing their meal, Kai led the party to the central gardens, where Fusette stood waiting.

The duchess looked elegant in a flowing aquamarine dress which complemented her neatly curled ebony hair. Her shawl was nowhere to be seen, leaving her ears and tails exposed for all to see. Since revealing herself at the assembly, Kai hadn't seen his cousin wear the shawl once, and it was obvious from her look of unrepentant glee she had no intention of donning the garment ever again.

"I trust everyone enjoyed their meal?" she asked. Smiling at the wave of nods, she continued. "Excellent! I know what we discussed with Lady Bidelga yesterday, but I hope you all are prepared. The outcome of today's Council meeting could change the entire landscape of the war."

Lucretia raised her hand. "Lady Fusette, I've heard rumors among the tacticians how the Liberators might reproduce that monstrous cannon we encountered at Havenfall. How will we address such a possibility?"

"Sadly, we have little recourse to deal with a weapon like that unless we can get close enough to destroy it. However, I will mention it to the Council."

Kai shivered. He still saw the crater that used to be his hometown in his dreams. Hakan's Shatterstar, while an engineering marvel, held no purpose but as an instrument of death. He'd lost count of how many times Maple or Orelia held him close after being jarred awake by the vivid nightmares his mind conjured of that day. Piles of scorched rubble, the scent of blood mixed with blackpowder and acrid smoke. In his mind, he swore to do everything possible to prevent such an atrocity from happening again.

"I can only imagine what the Libbies would do with another of those things," Teos mentioned. "After seeing what it did to Havenfall, who's to say they won't try turning the next one on Whistlevale?"

The entire party's faces turned pale at the suggestion. "For the love of Finyt, Teos," Ione gasped, "don't you speak that kind of horror into existence!"

"Ione's right," Orelia added. "Havenfall had a population of five thousand people, and it was only by pure foresight most of the town was evacuated before Hakan destroyed it. If they turn that thing on Whistlevale, which is over eight times larger—more if you include all the refugees and visitors surrounding the city—countless innocents will die."

Everyone shared uneasy glances, trembling at the thought Orelia's words put in their minds.

An eruption of muffled applause came from beyond the palace's southern walls, drawing the party's attention. "What in Finyt is going on out there?" Teos asked.

Kai's gaze twitched to Fusette, who signaled to the guards standing along the parapets with her hands. He quirked an eyebrow at the guard captain's answer, a series of signals he didn't recognize.

"It appears our guests have arrived earlier than we expected," Fusette answered, regarding the party's inquisitive gazes. "We should make our way to the chambers. At least Bidelga and Saredi will be able to stall them for a short while."

"What about the members of Parliament who weren't arrested?" Maple asked. "I reckon our visitors wouldn't appreciate being interrupted by a bunch of snobby nobles."

Fusette giggled. "That's part of why I declared Parliament disbanded. Until I call for the necessary session to reactivate it, they have no reason to be in the capital unless they have legitimate business or live here. As it is, I recalled the rest of the Exarch Knights following your return and all except Waveweaver have arrived. We'll have plenty of security scouring the palace in the event someone tries to interfere."

Nodding their heads, Kai's friends huddled together and muttered amongst themselves for a few moments before telling Fusette they were ready. Snapping her fingers, the duchess led the party through the doors leading to the rear half of the palace. The group marched along at a steady pace, passing by scattered groups of guards and servants, each of whom offered a respectful bow.

Approaching the large double doors leading to the Parliament chambers, the rest of the party broke off and continued further down the hall before scattering, leaving Fusette with Kai, Maple, and Orelia.

Casting a sweeping gaze over the hall, Kai nodded while opening the door and allowing the ladies to enter. Maple stepped through the doors first, followed by Orelia and Fusette with Kai bringing up the rear.

The hall led deeper into the main chamber, a three-story circular room with a raised wooden rostrum in the center. A series of five long, curved tables were set upon the platform to create a circle, with five chairs on the outside of each table.

Surrounding the central rostrum were three tiers of chairs where the members of Parliament sat, segmented by staircases placed roughly ten yards apart. Octagonal mosaic lanterns made of stained glass lined the walls on each tier, the glimmering flames within exuding a rainbow of color.

Fusette strode towards the far table and stood next to the center chair, with Maple and Orelia flanking her on either side. Kai took his place behind Fusette, just to the left, giving him a clear view of the entrance hall.

"Nervous?" Fusette asked.

Kai swallowed what felt like a lump of air lodged in his throat. "Perhaps. I'm surprised you didn't have Dewthorn or another Exarch here as your bodyguard."

"I could have, but I trust you more than them," the young monarch answered, giving the apothecary a warm smile. "When I think about what we have to do today, I feel much braver knowing I have family by my side."

Before Kai could respond, a sharp knock on the door cut him off. "Enter!" Fusette commanded.

The door creaked open and Kai licked his lips in anticipation, one hand resting on the handle of his mace.

Entering the central floor side by side, Bidelga and Saredi led a troupe of unfamiliar faces towards the rostrum with silent resolve. Many of the newcomers took one look at Fusette and blanched, their faces taking on a plethora of various states of shock and interest.

The Minister of State and Lord Chamberlain circled around to Fusette's table as the group came to a stop and stood at the end chairs on Maple and Orelia's other sides. The women took care to stand and bow.

Kai's eyes swept over the crowd, split evenly into a line of four smaller groups of five, though he did recognize a few faces. Skittering behind the four groups was a small squad of scriveners, quills at the ready. Hanblum and Ottoten stood among the five on the far left. A figure stepped forward from the group, a dark-skinned woman not much older than Fusette but was dressed in a glamorous robe of striking goldenrod yellow. Her wavy mahogany hair was done up in a high ponytail as a pair of round, cobalt eyes gazed upon Fusette with clear fondness.

"Fusette," the woman murmured in a soft, tender voice that felt like velvet to Kai's ears, "how wonderful it is to see you again. I only wish this meeting were under better circumstances."

"I share the sentiment, Your Majesty," Fusette replied, offering a demure curtsy to the other woman. "Still, I appreciate your swift response to our call for aid in these dark times."

"Come now, young lady, I know I've given you leave to call me Isolde," the woman rebuked with a thin, tilted smile. The sharp, angular lines of her face gave her the image of a stern matron.

"Yes, of course, Isolde. I only wished to convey the proper respect before making official introductions." Turning to Kai, she rested a hand on his shoulder and flashed him a cheeky grin. "As you can guess, this is Her Royal Majesty, Queen Isolde Graffeld of Galstein.

"Everyone, I know you've already met Lady Bidelga and Lord Saredi. However, I should introduce my other retainers for this meeting. The young man standing behind me is Kai Travaldi, otherwise known as Sir Gravebane of the Exarch Knights. He will be serving as both security and our on-duty apothecary to provide any needed medical aid. The ladies on either side of me are his wives, Lady Maple and Lady Orelia Travaldi."

A wave of murmurs rose from the different assemblies, several gazing at Kai with a mixture of contempt and distrust. There were some, particularly from the two groups in the middle, who regarded the trio with looks of approval.

"I'm surprised your branch of the church allowed their nuptials to take place," Isolde murmured. "You know how they feel about intertribal affairs."

Fusette shrugged, giving the older woman a cheeky grin. "I consider myself lucky our Archbishop doesn't agree with the official church doctrine on such matters. Besides, even a blind person can see how much those three care for each other, and Father always taught me true love has no boundaries."

A youthful female Norzen with almond-shaped eyes and golden fur emerged from the middle-right group, wearing an envoy's sash, introducing herself as Pelka while adjusting the round spectacles on her nose. "We never understood why Livoria and Galstein still follow such belief," she said in a crisp voice, "so I for one am glad to see this change. Intertribal marriages have been legal in Belomas and Rodekan for years, though I'll admit they're still quite rare. Tradition tends to lend itself to cultural and tribal homogeny, as I'm sure you're aware."

As Fusette nodded, the man at the front of the same group, a tall and muscular human who looked to be at least a head taller than Kai and twice as wide in the shoulders, stroked his neatly trimmed mustache while emitting a low huff. "So this is the legendary Gravebane?" he questioned, his eyes scanning the apothecary before settling on Fusette. "I've heard a bevy of rumors regarding him and yourself, Fusette, but wasn't sure of their reliability. It does seem as though at least two of them were right on the copper."

Offering a short bow, Kai gave a nervous chuckle. "With all due respect, sir," he mumbled, "I doubt the word 'legendary' should ever be applied to anything I've done."

A soft thump struck his mane as Fusette slapped him with an open palm. "As you can see, I'm still training him to accept compliments," she quipped to the others' amusement. "Everyone, this is His Imperial Majesty, Emperor Kabuji Aduleji of Rodekan." The emperor grinned and offered a respectful bow of the head. He wore a heavy steel cuirass over his chest, covering a resplendent black tunic with fur trim, and dark tan trousers tucked into a pair of calf-length leather boots.

From the middle-left group, an elderly Aerivolk man stepped forward. His weathered face was set in a wrinkled smile as his black and white feathers fluttered with each step. Compared to the others, his loose coral robe and sky-blue kilt looked drab.

"Kabuji does bring up a good point," he said in a muted but firm voice. "Our scouts have brought back many rumors flying about since we entered Livoria. Perhaps you could help dispel some of the fog, Lady Fusette. Though I will be honest, it does this old heart good to know I'm not the only faumen sitting on this Council."

Fusette giggled and bowed to the older faumen, both tails lashing behind her like whips. "I'll confess I'm curious about what sorts of rumors you've been hearing." Facing the others, she introduced the Aerivolk as Velibor, current head of the Chiefs Council from the Belomas Highlands.

"It seems gossip is the same, no matter which realm it hails from," Velibor continued. "The rumors I assume Kabuji referred to were the ones about you being Norzen yourself, as well as a Livorian faumen taking two brides outside of his tribe. Those, we can see the truth with our own eyes. Some of the more outlandish ones I've heard seem to say you and Gravebane are secretly brother and sister, explaining why you were so eager to grant him a Brand."

Kai and Fusette eyed each other before emitting nervous chuckles. "Well," said Fusette, "I can assure you we're not siblings, but..."

The man at the front of the far-right group narrowed his hazel eyes at the two. He was just under two yards tall and wearing a fine brown suit, his greying hair neatly parted in the middle. "Lady Fusette, are you insinuating you *are* in fact related to him?"

Taking a deep breath, Fusette met the man's stare with a firm gaze. "I'm unsure of how close the relation truly is, but Kai and I are quite certain we share a common ancestor from the days of the Desolation Wars, which would make us distant cousins. However, this had nothing to do with my decision to Brand him, as we only discovered the link less than a year ago."

"From the Desolation Wars?" Isolde asked. "But that was almost three hundred years ago! What evidence do you have to suggest you have a common ancestor from back then?"

The duchess' eyes twitched to Saredi and Bidelga, who both answered with uneasy looks. Reaching into the folds of her dress, Fusette removed a small tome that Kai immediately recognized.

The journal of Cacovis the Shadow. Found in the Citadel's underground archives, the tome offered a wealth of information written in Cacovis' own hand shedding light on the events of the Desolation Wars. After being translated from High Norzen to Centric by Lucretia, it appeared the scholar was eager to return it to Fusette's possession.

"This helped fill in some of the blanks. This tome is, in fact, the travel log of one of the Wind Saints." The other leaders' eyes widened at the revelation. "We had it translated and confirmed that Cacovis had two children, rather than one as was previously believed. The younger son, Tobiris, was already well known among the Norzen for changing his name and becoming the first Grand Duke of Livoria. What shocked us was discovering her elder son, Erklaus, as the original founder of Duskmarsh."

Kai thought he heard a low growl coming from the far-right group, drawing his attention. The man in the suit at their head gaped at Fusette. "Are you telling us," he whispered, "you and this knight are descended from the one responsible for the Desolation?!"

"Not that you're in any position to make demands of me, but this is correct. Kai and I are currently the only known living descendants of Cacovis the Shadow."

"And how exactly did you confirm the truth behind this link, outside of the journal's contents?" the man pressed.

Fusette's lips curved into a mischievous smirk. "Funny you should ask that question." Turning to Kai, she waved a hand towards the well-dressed man. "Kai, this gentleman is the Honorable Gideon Harmod, President of Corlati. Would you like to explain to him your experiences regarding the reason I called this summit? In fact...everyone, please sit! We have much to discuss today, after all."

Shifting his eyes to the glowering Harmod, Kai grinned. "Of course. I think the good president deserves to know about the murderous blighter using his realm as a scapegoat."

"What are you talking about?" Harmod demanded as he led his group to the table farthest from Fusette's and sat down. Isolde's group took the table to Fusette's left while Kabuji led the Rodekans to her other side. This left Velibor and the Belomian delegation to take the table between Fusette and Harmod.

Crossing his arms behind his back, Kai pinned the Corlatian leader in place with a fierce stare. "A forge master operating out of *your* realm has admitted to pulling the strings behind the Liberation Army and supplying them with not only equipment, but manpower in the form of sellsword companies. The name he used as a cover was Razarr. Ring any bells?"

Harmod's eyes bulged. "Razarr, as in the master of Ferden Ironworks?"

"So you know this man, Gideon?" inquired Kabuji, his countenance darkening.

"I've met him a few times during Senate sessions. He's one of the wealthiest forge masters in Corlati and has the ear of several influential Senators. He never struck me as a warmonger, though."

Pressing his palms on the table and leaning forward, Kai's gaze sharpened as he glowered at Harmod. "If his activities are a shock to you, perhaps it's a good time to mention he also happens to be a Norzen."

The entire chamber burst into choking gasps. One of Harmod's attendants, a hulking man with a wide scar on his right cheek, let out a bellow. "You can't be serious!" he shouted. "How can one of our most influential citizens be a sodding pelt—"

A deafening bang rippled through the chamber as Kai's fist struck the table with a boom. The wood splintered beneath his knuckles, the apothecary's eyes locked on the larger man. "This room gets one warning: I don't want to hear *anyone* say that slur in Lady Fusette's presence," he breathed. "It's bad enough I've been forced to endure that foul word for most of my life and have heard it more during this war than anyone has any business doing so. I won't tolerate it any longer."

"Gravebane!" exclaimed Bidelga.

Raising a wing into the air, Velibor consoled the minister. "No, the man has a point." Everyone's eyes turned to the Aerivolk elder. "We are here to discuss the facts of Livoria's situation and to get anywhere, we must be mindful of how we speak. Vulgar language has no place in this chamber, especially when the words may offend a sitting member of the Council. I guarantee you my companions would not be pleased to hear anyone refer to a member of my tribe as a vulture while I sit here."

Kai nodded, grateful for the Belomian chief's support. He remembered Maple mentioning that calling an Aerivolk a 'vulture' was as insulting to them as 'peltneck' was to the Norzen.

"I'm siding with Velibor on this," Kabuji added. "We're supposed to represent the best of our homelands. I don't give a damn what your opinion of anyone here is in private, but until this Council is dismissed I expect everyone to be polite and respectful. If not, the door's right there and I'll sit back laughing as Gravebane tosses you out ass over kettle. Hellfire, I'll probably help him!"

Rising to her feet, Fusette offered a contrite bow. "I appreciate the show of support. Truly." She shifted her eyes back to Harmod. "Now Gideon, I know this is much to take in, but Razarr revealed himself to not only Gravebane, but his entire party. A fair number of witnesses among the Hunter Corps also saw the man without his cloak. His real name is Hakan, and he declared himself the last living descendant of Berelmir."

Isolde shot to her feet, her sapphire eyes bulbous. "By the winds of Finyt, that man says he's descended from 'Black Heart' Berelmir?!"

Sweeping his eyes over the chamber, Kai noticed all the leaders staring at Fusette in unbridled shock as she nodded. "Unfortunately, this seems to be the case. The worst part is that his entire reasoning for instigating this war is because his family has desired to erase the entire Cacovis line ever since the Desolation. By Hakan's own admission, he means to gather the Norzen of Alezon under his banner to conquer the continent."

"So that's what your warning meant when you summoned us here," Isolde muttered. "Trust me, I don't think we have anything to worry about."

"Indeed," Kabuji added. "We've all taken measures to secure our capitals against potential insurrections. If anything, we owe you a debt of gratitude for warning us in the first place!"

Fusette accepted their graciousness with aplomb, her cheeks darkening in embarrassment. Kai kept his eye on the Corlati delegation, noticing several of Harmod's companions glaring at the duchess in silent fury. He brushed his fingers over Maple and Orelia's shoulders, tilting his head discreetly towards the other table when they glanced up at him. They offered brief nods while the leaders continued their discussion on how to deal with Hakan.

Kai's gaze switched to Velibor when the elder Aerivolk called to him. "Sir Gravebane, I apologize for shifting the topic of conversation, but I'm curious about something. I've read the reports my envoys acquired regarding the Battle of Havenfall. It seems there are witness accounts of individuals displaying rather shocking abilities during the fight on Tapimor's Crest. Abilities which may have helped mitigate the amount of damage caused by the Liberators' attack."

A tremor of unease arced through the apothecary's tails as Velibor sized him up, as if inspecting him for some sort of mischief.

"Before we continue, I was hoping you could explain how Livorian faumen managed to regain access to the powers of Origin."

CHAPTER VII

The silence following Velibor's question was deafening. Despite their tumultuous friendship, Kai found himself desperately wishing for Lucretia's presence in that moment. The stoic scholar had a much better understanding of the faumen tribes' connection to Origin than he did. Even taking his experimentation into account, Kai had little true understanding of how his abilities worked or why.

Beads of sweat prickled within his mane as he thought about how best to answer the Belomian chief's question. Playing ignorance wasn't an option; it was obvious the man knew what was going on, even if the expressions on the other leaders' faces made their bewilderment clear.

Taking a deep breath, Kai glanced at his bandaged arm—the result of his most recent experiment the day before—and met Velibor's stare. "I must confess to being caught off guard. I wasn't aware anyone else knew the implications of what we discovered leading up to the battle. My own comprehension of Origin is limited at best, so my friend Lucretia would be better suited to answering your question."

"Excuse me," Harmod interrupted, slapping both palms on his table, "but what in the name of Cadell are you talking about? Origin? What is that, some faumen legend from pre-Rebirth?"

A vibrating chuckle came from Velibor, who gazed at the Corlatian president with amusement. "Oh, it's more than just legend, Gideon. Origin is the collective term we faumen have for the elemental energies of nature forming our world. Origin runs in ley lines stretching all over Nixtral, converging in nexus points that result in various physical manifestations.

It was the tribes' greatest blessing, being able to call upon the elements of Origin through meticulous application of meditation and training."

"Well, Lucretia will be pleased," said Maple, drawing everyone's attention to her. "She was the one who translated the journal Lady Fusette is carrying. It mentioned some of the legends about Origin and what the faumen could do. Still, the actual experience is much different than what was described in that stuffy tome."

"Wait... experience?" Velibor asked. Kai bit back a wince as he saw Maple's eyes bulge at the realization of what she admitted.

The merchant met Kai's gaze and gave him a nervous smile. Releasing a low groan, Kai raised his arm and tore the bandage from it. Several gasps rang out as he showed them the array of tiny scars marking his limb that had yet to finish healing.

"Bloody hoarfrost," Harmod whispered. "What did you do to yourself, boy?"

Without speaking, Kai focused on the pulse of energy rippling within his chest. He allowed the sensation to spread down his arm and settle along his wrist. His eyes burst open, silver flashing within the grey as leafy vines burst from his wrist in tendrils, shooting towards the Corlatians.

Harmod shrieked, throwing himself backwards and collapsing in an undignified heap as the vines stopped halfway across the rostrum. The vines, while not the same woody ones of wisteria he used against Hemlocke at Havenfall, still ended in spear-like points with bright green leaves fluttering in the air along their length.

"By the Origin," Velibor whispered, eyes wide as saucers as he rose from his chair. He stumbled into the center of the rostrum, ignoring the raucous laughter of the other leaders towards Harmod, and inspected the vines with a critical gaze. His eyes flickered to Kai, who understood the silent question and nodded. Velibor ran his fingers along the vines, his lips curving into a wide grin. With a giddy stammer, he rushed towards Kai and grabbed the apothecary by the shoulders.

Kai's body tensed as the hand gripping his mace twitched, his eyes shifting toward a rising Orelia with a look telling her not to worry. He gave her a nervous smile and returned his gaze to Velibor, who had broken out into enthusiastic laughter.

"This is incredible!" he exclaimed. "I never would've imagined I'd be able to see a faumen outside the Highlands regain their connection to Origin before I pass. Things must be progressing better than we hoped."

A member of the Belomian delegation, a male Vesikoi with black and white mottled skin and wearing a bright orange full-body robe, rushed from his seat to gently pull the excited Aerivolk off Kai. His rounded cheeks and prickly stubble gave him the appearance of a genial pufferfish, and his diamond-shaped eyes were bright, despite being pinched together in frustration.

"Chief Velibor, please control yourself," the man pleaded. "We still do not know all the circumstances."

"Oh, yes. Right, right..." Velibor mumbled as he allowed the man to guide him backwards. "Please forgive my impertinence, Sir Gravebane."

Kai brushed the older man's apology off, tugging on the pool of energy in his chest and drawing the vines back into his arm. "No harm, Chief, though it might help if you can explain what is going on. According to Lucretia, faumen haven't been able to access these abilities since the Rebirth."

The Vesikoi at Velibor's side cleared his throat. "Allow me to explain. My name is Hibbel, a scholar serving the Chief's Council. I was brought specifically to address Chief Velibor's inquiry about your abilities. We've been studying the Origin phenomenon since shortly after the Rebirth, though until recent years, our success was limited. The Highlands' proximity to Nixtral's largest ley line nexus has provided us with numerous opportunities to study the fluctuations in generated energy. I'm aware of your church's, shall we say...contempt, for Madam Cacovis."

Fusette emitted a grim chuckle. "I wouldn't be surprised if my ancestor's name was known as far north as Feswili with the damage she caused, regardless of her good intentions in stopping Berelmir's army."

"Then it might surprise you to know that in Belomas, she's considered one of our most beloved heroes."

Kai and Fusette both slammed their palms on the table, gaping at Hibbel with wide-open mouths. "What did you say?" Kai choked out. His mind raced, trying to figure out why one of the most reviled individuals in Norzen history would be so well regarded outside of her homeland.

"Oh dear," Hibbel muttered. "I was afraid this would happen, Chief. Now you see why I was so adamant for us to share our knowledge with the other realms."

Stroking his beard, Velibor gave a slow, deliberate nod. "Yes, it appears the Council's isolationist stance is coming home to roost. You'd best give them the most important parts now. We can explain the details later once we adjourn."

"Very well, sir." After leading Velibor back to his seat, Hibbel stood in the center of the rostrum, giving each delegation a respectful bow. "Put simply, a sect within the ancient Rodekan Empire was responsible for what we know as the Rebirth. After discovering the local tribes could perform miraculous feats with elemental magics, this sect led a mass of soldiers into Belomas and subjugated them."

Kai's ears twitched as he heard a gasp from Maple. His eyes flickered to see her listening to Hibbel with a pained look on her face.

"What followed," Hibbel continued, "was ten years of terror. The tribes were subjected to horrific experiments to try and reproduce their magical feats in a way the Rodekans could use as well. We are fortunate their efforts proved to be in vain. However, what they did accomplish is something we've never quite understood: They corrupted the tribes' connection to Origin, forcing their human bodies to absorb more Origin than they were capable of handling."

The sound of a soft cough brought everyone's eyes to Isolde, who tapped her fingers on the table in a rhythmic pattern. "Is this how the faumen gained their current forms?" she asked.

Hibbel nodded. "Exactly, Your Majesty. Each tribe held a native connection to one of the six elements of Origin. When the Rodekans corrupted them, it was that connection which drove the formation of the tribes' bestial bodies we see today. The original names are lost to us, I'm afraid, but we've dubbed the elements by the names Timber, Breeze, Heat, Mist, Dust, and Spark."

"Lucretia mentioned this to us before," Orelia spoke up, resting a hand on Kai's arm while leaning her head on his shoulder. "She said something about the Norzen tribe being the guardians of the forest, so I assume their element was Timber." Kai smiled at her before a soft huff prickled his ears. His gaze landed on a Vesikoi sailor sitting next to Ottoten, who was scowling at Kai in obvious disdain.

Hibbel gave Orelia a beaming grin as his hands trembled in excitement. "Yes, that's precisely correct, young miss. Now, the corruption caused by the Rodekans transformed the tribes into what we now call faumen, leaving them unable to access their magical abilities. Our best guess is, with so much Origin locked within their bodies, they were unable to expel it without causing themselves irreparable harm. However, over the past three hundred years, our scholars have noticed a marked increase in the levels of Origin generated by the ley lines."

Eyes narrowing, Fusette muttered under her breath. "Three hundred years...but that would coincide with the Desolation Wars!"

With a snap of his fingers, the Vesikoi scholar gave a shout of triumph. "Yes! Our studies have determined that, since the Desolation, the world's Origin levels have been steadily rising to their highest levels since the Rebirth, focused around the ten major nexus points. The prevailing theory suggests the Desolation had some unseen effect on the ley lines. In turn, we believe this increase has resulted in more faumen being born with the *potential* to tap into their innate Origin, and some have managed to accomplish it in full. We think the tribes have finally evolved to a point where they can once again expel and manipulate their Origin. Sadly, not all faumen have this potential."

"You've lost me," Harmod admitted. After returning to his seat, the Corlatian watched the discussion in silence. Kai almost forgot his presence until the man decided to speak up. "What does the Desolation have to do with these Origin levels going up? Furthermore, how would you even measure something like that anyway?"

"Origin manifests in different ways," Hibbel replied. "However, one commonality among its manifestations is a highly reactive or potent physical form, capable of expelling tremendous energy if mishandled. It's the appearance of those formations which allow us to gauge the world's Origin levels, as larger and brighter manifestations typically coincide with higher energy levels."

Kai's breath hitched. Images of Havenfall coursed through his mind as he recalled Hakan's gloating. "The lekrite!" he hissed. The leaders' eyes all swung to him as he threaded his fingers through his mane. "Hakan said Cacovis caused the Desolation by igniting a massive vein of lekrite ore in the mountains where the Voidlands now sit. Could it be…?"

"What is this 'lekrite' you speak of, Gravebane?" Kabuji inquired.

It was Maple who answered, rising to her feet and bowing to the older man. "Your Majesty, the best way to describe it would be a glowing purple crystal. It usually grows out of slate or sandstone from what we've seen, and it tends to go '*BOOM*' if you're dumb enough to smack it. Hakan used a cannonball made from it to destroy Havenfall."

"When exactly did the Battle of Havenfall occur, Gravebane?" Hibbel asked. He removed a sheaf of parchment from his robe and was making annotations on it with a black-feathered quill.

Blinking, Kai shook his head as he tallied the days in his mind. "If I remember correctly, it was on the day of the Spring Equinox."

"Ah," the scholar mumbled. "Now it makes more sense."

"Wait, what makes more sense?" Orelia asked. Her ears were wiggling up and down in confusion.

"We've noticed the positioning of the moons has a profound enhancing factor on discharges of Origin. This lekrite certainly sounds like an Origin manifestation, so the energy expulsion would've been effected by the equinox. The Desolation also occurred on such a day; the Harvest Equinox, in fact."

Fusette leaned back in her chair, a pensive look on her face. "So you're saying the moons have an effect on Origin, just as they do the tides?"

Velibor nodded. "Correct. Eoria and Bucheron have a profound influence on many events on Nixtral, though we still don't understand how or why. Eoria, being the closer of the two, seems to have a more potent effect on regions laying along her path through the sky. It's in those regions where Origin manifestations are strongest."

Kai felt a dull throbbing in his skull while his desire to have Lucretia in the room grew with every sentence the Belomians spoke. The discussion continued, though the surrounding voices settled into alight buzz in his ears. He wasn't near smart enough to understand the deeper meaning behind what they were talking about, though he could at least comprehend the basic outline.

A cooling sensation bloomed across the back of his neck as he felt Orelia massage her fingers into his muscles. Kai emitted a contented purr as the former priestess kneaded his tightened neck.

Another pair of hands joined her as Maple reached up to rub his shoulders. The rumble in his chest grew louder, enough to draw Fusette's attention as she gazed at him with an amused expression. He quirked an eyebrow at the duchess and settled for giving her a happy smirk, preferring to relax under the ladies' attention.

"I love you two so much," he whispered, feeling the tension in his head melt away under their tender care.

"We know," they answered in unison. Kai could sense the smirk in Orelia's voice when she leaned over to whisper in his ear, "You made that very clear last night, darling. I hope you're prepared for a repeat performance once we return to our chambers."

Kai fought back the urge to sputter at Orelia's brazen statement. His cheeks flushed red, and a glance around the room told him Kabuji was watching the trio with a huge grin.

"You two are rather cheeky today," Kai mumbled, reaching up to thread his fingers through their hair.

"It's a talent," said Maple. "But we haven't heard you complain yet."

Kai grinned and leaned in to nibble the end of Maple's ear feathers, prompting a heavy blush from the cheery merchant. "Who do you take me for…?" he asked. "Morgan? I'm not *that* much of a dipwit." Both ladies giggled and ceased their ministrations, instead embracing his arms as they leaned against him. He noticed the same Vesikoi sailor from the Galstan table giving him a piercing scowl.

Other than the sailor and Kabuji, no one else seemed to be paying the three any attention, as they were more focused on the debate between Hibbel and Harmod.

A snappish comment from the president brought the trio's attention back to the discussion. "So if you're saying more faumen are able to tap into this, you must understand at least some of what it's capable of."

"We know only the basics of what faumen can do," admitted Hibbel. "The oral histories suggest they were able to perform much grander spells before the Rebirth. With how long it's taken us to reach this point, it may still be another few hundred years before the tribes can reenact those feats."

Stroking his mustache, Kabuji gave Velibor an intense stare. "Can you give us a rough idea of what the tribes can do at this time?"

The Belomian chief nodded. "Well, many are only capable of minor manipulation of the element in question, such as creating small fireballs or making plants grow as Gravebane did earlier. Also, we've learned that, despite each tribe having a connection to a specific element, it's possible for a faumen to be born with potential for an element not normally associated with their tribe. Due to the nature of their abilities, we've opted to call those faumen able to tap into Origin by the term Conjurers. Within this term, each element has its own name applied to its users."

"And what names have you provided for the different Conjurers?" Isolde asked.

"Those like Gravebane who can manipulate Timber are called Seeders. Heat Conjurers are known as Igniters. Breeze users are Drifters. Ashers can use Dust. Blitzers for Spark. And finally, Mariners can use Mist."

So I'm what they call a Seeder, Kai thought while glancing down at his arm. The tiny slits caused by the vines earlier were already healing over.

Fusette rose from her seat and offered a bow. "Scholar Hibbel, perhaps we best get back to the matter at hand. This has been an enlightening discussion, and I find myself quite interested in hearing more about it. However, this Council was called together for a reason."

Cheeks flushed, Hibbel returned the duchess' bow and retreated to his seat. "Oh yes, of course. Many apologies, Your Grace! I'm afraid I tend to ramble on when I'm engrossed in a subject."

"No apology necessary. In fact, I'd like to introduce you to Lady Lucretia after we adjourn. You two may have plenty to talk about."

"I look forward to the meeting, Your Grace."

After giving the scholar a quick nod, Fusette's gaze locked onto Harmod, who stared back with nervous apprehension clear in his eyes. Fusette took a long, wrapped parcel from Saredi and unfurled it on the table. A musket clattered to the table, it's bright red stock gleaming in the light. Harmod winced at the sight of it, as Fusette's breathing came out in heaving huffs, fingers steepled together in front of her face.

"I think it's time for answers, Gideon," she declared. "The man responsible for this war has produced weapons under your realm's banner and blatantly breached the Fulano Pact, instigating devastation which has caused my realm tremendous suffering that will take years to heal. All of this simply to kill two individuals. I want to know everything you do about what is going on. And so help me, if your answers aren't to my liking, I swear by the holy winds I will *strangle* you!"

Chapter VIII

Harmod's face paled as Fusette quirked an eyebrow at him, awaiting his response. Kai watched the man turn his gaze to the other leaders, all of whom were giving him equally curious stares.

"Are you three really not going to say anything to her?" Harmod asked, his eyes pinching together. "She just threatened me!"

Leaning onto his table with his knuckles resting on the thick wood, Kabuji gave a dark chuckle. "I think you should be more concerned with answering her questions, Gideon. As it stands, you're accused of breaching the Fulano Pact, whether you knew about it or not, and the weapon Fusette just dropped looks like it was crafted from *your* national tree. Our predecessors formed that pact specifically to protect the realms from outside interference. You know the ramifications of breaking it. Or need I remind you of Article Six?"

"You wouldn't!" Harmod shouted. "I had nothing to do with Razarr's plan. You lot all know I'm a moderate; I have no desire for war. Hoarfrost, I earned my election on the promise of *avoiding* it!" The president's eyes grew bulbous as he waved his arms while pleading his innocence.

"Gideon," Isolde warned with a steely hardness in her gaze, "anyone with eyes can see this weapon is made from rhubarb cypress, and Fusette's summons mentioned this particular flintlock was the one used to murder my Minister of Trade. Are you going to stand here, knowing this, and try to deflect responsibility?"

Ears twitching, Kai raised his hand. "You'll have to pardon my ignorance, but I'm not well-versed in the specifics of the Pact. What exactly does Article Six say?"

The emperor offered a dismissive wave. "No apology needed. Usually the only ones besides us who need to know the exact wording of the Pact are high ranking military officers and envoys. Article Six, at its core, says any realm not engaged in active hostilities with a nation affected by a breach is honor-bound to intervene on their behalf."

"To put it bluntly," Velibor added, his own eyes pinning Harmod in place, "as President, Gideon is liable for all actions undertaken by his realm's citizens, regardless of where they may have been originally born. Even if he were unaware of Hakan's actions, it's still his and the Corlatian Senate's legal responsibility."

Isolde stood and marched over to Fusette, drawing the younger woman into a hug. "The Holy Queendom of Galstein, for one, will always stand with Livoria. This genocide against the faumen stands to undue years of progress. If we don't stand up to such unrestrained hatred, then who will?"

Emitting a barking laugh, Kabuji slammed a fist to his cuirass. "The Rodekan Empire stands with Livoria as well! My realm may be blackened by its past as slave traders, but since my great-grandfather's rule, the Aduleji family has strived to improve conditions for faumen all over Nixtral. I refuse to stand by and allow this to continue."

Rising to his feet once more, Velibor gave a stiff nod. "The Belomas Highlands offers support to Livoria in its time of need. We stand to lose so much if this Liberation Army wins. This conflict isn't just about Livoria; it could incite a tribal war across Nixtral affecting all faumen and even humans, no matter where they may live!"

Harmod and his delegation stood stock still, frozen in the wake of their peers' outpouring of support. After a few moments, the president collapsed in his chair and cradled his head in his hands. His retainers appeared lost, unsure of how to respond when it was obvious the entire room was united against them.

"I don't know what to do," Harmod confessed. Lifting his head, Kai noticed his eyes looked hazy. As if he were fighting back tears. "I accept that I should've been more aware of what was happening, but at this stage, I'm not sure anything I say or do will have an effect. If I bring this to the

Senate, many of them will throw their support behind the Liberation Army. Less than thirty percent of the Senate seats are inhabited by moderates from the four major factions."

"Gideon," Fusette stated, pulling the president's eyes back towards her. "I have no desire to see your realm harmed by this. Despite my earlier anger, I do not truly want to hurt you. However, you must be aware: *My people are dying*! In less than a year, dozens of thousands of innocent people have lost their lives in the name of needless hatred. One of our church's own bishops slaughtered most of the children in his temple's orphanage, for Finyt's sake! Parliament did their best to tie my hands and limit the amount of authority I could wield just so they could usurp my throne. No more.

"I will not sit back and watch my homeland be torn apart by senseless bigotry and arrogance. Even if it means having to pick up a weapon myself, I'm prepared to defend this realm until my last breath. Now, are you willing to help us root out this insurrection and take back your pride? Or would you rather crawl back to the Presidential Hall in Elimoor and wait for us to come knocking on your borders with hordes of soldiers?"

"With all due respect, Your Grace," Saredi spoke up, "you shall not be picking up any weapons so long as I'm here. Your father would have my head if he were alive!"

Fusette turned to the Lord Chamberlain and leveled a flat stare at him. Kai quivered at the frigid aura his cousin emitted. "Saredi, I respect your guidance, but I'd love to see you try and stop me," she declared. "As for my father, you and I both know he'd be leading the charge at the head of a fleet himself." To Kai's shock, Saredi simply bowed his head with a pensive expression covering his face.

The large man from Harmod's table shot to his feet, his eyes wide with fury. "You wouldn't dare declare war on the Federation! You can't blame us all for a rogue forge master operating on his own and hiring sellswords to fight on his behalf."

The duchess' eyes swiveled to the man, narrowing. "Ah, but we can," Fusette reminded him. "Even if they were just sellswords, the fact remains their force was seen waving flags with the Federation's seal. Such an action insinuates their involvement had the government's backing."

The man's eyes bulged. "But—"

"She's right," said Harmod, causing the man to sputter in shock. "Razarr, or Hakan or whatever his name is, knew exactly what he was doing. By having those sellswords wave Corlati's flag during a battle, it gives the impression we've essentially declared war on Livoria. With everything going on, we now look like advocates for rebellion against the legal government of another realm."

"Then what do we do, sir?"

Raising his eyes to look at the other tables, Harmod gave an exasperated sigh. To everyone's shock, he marched to the middle of the rostrum and dropped to his knees, offering a contrite bow to Fusette.

"Lady Fusette, due to my ignorance, Livoria has suffered unnecessary atrocities and hardship. I beg your forgiveness and a chance to try and make things right. I don't know how much sway I can put on the Senate, but I'm willing to do everything in my power to prevent this from worsening."

"You want to help make this right?" Fusette asked with a leering grin on her face. "Then maybe you ought to put your foot down and stamp out the slave trade, for starters. Part of Hakan's plan revolves around selling most of the captured faumen to your realm's auction houses. We suspect it's one of his primary funding sources."

Harmod's face turned a sickly yellow. "The Senate would never permit that," he hissed. "I'm no fan of it myself, but the slave trade is too in-grained to just abolish!"

"Then perhaps you'd best let the Senate know something once this meeting adjourns," Kabuji spoke up, cracking his knuckles as a low growl rumbled from his throat. "They have two options: either they can give up their slaves on their own, or they'll do it at the end of our blades. As it stands, Corlati is surrounded by four potentially hostile realms! Unless the Senate agrees to work with us, we're authorized by the Fulano Pact to deal with any breaching nation via military force."

"You realize your suggestion will just create a black market for slaves, right?"

A scoff from Isolde brought everyone's attention back to her. "Gideon, you can't truly believe the slaves in Corlati are treated any better now than they would in a black market." Kai fought back a snicker at the unimpressed look on the Galstan queen's face.

Harmod's face drooped at Isolde's counter argument. "You may have a point, but how can I get them to listen? The anti-faumen factions retain enough of a majority to override any attempt I make to change the law. Even when I try to veto laws that seem unnecessary or cruel, they override me there too. It's pointle—"

A chuckle from Fusette stopped the president's rant short. "I doubt you have any method available to lessen their authority like how I dealt with Parliament, so perhaps you'd get better results appealing to their baser instincts."

"Baser instincts...?" Velibor asked, speaking up for the first time in a while.

"Survival," Fusette pressed. Her eyes darted among the room's occupants. "Unless they agree to our terms, there's a good chance few of them will survive the upheaval of an invasion. You say your election was earned on the promise of avoiding war, Gideon? Then prove it! Because of actions originating from your realm, war is a very real threat unless changes are made. We don't want to fight any more than you do, but we will do whatever it takes to protect our realms from this happening again."

"Speak for yourself, Your Grace," said Kabuji. Eyes narrowing, Kai saw the taller man looking over Gideon as if he were a wounded animal. "I reckon the nobility back in Rodekan wouldn't be very upset at an opportunity to annex Corlati again. Some of those families used to live in that region before the Federation went independent."

Kai wasn't sure how serious Kabuji was about annexing Corlati back into the Empire, but Harmod's paling face told him the president viewed it as a legitimate possibility. With a heaving sigh, Harmod nodded.

"Very well. I capitulate. My envoys and I shall draft a letter to the Senate for your review. I suppose I can count myself blessed you refrained from outright declaring war." The other leaders watched as Harmod sulked back to his table and accepted a sheet of parchment from the woman on the far left of their group.

As the Corlatians busied themselves with their task, the other leaders turned to Fusette. "With the most painful part of this summit now dealt with," Isolde murmured, "what help do you need from us, Fusette?"

Settling back into her chair, Fusette glanced at Kai and releasing a long sigh. "To be honest, any help at all would be appreciated. Admiral Basner's fleet alone will be a tremendous boon in fighting the Liberators directly. For now, my biggest concerns are dealing with the rampaging sell-swords and locating the captured faumen. My scouts intercepted enemy correspondence suggesting torture camps in western Livoria while they likely wait to ship the captives to Corlati, though there are no clues to their whereabouts."

Velibor raised his wing, casting a penetrating stare around the room. "Allow me to handle the camps, Your Grace," the elder Aerivolk pleaded. "The United Tribal Forces will scour every nook of the western provinces until we find those missing faumen, of that you can be certain."

Releasing a full belly laugh, Kabuji slammed a fist to his cuirass again. "Don't think for a moment I'm letting you have all the fun, Velibor! If Isolde and Admiral Basner are willing to help deal with the Liberators, the Imperial Army will take the vanguard against Hakan's sellswords."

"Can you muster a suitable number of soldiers quickly enough to handle such a task?" Fusette asked.

Kabuji chuckled. "We weren't about to be caught with our trousers down, Your Grace. Velibor and I already conspired to bring a full brigade of five thousand each. They're near the northwestern border, awaiting permission to cross the Danpa Mountains into Livoria."

Content to let the leaders discuss the details of handling the Liberators, Kai let his gaze roam over the rest of the chamber's occupants.

Ottoten and Hanblum offered him a respectful nod, though he could see the admiral was more interested in keeping a watchful eye on his daughter. Isolde's other two companions were muttering amongst themselves, though occasionally their eyes would flicker towards him for a moment before turning away.

Huddled together in a tight group, the Corlatians were mumbling under their breath as Harmod wrote his letter to the Senate. Kai hoped the Council's tactic would work, as he remembered the stories of the slave houses shared by Hakan and Duarte. They may have been his enemies, but Kai wouldn't wish those horrors on anybody...well, except maybe Hemlocke. Thinking of the traitorous Aerivolk made his blood boil.

The Rodekan delegation was quiet compared to the hushed conversations occurring elsewhere. Instead, Kai noticed they were surveying the room with a quiet intensity. A Soltauri on Kabuji's left was focused on the group from Belomas, which caused Kai's gaze to flicker towards them as well.

The Belomians were engaged in a hurried conversation, many of them chattering as Hibbel jotted their comments down on his parchment. Kai's ears twitched, hearing an occasional word, but their conversation was too rushed for him to hear exactly what was said. He did spot a younger Aerivolk in leather armor, an obvious bodyguard, glaring at him. His eyebrow quirked upwards at the unusual show of aggression.

What did I do to piss him *off?* Kai asked himself.

Ignoring the belligerent guard, he swiveled his ears towards Fusette, hearing her thank the others for their offers of support. A tug on his robe had him glancing down at a grinning Maple, though the muscles in her jaw looked tighter than usual.

"What's got you in such a mood?" he asked.

She rose from her chair and gave him a swift peck on the cheek. "It just feels like so many things are going better for us now. Without Parliament getting in the way, Fusette can actually focus on ending this war."

Scratching behind his head with a shy grin, Kai ruminated over her words. "You may have a point. And with the other realms lending a hand, I reckon we won't have to shoulder as much of the heavy lifting in battle."

A braying laugh from Kabuji cut the pair off, as everyone watched the tall emperor clap Fusette hard on the back. "So what's your next big plan, Your Grace? I hope you weren't planning to sit back and relax now!"

To her credit, Fusette weathered the blow without flinching. Instead, she regarded the older man with a solemn gaze. "Hardly, Your Majesty. I do have something in mind, and it's a task I would've done years ago, if not for Parliament's meddling."

Everyone's eyes spun to her as she turned to Kai and tilted her head, giving him a bright smile. "Kai, I have an important request for you. I humbly ask for your party to escort me to Duskmarsh. It's time to recruit the Norzen of Livoria to our cause."

Chapter IX

As the Liberation Army trudged along a familiar forest trail, the sounds of twittering birds in the forest canopy above made Agosti want to shoot someone. He'd never liked the feathery creatures' singing ever since he was a sprout. The shrill chirps felt like a miner's pickax being driven into his skull, and the enmity had only grown as he aged. The only reason he tolerated wirochs was knowing they were often quiet as mice unless agitated or spooked. Glancing into the trees in a vain attempt to spot the infuriating pests, he pulled a pistol from his belt and aimed upwards, firing a single shot.

Mixed with the fluttering of wings, several squads of soldiers scattered among the trees at the sudden blast. Many looked around wildly, some drawing their own flintlocks while searching for the enemy. Standing beside him, Adalbard stared at the general with an exasperated expression. Agosti chuckled to himself as he saw the men scrambling like insects exposed to the light.

His amusement came to a swift end when Vice General Medoro rode alongside him on a brown-feathered wiroch, a fierce glare on his face. "What in bloody Nulyma are you doing?" he snapped. "Do you *want* the Royalists to know we're here?"

"Oh, shut your damned trap," Agosti barked back. "I doubt those Royalist bastards are anywhere near here. So what if I take a potshot at some stupid birds?"

Medoro's face twisted into a look of unrepentant malice. "Birds…?" he whispered. "You just scared the piss out of our army over a bunch of bloody *birds*?!"

The former river pirate rolled his eyes, shooting a hesitant glare at the vice general's mount. "Hey, I despise them, alright. Doesn't matter if it's the little ones or those damned Aerivolk. The only thing they're good for is roasting over a campfire."

The two stared at each other in clear disdain while the soldiers settled into a nervous silence as they looked on, their faces filled with apprehension. Not a sound was heard as the standoff continued, until Medoro began chortling. The unexpected response sent a tremor of unease through Agosti.

"What the hell is so funny?"

"I think I get it now," the other man replied, a gloating smirk on his lips, "you're scared of that Aerivolk working for our benefactor. The one with the white wings. I remember seeing how you acted around him the last time we saw Razarr."

It took everything Agosti had to bite back a sneer. He didn't think anyone noticed his reticence around the shorter faumen. "Listen," he hissed, "I don't give a damn what you think about me, but there's something about that bastard what gives me the fucking heebies. Not even the damned peltneck who keeps giving us trouble unnerves me the way he does."

Medoro stared, his face scrunched up in confusion. "You're serious, aren't you?"

"You're damn right I'm serious. Whatever you do, don't let your guard down around him. You might not live long enough to regret it."

"General Agosti!" a soldier shouted as he urged the wiroch he was riding towards the two officers, the pin on his uniform marking him as a forward scout. The massive bird emitted a gasping squawk as it came to a stop, its sickle-like beak bobbing up and down with its breathing. "There's a town perhaps three thousand or so yards west of us, on the riverbank. A small one, and the scouts say there's a larger one perhaps an hour or so north of us. Do we skirt around them or attack?"

Stroking the light stubble growing on his chin, Agosti weighed his options. "How low are we on supplies?" he asked Medoro.

"Low enough that our weakest men will likely starve to death by the end of the week, assuming the beasts don't get them first. And we've already run out of prisoners to use as a 'secondary' food source."

The general cursed. "Damn, I was hoping we could avoid having to attack anything larger than a village. Guess we don't have much of a choice. What are the names of both towns?" Agosti looked around with a fierce scowl as a young officer approached carrying a rolled-up map.

"Well, sir," said the man, unfurling the large parchment along the ground and examining it, "considering how far we've traveled, I'd estimate the larger town is the river port of Glimmerdale. The smaller one is called Brightwise."

With a snap of his fingers, Agosti grinned. "I know the first name! I ran into that sellsword lackey of Razarr's around here before the Havenfall battle. I think his name was Obram. The locals shouldn't be too much trouble. Apparently, the whole town was laid low by some illness the last time I was in the area, so they're probably still weak enough to deal with."

Medoro released a heavy sigh, his shoulders slumping. "Then what's your plan?"

"Do we really need one? Just storm the damn gates and round everyone up." Agosti snickered at the other officer's pinched glare. "Tell the men not to use too many of our stonehood bombs, though. I'd rather save them for the Royalists."

"Uh, General...sorry for interrupting, but do you hear something?" the scout asked, swiveling his head. Agosti frowned and closed his eyes, focusing on the surrounding sounds of the forest. He was moments from rebuking the scout when he heard it.

A low whistling sound that grew louder with every second. Agosti's eyes widened when he recognized it.

"Arrows!" he shouted, twisting his left arm up to shield his head with the tiny buckler strapped to the wrist.

Agosti's warning came too late for one, though, as a gurgling cry rang out when an unprepared soldier took an arrow to the throat, collapsing to the dirt in a heap. Several metallic clangs echoed through the trees when a volley of a dozen more arrows fell from the sky, pinging off the Liberators' shields.

The loud, bone-rattling bray of a war horn reverberated above the army's din, freezing them in place with a melody Agosti swore he'd heard somewhere before.

He felt a sting when Medoro gave him an open-palmed smack across the back of his head. "Damn you, Agosti! That's a Royalist horn call," the officer bellowed, "and not just any call, either. It's the bloody Marine Cavalry!"

Spitting out a curse, Agosti rubbed his head as the declaration sent the men into a blind panic. Their frenzied attempts to flee soon spread to the rest of the army. As much as Agosti detested Medoro, he knew the man was a Royal Navy vice admiral for years and so would know the different fleet calls. "Damnation," the former pirate snapped, "I thought those bastards would be further north. What are they doing out here?"

"If I may," Adalbard cut in, drawing the officers' attention to him. "Perhaps we would be best served getting to Brightwise as swiftly as possible, as it's the closer and smaller of our potential targets. We can barricade ourselves within the walls and escape across the river."

Medoro cast a scathing sneer at the priest. "And what are we supposed to do if they draw us into a siege?"

Adjusting his dirty vestment, Adalbard gave the vice general a sharp poke in the chest with his staff. "I doubt we're in much immediate danger. If my memory is correct from listening to the battalion practices at Faith Hollow, that call sounded more like an alert than a command to charge. It's more likely we're being pestered by a scouting squad and they're informing the main force of our location. So long as we hurry, we should be able to barricade the town wall and make our way across the Great Ardei before the bulk of the enemy fleet arrives."

The vice general scowled but nodded to Agosti's relief. The last thing they needed was to break out into a fight amongst themselves with the Marine Cavalry so close.

Nodding to Medoro, Agosti ordered him to begin herding their men towards Brightwise, directing the scout to lead the way. "It's not a half bad plan, priest," he admitted, "but what do we do if the townsfolk rat us out and tell them where we went? You know they will the moment that fleet shows up."

Adalbard chuckled. "I'm surprised at you, Agosti. I figured you'd be the first one to realize our best bet is making sure there's no one left to inform the Royalists of our whereabouts."

A malicious grin spread over Agosti's lips as the men finally began rushing west. "You know, priest, sometimes we think so much alike I wonder if you're a long-lost uncle of mine. Did you have any siblings?"

"By the winds, no! I was an only child."

Riding back towards the pair, Medoro's glare deepened, making Agosti wonder if the man's face was permanently stuck that way. "The good news is," the officer growled, "the men are heading the right direction. Now what do we do once we storm the gate?"

Agosti clapped Adalbard hard on the back. "We'll build on the priest's suggestion. Have half the men seize every useful item they can find. Food, clothes, and supplies take priority. Have the rest capture as many townsfolk as they can, human or faumen. We'll keep using the beasts as extra food while the human civilians will make nice hostages until we can getaway."

"And what will we do with them once we escape?"

Both the priest's and general's faces shifted into dark smirks. "Kill them, of course," Agosti replied as if it were the most obvious answer in the world. "We hardly need *more* mouths to feed, after all."

It was hard for Hemlocke to keep from chuckling at the bewildered look on Obram's face. The two stood at the outskirts of a small village, though not a sound could be heard from within. They had passed by this same hamlet perhaps four or five days ago while circling the trail, and back then it looked perfectly fine. Now, nothing stirred among the throng of half-timbered buildings except the occasional tree ferret or wild rabbit skittering about. Behind them, Grimghast lay curled up in a ball fast asleep, looking like a mangy black boulder except for the occasional snore she emitted.

"By the ancient gods," Obram muttered, "what in bloody hell happened here?"

Looking at it from the outside, one would simply think the village was tucked in for a quiet night. Such a theory was disproven, however, by the fact it was midday, with the summer sun beating down on the two companions enough to leave a light sheen of sweat coating their skin.

The Aerivolk's grin carried a hint of madness as the pair entered the village, their eyes searching for any movement. The ominous silence sent a shiver of glee down Hemlocke's spine as his gaze swept over the village. A lingering rancid odor wafted across his nostrils. Taking a deep breath, he ruffled his feathers, embracing the stench.

"Beautiful, isn't it?" Hemlocke cooed, his chest rumbling in a trilling cackle.

"It's damned creepy is what it is."

Both men wandered among the silent buildings, though only Hemlocke walked with a quiet certainty. He saw Obram tiptoeing over the dirt, his head swiveling about in apprehension. The further they walked, the more powerful the scent from before grew.

"Obram, my friend, you're far too nervous. There's nothing dangerous here. Well, dangerous to *us*, at any rate."

The Risbado turned and leveled a burning glare at Hemlocke. "Forgive me if I don't believe y—what the piss!" Obram turned away from the other man for a moment, only to jump backwards when he spotted a body lying on the ground, sticking halfway out of the doorway to a house. The person wasn't moving, and it didn't look likely they ever would again.

Hemlocke emitted a giggle at Obram's reaction, his own gaze roaming over the corpse. It was an adult human male, possibly in his forties, though the body's withered appearance made it hard to tell. Splotches of red, corroded flesh peppered the neck and torso. Pulsing boils the size of chicken eggs were scattered over the entire body, several of which looked to have already burst. An inky black slime oozed from the broken blisters, trickling down the sides like ebony tears.

Sucking in a breath, Obram inched away, his paling skin contrasting against the dusky grey of his fur. "What is this...?" he asked, pointing a meaty finger at the decaying body.

"This, my friend," Hemlocke answered with a wide toothy smile, "is poetry in action. Remember the poison I told you we would be using to wipe out our enemies? This is the result, and the agony its victims suffer through makes my troubles seem like a common fever in comparison. Look."

Raising his arm, Hemlocke gestured towards a fountain at the village square's center, his eyes lingering on a small crate bearing the Liberation Army's banner near the fountain's base. The crate was covered in tiny claw marks, and looked to be filled with mounds of hay, fur, and leavings.

Obram's gaze followed the Aerivolk's arm, choking back a gasp at the sight.

Dozens of corpses, human and faumen, littered the ground. All sported the same rotting appearance as the first. At least three were lying inside the fountain, the water a sickly grey from a mix of black ooze and blood. Obram looked ready to retch as he remembered to breathe, drawing the overwhelming stench of feces and decay into his nose and mouth. His eyes bulged, spotting a building directly across the plaza that looked like it had been a school. A woman's body lay in front of the doorway and behind her, across the threshold, were several smaller figures.

"What kind of hell-damned sickness is this, and where did you get it from?" Obram whispered. "I've never heard of anything so horrific back in Feswili."

Releasing a demented trill, Hemlocke whispered in the sellsword's ear. "Most Livorians who are old enough will remember this from nine years ago. As for where it came from...well, you already know I dabble in poisons after what I did to Kai's wench. It took some time, but I managed to procure a vial of this from an old black-market contact. I arranged our couriers to drop off a package here the last time we passed."

Obram's jaw clenched. "The last time we passed? Are you telling me that illness did all *this* in less than a week?!"

"Indeed. The pestilence spreads like wildfire if the infected are not contained, and without certain remedies, this is the result. Now imagine if we introduced it somewhere on a grander scale. Somewhere like say...Whistlevale?"

Tilting his sallow face to gaze at the feathered migrant, Obram clicked his tongue. "Hemlocke, I mean this with all due respect, but you are one terrifying son of a bitch."

"What can I say? It's a gift."

Chapter X

The twittering of wirochs filled the air as Kai and the party hustled through the royal stables, saddling up a small flock of birds in preparation for the trip to Duskmarsh. Kai felt a tremor of nervousness make its way down his spine. This would be his first time seeing the Norzen city since his birth parents set him adrift on the Great Ardei as an infant.

After the Council officially adjourned, the rest of the party met up with Kai's group, the seven friends surrounding the leaders like an honor guard. Fusette and Saredi made sure the other rulers and their delegations were assigned spare rooms in the palace's southern wing, where guests were kept. Kabuji proved to be the most curious of their visitors as they settled in, battering Fusette with questions on why she requested Kai's party specifically be the ones to escort her to Duskmarsh, as opposed to a full guard of sailors.

The Grand Duchess' response caused Kai's entire party to flush red in embarrassment.

"First of all, Your Majesty, I'd rather keep this mission limited to as small a group as possible. Having said that, these seven are far and away the best my realm has to offer. Remind me to show you the reports of their exploits sometime."

Behind them, Saredi led a gaggle of servants in harnessing a team of wirochs to Fusette's personal traveling coach. Crafted of black-painted oak and lined with silver trim, the coach rested on two smaller yard-tall, six-spoke wheels in the front and a pair of eight spoke wheels over five feet tall in the rear. The interior was bedecked in fine nobletusk leather with silk curtains covering the windows. Small sacks and two cubic crates were secured to the back of the carriage, a variety of faint smells coming from them. Fusette herself sat in the driver's box, watching everyone bustle about with a forlorn expression and her chin cupped in her hands.

From his spot near the back of the stable, Kai noticed one of his partners approaching the duchess as he finished securing the tack to his wiroch.

"What's wrong, Fusette?" Maple asked, hopping into the box and sitting next to her, a terse frown on her lips. "You look like someone just told you your birthday was cancelled."

"Nothing quite so silly, Maple," Fusette answered, regarding the merchant with a slanted grin as she stretched out. "Besides, my birthday isn't until the end of this moon. No, the palace weapon smiths informed me they finished copying those muskets the Liberators have been using. They even said they developed a new variant. I just hoped I could see the thing before we left."

Maple burst out into a soft laugh as Kai's eyes widened. He'd almost forgotten Fusette's birthday was a mere eighteen days away—a full three weeks— on the 24th of Regemond, the first moon of summer. "Well, even if you can't see it now, we'll be back before you know it."

As if to prove Maple wrong, a middle-aged man in a blacksmith's apron rushed into the stable, a long bundle wrapped in cloth clutched within his arms. Seeing him bent at the waist gulping down breaths of air, Kai wondered if the man ran all the way down from the palace basement, where the smithy was.

"Wait, Your Grace," the man gasped out, stumbling towards the coach as both women leapt from the box to approach the man. Maple held out a canteen and bit back a chuckle as the newcomer emptied the vessel in seconds. "Thank you," he gasped.

Folding her arms in front, Fusette regarded the man with curiosity. "I recognize you," she said, "you work for Master Mica down in the smithy. Is this the flintlock he mentioned?" The duchess gestured to the man's parcel, her eyes roaming over the wrapped bundle in hesitant curiosity.

"Correct, Your Grace," the man replied, doing his best to stand up straight in front of the monarch. He held out the bundle towards her while bowing his head. "It took some doing, but this is what we came up with."

Curiosity piqued, Kai patted his wiroch and ambled towards the group, watching as the man laid the bundle on a tack table and removed the cloth wrapping with a flourish. The apothecary's eyes widened at the sight of it.

The gun was shorter than the yard long Corlatian musket by a third, but much bulkier. The stock was thick, made of brilliant white sun birch with a brass priming plate affixed to the right side. A small rod was nestled under the barrel, the end of which flared outwards like a trumpet.

"What in Finyt is this?" Kai asked, leaning on the table as he inspected the strange gun. A course on firearms had been part of his Hunter training, so Kai was familiar with the basics of how they worked. This new weapon, though, was unlike anything he'd ever come across.

"We call it the blunderbuss, Sir Gravebane," the man said, offering a bow and a pained wince. "Don't ask about the name, though; all I can say is we lost a bet with the kitchen staff. To be honest, after running some tests with the musket Her Grace provided for us, we wanted to make something a bit easier to use."

Picking the weapon up, Kai was surprised by its weight, which he estimated at six kilos. "It's a tad heavy if you wanted it simple. Wielding this thing would be a chore for mounted cavalry soldiers."

"True, which is why we designed it for infantry use. The recoil on this beast would knock a wiroch over. However, it does mitigate some issues we noted in the musket."

"Issues?" Fusette asked, leaning over Kai's shoulder as the party ambled over.

"For one, like pistols, the muskets can only fire a single shot before requiring a reload, which takes roughly four times as long as a pistol. The blunderbuss takes perhaps the same reload time as the musket, but the larger bore allows it to fire multiple projectiles at once. We also hope the bore size will keep it from jamming as much as the muskets are prone to.

The best benefit, if you ask me, is that it's not limited to standard iron ball ammunition."

Kai's eyebrow quirked upwards. "Not limited to standard ammunition? What do you mean?"

The weapon smith's lips curved into a wide smile. "It's not meant to be used regularly as overusing this feature can damage the gun, but if a sailor runs out of iron balls, the large bore makes it possible to use anything within reach as potential ammunition in a pinch. Stones, broken glass, nails, anything small enough to fit down this barrel can be used as a weapon."

"Interesting," Fusette said, plucking the weapon from Kai's hands and lifting it up and down. "This blunderbuss may be just the thing we need to counter the muskets."

The man gave an uneasy chuckle. "It does have some weaknesses compared to muskets, the most notable of which is the range. Muskets can be accurate up to perhaps seventy yards with a competent marksman. However, the blunderbuss is meant to be a close-range weapon like pistols, with an effective firing range of only ten yards. Still, the flared barrel spreads the ammo out over a wider area, which should make it devastating in close quarters."

Nodding along with the man's words, Kai's hand curled into a fist. He could imagine the damage a weapon like this could do to flesh if loaded with glass or nails.

"Your Grace," Saredi said, sidling alongside the group, "the coach is ready for departure. Are you certain you don't need me to come along?"

Rolling her eyes, Fusette thumped Saredi in the shoulder. "I can assure you, Saredi, everything will be fine. I appreciate your concern, but I'm not a little girl anymore. I seriously doubt Gravebane and his party will let anything bad happen."

A shiver ran down Kai's spine as the Lord Chamberlain regarded him with an unyielding stare. "For his sake," Saredi intoned, "he'd best make sure you return in perfect health."

Another hand came from behind, this time Orelia's, cuffing the Vesikoi noble in his slicked back hair. "Lord Saredi, I'd appreciate it if you'd stop glaring at my husband as if he offended your mother," the young woman remarked.

Rather than snap back, Saredi nodded and stepped away while nursing his head.

"Saredi," Fusette continued with an exasperated sigh, "you're the only one I can trust to make sure things are run properly while I'm gone. With Parliament disbanded, the palace needs a steady hand to guide it and direct the war effort until we return. Besides, someone must ensure our guests are well taken care of while I'm attending this matter, and no one is better than you at such tasks."

"I understand, Your Grace. I shall pray every day for your safe return." Kai swore he saw a hint of a blush in the Lord Chamberlain's cheeks alongside a proud smile.

"Thank you, my friend. We'll be back as soon as possible." Turning to Kai, Fusette smiled. "Now how long will it take for us to reach Duskmarsh?"

Kai's gaze twitched over to Lucretia, who unfurled a map of Livoria on the tack table with a sigh. Several markings were made on the map, including three red crosses. "On a normal trip, the trek to Duskmarsh would take roughly five days. However, we will likely need to add one more to account for a necessary detour."

The duchess' nose crinkled in confusion. "Why do we need a detour?"

"There have been reports from nearby Navy patrols citing attacks on caravans along the main road leading to Duskmarsh. No survivors. These red markings indicate where the attacks occurred. Our plan is to skirt around the main road at this point," she explained, pointing to a green circle, "and curve through the forest until reaching the Rustclaw River at this point." Here she tapped a blue circle. "Once there, we can follow the Rustclaw south all the way to Duskmarsh."

"Very well. If you believe that's the best route, then this is what we'll do. I trust your judgment, Lucretia."

After rolling up the map, Lucretia bowed and returned to finish saddling her wiroch. Maple and Orelia, both having already mounted theirs,
cantered past Kai and leaned down as they passed, brushing their lips
against his forehead. He felt a wide smile curve into place, watching as
they passed out of sight through the stable doors.

A soft giggle drew the apothecary's attention to Fusette, who waggled
her eyebrows in a teasing manner.

"Oh don't you start," Kai mumbled. "I get that enough from my sister."

"Hush you. I happen to think you three look adorable together, but if
Serafina is permitted to tease you, then I most certainly am as well. I truly
am happy for you, Kai. Ever since the Runegard incident, you've looked
more cheerful than ever, and I'm positive those ladies are the reason why."
His cheeks flushing red, Kai fought to ignore Morgan's snickering and led
Fusette to the coach.

As his fingers curled around the door handle, the peppy atmosphere
was shattered by a pair of screams from outside, sending the wirochs into
a frenzy.

Kai turned towards the stable doors, his blood running cold with eyes
wide and rimmed in red as the rest of the party bolted outside. He
recognized those shrieks.

"Maple! Orelia!"

Chapter XI

Rushing for the stable exit, Kai's hand slid down to grasp the handle of his mace. Thoughts raced through his mind, wondering what could have caused both his partners to scream. He heard the others shouting in unison, creating a din that rattled his skull, as Fusette ran alongside him. Huffing along behind was the weapon smith, the blunderbuss clutched tight in his arms. The unease in Kai's chest thickened when he heard Teos spouting vehement curses in his native Soltish.

Sprinting into the sunlight, Kai contracted his pupils to avoid being blinded by the sudden sunlight. His gaze swiveled at once to the group of bodies surrounding the wirochs he saw his wives riding.

Another pair of wirochs were standing beside them, the riders leaning towards Maple and Orelia who were trying to urge their mounts backwards. Kai's vision turned a pale, hazy red when he saw the anxiousness in their eyes, though Maple's teeth were clenched in obvious fury. The urge to slip into a Frenzy Haze pulsed when he recognized the other riders as the Vesikoi sailor and Aerivolk guard from the Galstan and Belomian delegations, respectively.

"Cease this uncouth behavior at once!" Lucretia snapped, grabbing hold of the reins for Orelia's wiroch while Ione secured Maple's. Together, the two women coaxed the skittish birds backwards, though the two men remained undaunted in their pursuit.

The Aerivolk's face was curled in a sneer as he swiped his talons at Ione, who brushed the claws aside with her shield. "You lot stay out of this! We just want to show the ladies a good time," he trilled, casting a sinister leer at Maple.

"Too right," the Vesikoi added, his eyes roaming over Orelia with a gaze that had Kai's tails tingling in disgust, "we ain't trying to hurt them…just show them what they're missing with some real men!"

He wasn't surprised to hear the former priestess snap at the sailor, "If you touch either of us again, I won't bother holding Maple back a second time."

Hearing a clamor from the palace, Kai spotted the other realm leaders rushing towards them with an entourage of Fusette's guards scampering after them. Tapping Fusette on the shoulder, he tilted his head towards the incoming group. She nodded, stomping past the party with Saredi on her tails. The moment she sidled alongside Maple's wiroch, Fusette put her fingers to her lips and blasted out a shrill whistle.

Everyone in the immediate vicinity came to a sudden stop, all eyes veering towards the duchess. From his place in the back, Kai turned to the weapon smith, his eyes flickering to the gun.

"I demand to know what exactly is going on!" Fusette bellowed, her grey eyes flashing silver.

Orelia gave an annoyed huff, jabbing her finger towards the two men with one arm crossed over her breasts. "Maple and I were talking amongst ourselves while waiting for the rest of you. Then, without provocation, these two brutes came over and put their hands on us!" Pointing at the Aerivolk, she continued, "That fool should consider himself lucky I held Maple back from gutting him like a fish."

Clenching his hand into a fist, Kai dug his boot into the dirt as a low rumble echoed from his chest. Maple had yet to say anything, the unusual silence a clear indicator of how furious she truly was. He was relieved to see the leaders stepping in, none of whom looked pleased. If he were lucky, they would diffuse the situation without him having to step in. Because if he had to deal with these two…

Feathers flaring, Velibor glared at the Aerivolk guard. "Sibora, what is the meaning of this?" he demanded. "Have you lost your damned kettle?"

Isolde stood at the Belomian chief's side, Ottoten on her other side, and frowned at the Vesikoi. "Ensign Elkrud, I pray you have a good explanation for your actions. I am deeply disappointed to see you accost a citizen of our greatest ally."

The queen's vague rebuke caused Kai's muscles to tense. He turned to the weapon smith as Sibora began speaking.

"Chief, you can't possibly think we can allow this farce to continue," he said, his eyes roaming over Maple. "An Aerivolk and a Norzen, married? It's the most absurd thing I've ever heard of! Even in the Highlands, this would be considered a scandal. No, this young lady's better off coming back with us. I promise I can provide for her."

Elkrud nodded while pointing at Orelia. "The same goes for Lady Basner," he added. His eyes met Ottoten's glare. "Come on, Admiral! You can't think this is appropriate for a lady of your daughter's stature. She'd be much happier returning home with me."

Shaking his head, Ottoten glowered at the young officer. "Ensign, it's not my, *or your*, decision to make. I've already had this discussion with my daughter and yet you're standing there, bringing shame on our entire realm." The bronze-skinned admiral looked ready to breathe fire. "Damn it, Elkrud, give me one good reason why we shouldn't let Lady Fusette tan both your hides!"

"Why would I be the one they need to worry about?"

The sudden question had everyone spinning to face the Norzen duchess, who regarded them with a sly smirk while pointing her thumb backwards. A light pinging sound drew everyone's attention further back.

Kai stood there with blunderbuss in hand, a clawed finger tapping the lock plate while pointing it at the two wiroch-mounted men's chests. "I'm not one to normally use firearms," the apothecary growled, his voice low and unyielding, "but please, give me an excuse to pull the trigger and see just what this thing is capable of."

With a haughty sneer, Sibora chuckled. "You wouldn't dare. Our realms are here to provide yours with assistance and as delegates serving our leaders, we have diplomatic immunity."

Two pairs of grey eyes met as Kai glanced at his cousin. "Immunity?" he asked.

Velibor shook his head, sending the other Aerivolk a stern glare. "Diplomatic immunity offers no protection against this type of foolishness," the chief answered. "Sir Gravebane, I must apologize to you personally for this assault on your family. Please, allow me to handle Sibora's disgraceful behavior."

"The same goes for me," said Isolde, bowing to Kai. "Ensign Elkrud's actions are unacceptable, and I must beg you to allow me to punish him." Seeing the two leaders be so contrite with him stunned Kai for a moment. His gaze flickered to Orelia and Maple, who stared back with worried expressions.

Another glance at Sibora and Elkrud hardened his resolve. Neither one looked apologetic in the least, continuing to stare at the women with obvious lust. Lowering the blunderbuss, he snorted.

"I accept your apologies, but I'm afraid I cannot allow anyone else to deal with this." Turning to Fusette, he handed the firearm back to the weapon smith before clapping a closed fist to his chest. "Your Grace," he intoned, causing the duchess' eyes to widen at his sudden solemnity, "I hereby request the right of a formal Honor Duel."

Most of the party broke out into sputtering coughs, though Morgan looked confused, as was often the case when the sellsword was exposed to Livorian customs.

Fusette and Isolde blanched at the request. "An Honor Duel," the Galstan queen murmured, frowning as she stepped forward. "Sir Gravebane, are you certain you wish to take that path? If so, may I please request a prohibition on mortal injuries? I think we've seen enough death already in this war."

Offering her a nod, Kai rolled his shoulders. "That's fair, Your Majesty. I won't kill them, but it seems an example needs to be made. These men made unwanted advances towards my partners. I refuse to allow such an insult to stand without formal response."

Emitting a wheezy cackle, Sibora swept his eyes over Kai. "Judging from those robes, I'm guessing you're an apothecary. What can a plant peddler like you do against not one, but *two* professional soldiers?" The rulers, sans Fusette, all shared uneasy glances as they watched Kai regard the two men with frigid silence.

Curling her lips back in disgust, Maple moved to shout at Sibora, only for Orelia to press a hand over her mouth. The merchant turned her head in confusion, though Orelia only shook her head with a smug grin plastered over her lips.

Kai shrugged, refusing to rise to the guard's baiting words. He instead turned to Fusette. "Milady, I'm afraid I must deal with this before we can depart. May I have your permission to make use of the Coliseum?"

Fusette blinked. "The Coliseum? Are you saying you want to…?"

"Yes. If need be, gather any of the Exarchs who wish to watch in the stands with everyone here. Even if it's a small audience, I want there to be witnesses."

The Ardei Coliseum was a grand building, easily the second largest in Whistlevale by area after the Royal Palace. Hexagonal and constructed of a mix of limestone, granite, and basalt, it towered over the city's West District in much the same way the Citadel loomed over Runegard.

The outer walls, with an array of pointed arches surrounding the entire exterior, were painted in a pale saffron with carmine edges. The interior halls were unpainted, though many tapestries lined the walls on all four floors. Each of the building's six sides contained four wide, spiraling staircases set equidistant from one another and attached to landings on the upper tiers.

As Kai strolled through the halls of the Coliseum's northernmost side leading towards the arena, Maple and Orelia by his side, he released a frustrated sigh. "I truly wish you two hadn't gone through that," he muttered. His eyes flickered among the racks of weapons hanging from the walls.

Rolling her eyes, Maple nuzzled her face into his shoulder. "Don't you start blaming yourself for other peoples' stupidity. This is probably for the better, anyway. If I'd spilled that idiot Sibora's entrails like I wanted, Fusette would've had to arrest me!"

"You and I both know she wouldn't," Kai responded, tapping her on the nose, "though she'd definitely have to call in a favor to smooth things over with Chief Velibor."

A firm grip on his mane turned Kai's eyes to Orelia, who pinned him in place with a steely gaze. "Regardless, you've gotten yourself into this mess, so now you can get yourself out," she lectured. Emitting a tired huff, her eyes softened as she hugged him close. "Please try to avoid drawing this out too long. The quicker it ends, the less we have to worry about you getting hurt."

"I'll be fine. I already have a plan."

Maple's eyebrow quirked upwards. "*You* have a plan? Sweet Finyt, Ora, we might have to be concerned, after all."

"Oi!" Kai sputtered. "My plans work... usually."

Giggling, the two women patted Kai on the head with a soothing touch. Maple pulled a mace with a rounded head from the rack lining the wall and tucked it into Kai's hand before they both rushed up the nearest staircase. It felt much lighter than his normal weapon; likely made of aluminum. He shook his head and stretched back, feeling a slight pop in his lower spine.

"That felt good," he muttered, setting the mace down and drawing a set of fur-lined domed gauntlets like Orelia's over his forearms. The chill of the metal and leather prickled his skin as they slid into place, making the fur of his mane stand on end. Both bracers gleamed in the sparse sunlight peeping through the arches above as he ducked into a stance and gave a few slow punches. The mace lay forgotten on the ground as he stepped towards the point of light at the end of the hall signaling the arena entrance.

"Let's do this."

"There you two are," Fusette declared as she noticed Maple and Orelia entered the royal box from a nearby door. "We might have a few more people than anticipated."

Tilting her head, Maple asked what the duchess meant, only to peer over the edge of the box and gasp at the scattering of small crowds filling the two tiers below them on the northern side. The groups on either side of the lower tiers looked to be made up of palace servants mixed among several troops of ordinary citizens who wandered in from the city proper.

With a giddy laugh, Fusette pointed out the other rulers and their delegates taking seats on either side of the royal box. Gideon and Velibor's groups sat on the left side, while Isolde and Kabuji settled into the seats to the right. Directly below them sat several lines of people, most of them human, though some faumen were scattered among the mix.

Orelia tapped Maple's shoulder and pointed at three familiar figures in the far end of the group: Dewthorn, Burnsong, and Swiftlock. Taking a close look at the rest, their eyes widened when they noticed every single member of the center crowd wearing recognizable brass watches around their necks.

The Exarch Knights.

Adjusting her ears, Fusette turned her head to listen in on some of the conversations taking place below them.

"Any idea why Her Grace called us out here?" a woman Exarch directly beneath the royal box asked.

A Soltauri man next to her snorted. "I heard something about Gravebane calling for an Honor Duel and witnesses were needed."

Several of the surrounding Knights broke out into irritated mumbling. "What in Nulyma is that bloody fool demanding an Honor Duel for?" another wondered.

"No clue," the Soltauri answered, "but I've been seeing his name in the newsletters a lot since the Battle of Havenfall. Then there's that business with the church and Her Grace..."

A fourth Knight, this one a barrel-chested man in his forties wearing a crisp Navy uniform with a commander's rank on the epaulets, emitted a low growl Fusette almost missed. "I could've sworn we ordered that damn hellcat to keep his head down if he knew what was good for him..."

Fusette's eyes widened before pinching together in anger, her gaze twitching to Maple and Orelia, both of whom were glowering at the officer. At least now she knew why Kai kept to himself following his Branding Ceremony.

"Enough, Bronzefoot," Dewthorn commanded, his admiral's rank glinting in the sunlight. "I don't care about your personal feelings towards the man, but Gravebane is still one of us, so I expect you to hold your tongue."

"We're not on official Navy business, Dewthorn, so don't patronize me," the younger officer snapped back in a hushed tone, giving his superior a haughty smirk before spitting on the floor. "Besides, why should I care about giving the fool respect?"

Unable to hold her tongue any longer, Fusette leaned over the box wall and leered down. "Because I can hear you, Bronzefoot," she chided. The Exarchs all turned their wide-eyed gazes upwards in unison, almost sending the duchess into a fit of giggles.

Eyes locked on her twitching ears, Bronzefoot fell into a stammering mess, unable to string a coherent sentence together. Fusette frowned and held up a hand, silencing him. "Just so we're clear, I never *ordered* anyone to come here," she explained, "it was a request. Nothing more, nothing less. If you have no desire to be here, Bronzefoot, you're more than welcome to leave. The door is right behind you."

The man uttered some foul words before settling into his seat with arms crossed over his chest, reminding Fusette of a cranky toddler.

"Your Grace," a peppy voice called out from further down. Fusette leaned further forward and spotted a young Aerivolk woman around Orelia's age at the stands' edge, dressed in a flowing dress and carrying a warhorn in one hand; the Coliseum's chief announcer, if the duchess' memory served. "I believe the participants are ready."

Fusette nodded and gestured with a hand signal. The woman grinned and blew a deafening blast on the instrument that captured everyone's attention. As the gathered masses turned their heads towards the royal box, Fusette's face settled into an intense, stern expression. Picking up a warhorn from next to her seat, this one with a wider mouthpiece, she brought it to her lips and called for the crowd's attention.

"Thank you, everyone, for coming on such short notice," she began, her tails twitching behind her as she swept her gaze over the throng of people. "For those visiting from the city who may not know what's going on, I'm afraid this isn't a joyous occasion. A formal Honor Duel has been declared and accepted."

Several muffled gasps were heard from the crowd.

Casting her gaze down to the arena, Fusette noticed a pair of figures stepping into the light from the northwestern side to her right. "Ah, it appears the two challenged are making their appearance. I suppose introductions would be appropriate. These two gentlemen are Ensign Elkrud of Galstein and Guard Captain Sibora of Belomas."

Dozens of eyes spun to watch as the two men marched into the arena's center, their stances confident. Both carried plain longswords with curved guards.

"Wait a tic," Morgan piped up from the corner of the royal box, "I thought this was supposed to be a non-lethal duel! Why are those two carrying swords?"

Fusette chuckled. "Do not worry, Sir Morgan. They were given swords specifically crafted for use by gladiators and other competitors; the blades are purposefully dulled. The worst they could cause is some nasty bruising."

The Exarchs broke into an animated chatter. Her focus shifted as Fusette saw Maple and Orelia giving excited squeals while pointing downwards. A quick glance showed a familiar form emerging. "Excellent! Viewers, it seems our challenger, Sir Gravebane, is now entering the arena."

Taking a closer look, the duchess' eyes narrowed, shrinking to pinpricks when she realized Kai was stepping onto the field empty-handed.

"What in the winds?" Fusette muttered. She stormed to Maple on the far-left side of the party's group and tapped the merchant on the shoulder. "Maple, I know we made sure a plain, aluminum mace was provided for Gravebane's use. Why is he engaging his opponents without a weapon? He's putting himself at an unnecessary disadvantage!"

Maple's face pinched inward, her mouth drawn taut. "What are you talking about, Fusette? I handed him the damn mace myself. Ora saw me!" Turning back to the scene below, her mouth dropped open in horror when she saw Fusette was right. "Oh merciful Ausrina," she whispered.

The rest of the party gaped in wide-mouthed shock as Kai strode a third of the way towards his opponents. Digging his boots into the dirt, he curled both hands into fists and hammered his knuckles together. In the stands, Fusette could hear most of the Exarchs braying in laughter, some even pointing at Kai with one screeching how he was an incompetent pebblewit.

"What is that brazen fool trying to do?" Lucretia asked, her spectacles almost slipping from her face. "Even if those swords are dulled, they can still cause severe damage if he has nothing to block with. He knows this!"

Ione trembled on the scholar's left side, her hands covering her mouth. "D-did he forget to bring his weapon?"

"I doubt it," Maple retorted, "not when I handed it to him right before we came upstairs. He had to have left it behind on purpose, though I can't imagine *why*."

A mirthless chuckle came from Maple's right. Everyone turned to see Orelia staring at the arena with her lips curved into a tilted, toothy grin. "Maple, I'm surprised you haven't figured it out yet. I wasn't sure if Kai would really go for it, but it seems he wasn't joking, even if I'm not happy with his decision."

"Not joking," Maple mumbled, "wait, what are you talking about? Do you know what he's up to?"

The sound of a cleared throat startled the group, causing them to turn towards Isolde, who was gazing at the arena in confusion. "Fusette," the queen droned, "do you know why your Exarch is standing there defenseless? Should we not call this off until he retrieves his weapon?"

"There's no need," Orelia urged. Isolde regarded the Vesikoi mixblood with bewilderment. "He's not as defenseless as you think. Besides, Kai would be insulted if you tried calling the fight off now to try and protect him."

"Orelia," Teos spoke up from the party's center, between Lucretia and Morgan, "what is that idiot doing?"

"Remember how he said an example needed to be made?"

"Yes, but what does it have to do with anything?"

"Kai is going to humiliate those two in front of all these people...by beating them into submission with his bare hands."

A loud choking cough resounded from Kabuji. "With his bare hands?" the emperor questioned. "He's a bloody apothecary! What in hellfire makes him think he can pull that off? He's facing two opponents, both with a range advantage."

Orelia's smirk only grew wider, sending a wave of foreboding through Fusette's tails. "If there's one thing our party has learned since meeting Kai, it's that underestimating him tends to have painful consequences. Just watch."

Ears swiveling forward, Kai ignored the laughter of the Exarchs above him. Instead, his entire focus was on the two cackling men in front of him.

"Is he serious?" he heard Sibora ask, twirling his sword. The Aerivolk turned to Elkrud with a cocky smirk. "You reckon he's trying to convince us to go easy on him?"

The sailor emitted a dark chuckle. "If he is, it isn't working very well. I'm still going to give him everything I've got when it's my turn."

Fusette's voice echoed from the royal box. "Exarch Gravebane," she intoned with a firm voice, "are you intending to engage in this duel without the benefit of a weapon?" Kai's ears picked up the gasps from his friends when he wordlessly nodded. "I see. Which of your opponents will you face first?"

Releasing an amused chuff, Kai grinned. "Why draw this out? I'll fight them both at once."

He didn't have to turn around to know his friends were probably looking at him as if he'd lost his kettle. "Are you certain?" Fusette asked. "You won't be able to retract once approved." He nodded again.

His opponents' faces settled into malicious sneers, watching Kai with the predatory hunger of a wolf stalking a lamb.

"Very well. Let the duel commence!"

Clanging their blades together, Sibora and Elkrud circled around Kai to the left and right, respectively. "I thought apothecaries were supposed to be intelligent," the Aerivolk snickered, "but it seems you're just another stupid peltneck."

Kai's eye twitched, his gaze lingering on the Belomian guard for a moment before shifting to his blade. The Norzen's eyes narrowed.

"Any last words before we put you out of your misery?" Elkrud asked, raising his sword, and closing the distance. Without waiting for a response, he lunged forward thrust the blade towards Kai's head...

Only for Kai to simply tilt his head to the side and allow the steel to pass by his cheek harmlessly. With an unblinking stare, Kai met Elkrud's stunned gaze and uttered a single sentence.

"If strength were measured by hubris, you two might've actually had a slim chance at winning this."

In the blink of an eye, Elkrud was blasted off his feet and sent skidding across the arena dirt, stopping in an undignified heap while somehow maintaining a grip on his weapon. Kai had a single arm outstretched, his fist resting where Elkrud had stood moments before.

Sliding a foot along the ground, Kai turned to face Sibora, who trembled in place with sword raised and jaw clenched. The apothecary smirked and held an open hand forward, beckoning the guard to attack.

Sibora growled and charged forward, twirling his blade. The midday sun glinted off the steel, forcing Kai to contract his pupils to keep from being blinded. Stepping in range, Sibora swung for Kai's neck in a wide arc.

A loud clang rang out when Kai blocked the attack with a raised arm, the sword bouncing off the curved dome of his gauntlet. Sparks flew past Kai's head, a low growl escaping his lips. He glanced over and saw a thin cut in the metal.

I thought those swords looked too pristine. They're using real *blades.*

Stepping back, Sibora opted for quick, lightning-fast stabs towards the apothecary's chest. Not a single blow landed as Kai weaved around the sword with the grace of a dancer. With a frustrated roar, Sibora ruffled his feathers and lunged, aiming for Kai's face.

Like with Elkrud, this proved ineffective when Kai pivoted in place, turning his whole body out of the way and letting Sibora's attack sail past. Unlike before, this time Kai grabbed Sibora by the wrist and twisted hard. The Aerivolk yelped in pain, dropping his sword with a clatter.

"Let go, you stupid peltneck!"

Without a word, Kai yanked Sibora forward and raised his other arm. As the guard struggled to free his hand, Kai opened his fist. Releasing a snort, he smashed the open palm into Sibora's prone elbow while pulling back.

The Aerivolk's agitated shouts morphed into howls of excruciating pain as a loud crack rent the air, his wing clearly snapped in two. He stumbled backwards, eyes pinched shut while his right arm hung limp at his side. Kai gave a quick whistle, drawing his opponent's gaze upwards. Lifting his leg, he launched a devastating side kick straight into the other man's rib cage. Sibora's armor offered little protection as he was sent flying, his back striking the arena wall hard.

A roar from behind sent a pulse of pain through Kai's ears. Flattening them, he curved them enough to pick up the sounds of heavy footfalls approaching behind him. The whistle of a blade slicing through the air reminded him of his first battle with Duarte in the woods outside Mistport. He ducked at an angle, the gleaming silver of Elkrud's sword passing by the edge of his vision.

Launching himself back, his shoulder hit Elkrud's solar plexus and knocked the sailor off balance, arms flailing backwards. This gave Kai an opening to slide across the dirt to Elkrud's flank, lifting one leg and smashing a boot heel into his opponent's kneecap. Another booming crack reverberated as Elkrud collapsed to the ground shrieking, curled into a ball and clutching what remained of his shattered knee.

His gaze flickering between the two fallen men, Kai cracked his knuckles with a grim smile slipping into place.

In the royal box, Fusette shivered as she watched Kai take his opponents apart piece by screaming piece. The sounds of metal striking flesh and cracking bones echoed from the cavernous arena, mixed with the pleading wails of Sibora and Elkrud. The duchess fought back the urge to retch. Sweeping her eyes over the stands, she saw most of the women watching were turned away, refusing to watch. Her gaze settled on Orelia and Maple, both staring with the same grim leer their husband wore.

An irritated grumble drew her attention down to Dewthorn, who was watching the scene with an exasperated glower.

"I'm beginning to wonder if that boy was holding out on us," said the admiral.

"I doubt it," Maple replied. Dewthorn matched her stare as Burnsong and Swiftlock watched with keen interest. The other Exarchs tried to discretely listen in, though they were rather obvious about it. "It was his training with you three that got him to this level, and I reckon none of you would brass him off enough to make him use his full breadth of knowledge like this."

Bronzefoot piped up, sneering at the merchant. "What are you talking about? We know Norzen are one of the strongest tribes in terms of physical ability, but he shouldn't be anywhere near this good."

A tittering giggle from Orelia had everyone turning towards her. "Did you forget Kai also happens to be an apothecary?"

"So he's a plant peddler...what of it?"

Maple crossed her wings and looked down at Bronzefoot with an eerie smile. "Would you agree apothecaries are good at putting people back together when they're ill or hurt?"

"Well...yes." Bronzefoot and several other Exarchs shared a confused glance. Anyone with sense knew apothecaries had to be just as adept at setting bones and stitching wounds as they were at medicinal blending.

Orelia leaned over the box and tilted her head, chuckling. "Did you ever consider the idea that the same knowledge he uses to heal a body might also make him proficient at *breaking one apart*?"

It was easy to see who was listening in as everyone who heard Orelia's statement turned sickly pale. The Exarchs seemed to be staring at Kai in varied states of befuddlement, obviously unsure if they should be worried or impressed.

By the time Kai was finished, Elkrud and Sibora both lay in the dirt with blood and dark purple bruises covering most of their bodies. Neither man moved, though their groans of pain could be heard echoing throughout the Coliseum.

Kai snorted, leaving the pair where they lay as he approached the royal box. Dropping to one knee, he clapped his hands together and bowed his head.

"Your Grace," he said, "the honor of my family has been sufficiently restored. Thank you for allowing me to correct this insult."

Fusette nodded, rising to her feet. "I am glad to hear it, Gravebane. It's my hope we won't have to witness a repeat of this in the future." Kai's gaze flickered to the scriveners scattered among the crowds, their quills moving at a frantic pace. At least half of them kept glancing back at the two broken soldiers, making Kai wonder just how bad a light the newsletters would paint him in. Not that he cared too much about it at this point.

He was surprised when Kabuji stood, regarding him with an intense stare. "Sir Gravebane," the emperor called out, "if I may ask, was it necessary to inflict so much damage to your opponents? It's clear you could've ended this much earlier, yet now it's possible these two may never fully recover. Why would you be so harsh?"

From where he stood, Kai could see Lady Bidelga in the back of the royal box shaking her head and flailing her arms about. Biting back a chuckle, Kai almost felt bad for the amount of stress he had put the older woman through since the party's return to Whistlevale. The only reason he didn't was because he was too stubborn to renege on his principles in favor of being politically sensitive.

There was a reason he wasn't a diplomat, after all.

"Yes, Your Majesty, it's true I could've stopped much earlier," Kai admitted. "However, I find myself unwilling to care whether those two make a full recovery." A multitude of gasps rose from the stands. "I may be an apothecary but be aware I'm also a devoted husband, if I may be so bold. If they wished to leave this city in good health, then they should've thought twice before putting their hands on my wives without consent."

Kai's ears twitched as he heard the scriveners' quills scratching at a furious pace. They all watched him with wide eyes, leaning forward to try and catch every word. Half of the other Exarchs cast heated glares at him, though Dewthorn's group eyed him with amused smirks.

"I love Maple and Orelia more than anything. As their husband, my duty isn't *just* to provide their necessities. My greatest desire is to ensure their safety and, most importantly, their happiness. The fact we're of different tribes doesn't matter a whit. What those two men did was essentially spit on not only their honor but my vows to cherish and protect them. Can you stand there and say you wouldn't do as I did if someone dared to lay an unwanted finger on your Empress?"

If Bidelga's eyes grew any wider, Kai was sure they might fully burst from her head. Everyone in the stands turned to watch Kabuji's reaction. Several moments went by in silence as the two stared at each other.

To the crowd's shock, the Rodekan emperor burst into braying laughter, his eyes pinched shut. "You know what, Gravebane, I like you!" he exclaimed.

Kai was unsure of how to take the older man's sudden declaration, though he was at least grateful his words hadn't offended the monarch.

"You bring up a perfectly good point. I damn well *wouldn't* sit back if someone treated my Liko in such a manner. I only asked because I wished to ascertain the reasoning for being so vicious in your response. And quite frankly, I think you were rather restrained, given the circumstances."

One of the scriveners, a regal looking Wasini woman with indigo scales and white feathers, rose up and made use of a provided warhorn to draw Kabuji's attention. "Your Majesty," she said, "are you saying you support Gravebane's excessive use of force in this duel?"

Turning to the woman, Kabuji cast a tilted smirk. "Ma'am, not only do I support his decision, let me point out that any husband who truly loves their spouse should defend their honor with equal or greater fervor. Besides, Gravebane left both his opponents alive when, despite agreeing to a non-lethal duel, he was perfectly within his rights to snap their necks. Trust me, if anyone dared harass my wife the way these two did to those young ladies, there wouldn't be bodies left to bury, agreement or not!"

Kai was stunned to see numerous people across the stands nodding to the emperor's words. Many men were hugging their wives close and gazing at them in love. Glancing back at Fusette, he couldn't help but blink in confusion at the wry smirk she was sending him.

A small flood of people began exiting the Coliseum as the duchess declared the duel officially over, though Kai noticed some of the citizens remaining behind and chatting with the scriveners. Casting one final glance at his fallen opponents, the apothecary marched through the doors leading back into the maze of hallways.

He had a feeling Maple and Orelia would want to make sure he was fine after his most recent battle.

Chapter XII

Upon returning to the palace stables and finishing up the preparations to leave for Duskmarsh, Kai found himself wishing he were back in the Coliseum.

On the one hand, he was correct in assuming his wives wanted to ensure he was still hale and healthy after the one-sided beating he gave Elkrud and Sibora. However, their reasoning soon became apparent as the two women grabbed their husband and began throttling him themselves the moment they set foot in the stable.

"You complete and utter dipwit!" Maple shrieked, pounding Kai on the chest with one hand while the other held him in place by the mane. "What were you *thinking*, going in there without a weapon? You could've been seriously hurt! Or killed!"

Orelia nodded while inspecting his gauntlets with a critical eye. Her gaze narrowed as she saw the thin scratch from Sibora's sword, giving Kai a simmering glare. "It was unusually reckless of you," she said, her grip on his arm tightening. "While I know why you did it, it was an unnecessary risk and I trust we won't need to have this conversation again." Even though her voice was level and calm, it was clear she was holding her anger back.

Despite their obvious frustration, Kai could sense their hearts weren't in it as their blows were mere taps compared to what he knew they were capable of. It didn't stop him from feeling like a fool for making them needlessly worry.

Glancing up at the rest of the party, he ignored their snickers and drew the pair into a tight hug. "I know. I'm sorry I made you both worry. I let my pride get the better of me and it caused you nothing but grief. No matter how confident I was in dealing with those two, I should've considered how you would feel about my actions."

Maple pushed away, her eyes narrowed while jabbing a finger into his cheek. "Yes, you should have," she growled out. "It's bad enough we worry about you when we get caught up in a battle. The last thing I want is to become a widow because you decided you had to win some winds-be-damned pissing contest and got careless!" Slapping her wing against his chest one last time, Maple trudged away and mounted her wiroch, pointedly ignoring Kai's wilted expression as she spurred the bird to the other side of the stable.

Releasing a sigh, Orelia gave the apothecary's ear a firm tug, jerking his gaze back towards her. "Give her some time before you say anything. I can tell something has been bothering her the past few days, but she won't admit what. Just be patient. But if you ever do something so stupid again, we'll set you adrift in a dinghy and you can sleep out on the ocean for a few nights. Understood?"

Kai gave a slow, deliberate nod while eyeing the former priestess with trepidation. He had no desire whatsoever to sleep in what he considered a floating coffin for even one night. "Yes ma'am," he said. His fur stood on end as Orelia pinched the edge of his collarbone, digging her nails into the skin.

"Good," she murmured, her gaze softening as she leaned in and pressed her lips to the base of his ear. "For the record," Orelia whispered, "I thought your performance was rather impressive, despite how foolish it was."

Opting for the safer route, Kai bit back his comments and settled for kissing Orelia on the cheek. His heart swelled at seeing her wide smile return.

"I'll try to have a chat with her first," she continued, "so just hold your wirochs until I can calm her down a bit." Tapping Kai on the nose, she sauntered after Maple with a sway in her hips. That left Kai standing in the center of the stable as Fusette marched beside him, Velibor and Isolde flanking her.

The duchess cleared her throat, bringing Kai's gaze to her as she turned to the Galstan queen. "Isolde," said Fusette, "I know this trip is rather important, so I wanted to get your opinion. How do you think we should approach Duskmarsh? I've shared correspondence in the past with the city's headman, Osko, but his replies have always come off as dismissive. I truly don't want to make things worse."

"Fusette, you must try to see things from their point of view if you hope to get anywhere," Isolde advised. "Given the sensitivity of the situation, the last thing you want to do is offer anything that sounds like an excuse or deflecting the blame elsewhere."

Velibor nodded in agreement, his dorsal feathers fluttering in the breeze coming in through the open doors. "Isolde speaks with much wisdom, young lady. I know it isn't much, but I shall be sending Hibbel with you as a representative of the Highlands. He does have some level of diplomatic training, which may serve you well."

"Thank you very much for your guidance and suggestions," Fusette replied, bowing her head to other leaders. "My intention is to be as open and honest as possible with Osko. I know the citizens of Duskmarsh are likely angry with me, and I must accept responsibility for that."

Standing at attention, Kai was surprised to see Isolde envelop Fusette in a tight embrace. "And that is proof of just how far you've come as a leader, Fusette," she said. "Galen rest his soul, but you and I both know your father would've been stubborn about taking the blame for the troubles Parliament caused you."

Fusette let out a soft giggle. "That's true. For all his endearing qualities, Father could be rather bullheaded about such things." Turning to Kai, she reached up and smoothed out his tousled hair. "Kai, I won't mince words. This is going to be a tough mission. Neither of us has been to Duskmarsh as adults, and we have no idea what kind of reception we'll receive. I'm trusting you and the others to watch my back while remaining on your best behavior."

Nodding, Kai emitted a nervous laugh as his tails thrashed about behind him. "You can count on us, Fusette. To be honest, I can't tell if I'm more nervous or excited about making this trip."

"I know. I can't help but wonder what we'll see there."

A sharp tap on his shoulder shifted Kai's focus to Velibor, who regarded the apothecary with a raised eyebrow. "I'm surprised to see you being so informal with Lady Fusette. Have you forgotten the proper protocol for addressing a woman of her station?"

Kai bit back a snort. "With all due respect, sir, she gets snappy if any of us are formal with her outside of official functions. I get in enough trouble with my wives as you've obviously seen, I don't need to irritate my last known friendly living relative as well."

The Aerivolk chief swung his gaze to Fusette, who returned it with a cheeky grin. "He's family, Chief Velibor. I know what the protocol says, but I'm not going to make anyone I consider family or a dear friend jump over fences just to adhere to strict formalities. I'd much prefer to give you and the other leaders leave to address me informally, but I know only Queen Isolde would take the offer."

With a light chuckle, Velibor shook his head. "You'll find us old folks tend to be a bit set in our ways, young lady. I reckon Her Majesty wouldn't see a problem with it because she's not that much older than you. Now then, I'll go make sure Hibbel is ready to depart while you finish up here." Bowing his head, Velibor shuffled away with his talons clicking against the wooden floor with each step.

Kai and Fusette shared a look before snickering. The duchess gave Kai a soft punch to the shoulder as she tilted her head in the direction Maple and Orelia had gone, towards the carriage. Biting his lip, he nodded and slunk away without a sound.

He wondered how much groveling he would need to do to get back in their good graces.

After passing by Lucretia and Ione, the latter of whom gave him a sharp pinch on the cheek with a stern gaze, Kai grumbled under his breath as he approached the carriage. He could hear Maple and Orelia talking on the other side, prompting him to stay where he was to avoid drawing their ire again.

"Dang it, Maple," Orelia growled, "I know what Kai did was stupid, but don't you think you were being a bit too hard on him?"

Maple's voice, her drawl out in full force, barked back with more anger than Kai could remember hearing from her. "Ya think I don't know this, Ora? I regretted it as soon as I pushed him away, but I felt so angry, and I can't bear the thought of losing him! I already got enough in my ruck without worrying if my own husband is gonna get himself killed. He can't keep getting lucky forever..."

"Mapes, we all saw what he did to those bastards," Orelia retorted, "and that wasn't luck. It was pure, ruthless skill. Also, what has gotten your feathers all in a twist lately? I've never seen you this crabby before. For Galen's sake, you're acting like *Lucretia* back when she was as cuddly as a battleaxe!"

Kai's ears twitched as he heard a soft thump followed by the distinctive sound ruffled feathers. "Have I really been that bad?" Maple asked, her voice cracking. Though she said nothing, Kai could detect the faint sound of Orelia's hair shifting as he saw her nodding through the reflection in the carriage window. "I guess I can't really hide it anymore. The truth is, I'm worried about my parents."

"Your parents? I thought you said you regularly exchange hawk post with them."

"Aye, but I haven't gotten a single hawk in over a week. It'd be one thing if it was just Papa. He's not one for writing letters too often. But I've never gone more than four days without hearing back from Mama. The last letter she sent said they were packing up to leave Shiverhill and batten down in the capital until the war ends. Now I'm wondering if the Libbies or those sellsword bastards snatched them up along the way."

Orelia emitted a drawn-out groan. "You haven't bothered to tell Kai any of this, have you?"

"Of course not! He has enough to deal with. I don't want to make him worry about my problems with all this mess still going on."

"Bloody Nulyma, Maple!" the former priestess hissed. Kai flinched, hearing a pained chirp from his older wife that only could've come from having her feathers pulled. "I love you, Mapes, but you run a greater risk of losing Kai if you shut him out like this. Even if we can't physically do anything about your parents, at least he'll know why you're feeling so down. If he doesn't know anything, what's to stop him from thinking he's failed you in some way and start blaming himself for your attitude?"

Peering through the window, Kai frowned at seeing the dejected expression on Maple's face. He couldn't fault Orelia's reasoning, as blunt as it was. He had been wracking his mind wondering what he did to agitate the merchant, even before the duel.

"Oh pish, Kai *would* blame himself, wouldn't he?"

"Of course he would! We've all seen how that's just the type of person he is, trying to carry everyone else's burdens no matter what it may do to him in the process."

The apothecary's legs twitched as he heard sniffles coming from Maple. The urge to rush over and comfort her was overpowering, though Orelia's warning kept him rooted to the spot. He had a feeling jumping in now would only earn him a smack to the head, courtesy of the younger woman's staff.

"I've really made a mess of things, haven't I?" Maple asked.

"I told Kai to hold back until we could have this little talk, and I'm glad we did. Just...let him come to you. I won't say anything about the specifics, but I'll reassure him it's not anything he did outside the obvious. You're always telling us to be honest and open with each other, so now it's time you follow your own advice. And don't worry. We'll be fine. We've weathered worse problems than this."

The sound of rustling clothes prickled Kai's ears as the two women embraced each other. Stepping away from the carriage, he bustled over to his wiroch and began fiddling with the tack to make himself look busy. He saw the pair emerging from behind the carriage from the corner of his eye and noticed Maple giving him a shy, drained smile with Orelia marching in step right behind her.

He cast a gracious smile of his own in return. Maple said nothing as she walked past, though Orelia came to a stop next to him, her frown pinning him in place more effectively than Saredi's scowls ever could.

"How much of that did you hear?" she asked once Maple was out of range, her eyes flickering to his ears. Kai's flinched; he should've expected her to suspect what he'd been doing.

"More than enough," he said in a clipped, formal tone. "I'll talk with her once we get outside the city and have fewer loose ears waggling about."

Orelia only nodded as her lips curved upwards. "You'll be fine. Just be your normal, charming self," she whispered, planting a peck on his nose before rushing off.

A low chuckle from the other side of the tack table drew Kai's attention to Teos and Morgan, both of whom were leaning against the wall next to their own wirochs while giving the apothecary identical smug grins.

"So how boned are you with those two?" Teos pressed, twirling his mount's reins in one hand. "Maple looked plenty brassed off. Granted, that little stunt of yours was damned stupid." Morgan bit his lip in obvious mirth, running a hand through his thick beard as he asked Kai if they needed to smooth things over for him.

Rolling his eyes, Kai waggled his pinky at the two and finished stuffing the last of his provisions into the saddlebag hanging from his wiroch. "It's not as bad as you pebblewits are making it out to be. Besides, are a pair of dry bones like you in a position to be giving me advice on romance or butting into my love life?"

"That was a low blow, 'pothy, even for you," Morgan grumbled, though the smile never left his face as he gave Kai a playful shove.

Kai pushed back in jest as the three led their mounts outside, where Saredi was directing the palace staff in bringing the carriage out for its final loading. The rest of the leaders were surrounding Fusette in a circle, shaking hands and wishing her luck.

"Don't you worry a lick about Whistlevale," said Kabuji with a face-splitting grin. "We'll keep an eye on things for ya while you're gone and keep you updated by carrier hawk. And we'll do our best to protect your people as if they were our own. I put my eldest son, Matagu, in charge of the Imperial brigade while I'm here, and he's no slouch on the battlefield."

"Indeed," Velibor added, folding his wings in front of his chest as he bowed. "I've left the Belomian forces in the care of General Zelik, one of our brightest commanders who I daresay could be a match for Admiral Basner himself."

Ottoten smirked from his place next to Isolde, tipping a hat towards the Aerivolk chief. "I remember Zelik. We met during a training exercise back when we were young, dumb officers. He may not look like much, but he's crafty and I doubt any commanders the Libbies left behind in the western provinces will have an answer for him."

Fusette offered a contrite bow and thanked the leaders for their assistance, though Gideon remained separated from the rest of the group, his associates surrounding him while eyeing the others with skepticism. Enduring one final embrace from Isolde, the Norzen duchess climbed into the carriage, dragging Ione along while stating, "I have no intention of making this journey without at least *someone* to talk with along the way."

After making sure the tavern maid wasn't planning to bolt and getting the party to agree on swapping off sitting with Fusette at regular intervals, she pulled the curtain aside and waved to Saredi and the others, most of whom returned the gesture.

Spurring his wiroch in front of the carriage, Kai directed the rest of the party to their positions surrounding the vehicle while Hibbel perched himself in the driver's box. With Kai in the vanguard, Maple and Morgan rode beside the left side of the carriage, as Lucretia and Orelia covered the right side and Teos took the rear. With a snap of the reins, the wirochs emitted a series of sharp squawks as they trudged along.

A sudden flicker of movement on the carriage drew Kai's gaze back, only to see a brown-skinned human woman in a pristine white Holy Navy uniform planting herself at Hibbel's side. He recognized her as another of the Galstan delegates accompanying Isolde during the Council, though her bright smile was much friendlier compared to Elkrud. The woman looked to be around Ione's age with an oval face that was just beginning to wrinkle, piercing brown eyes and sleek, wavy black hair flowing to the base of her back. A yard-long metal spear with a broad head was strapped to her back.

"Gravebane," said Isolde as she approached with a slight bow of the head. "This is Captain Yulia Ruhl. Just as Hibbel will accompany you on behalf of Belomas, she will represent Galstein on this mission. She's also quite handy with a spear, so she can provide battle support should you run into any trouble."

Leaning to the side, Kai reached out and shook the woman's hand. "We're glad to have you. It never hurts to have an extra pair of eyes considering where we're going."

"Good to know I'm not the only one who thinks that way," Yulia replied in a refined, plummy voice that suggested a noble upbringing. "We in Galstein have heard many rumors concerning Duskmarsh. It'll be fascinating to see what it's truly like."

It was impossible for Kai to disagree with her. In six years, his travels as a Hunter had never taken him to Duskmarsh, despite a lingering desire to visit the city he now knew he was born in. A well of excitement bubbled within his chest, along with a glimmer of hope that this journey would provide him and Fusette with answers to at least some of the remaining questions about their lineage.

The apothecary glanced over at Kabuji, who gave an amused chortle before gesturing to the Norzen woman he remembered seeing during the Council. "Of course, Rodekan wishes to send assistance as well," he said. "Pelka is easily our best diplomat and the fact she's Norzen may even help in your negotiations with Duskmarsh."

Kai conceded the point and thanked the emperor for his support thus far. Pushing her spectacles further up her nose, Pelka hopped into the carriage with Ione and Fusette, immediately drawing the other two women into an animated discussion.

A quick peek at Gideon and his glowering delegates made it clear the Corlatians would not be sending a representative of their own. After giving the group one final glance, he nodded to Fusette and led the party through the palace gates and into the city proper.

The streets were teeming with people as crowds flooded both sides of the main road to watch the carriage make its way towards the city wall. Kai noticed many watching him, their eyes full of curiosity and wonder. It was a marked difference from the wariness and doubt he was used to seeing, and while it was a preferable divergence, it felt strange. Emitting a soft chuckle, he waved to the crowds as they moved forward.

A small group of children ran alongside the carriage while remaining on the walkway's edge, cheering and waving to Fusette. The duchess giggled and waved back; her lips curved into a jubilant grin. The children's parents corralled them back by the time they reached the gates. Snapping to attention, the guards hammered closed fists against their chests in a crisp salute before pulling the gate doors open.

The massive gate's loud groaning rattled Kai's ears, forcing him to flatten them against his head. He shook his head to dispel the sharp ringing continuing to vibrate through his skull. He was partly mollified by the sincere apologetic looks on the faces of the guards as they rode past.

To Kai's surprised appreciation, the guards waited until the party had ventured a fair distance away before shutting the gates again. Sharing a look with the rest of his friends, he shrugged and cast his gaze ahead once more.

The sprawling, cliff-laden hills of Ballad's End lay directly ahead, down the main road leading south. That, however, wasn't their goal as the small caravan turned its way down one of the thinner roads going west.

While he had no idea of what exactly awaited them in the Videring Forest's expansive swamps, Kai knew one thing for certain.

Their success or failure on this mission could very well determine the outcome of the entire Faumen War.

CHAPTER XIII

A light breeze drifted over the party as they traversed the dirt road leading to the Videring Forest's northern edge. Kai tilted his head and inspected the darkening clouds overhead with a light frown. It looked like they would have to set up camp soon to avoid getting caught in the coming storm.

Glancing back, he gestured to Morgan and offered to trade positions. Morgan nodded and urged his mount forward while giving Kai a smug grin, the bird emitting a gentle chirp.

Shaking his head at the blatant teasing, Kai ordered the mixblood to scout out potential campsites as he sidled his own wiroch next to Maple, who shifted her gaze at his approach.

"Maple," he murmured in a gentle tone, drawing her eyes to his. "Listen, I know I messed up back at the Coliseum and should've warned you about what I was planning. I'm sorry for worrying you. Ora hinted at something else troubling you, but she didn't say what it was precisely. I'm all ears if you want to talk about it." As if to prove his point, Kai fluttered his ears, the furry appendages swiveling back and forth like door hinges.

A soft sniffling noise prickled Kai's ears along with what sounded like a giggle. He watched as Maple's body shook in the saddle before lifting her gaze. She leaned over to rest her head on his shoulder. "It's my parents, Kai," she whispered. Tears streaming down her cheeks, she explained the lack of communication from her parents and how long the silence had been going on. "I'm scared," Maple chirped. "All my mind can think up is that they got snatched off the road by the Libbies or bandits."

Kai wrapped a soothing arm around the merchant's shoulders, pulling her close as their wirochs plodded along chattering to each other. "I can't say I know exactly how you're feeling, honey, but I know if it were my mom and Serafina in their place, I'd be scared out of my fur. We may not be able to do anything now, but I'll have everyone keep their eyes peeled just in case. Who knows, maybe we'll get lucky and come across them along the way. Why don't you tell me a little about what they're like?"

Wiping the tears from her eyes, Maple nodded. "Their names are Cress and Willow. Papa was a sailor in the Navy before I was born and has dark yellow feathers like mine. Now he does carpentry work and builds houses. Mama's a seamstress but her feathers are black and red."

"So you take more after your Da?" Kai asked, his lips tilting into a smile.

Maple emitted another sniffle, her eyes flickering upwards. "Yep, though Papa always joked the only thing I got from him was my feather color. He says I get everything else from his mom, Grammy Loralei."

Fighting back the urge to roll his eyes, Kai pressed his lips to Maple's forehead. "Is that the human grandmother you told me about before?" When she nodded, he ruffled her hair. "She must've been an impressive woman if she helped create someone as amazing as you."

He let out a playful yelp when Maple smacked him in the arm. "Flatterer," she grumbled with a tilted smile back on her lips.

Kai's face nearly split in two, pulling her into a sensual kiss. "There it is," he said, "that's the smile I fell in love with."

She gave a wistful sigh as she leaned over further, nuzzling against him. "What can I do, love? My temporary exile from Shiverhill was supposed to end last winter. If something *did* happen to my parents before I got a chance to see them again..."

"We don't know anything for certain. Like I said, we'll keep our eyes open and our hope strong."

Maple snorted. "If it were anyone besides you saying that, I'd tell them to fall back to reality. But after all we've been through together, hearing it from you makes me think we might get lucky. You do have a knack for doing things others would cast off as impossible, after all."

"Only because I have something worth defying the impossible for," Kai answered, his eyes flashing with adoration. "Two wonderful, beautiful ladies who put up with my stupidity despite all logic and reason."

Her grin now back in full force, Maple threw both wings around him tightly and buried her face in his mane. "I love you," she said, her voice muffled by Kai's fur.

"I love you too."

"Oi, lovebirds!" Morgan called out, his voice snapping the pair's heads to the front. "Let's stop here and set up camp in that clearing just inside the tree line. That storm's gonna hit soon and I'd rather not get soaked while putting up the tents." Rolling his eyes, Kai shouted his agreement and directed Hibbel to follow Morgan off the main road and into the clearing.

His eyes met Maple's and he felt a sense of relief wash over him, knowing that even if they had disagreements at times, their love still burned strong.

To everyone's surprise, they managed to finish preparing the camp with plenty of time before the downpour began. Settling underneath a broad, wax-coated leather tarp secured to wooden poles, the party got to work on dinner with Ione directing everyone in preparing the ingredients for fish stew. All the while, the rain pounded at the tarp, producing a strangely relaxing pattering to accompany their tasks.

To Hibbel and Yulia's shock, they saw Fusette and Pelka in the corner, learning from Kai the proper way to dress and de-bone a fish. When the two foreign delegates questioned the monarch on why she was learning something so unnecessary, Fusette regarded them with a tilted smirk.

"There is no such thing as unnecessary knowledge," she replied. "All learning, even that which is scarcely used, helps a mind to grow and our minds, unlike our bodies, are capable of growing throughout our entire lives."

Lucretia nodded, her eyes glimmering with passion. "Lady Fusette is correct. All knowledge has purpose but what matters most is how we choose to use it. Dolmaru used to say, 'Knowledge carries no bias at its start. Its winds of flight rely on the heart.' That quote serves as the cornerstone of the Citadel's entire teaching philosophy!"

"But Her Grace is royalty!" Yulia exclaimed, her eyes narrowing in confusion. "She shouldn't be learning a commoner's task."

Snorting, Fusette pointed to Kai, the boning knife still clutched in his hand. "If that's the case, perhaps I should forbid Kai from continuing further."

Now the Galstan sailor looked utterly befuddled, her gaze shifting between the two Norzen. "Why would he need to be forbidden? I understand the Exarchs are classed as nobility, but they still function as high-ranking soldiers to my knowledge and need to know how to survive in extreme conditions."

If Fusette's grin gets any wider, Kai thought, *her head might split in two.*

Sure enough, Fusette stared at Yulia and Hibbel with unabashed glee. "Oh, did you forget what I mentioned at the Council? Kai happens to be my cousin. A rather distant one, but still my only blood relative through the royal line, which technically makes him the *crown prince*. Thus, until I produce an heir, he remains the only one with a claim to succeed me as Grand Duke."

The two paled and turned to Kai, who offered a shrug in response. "She's not wrong, though I've lost count of how many times I've mentioned I have no desire to be Grand Duke," he muttered.

"You certainly don't act like a prince," said Pelka as she drew a short-bladed knife over the fish, removing its scales and bones before cutting the meat into smaller pieces for Ione to dump into the cauldron. "Looking at the two of you, the only similarities I see are in your facial features and fur color."

Glancing at Fusette, Kai couldn't argue the point. They shared the same deep ebony hue in their fur, and while the duchess' heart-shaped face carried a rounded softness, both her chin and dusky grey eyes were sharp and angular like his own.

Kai chortled, noticing the rest of the party gazing at him in amusement. "Ma'am, until the disaster in Runegard, I truly believed myself to have no family other than the humans who raised me. Up to that point, I was nothing but a fledgling apothecary and Hunter who bumbled into being named an Exarch by pure chance.

"Since then, I've discovered a family that means the world to me. Sure, we all look different, and our collective personalities are like night and day. It doesn't change our dedication to each other. I will admit though, I still feel unworthy of them at times, never mind being mentioned in the same breath as Fusette. Compared to her, I'm just a two-copper hack—"

The apothecary's rambling was cut short when three hands—one each from Fusette, Maple, and Orelia—all struck the back of his head in rapid succession.

"One of these days," Lucretia quipped from the opposite side of the shelter, a thick tome nestled in her arms, "your self-deprecation is going to earn you a head injury from one or all three of them."

Rubbing the back of his head, Kai cast a stern frown at the scholar and stuck his tongue out. He quickly regretted this when Ione reached over and pinched it between her fingers, slathering a spoonful of castor oil over it.

"Bleh!" he gagged while spitting the oil out and guzzling the contents of his canteen. The entire group burst into laughter, though Kai gave Ione a look of betrayal. The tavern maid only waggled her spoon at him with a smug smile before returning to tending the cauldron.

A quick glance at Morgan and Teos told him neither would be any help either, as the two men muffled their snickers as they focused on prepping the pile of vegetables in front of them. Biting his lip, Kai opted to take his lumps in stride and go back to teaching Fusette and Pelka.

As the storm continued to rage around them, Kai was happy to see the foreigners interacting with the others with little issue. Yulia seemed most comfortable with Orelia, which made sense considering both women were from Galstein and it was likely they knew each other through Ottoten.

He wasn't surprised either to see Hibbel conversing eagerly with Lucretia. The two scholars looked cheerful as they discussed the former's ideas on Origin theory in technical terms Kai admitted to having no knowledge of.

The real surprise was Pelka. While seeing the Norzen envoy chatting with Fusette was to be expected, Kai was happy to see her also drawing Maple and Morgan into the discussion. He had an inkling as to what they were talking about, considering the four would chatter for a few moments, glance over at him, then look between each other and erupt into a fit of laughter.

Soon enough, a round of heavy bowls made its way throughout the group as Ione filled them to the brim with stew. The eleven travelers settled into a comfortable camaraderie, chatting amicably while waiting for the storm to abate.

Kai felt a pleasant sense of surprise growing over the next few days. Thus far, their detour around the main road had avoided any snags, and the road leading over the surrounding swamp was oddly empty.

Due to the area being perpetually flooded, in Livoria's early years massive amounts of stone and dirt were hauled into the Videring to build intersecting roads connecting Duskmarsh and the rest of the swamps to the region's main trade routes.

The strangest thing about the situation was how the road looked as though it had seen recent heavy use, yet there was little evidence other than a mass of faded footprints hinting at who may have passed through before them or when. The only sounds accompanying the party were the constant chattering of the birds, hidden among the mass of cypress trees rising from the burbling water, and the occasional splash of some unseen animal swimming through the murky swamp. A quick glance towards the setting sun told Kai moonrise would be on them before long.

Marching next to him in front of the carriage was Teos, the smuggler's eyes darting about with a quiet intensity. "How far out do you reckon we are from Duskmarsh?" he asked.

Pulling the map from his saddlebag, Kai unfurled it and traced a clawed finger over the path they were currently traversing. "If we keep up our current pace, we should arrive by mid-morning tomorrow. I reckon we're close enough to the city to not worry about running into any bandits either."

"Why is that? Aren't most bandits in this part of the realm Norzen?"

Kai flashed the smuggler a lopsided smirk. "True, but Duskmarsh likes to keep a low profile and, from what I've heard, tends to treat banditry much more harshly compared to other cities because of the negative connotations it brings towards them. If this holds true, most thieving bands will avoid the area to keep from drawing the city's attention, Norzen or not."

Releasing a chuckle, Teos nodded. "I suppose that makes sense. The Norzen already have a foul reputation to start, so they wouldn't want anything nearby that stokes the fire, so to speak."

"Kai!" Ione called out, spurring her wiroch forward. "Fusette says she wants to come to a stop soon so we can discuss a plan for tomorrow. Where can we settle down for the night? All I see is this one road going in a straight line and we're surrounded by swampland."

Scratching at the fresh stubble on his chin, Kai considered their options. Referring to the map again, he frowned. There didn't seem to be anything suggesting a place to stop for rest, and he wasn't sure if camping on the main road was smart.

Despite his and Teos' conversation, there was still a slim chance of bandits roaming the area, particularly at night when patrols by the Navy and provincial constables were few and far between. Camping on the road would leave them vulnerable to anyone who might pass them by as they slept.

Glancing back, he called for Lucretia and Maple, releasing a sigh of relief when the two women ambled over. "Do either of you know of any places to rest on these swamp roads? I've never been out this way and you know the trading routes far better than I ever will."

Lucretia stared at the map with a slight frown, admitting she wasn't familiar with the roads surrounding Duskmarsh due to the hatred she once harbored for the Norzen.

Plucking the parchment from his hands and trailing a long finger over their current route, Maple clicked her tongue. "I've never traveled this close to Duskmarsh myself, but I remember hearing other merchants mention resting plots along the roads running through the swamps. They were made specifically for caravans, so it would be more than spacious enough for us. We likely haven't seen any yet because we only just entered the swamps this morning and from what I heard, you gotta keep your wits about you to find them. I'd be willing to wager we'll find one before long if we look around."

Kai tucked the map back into his bag and gave them both an appreciative smile. "Thanks. If we can find a dedicated resting space, that would be best. Let Fusette know we're gonna keep going for a bit longer. If we can't find one of those plots before moonrise, we may have to take our chances camping at the edge of the main road."

"Wait a tic," Maple muttered, raising a hand over her eyes as she peered at something down the road. Moments later, she broke out into a cheerful grin and pointed. "I think I see something! It's hard to tell with all the trees, but it looks like there's a separate path a thousand yards or so up ahead. The road seems to be wider in that area too."

Sharing a look, the two men snapped their reins and surged forward, ordering the others to continue at their current pace. Kai narrowed his eyes, biting back a flinch from the stinging evening breeze. They soon spotted the path Maple mentioned, branching off the main road to the left and cutting through the mass of dangling cypress branches.

"Ya know something?" Teos asked as they stared at the path, catching a glimpse of a sizable open plot of dirt several dozen yards further in. "I always knew that girl had some damn good eyes, but I reckon most folks would've completely missed this dirt path unless they knew what to look for, especially at that distance."

"No fooling," said Kai. "Then again, that's part of what makes our little family such a good team; we can cover each other's weak spots where it counts."

Sensing movement on his side, Kai glanced over to see Teos staring at him with a warm expression he couldn't remember seeing on the older man's face. "We really *are* like a family, aren't we?" he finally mumbled, his gaze swiveling back towards the approaching carriage.

Nodding once, Kai felt his lips curve upwards as a warm sensation bloomed in his chest. "I've learned there's more to that word than blood. Fusette may be the only one here who's my blood kin, but the rest of you are just as precious to me as Ma and Serafina and, to me, that counts for more than all the jewels and gold in the royal treasury."

It took some time for the party to hack away enough overhanging branches for the carriage to fit down the path without snagging, but they managed it and even finished settling in before the swamp was plunged into darkness with only a campfire and the soft glow of Eoria and Bucheron overhead to provide light.

The group sat around the crackling fire, its orange flames whipping about in a sinuous dance while filling the travelers with warmth. They had long since finished their dinner and were staring around the makeshift camp in pensive silence.

Nestled between his wives, Kai sensed someone watching him and glanced up to see Fusette smiling in his direction with an inquisitive expression. Tilting his head, he parted his lips to ask what she was thinking, only for Pelka to beat him to it.

"Your Grace," the Rodekan envoy muttered, pulling Fusette's gaze to her. "Is it true you've never been to Duskmarsh once during your entire reign? I overheard Queen Isolde mentioning it to the emperor before we left."

Fusette emitted a heavy sigh, her shoulders sagging as if bearing a tremendous weight. "It's true. Father never let me accompany him during official visits and even after ascending to the throne myself, I couldn't find time to make the trip no matter how much I wished to do so. I suppose I only have myself to blame for getting drawn too deeply into Parliament's power squabbles, hoping to gain at least a fragment of the respect they showed my father. Of course, I was young and foolish back then."

A sharp cough came from Teos, who regarded the duchess with a stern gaze. "You shouldn't be trying to compare yourself to your father when it's still so early in your own reign. Remember, Vonlo held the throne for twenty years before he passed. I'd wager he had his own troubles as a young Grand Duke, considering he was only twenty upon his coronation, a couple years older than yourself when you ascended."

"Perhaps, but it's hard not to set myself against him when he's the sole example I have experience with. I never knew my grandfather, after all, though I've heard numerous stories. I assume Parliament saw me as weak compared to Father and hoped to depose me without a struggle. Unfortunately for them, Father was adamant I memorize the entirety of the Livorian Codex, so I knew what options I had in dealing with their little attempted revolt. And now, thanks to their silly ambitions, I wield more authority than any monarch in the realm's history. Authority I don't even desire."

"That seems like a bit of a contradiction," Hibbel remarked. Adjusting his spectacles, the Vesikoi scholar leaned forward with eyes sparkling in interest. "If you truly don't desire the authority, then why take it upon yourself in the first place?"

"To protect the people," Fusette answered without hesitation. "Had I allowed myself to be deposed, I've no doubt Remigo would have attempted to parlay with the Liberators, possibly even allowing them to annex a portion of the realm for themselves and continue their genocide against the faumen."

Ione shivered, her eyes darting between the rest of the group. "Do you really think Parliament would have done such a thing?"

With a noncommittal shrug, Fusette snorted. "It wouldn't surprise me, considering their desire to maintain their own wealth and power, no matter the cost. While I may not be a leader on the same level of my predecessors, I'm certain many more lives would be lost if I allowed Remigo to take over. Father used to warn me that power is magnetic to the easily corruptible, and Parliament was his primary example of the proof in that statement."

Yulia turned her gaze on Fusette, eyes narrowed while drawing a whetstone over the edge of her spear. "Are you saying you're easily corruptible, milady?" the officer asked, her regal voice taut and firm. "You did invoke your wartime authority of your own will, after all."

"I like to hope I'm not as easily swayed by its siren song, but I'll confess to hearing the whispers in my mind, hinting at the possibilities. What I know for certain is many of the worst tyrants in history began their reigns seen as benevolent leaders, only to be corrupted when the fear of losing all that power bound their hearts. My greatest wish is to end this war quickly, if only so I may begin the task of rebuilding Livoria and relinquishing this absolute control."

Yulia's hardened stare didn't waver. "And what if you *can't* let it go?"

A tremor of unease rattled Kai's nerves when Fusette tilted her gaze towards him. Her eyes were soft and warm but also filled with an emotion Kai had become far too acquainted with during this war.

Fear.

"If that were to happen, then I can only think of one recourse available. Kai!" Fusette barked, causing the apothecary to stiffen. "Consider this an absolute order, not to be rescinded under any circumstances."

Kai bit his lip, feeling beads of sweat slipping into his mane as the others watched him with bated breath. He wasn't sure what she was about to tell him, but he already knew he wouldn't like it one bit.

"Speaking from the depths of my heart, I believe maintaining the health and safety of the people to be the supreme law of our realm. Should I become corrupted at any point and attempt to wield my authority in a way that would cause irresponsible harm to Livoria or her citizens...I order you to strike me down."

The party erupted into a furor. Maple and Orelia gaped at Fusette, their mouths hanging open in unrepentant shock. The foreigners looked equally stunned, their eyes wide as saucers.

Releasing a heavy sigh, Kai laid a hand on his mace while returning Fusette's expectant stare. His throat felt tight, as if a ball of lead were lodged in it. "You really think I have what it takes to do something like that?" he asked in a low croak.

"You're the only one I would trust with such a task," said Fusette. Tears glistened at the edge of her eyes. "If I truly fell to the darkness, then at the very least I'd prefer to have a family member be the one to end me rather than some bloodist bastard."

Kai shrugged. "As much as the idea chafes my fur, I understand your reasoning. Very well. If it ever comes to that point, I'll do it. I must confess something, though."

Everyone turned to him, the questions dancing in their eyes.

"The only reason I'm even agreeing to this is because I'm confident you've given me an order I'll never have to carry out."

A muffled chuckle brought Kai's attention to Pelka, whose eyebrow was cocked upwards in amusement. "You are *that* certain of Her Grace's character?" she queried, her fingers steepled under her chin.

"Absolutely. It's true that, in the past, she was never as decisive as I've heard Duke Vonlo was during his reign. However, this war has forced the people of Livoria to decide if they would rise and meet the calamity head-on or fall in its wake, and no one has risen to the task more soundly than Fusette."

The three foreigners shared a look as the rest of the party broke out into subdued cheers. Kai's face flushed when his wives leaned in and kissed his cheeks, then he found himself nearly knocked over when Fusette threw her arms around his neck.

"Thank you," Fusette whispered, her tears now falling freely while Kai patted her back.

From her spot next to Hibbel, Lucretia slammed the tome in her hands shut and cleared her throat. "From my own experience with Lady Fusette, I find myself agreeing with Kai, strange as it sounds. I am curious about something, however." Her eyes locked onto Kai. "How do you feel about returning to the city where you were born? You did admit to never having a reason to go to Duskmarsh yourself until now."

Noticing everyone's attention now focused entirely on him, the tightness in Kai's throat intensified. His fingers curled into fists, the slick sensation of sweat on his palms standing out against the clammy chill spreading through his body. "If I'm being honest, I'm nervous. I really have nothing tying me to the city except a sense of curiosity about what it's like. The most important thing for me is ensuring Fusette's safety. We have no idea what's waiting for us, so we need to be prepared for anything."

It was Morgan who verbalized a question which, while rarely at the forefront of Kai's mind, still tingled at the edges of his thoughts ever since he first heard what happened to his birth parents. Like a fly that refused to go away.

"We know what Hakan said about your folks, but what if they weren't the only ones? What if you've got other family hiding away in there?"

Grasping his arm in a firm grip, Orelia gave him a soothing smile while running her other hand through his mane. "He does bring up a valid point. Still, no matter what awaits us in that city, Maple and I will be at your side every step of the way."

Maple hooked both wings around Kai's neck, drawing him close enough to nuzzle his ear with her nose. "Ora's right. You're stuck with us, for better or worse. Now maybe we ought to pack in this depressing talk and get some shut eye. Tomorrow's a big day, after all, and we want to be at our best."

Nodding as one, the group stood and scattered to their tents, organized in a circle around the fire pit as Kai and Teos smothered the small blaze. Wishing the Soltauri good night, Kai ducked into the tent he shared with Maple and Orelia.

"You really are something, you know that, right?" Orelia mumbled as Kai tied the opening to their tent shut before joining the women in the pile of woolen blankets spread along the ground. "I can't believe Fusette would ask you to do such a thing! Or that you would agree to it!"

The apothecary let out a tired groan and nestled himself beneath the thick fabric. The warm softness of Maple's feathers was soon draped across his chest while Orelia's cool fingers slipped over his lower abdomen. Pulling the two closer, he gave each a kiss on the forehead and let out a contented sigh. "I know what you mean," Kai whispered, "but think about it from Fusette's side. She's clearly smart enough to see the potential danger in having wartime authority for too long. Most nobles would chomp at the bit for even a sliver of that much power. Bloody Nulyma, they even tried taking it by force back at the palace!

"I doubt Fusette would ever do anything to make me follow through on such an insane order, and I trust her. I only agreed to it for two reasons. First, it soothed her worries about the possibility. More importantly, I understand how she feels. If our roles were switched and I went off the deep end, you two and Fusette are the only ones I would trust to stop me from breaking my oath and harming innocent people."

Maple and Orelia stared at him with gentle eyes, both women cooing and curling their bodies against his. "When you put it that way, it makes more sense," said Maple. The merchant's eyes swiveled to her sister wife as her face broke into a wide grin. "So, what are you planning to do now that you're not a priestess anymore, Orelia?"

"I'm not quite sure yet. Truth be told, I'd love to work with children again in some capacity, but I doubt I'd have the disposition to be a nursemaid or midwife. I suppose I could always open an independent orphanage like I originally planned when we were still traveling to Runegard."

Kai let out a soft chuckle. "What about becoming a schoolteacher?" He looked down to see Orelia watching him with keen interest. "Think about it. You're one of the smartest people I know, and you're good at explaining things in an understandable manner. It's true you can be a bit firm at times, but it's clear to anyone how much you adore children. I think it'd bean amazing fit for you."

The redheaded Vesikoi hummed, tracing her fingers over Kai's abs with an intense expression on her face. After an extended silence, she glanced up at him and smiled, kissing the edge of his mouth. "You might be onto something, my dear. I'll talk to Fusette about it later and ask who to speak with about attaining the proper apprenticeship and certification crest."

Maple let loose a throaty trill next to Kai's ear. His body reacted instantly as the Aerivolk's warm hand slipped down his chest with clear intentions. "Perhaps we should celebrate this progress in the best way possible," she purred, her eyes shining with mischief.

Despite a growing desire to submit to her advances, Kai leaned his head over and gave Maple a sharp nip to her ear feathers. "As tempting as that offer is, honey, we all know Lucretia would cut that tent flap open and skewer us in a heartbeat if we woke her up. And let's face it...you can be rather loud when we're having fun."

Kai bit back a groan seeing Maple's grin refuse to leave her face. "Only because you know how to flip my lever, love," she giggled. "Very well, I'll refrain from ravishing you for now. But the moment we have a room to ourselves, you're getting put to work."

Rolling his eyes, Kai muttered an eager agreement before kissing both women and clutching them tight against his body. The three fell asleep in each other's arms, their soft snores serving as the only sound in the dark tent.

Chapter XIV

Saredi Bastion liked to consider himself a simple man, at least when compared to other high-ranking nobles. But then again, he had come from more simple roots. The Vesikoi was a proven example of meritorious court advancement, working his way up the ranks through years of faithful service.

The third son of an archbaron from the northern coast, he began work as an apprentice secretary in Duke Vonlo's household shortly after the man's coronation. His decorum and organizational skills were quickly noted by the young Grand Duke, leading to Saredi being appointed Lord Chamberlain in AR 1012, following Princess Fusette's twelfth birthday. Despite the promotion technically giving him the title of Count, he indulged in few of the luxuries and advantages his peers did.

He didn't enjoy most foods preferred among the entrenched high nobles, such as bulwark deer venison and rare imported sweets like the Belomian wavefruit, thinking them too rich and heavy for his stomach. Instead, he preferred lighter fare like rabbit and leek stew, freshly baked bread, or cabbage salads garnished with carrots, onions, and nuts.

Pulling rank was another common pastime of the nobility, and one which the Lord Chamberlain thought to be the height of disrespect. Despite how hard he was on the man, Saredi held a deep respect for Gravebane for his adamant refusal to invoke his status as an Exarch over others unless lives were at stake. Few in the order could resist the temptation at least once—even Larimanz admitted to doing so several times in his impetuous younger days—and yet the Norzen's reputation remained unblemished.

Lastly, he harbored true faith in House Ardei's dedication to the Livorian people, having seen both Vonlo and his daughter's efforts in closing the gap between not only nobles and commoners, but also humans and faumen of all tribes. It was that faith in Fusette which pushed him to accept her ridiculous order to direct the Royalist court in her absence.

And now, after only five days, he was already wishing for the young monarch to return and take the reins back before he lost his mind. Whatever was left, anyway.

"By the winds, Saredi," Hanblum commented as the envoy accompanied him through the halls, "you look like a corpse just pulled from the river. Are you not sleeping well?" Hanblum's voice was laced with genuine concern and one wing rested on the other man's slumped shoulder, an act which filled Saredi's heart with gratitude.

The two men were enroute to the Parliament chamber to meet with the new 'allied war council,' as Isolde had taken to calling it, and discuss their next moves. Kabuji and Velibor also reported receiving news from their respective brigades and the older rulers had looked positively giddy at breakfast that morning.

Shaking his head and massaging his fingers into the bags beneath his eyes, Saredi emitted an exhausted groan. "Sadly, my friend, sleep has become a rare bedfellow these days. I find my respect for Her Grace increasing every moment she's gone," the Vesikoi confessed. "How she has maintained her sanity while keeping those court buffoons in line, I will never know. The terrifying part is that things are drastically *simpler* now that the opposition forces in Parliament and the church are out of the way."

Hanblum winced. "That is true. I remember seeing Her Grace coming close to throttling a rather belligerent noble during the first session I observed after arriving, right before she sent Gravebane on that mission to Havenfall. I doubt I would have been able to resist the temptation."

Unable to hold back a snort, Saredi gave the envoy a sideways glance as they entered the hall leading to their destination. "I remember that day as well. Kendela was one of the most aggravating members of Parliament and he had no qualms about throwing his wealth around to get what he wanted. It was practically an open secret in the court that he bribed his way to receiving a Margrave title."

"How does one even attain such a prestigious rank, anyway? This Kendela was a merchant, was he not?" Hanblum asked, eyes sparkling with curiosity.

"He was. At the moment, titles can be obtained in one of two ways. First, an individual could advance by proving both a substantial level of personal wealth and engagement in an enterprise which could be considered crucial or fulfilling a growing need within the realm. This is how Kendela gained his title."

"What did that ghastly man do to be considered important enough for a provincial territory?"

Saredi sighed. "Kendela was a lout of the highest order, but even I admit he was a shrewd businessman. He owned over three quarters of the spice farms in central Livoria and oversaw their export to other realms. Saffron, peppercorn, and juniper formed the bedrock of his trade, and each of those are expensive enough individually, let alone combined."

"And the other method?" Hanblum continued.

"A noble family may elevate their rank by finding favor with the royal family, typically through meritorious service or performing deeds beneficial to the realm. The Exarchs are an example of the latter, though lower ranking noble families or even commoners may rise through the court in the same manner via other means. House Babarrio in Everstill is a good example. It was Baron Alpardo Babarrio who invented the steam engine back in AR 975, thanks to financial assistance from Duke Gunnar, Lady Fusette's grandfather. The family was elevated and Alpardo became the viscount in charge of Everstill, where the family has remained to this day."

"Fascinating," Hanblum murmured. "Perhaps I shall speak to Her Majesty about conducting a review of Lady Fusette's reforms once this terrible mess is sorted out. I'm sure Galstein would benefit from a more modern approach to regulating the nobility."

The pair approached the entrance to the Parliament chamber and Saredi swung both doors open in a fluid motion. He felt a smile slip into place when he noticed all the other rulers already seated on the rostrum. Bowing low, he and Hanblum settled into place next to Lady Bidelga, who gazed at Saredi with a disappointed frown.

"You're late, Lord Bastion," the minister snapped.

All eyes spun to Kabuji when the hulking emperor burst out into his signature barking laugh. "Don't give the man grief for such a piddling thing, Bidelga!" said Kabuji. "You know very well we only just arrived a few minutes ago ourselves."

To the Lord Chamberlain's surprise, President Harmod was also present, though he was only accompanied by one of his delegates: a meticulously dressed man in a black suit that contrasted against the president's brown ensemble, with rounded cheeks and a look of intense focus in his eyes. Harmod introduced him as Tarmel Lattier, the Corlatian Secretary of State.

"I believe we should begin our deliberations. After all, time is of the essence," Tarmel urged in a sharp, clipped tenor.

Kabuji uttered a brief apology and settled into his seat as Saredi and the others followed suit. Bidelga gestured to both the Rodekan and Belomian leaders, gently requesting them to share their news.

It was a shock to everyone when the bombastic emperor deferred to Velibor. "I suppose I should start off with the good news," the elderly Aerivolk began. "General Zelik and Prince Matagu have entered Livorian territory and begun the march southward. Zelik informed me the two armies would be separating by today and seeking out their objectives."

Isolde clapped her hands together. "Oh, this is wonderful news. Perhaps it's time we begin making our own moves." Turning to Ottoten, who sat on her left side, she rested a hand on his epaulette. "Admiral Basner, I'd like you to take half our fleet and make for Duskmarsh to provide Fusette support."

The admiral rose and snapped off a crisp salute, slamming a closed fist to his chest. "Of course, Your Majesty. I was hoping to suggest such an action myself, though you beat me to it. I shall begin preparations as soon as we adjourn."

A soft tapping sound drew Saredi's attention to Harmod, who was staring at a pile of parchment in front of him. The man was visibly sweating, his cheeks flushed and yet sunken at the same time as he shifted from one page to the next. While one hand was tapping a finger against the table, the other was overcome with jitters, shaking enough for the Lord Chamberlain to wonder if he was having some sort of fit.

It concerned Saredi enough to raise his hand, calling for attention before addressing the Corlatian leader. "President Harmod, is there a problem? You seem to be distressed."

Harmod's eyes rose to meet Saredi's, his brown orbs wide and unblinking. "I suppose I am. I've just received disturbing news from Deron Robell, a political ally back home in Elimoor. I had wondered why I haven't heard from them since I left, but this certainly fills in some of the blanks."

Leaning back in his chair, Kabuji cast a side eyed glance towards Harmod. His fingers were steepled together, resting just underneath his chin. "What kind of disturbing news?" he asked. "Don't tell me the Senate is opting to throw their lot in with the Liberation Army, Gideon."

"No, they aren't," Harmod answered. "Not officially, anyway. However, it might be more problematic." He slid the parchment over to Tarmel, who gave the documents a quick look before his own face shifted from a deep tan to pale.

"Well spit it out, man! What in hellfire is going on?"

Harmod slumped in his chair, his shoulders drooping and his entire countenance emitting an aura of confusion mixed with despair. "It appears Hakan's plan has been executed against Corlati. Shortly after our delegation reached Whistlevale, a small army of Norzen with no identifying markers infiltrated Elimoor and made an assault on the Presidential Hall."

Gasps echoed throughout the room.

"By the holy winds," Isolde murmured, her mouth hanging open. "I can't imagine that going too well for them."

A dark chuckle came from Harmod, sending a tremor of anxiety through Saredi. "It somehow gets worse. While the attackers were wiped out, they did manage to murder my Vice President. Once the dust settled, the Senate's anti-faumen contingent, led by the Purity Party, took the ensuing pandemonium as a chance to attempt a coup of their own. The moderates have been driven out of Elimoor and I've been technically removed from office due to, and I quote, 'seditious acts and attempting to form political alliances with known enemies of the Corlatian realm.'"

Silence reigned as everyone stared at each other, utterly flabbergasted. It was Velibor who broke the quiet with a rough cough. "Gideon…does this mean the Federation is now officially our enemy?"

Saredi awaited Harmod's answer with bated breath. He was not looking forward to sending a hawk to Fusette informing her of this unfortunate development.

"To be honest, Chief Velibor, I don't know. The Corlati Federation is officially fractured right now. Deron says the largest populist groups, my own Industrial Union and his Progressive Party, have declared the new government to be illegitimate and taken a large chunk of the military with them."

"Taken them?" Kabuji asked, his eyes narrowing. "Where?"

Harmod rested his elbows on the table and cradled his head. Saredi could see his fingers digging into his temple as he let out an exasperated sigh. "According to this, the moderates decided to form a new nation, electing me as its first President with Deron serving as interim Vice President. A map was included showing where the new declared borders are located. They've annexed the northern and eastern provinces of Corlati, setting up the start of a new capital in Edney."

"Edney?" Saredi questioned. His gaze swiveled to Bidelga. "The name sounds familiar, but I can't recall the location."

The Minister of State looked over at Harmod. "If I remember correctly, it's the largest city in the southern half of Corlati, on the north shore of Lake Buxlow," she said.

"Correct," Harmod replied with a soft titter. "Oddly enough, my allies have taken to naming the new territory after that exact lake. They're calling it the Buxlow Republic."

"Wait, why would they create an all-new nation if they're calling the usurpers illegitimate? Why not simply call themselves the true Corlati Federation?" Saredi pointed out. To the Vesikoi nobleman, the idea seemed rather unusual.

"I'm afraid I won't learn the specifics of that until I return to Edney and hear the full story. Speaking from a moderate's point of view, however, I would guess our side sees the Corlati name as tainted by years of horrors wrought against the faumen. Many Corlatians, particularly in the farmlands and savannahs, want to live in peace with the tribes but the Senate has been traditionally infected by the wealthy, who see the tribes as no better than beasts."

Nobody spoke. The silence permeating the room was deafening as everyone took the time to absorb Harmod's revelations. Soon, muffled conversations sprung up between the five groups. Saredi and Bidelga agreed that Fusette needed to be informed of this, though the Lord Chamberlain wondered how the young monarch would react.

"I am curious about something," Kabuji said, rising to his feet while spinning towards Harmod. "Gideon, you said your faction took a large portion of the Corlatian military with them, right?"

Harmod nodded.

"Well then, how likely would it be for the usurpers to make a run at subjugating your allies?"

"Considering they still have to consolidate their own power base in the areas still under their control? Not bloody likely. In addition, the military forces they retained aren't quite as large as ours, so it would become a battle of attrition, and I reckon they'll want to avoid that if they want to pass themselves off as legitimate."

"So how will you approach this, Gideon?" Velibor asked, ruffling his feathers and eyeing the younger man in curiosity. "While this situation makes a potential conflict easier for our side, you do still need to address it. Should you need to return at once, I'm sure everyone will agree your troubles are sufficient reason to leave." Around the room, everyone's head bobbed in agreement.

To Saredi's surprise, Harmod shook his head. "As tempting as the idea is, I must decline. Deron and my allies can handle things on that side of the border until we end the conflict here."

Harmod took a blank sheaf of parchment and scribbled a note down. Rolling it up, he handed it to one of the couriers and requested it be sent to Deron immediately. Turning back to the others, his lips curved upwards in a toothy grin.

"What are you planning, Gideon?" Kabuji asked, a matching grin forming on his own face.

"I'm sending orders for Deron to divide our forces into three groups. The largest will be on standby to defend against the Corlatian Army in case they decide to attack. The second will serve as border patrol. With Buxlow now forming a buffer between Corlati and Livoria, our men can roam the border and prevent any additional sellsword companies from marching to the Liberators' aid."

"And the final force?" Isolde inquired.

Harmod's grin shifting into a nervous smirk. "The last group, a company of about six hundred, will be ordered to march to Whistlevale at once using one of our more recent inventions: a steam-powered carriage. I know it's not much, but I'd like to offer their services in the immediate defense of the capital."

Sharing a look, Saredi and Bidelga nodded. "That would be much appreciated, President Harmod," said the Minister of State. "Such a boon would permit us to divert more sailors to combating the enemy directly."

A wheezing cough came from Velibor, pulling everyone's gazes to the elderly Aerivolk. "I suppose if this is how the dice are going to fall, then perhaps we should make everything formal and binding. I'd like to be the first to offer official recognition to the Buxlow Republic and accept them as stalwart allies of the Belomas Highlands."

Erupting into another of his booming laughs, Kabuji slapped a palm on the table while fixing the Belomian chief with a teasing smile. "Damn it, Velibor, you beat me to it! In that case, the Rodekan Empire officially recognizes the Buxlow Republic as well."

Rising from her seat, Isolde bowed to Harmod and cast a sweet, tilted smile his way. "This will certainly be an interesting development. The Queendom of Galstein also recognizes the Buxlow Republic as an independent nation and I for one would love to discuss a potential alliance once the hostilities in Livoria are over."

Glancing at the others, Saredi released a heavy sigh. "It would be so much simpler if Her Grace were here to handle this. Seeing as how she's busy, though, it seems I must fulfill such obligations until her return. As Lady Fusette's representative, I offer the Grand Duchy of Livoria's tentative support of the Buxlow Republic. Once Lady Fusette returns, she will likely offer formal recognition."

Bowing to everyone, Harmod thanked them for the outpouring of support. "We will do all we can to limit Hakan's allies from continuing to pour into Livoria. Now then, have you heard any updates from Lady Fusette?"

Saredi nodded. "We are fortunate Duskmarsh is less than a day's flight by carrier hawk. According to the missive she sent I'm assuming yesterday, the delegation will reach the city sometime tomorrow."

"How confident are you she'll be able to convince the Norzen to fight?" Velibor asked. The chief stroked his feathers, casting a sharp gaze around the room. The question brought a tense aura to the room, as Duskmarsh's allegiance could shift the tide of the war in either direction.

Kabuji let loose a hearty chuckle. "Hey now, I sent Pelka with them for that very purpose," he reminded them. "She's a competent envoy and I'd wager she knows more about Norzen traditions than anyone outside Livoria or Belomas."

"That may be," Saredi said, "but the headman of Duskmarsh, Osko, is not one for the flowery language employed by most diplomats. He's crafty, and I worry he'll try to pressure Her Grace into making excessive concessions just to return to his good graces."

A scoff came from Bidelga to the Lord Chamberlain's side. "I'm more concerned about sending Gravebane along. He's a competent apothecary, but a diplomat he is not."

Saredi smirked. "Then I suppose it's a good thing he isn't there to be a diplomat. You should remember that, despite his flaws, he takes his duties as an Exarch seriously."

"Are you feeling well, Saredi?" Bidelga questioned. She pressed an open palm to the noble's forehead, though he brushed it away with a withering look. "You sound almost *proud.*"

"I wouldn't say I'm proud, but I respect the man's ability and, as Lady Fusette is fond of saying, he has proven himself in spades. The frightening thing is that each of his friends are equally capable and terrifying when provoked. Should Osko attempt anything untoward, he won't have an easy time of it against them."

CHAPTER XV

Kai's entire body quaked as the delegation approached the massive wall surrounding the city of Duskmarsh. Formed from intersecting logs, the bottom layer of which vanished into the murky waters of the swamp, the wall extended at least fifteen yards above the water's surface and loomed over the party.

With Maple and Orelia flanking him, Kai noticed a small squad of armored guards, all Norzen, milling about in front of the open gate. The caravan was swiftly noticed, however, and the entire squad turned to face them. Even at a distance, Kai could see the tension in their bodies, tails coiling in anticipation and hands grasping their spears tight.

A small cloud of dirt rose from the ground when Pelka urged her wiroch forward, pulling alongside the trio. Kai suppressed a frown at the worried expression on her face.

"They seem nervous about something," the Rodekan commented.

Orelia nodded. "So it would seem. I hope they permit us to enter."

"They bloody better," Maple grumbled under her breath. "Be a bit of a pain if we came all the way out here only to be turned away at the gate." Kai silently agreed with her, though his ears twitched as he heard confused mumbling among the guards before two began approaching the incoming group.

A quick glance back to the carriage and his gaze met Fusette's through the hole behind the driver's box. Her face was set in grim determination, which lit a fire in the apothecary's chest. No matter what, they came here for a reason, and he would do his best to make sure they fulfilled that mission.

"Halt," snapped the guard on the right. He was a young male, around Kai's age, the bright orange fur on his tails bristling and short ears folding forward at the tips.

His accomplice, a sharp-eyed woman in her early fifties with silver and black fur and wearing a black sash with gold trim none of the others were sporting, tapped the tip of her spear against his cuirass while eyeing the group in unrestrained curiosity.

"What business do you have in Duskmarsh today?" she asked.

Pelka moved forward and held up her left hand, palm inward, then proceeded to tap her own right shoulder, then her left, and finally placing a closed fist directly over her heart. "At ease, Madam. We are escorting Her Grace, the Lady Fusette, to speak with the headman of your fair city. None here mean you any harm."

The male guard focused his attention on Maple and Orelia, staring at them with a glimmer in his eyes that rankled Kai's fur. "I hope you lot aren't expecting us to let the rest of these faumen in," he groused. "We've had enough trouble with wayward fools thinking they can sneak in, and that ain't even considering the—"

His tirade was cut short when the woman struck him in the back with an open palm. Kai thanked the woman in his mind, as he felt an urge to slap the man himself. "Shut yer yap," she growled. "What did I tell you about opening your fat gob?"

To Kai's amusement, the man's face turned a ghastly shade of white. "S-sorry, Vice Commander Guri. I swear to Cuballa it won't happen again."

Kai's eyebrow shot up as he glanced at Pelka. "Cuballa?" he asked.

"The Norzen's traditional vision of what you Windbringers call Finyt," she answered with a cheeky grin. "It appears I might have to give you a beginner's course on ancient Norzen customs at some point."

Their gazes were drawn back to the guards when Guri barked, "See that it doesn't."

Turning back to Kai, she inspected him closely, her eyes lingering on his face. "I don't know why," Guri murmured, "but something about you looks bloody familiar. I am Guri, Vice Commander of Duskmarsh's illustrious city guard. What's your name, boy?"

Eyes narrowing, he tilted his head. "Kai Travaldi, ma'am. And I'm quite certain we've never met. This is my first time visiting the city, after all, so I'm unsure why I would look familiar to you."

Both guards' eyes widened. "What self-respecting Norzen uses a house name like a damned human?" the male asked.

Kai's lips curved upwards, his fangs poking out, when he heard the carriage door burst open behind him followed by the audible thump of boots hitting the dirt.

"Considering I also have a house name, I want to know if you'd care to *repeat* that question?" Fusette drawled, her pupils contracted and locked on the two guards as she strode forth raising an emblem of the royal family's seal.

In a flash, Guri's spear swung in an arc behind her comrade, its shaft striking the guard behind both knees and dropping him to the ground. Guri herself followed suit, clapping a fist to her cuirass mid-kneel.

"Your Grace!" she exclaimed.

It was clear the rest of the guards near the gate had heard her, as all their knees hit the ground in unison. Kai would've been impressed at the synchronization of it all if he wasn't so busy trying not to laugh.

Fusette strolled towards the two, tapping Kai on the knee. With a quick nod he urged his wiroch forward, falling into step behind his cousin. Ordering Guri to stand, she faced the older guard with a firm countenance.

"I know the proper protocols haven't been followed for announcing my arrival ahead of time," the duchess said, "however, time is against us, Vice Commander, and this visit has been woefully needed for years. You will take us to speak with Headman Osko at once. If he cannot speak due to prior commitments, then we shall find accommodations in the city until he is ready."

Guri's eyes swept over the rest of the party, who were watching the scene with hints of mirth hidden in their smiles.

"With all due respect, Your Grace, do you intend to bring these others into the city as well?" she asked.

"Are you telling me I'm forbidden from bringing my bodyguards and the chosen representatives of our realm's allies to meet with Osko?" Fusette replied, her voice flat and unamused. A shiver ran through Kai's spine, thankful the monarch's piercing gaze wasn't focused on him.

Waving her hands in front of her, Guri stepped back. "O-of course not, Your Grace! It's just... things have been rather unsettled of late, so we've been forced to take extra measures to secure the city against invaders."

"The fact you're suspicious of my personally selected security makes me wonder if Duskmarsh considers *me* an invader," Fusette pressed. The duchess looked ready to spit fire if the hitch in her voice was any indication.

Guri's face paled even further, her shoulders slumping as she hauled the other guard to his feet. "No, Your Grace, we do not. Please follow me and I shall take you to the chancery to speak with Headman Osko."

Giving a single curt nod, Fusette returned to the carriage and climbed in, instructing Hibbel to follow Guri with the party covering the sides and rear. Once in place, everyone followed the older woman through the gate.

As they passed the guards, Kai spotted them eyeing the party with fierce glares.

Lovely, he thought. *Like we didn't have enough to worry about.*

Ever since he was a sprout, Kai had wracked his mind imagining what it would be like visiting the city of his birth. From the differing opinions he'd heard over the years, he knew seeing it with his own eyes would be the only way to know the truth.

Thus, he was pleasantly surprised by how normal it all looked, despite the obvious differences. As Guri led them into the city proper, Kai noticed his companions were just as transfixed as he was, everyone's eyes drinking in the sight of what many regarded as the center of power for Alezon's Norzen.

Duskmarsh, being a city built on a swamp, was sprawling and widespread in a manner reminding him of Havenfall. Only a few scattered buildings stood higher than two stories tall, and those stood out among their shorter brethren like black-wooled sheep.

Many of the largest structures and even groups of houses were set on broad pyramidal mounds of dirt, each over a hundred yards in width, covered with grass and clumps of brightly colored wildflowers. These mounds were connected to each other via an intersecting web of bridges built with stone archway frames layered with dirt and grass.

Wooden walkways branched off the larger mounds intermittently, leading to wooden platforms with each supporting what appeared to be various shops and smaller houses. Connecting the entire city between these various structures was a series of wide canals, larger than the ones he had seen in cities like Whistlevale or Runegard and all leading out to the surrounding swamps through arches in the city wall.

Kai was intrigued by the long, flat-bottomed boats dispersed throughout the canals, ferrying people among the larger mounds and smaller platforms. The oarsmen operated with efficient movement, using long rowing oars to propel their craft through the water in silence. He turned to Guri and pointed them out.

"Pardon my ignorance, but what are those?"

The older Norzen regarded him with mirth. "You really *are* a stranger here," she muttered, a smirk splayed across her lips. "Our grand city is known for many things, but our greatest pride is the gondola. They require a skilled hand to pilot, but you'll never find a more trustworthy craft for navigating anything smaller than the ocean."

A shiver ran down Kai's spine as he watched the boats glide over the water's surface in tranquil silence. They reminded him of watching wild ducks swim on the river outside Havenfall growing up.

With every bridge the group crossed, it became apparent more people were growing aware of their presence. Mumbled whispers among the populace followed them with each step. Kai felt hundreds of pairs of eyes on them, his gaze roaming in a sweeping pattern.

Large crowds were gathering at the walkways' edges, filling the streets with Norzen of all ages. Many were staring at him with a mixture of confusion and curiosity, though they would cast suspicious frowns at the rest of the party. Kai's body stiffened feeling his wives sidle their wirochs alongside his, their hands resting on his arms. He gave them both a reassuring grin, struggling to ignore the chill in his gut.

Trying not to focus on the growing attention, Kai let himself take in the sight of things which reminded him of other cities he'd seen throughout Livoria.

In the corner of the mound they were walking across, he noticed a blacksmith hammering away at what looked to be a broadsword. On the opposite side, he saw a busy meadhouse in full swing, several tavern maids bustling about with arms weighed down by plates full of food.

Kai's gaze shifted to Ione and the two shared a nostalgic smile, the scene reminding them of the fateful day they met. He also spotted Lucretia staring at the meadhouse with a forlorn smile forming on her lips.

Swinging his eyes to the front, he led the group after Guri, Fusette's carriage rattling along with Morgan and Teos bringing up the rear.

After walking a distance that left Kai grateful for their wiroch mounts, they reached what Guri declared as the very heart of the city.

The mound they were approaching was the largest by far, at least triple the size of the others. The pagoda at its center was impressive, easily the tallest building in the city at six stories tall and constructed of stone and wood in a pyramidal tower design with each tier slightly smaller than the one below it. Several smaller buildings surrounded it, and the doors of each were in constant motion, numerous Norzen flitting in and out.

"This is the central chancery," Guri explained, her eyes glazed over. "Headman Osko's office sits on the top floor, but you shall meet with him in the audience chamber on the second."

Kai glanced over when Teos stopped his wiroch alongside him as they came to a stop in the square just outside the chancery. The smuggler stared up at the colossal structure, scratching the base of his horn under his hat. "Looks a fair bit taller than the Royal Palace," he said.

A chuckle could be heard from the carriage, its door opening wide. Hibbel leapt from the box and rushed to hold his arm out for Fusette and Ione, who stepped out one after the other.

"Thank you, Hibbel," Fusette muttered while smoothing out her dress. She gazed up at the towering chancery with an approving nod. "That is true, Sir Teos," she continued, "however, the palace is much more widespread despite being only three stories high at its apex and takes up more than triple the area of this cluster of buildings. Still, I must confess to being fascinated by the beautiful architecture."

"The headman will be pleased to hear your praise, milady," Guri tittered. "We Norzen take pride in our architectural and engineering expertise, though many others around the world fail to appreciate them."

Kai couldn't help but notice the older woman's attention lingering on Maple and Orelia as she spoke, her eyes pinching together in visible befuddlement.

"Yes, well," Fusette murmured, "my greatest hope is such foolish thinking will be a thing of the past once this war is over and done with. We leave ourselves in your capable hands, Vice Commander."

Bowing low, Guri beckoned the group to follow. Dismounting their wirochs, everyone ambled after her at a brisk pace. As they stepped through the freestanding gate leading to the chancery's stairway, everyone's head was on a swivel.

I'm pretty sure we all *look like country bumpkins,* Kai murmured to himself with a chuckle. Even Fusette wasn't immune, her royal demeanor abandoned as she spun around taking in as many sights as she could.

If he were honest, though, he couldn't fault them for their gawking. His own eyes darted from place to place, though they always returned to the gondolas, gliding over the otherwise still waters of the swamp.

The chancery interior was luxurious, though it retained a rustic charm Kai appreciated. The furniture was crafted of solid wood, likely harvested from local cypress trees. Each cushion was made from fine leather, and the overhanging lanterns from glimmering, stained glass in a variety of colors. Tapestries lining the walls were covered in flowing script that Kai recognized as High Norzen.

Not that he could read any of it, but he'd looked at Cacovis' journal enough to recognize his tribe's native script at a moment's notice. If anything, the sight only served to remind him to ask Lucretia if she'd mind teaching him the language at some point.

Guri led the party upstairs, with Kai and Fusette at the front, Pelka forming a line with Maple and Orelia just behind them. Yulia and Hibbel brought up the rear, while the rest of the party formed a scattered group in the middle.

Tilting his head, Kai saw Ione glancing about, her shield resting on her arm and ready to move at a moment's notice. Morgan and Teos looked equally tense, their eyes monitoring the curious crowd building along the walls as they climbed upstairs. Lastly, Lucretia was in the center of the group. The scholar's body trembled, her eyes refusing to stop moving.

Releasing a sigh, Kai felt a wave of empathy for the woman. Given her history, being in the middle of Duskmarsh had to be causing undue levels of stress. He leaned back and murmured to Orelia, tilting his head towards Lucretia. His wife nodded, brushing her fingers down his cheek before falling back to walk with the young noble.

Kai bit back a grin when he saw Lucretia give Orelia a confused stare before turning to him with a petulant frown. He shrugged and rolled his eyes at her in jest.

"Here we are," Guri announced, coming to a stop. The double doors were wide and ornate, with dozens of various jewels and precious stones set into the wood. Guri gripped both handles and hauled the doors open, leading the group into the chamber.

The expansive room reminded Kai of the Parliament chambers back at the palace, though square-shaped rather than circular. In addition, there were no seats arranged in rising tiers, with tables and chairs instead being spread out in lines along the walls. The room was minimalist in its furnishings outside the seating, with the only other notable ornamentation being pedestals set equidistant around the wall, each holding a lit glass oil lamp.

At the far end of the chamber was a raised platform, upon which sat a large oak desk decorated with brightly colored baubles, none of which seemed to have a use other than looking pretty.

A tall man was seated behind the desk in a broad, high-backed chair that Kai thought, in a small corner of his mind, looked disturbingly like a throne. He looked roughly equal in age to Guri, perhaps even a few years younger. His dark grey, almost black, fur was fading to a brilliant white in places with age, long bangs hiding a leathery face covered in wrinkles. Two sharp grey eyes hidden behind round spectacles were fixated on a piece of parchment he was scribbling all over in front of him, though his gaze flickered upwards towards the party every few moments.

After several of these fleeting glances, his quill stopped moving. Pushing his glasses further up his nose, the man raised his head and took a deeper look at the party. Kai noticed his gaze linger on Fusette before his lips parted in a sudden gasp.

"By the forest's blessings," he mumbled in a soft, withered voice. Kai was forced to strain his ears to hear what the man had said before he clambered out of his chair and bustled around the table. Several guards moved to assist him, but the man brushed them off.

Stopping in front of Fusette, he looked the duchess up and down with an expression of disbelief. "Lady Fusette is it really you?" he asked.

Bowing her head in respect, Fusette's lips curved into a confident smile. "Indeed, Headman Osko. It's a pleasure to see you again. I haven't enjoyed your company since my coronation ceremony."

"Quite so," Osko answered while lowering himself onto his knees. The man's actions inspired the guards and other Norzen within the room to follow suit. Osko returned to his feet and cast a sweeping gaze to the rest of the party, his fingers curling into half-closed fists. "I apologize if the guards gave you a rough time. Emotions have been high in the city since our recent skirmish with the Liberation Army several moons ago, among other things."

As the party broke out into confused muttering, Fusette nodded. "I was afraid of that. Admiral Larimanz mentioned in a report how a smaller force had broken off from the main army and was heading this way. I trust you dealt with the situation?"

"Of course, Your Grace. We are quite capable of defending ourselves. It comes with the territory of being a Norzen, as I'm sure you're aware."

"Yes. Sadly, I am aware of the difficulties facing our tribe." Turning to the others, Fusette gestured the older Norzen with a wide arcing swing of her arm. "Everyone, this distinguished gentleman is Osko, headman of Duskmarsh." She then proceeded to introduce each member of the party individually, her smile growing as Osko offered them all a firm handshake.

When she got around to Kai, Fusette was positively glowing in happiness. "Osko, you may have heard of this one even if you two haven't been formally introduced. This is Kai Travaldi of Havenfall's Hunter Corps, though he also goes by another name: Gravebane of the Exarch Knights."

Osko's eyes widened, pivoting to face Kai. "So this is the sprout we've heard so much about! We weren't sure if we believed the rumors floating about over the past few years. It wasn't until the newsletters started coming in from Whistlevale after you revealed yourself that we saw the proof on the parchment."

Unsure of how to respond, Kai stood still, though he sensed his wives shifting behind him. He felt a gentle pressure on his back in two places, the sensation filling him with a sense of relief.

His shock returned, though, when he heard a heaving gasp from Osko. The headman stepped back with bulging eyes and a pale face. For a moment, Kai worried the man might pitch backwards in a dead faint. His hand trembled, rising until a jittery finger pointed at Kai's chest.

"It can't be," Osko whispered. "...Ulfrik?" Now it was Kai's turn to stumble back. He met Fusette's gaze before gaping at Osko. He could hear his friends gasping in surprise behind him as well, though he didn't dare turn around. He did, however, see Guri standing behind Osko with her mouth hanging open.

"By Cuballa's shores," the guard breathed, "*that's* why he looked so damned familiar."

Kai hadn't heard the name Ulfrik since his battle with Duarte in the royal archives beneath the Citadel. That night, the monk had revealed it as the name of his biological father, murdered by Hakan when Kai was still a young infant.

"D-did you know Ulfrik?" Kai asked, his breath catching in his throat. "I was told that was the name of my birth father...but that's about all I know of my parents."

The headman's wrinkled face slipped into a tight smile. "Young man," he said, "If I hadn't already seen the man's corpse years ago, seeing you would've convinced me he'd finally come back after a long trip. That's how much you resemble him. Ulfrik and your mother Frida were among the most respected members of our city."

Kai stepped back, feeling Orelia guide him to sit in a nearby chair. A torrent of emotions surged through him, not the least of which was unfettered joy.

Frida. The name kept repeating in his mind like a mantra. *My birth mother's name was Frida.*

Tears prickled the edge of his eyes, though he soon felt the soft touch of Maple's wings on his face. The gentle caress was enough to soothe him, even if he had thousands of questions fluttering around his mind.

A gentle weight rested on his shoulder, drawing his attention up to Fusette. His cousin gave a soothing smile that, combined with the ministrations of his wives, filled him with warmth.

"Thank you, Osko," Fusette said while bowing. "I think Kai needed your words more than even he realized. Now, I'm afraid the reason for my visit isn't as pleasant as I would wish."

Osko and Guri shared a glance. "I was afraid you'd say that," the headman replied. He returned to his seat behind the ornate desk and plopped onto the cushion with a heavy sigh. "I assume you are seeking Duskmarsh's assistance against the Liberation Army?"

"Correct," Fusette confirmed. "You've already been forced to face them yourself, though I'm unsure of how much you've seen of their atrocious weaponry."

"We did see those strange long flintlocks they've begun using," Guri offered. "Where did they acquire such an unusual weapon?"

To Kai's surprise, Osko waved off his subordinate's question. "How they came to acquire those guns matters not. What I want to know, Your Grace, is why we should raise arms in this conflict when you've ignored our past pleas for communication."

Kai grimaced, a look matched by the monarch. They suspected this argument was coming, but it didn't mean they relished the thought of debating it.

"I'm afraid I must beg your forgiveness on that front, Osko," Fusette answered with sincere regret in her trembling voice. "I let myself get caught up in Parliament's foolish political games and it has caused my family's relationship with your city to sour. I reckon the only good thing to come of this is that Parliament forced my hand."

A contemplative hum came from Osko. "Is that so? What happened, milady?"

Fusette emitted a heavy sigh. "They attempted to rise against me in a coup, assisted by the Windbringer Church's Quorum of Bishops." Kai's gaze twitched to Guri when she let out a hiss. "However, the attempt was foiled and Parliament has been disbanded until the end of the war. This may well be a boon for your city, as without the nobles interfering, I can make real changes towards reintegrating the Norzen back into main-stream Livorian society."

"Impressive. Not even your father, may the forests rest his soul, had the stones to stand up to Parliament in such a manner."

Kai felt a chill and turned to see Fusette's mouth set in a taut line. "With all due respect, Osko, I am *not* my father. You'd do well to remember that.

Now you mentioned other issues beyond just the Liberators assaulting the city. What specifically have you been seeing?"

The way Osko chortled and waved a dismissive hand at the question as he paced back and forth rankled Kai's fur, though he couldn't pinpoint why.

"Nothing you need be concerned with, Your Grace. Just a few groups of vagrants caught trying to sneak in after getting lost in the swamps over the past few moons."

The headman sounded *far* too pleased with himself for Kai's comfort. His mane was beginning to itch, and he'd learned long ago to trust his gut.

"These vagrants wouldn't happen to be faumen of other tribes, would they?" he asked.

Coming to a sudden stop, Osko's gaze shifted to Kai with an intense stare. "That's correct, but how do you know that?"

"Simple logic, really. With the Libbies being stretched thin the longer the war goes on, it's not outside the realm of possibility to think faumen from the western provinces would try fleeing the region to avoid getting snatched up, and the roads leading past Duskmarsh would offer the quickest route east. If that's the case, those aren't vagrants you've been capturing...they're innocent people seeking refuge."

A loud thud echoed through the chamber, drawing everyone's eyes to Osko. The older man glared at Kai, his eyes dripping with venom.

"Mind your tongue, boy! You may be Ulfrik's son, but you know nothing of how things are done here." He snapped his fingers towards a young guard, who approached and gave a crisp salute. "Bring in the three we captured last week," she ordered. "I want him to see what happens to those who violate our sanctuary."

Nostrils flaring, Fusette watched the guard rush off. She spun to Osko. "You can't be saying you've been tossing Livorian citizens into the gaol without informing the capital. You know the protocols, and I haven't seen a single report coming from Duskmarsh regarding imprisonments."

"We like to handle things ourselves, Your Grace," Osko supplied. He strode back to the desk, tracing a clawed finger along the edge. "It's been that way since the great Erklaus founded our city." The headman's eyes flickered to Kai as he spoke. "Besides, the way I see it, you forfeited any authority to make demands of us with your neglect."

"You're striding the same treacherous line as Parliament, Osko," Fusette warned.

Kai's eyes swept over the rest of the party. Lucretia carried a defeated look on her face, though Teos and Morgan both looked ready to spit nails. Ione stayed close to Fusette, one hand resting on the grip of her cutlass. Maple and Orelia were huddled together with Pelka, mumbling amongst themselves. Off to the side, Yulia and Hibbel were watching the parlay with worried expressions.

It took almost fifteen minutes for the guard to return, but when Kai saw the figures he was leading in, it was enough for the familiar cloud of a Frenzy Haze to settle over his vision.

The guard was dragging two older Aerivolk along, an obvious couple, along with a single younger female, their wrists shackled together and wearing ratty prison tunics. The older female bore feathers the shade of polished garnet and ebony, though her pale face and exposed talons were covered in dirt. The blonde male was much taller than his companion, equally dirty with deep yellow feathers that sent a frigid tremor down Kai's spine. Lastly, the younger woman's sky blue feathers were caked in dust and her round face pocked with tiny scratches.

The apothecary could hear all three emitting ragged breaths with each step and could tell they hadn't been allowed to bathe in who knows how long. He wasn't sure what they'd endured during their imprisonment, but he also wasn't sure he *wanted* to know.

Beside him, a heavy rumble echoed from Fusette's chest, her eyes flaring with rage. "Osko..." she growled.

Just when Kai didn't think the situation could get any worse, he sensed movement behind him and heard a horrified trill from his wife.

"Mama?!" Maple shrieked. "Papa? Clove!"

The trio's heads shot up, their eyes widening in terror when they saw Maple's open-mouthed gape.

"It can't be," Clove muttered in delirium. Her eyes were locked on Maple's, an expression of uncertainty marring her features. "Is that really you, Featherbolt?"

"Maplyne?" the man, Cress if Kai remembered correctly, gasped in a hoarse voice he had trouble hearing even with his sensitive ears. "Oh Finyt, don't tell me they caught my little girl, too…"

The woman, Willow, stared at Maple in shock, a thin line of drool mixed with what could only be blood trickling from the corner of her mouth.

If Kai was angry before, hearing the man's words rendered him volcanic. Taking a closer look, he realized they looked exactly as Maple described. He spun towards his cousin with eyes rimmed in crimson.

"Fusette," he hissed, locking eyes with the duchess, "I suggest you speak up before I take this into my own hands." The iron tang of blood overwhelmed Kai's nose as his nails bit deep into his palms.

He wasn't disappointed by the monarch's explosive reaction.

"Osko!" Fusette bellowed. She and Kai stood shoulder to shoulder facing the headman, their fur bristling in fury. "What in bloody Nulyma is the meaning of this? These three look as though they've been beaten. Repeatedly. Release them at once!"

The surrounding guards broke into a disorganized tumult, glancing between Osko and Fusette while the two stared each other down.

Kai wasn't sure if he was more impressed or concerned when Osko scoffed at Fusette's command. "I think not, Your Grace," he retorted. "These three, among others, were found violating our borders and they will be punished in accordance with our laws. Your father should've explained to you the truth of our struggles against the other tribes. I watched my predecessor explain it to him in depth during his first visit following his coronation. That he didn't tell you before his passing is a shame on his memory."

Quaking with rage, Fusette stormed forward until only Guri stood between them and jabbed a pointed finger around the other woman into Osko's nose. "That you think the other tribes are our enemies is the true shame," she said. "I don't rightly care if this is how you've always done things. I am the reigning Grand Duchess, and I refuse to brook such unrestrained hatred any longer. Not from you, or anyone else for that matter, with all the damage it has done to our realm."

Osko's eyes flickered to the prone Aerivolk. All three stared at Fusette with wide eyes.

"Are you really Lady Fusette?" Cress asked, his gaze lingering on her twitching ears.

She turned to the pair with a soft smile. "That is correct, sir. I must apologize for how you've been treated. We will be taking you back to the capital with us once our business is done here."

"They're not going anywhere except back to the gaol," Osko snapped.

Before Kai could think to stop her, Maple barreled towards her parents, her feathers brushing his arm as she passed. His eyes bulged when he saw the young guard covering the three prisoners step in front and raise his spear towards Maple's heart.

The bladed head didn't make it above the guard's waist before Kai was on him, slamming his mace onto the weapon's shaft to snap it in twain. He pinned the paling youth in place with a dark glower that promised death.

"You lay one finger on them," Kai intoned, "and I promise they'll be scraping what's left of you off the wall."

The glimmer of polished steel shone in Kai's peripheral vision, his eye shifting to see a second guard swerving around Fusette to press her own spear against his neck.

"Put the mace down, boy," she commanded. "What kind of Norzen protects an *Aerivolk* of all things?"

The woman let out a sharp yelp when Orelia appeared from her blind spot, striking her in the wrist and sending the spear clattering to the floor.

A firm scowl slid into place on Kai's lips when Osko hammered both palms on his desk and shouted, "Have you lost your kettle? Your parents would be ashamed of this!"

Muffled gasps resounded from the party. Kai was impressed at the vitriol Morgan and Ione were spewing towards Osko, using multiple curses he'd never heard of before.

The apothecary turned and faced Osko with his back straight and head held high. "You say my parents would be ashamed of my actions. Well, who decided that? I never knew them thanks to the grudge of a bitter, hateful maniac. When I was a sprout, I always wondered what it would be like to have grown up here among other Norzen. Now, after seeing how you act and treat others the same way as the bastard who murdered my parents...I'm glad things turned out the way they did."

The Norzen headman began sputtering with indignation. "You dare say such a thing?" Osko spat. "Have you no honor or pride as a Norzen?"

"Whether I'm Norzen or not doesn't matter a lick. What matters is that I consider life a sacred blessing, no matter what tribe someone hails from." Kai's gaze flickered to Maple and Orelia, giving them a cocked grin. "A body is naught, but a shell meant to house the heart and soul, which are how a person *should* be judged. There's proof in this very chamber of our ability to befriend and love others, no matter our differences."

Osko stared at Kai, a befuddled expression on his face. "Love? Don't be daft, boy. We follow few of the Windbringer teachings, but one thing we agree on is that love between different tribes is not only impossible, it's blasphemy."

Sensing his friends and loved ones surrounding him, Kai smirked at Osko and shook his head in amusement. "That's where you're wrong."

Then, to the shock of everyone present not in the know, Kai and his wives raised their arms in unison. The sheen of their wedding ribbons glowed in the lantern light, the ends fluttering in the breeze drifting through the open windows.

"Love is a force which knows no boundaries," Maple declared, her gaze meeting her parents' with a tilted smile. "It is both the greatest power we hold and our strongest shield against fear and hatred."

"You say love between the tribes is impossible," Orelia continued, "but Kai has a habit of proving that word wrong with every action he takes. His capacity to love and care for others not only draws people to him like a flame but makes him the finest apothecary Nixtral has ever seen."

Kai stepped forward, his lips curving into a confident grin while meeting Osko's gob smacked stare.

"You seem like a betting man, Osko. What say we make a little wager?"

Chapter XVI

Silence reigned in the audience chamber as Kai and Osko stared at each other. The apothecary's grin widened when he saw the headman considering his challenge. The rest of the party stood in a curved arc behind him, hands resting on their weapons.

"A wager?" Osko finally murmured, fingers threading through his mane as his eyes narrowed. "First of all, what kind of wager are you suggesting? Furthermore, give me one good reason why I should make any kind of deal with someone who would so brazenly spit on their familial history. By Cuballa, boy, do you truly know *nothing* of your family's legacy?!"

Kai shrugged. "I know more than you probably think I do. But let me warn you. You can either make a wager with me and try to save face, or I can stand back and let Fusette do as she wants. And considering how brassed off she is, you'd probably suffer less dealing with me."

Eyes widening, Osko's gaze flickered over to Fusette, who was eyeing him with a confident smirk. He met Kai's stare and gave a quick nod. "Very well. What are the conditions of your wager?"

"Simple. I'll take on any fighter you're willing to set against me one-on-one. No conventional weapons. Victory conditions to be determined at the battle site. If I win, you set these three and the rest of the captive faumen free."

He heard several Norzen emit a hitched breath. Osko chuckled. "I see. And if my fighter wins?" he pressed. The older man snapped his fingers at Guri, who rushed out the door in a flash.

"Then I suppose you'll get to add me to your collection of prisoners."

The party broke into a furor at his words.

"Kai, have you lost your bloody kettle?" Lucretia shrieked. The others made similar shouts, though their voices blended together in a headache-inducing cacophony.

"Silence!" Fusette barked, bringing everyone's attention to her. She pinned Kai in place with a severe frown. "Kai, are you certain about this?"

He nodded, reaching across to grip his bandaged left wrist with his right hand. His eyes twitched, meeting Maple and Orelia's unhappy stares.

"Darling, do I need to remind you about the dinghy?" Orelia warned, arms crossed under her chest and a firm scowl in place. From her spot next to the Vesikoi, Maple looked torn between wanting to throttle him and kiss him, her gaze constantly twitching towards her prone parents and friend.

Biting his lower lip, Kai nodded. "I know, Ora, but I'm asking you and Mapes to trust me on this. I have no intention of losing."

A new voice, a heavy bass even deeper than Duarte's, boomed from the chamber entrance, "You seem rather confident for someone so small!" Pivoting on his heels, Kai turned to the door and felt his eyebrows jerk upwards.

The man standing next to a gasping Guri was easily the tallest and bulkiest Norzen Kai had ever seen. He looked to be even taller than Teos, with a barrel-like chest straining against the leather cuirass strapped to his body. His arms were layered with thick muscle and clawed fists the size of melons, one of which carried a greatsword. He was covered in dark amber fur with two long, thin tails and a short bushy beard.

Kai noticed Fusette eyeing the newcomer with curiosity, her own tails thrashing as she took in the man's intimidating appearance. "I assume you will be my opponent?" he asked, eyes roaming in search of potential weaknesses.

"Obviously," Osko chortled from behind Kai. The older Norzen's voice broke into an imperious cockiness that produced a deep rumble from Kai's chest. "This is Rorik, Commander of the Guard and our city's sworn champion. If you wish to back out and head straight to the gaol, boy, I won't hold it against you."

A firm tug on his ear drew Kai's gaze to Maple, who emitted an audible gulp. "Kai...are you sure about this?" she whispered. "He has to be bigger than Duarte!"

The apothecary's gaze twitched to Clove, Cress, and Willow, all of whom were quaking in fear so much their chains rattled. The metallic clink solidified his resolve, his hand cupping Maple's cheek.

"I'm sure," he said. "I promise we'll get them out of here."

"We?" Orelia questioned, glancing at him. "But I thought you said you'd face him alone?"

Kai's face split into a wide grin. "As long as I have you two waiting for me, you both give me more strength than I could ever have on my own."

Letting out a happy trill, Maple tucked her head into his neck. "I knew there was a reason I married you. Just remember...if you lose, Ora and I are plucking every strand of fur off your ass after we break you out."

He rolled his eyes. "I wouldn't expect anything less."

A loud scoff rose from Osko, who stared at the triad with disdain. "Enough of your disgusting banter. Now come. We best get this over with."

The party followed Osko through the city, the headman flanked by Rorik and Guri with Fusette and Kai leading their group just behind. The procession drew many curious eyes, with multiple Norzen lining the street edges on their path. Some bid Fusette pleasantries with wide smiles, while others remained silent, their eyes dim as they cast furtive glances towards Osko.

Seeing how the townsfolk reacted to their leader's stony glare filled Kai with concern. His hands curled into tight fists thinking about the upcoming fight. He peered at Rorik, who ambled at a brisk pace with a relaxed, uncaring posture. It was as if the larger Norzen wasn't the least bit concerned about what was coming, and Kai didn't know if he should be worried or offended by it.

What Rorik's response did do, however, was remind him that this was one battle he couldn't afford to lose.

After a fair distance, they arrived at what looked like a stadium dug into the swamp itself. A circular wall of logs a hundred yards in diameter and five yards high formed the perimeter. The water had been drained, leaving a broad field filled with grass, boulders, and more than a fair number of various trees. Some had thick, broad trunks with expansive canopies. Others were tall and thin with short branches. The water outside lapped against the wall, leaving the dirt at the arena's edge constantly soaked.

For seating, a pyramidal set of stands four tiers high was constructed around the stadium, built from a stone frame with wood seating. Entrances to the stands were connected to the main road via an intersecting web of wooden bridges and piers with docks for those arriving on the canals. A sizable crowd followed the group inside, branching off into the stands while Osko led the party to a central box overlooking the arena's center. Kai and Rorik were directed through a small gate which opened to a staircase leading to the arena.

It was clear Rorik was in his element, waving to the growing crowd with a happy smile as they cheered. He left Kai and took off at a light jog, circling the arena. The throng of Norzen lapped it up, each section cheering louder as the bulky warrior ran past. After doing a full lap he tore the leather cuirass from his body, quickly followed by his tunic, leaving him bare-chested. The crowd erupted into a thunderous racket, their applause forceful enough to cause the arena walls to vibrate.

The din forced Kai to flatten his ears. Having left his mace with the others, he slipped a pair of thick leather gauntlets over his hands. The sensation of warm leather calmed him somewhat, his eyes turning towards his opponent.

Rorik gave him a bemused smirk. "You still have time to quit, my young friend. I can tell from your robes; you are an apothecary. I respect you as a man who uses your hands to heal and nurture. However, I cannot in good faith respect you as a warrior without proving yourself."

Quirking an eyebrow, Kai began stretching while not taking his eyes off the larger Norzen. "May I ask why not?" he asked. Kai knew there were many reasons for Rorik to say such a thing, but he wanted to hear it from the man's own mouth.

"Have you not looked in a mirror?" Rorik responded with a booming laugh that reminded him of Kabuji. "You have modest height for a member of our tribe, but you remain far too thin to be considered a proper fighter."

"I think I might surprise you," Kai shot back, sliding into a stance.

"The only thing that would surprise me is if you are somehow still conscious three minutes after this begins."

Glancing upwards, Kai noticed Osko and his entourage, with Guri at its head, sitting on one side of the central box. Fusette and the rest of his companions filled the seats on the other side. The captured faumen, with Cress, Willow, and Clove at the front, were shackled to iron bars set into a platform just below the central box.

Stepping to the fore of the box, Osko raised his hands outward and lowered them slowly. The crowd settled into a tense silence.

"Citizens of Duskmarsh," the headman crowed, "today is a rather momentous occasion. Our Grand Duchess, the Lady Fusette Ardei, has *finally* decided to grace us with her magnanimous presence." Waving his arm towards the monarch in a sweeping motion, the crowd burst into cheers, though their joy was swiftly deadened when Osko turned towards them with a blistering glare.

Kai bit back a growl at the disrespect the headman was showing towards Fusette. While he could understand being upset with her inability to visit, such blatant contempt was beyond the pale.

"With her, she has brought back one of our missing sons: the only child of our dear Ulfrik and Frida, last of the illustrious Erklaus line!"

The throng became louder than ever if Kai thought it were even possible. He suppressed a pained hiss, his skull vibrating in pain at the tumult.

"However," Osko continued, "this same son of our noble tribe has committed blasphemous acts against all Norzen. He now stands before us, wed to not one but two females outside of the tribe and willing to fight for the sake of other faumen. Lady Fusette has given her approval of his debauchery, selecting him as her own chosen champion, and he has offered us a wager through which we shall regain our honor."

Kai snorted. The irony in Osko saying anything about honor was not lost on him.

"Commander Rorik has been our city's steady guardian for nigh on eight years now. It is he who will restore the Norzen tribe's pride in defeating this heretic in gladiator combat. Son of Ulfrik, do you have anything to say in your defense?"

Rolling his eyes, Kai gave a passing glance at Rorik. To his surprise, the warrior was frowning in Osko's direction while cracking his knuckles one at a time. His ears twitched with every pop from the other man's hand. He took a deep breath and decided to think about it later. His gaze swung up to meet Osko's.

"First off, I wasn't aware I needed to defend myself from anyone other than the man across from me. Unless you plan on jumping into the arena in his place, that is."

The audience burst into titters. Even Rorik couldn't hide the minuscule grin forming on his lips. Kai's ears twitched, hearing Osko growl from the box. He knew it was probably dumb, but he was losing patience with the aging headman.

"Second, I have nothing to be ashamed of. In fact, I freely admit it: my wives are of different tribes, and I love them both with all my heart." The crowd burst into stunned gasps and whispers. Kai watched as many gazed towards the box in confusion. He bit back a laugh at seeing Maple and Orelia milking the shock for all it was worth, standing and waving to the crowd with joyful smiles while blatantly ignoring Osko's stammered shouts to sit back down.

Good luck getting those two to listen, given how you've acted thus far, Kai thought. If anything, the headman's embarrassment would only provoke them further.

After several more failed attempts, Osko gave up the pot and rounded on Kai, nostrils flaring. "You will keep those...females...under control, boy, or so help me—"

The older Norzen's breath hitched at the frigid stare Kai gave him. "Or you'll *what*?" he growled, his voice freezing the entire crowd in place. "Finish that sentence and I'll come up there and hang you with your own tails, champion or no champion."

Osko dropped into his chair with one hand clutched over his heart. Kai noted Fusette giving Osko a dismissive shake of her head. He turned back to Rorik and fought the urge to step back at the taller man's intrigued look.

"It seems there's more to you than meets the eye," Rorik said, cracking his knuckles. "Elder Osko is not an easy man to cow, yet you silenced him with little effort."

Both men slid into a stance. Rorik's posture was more relaxed, leaving his arms hanging loose and both hands curled into half-fists. Kai assumed a left-handed boxer's stance, right fist held in front with the elbows tucked in and his left fist nestled next to his cheek.

Kai grimaced at the almost dismissive stance his opponent was taking. He knew his normal methods of fighting would have little effect against a man Rorik's size. The Norzen champion easily outstripped him in both height and reach. His best chance would be to hope Rorik was as slow as his bulky body looked and wear him down long enough to land some good blows.

With Osko still shivering in his chair, Guri stepped to the front of the box and looked over the two opponents. She gave Kai a stern frown before raising her arm.

"The match will continue until one competitor surrenders or has been rendered unconscious. Is this acceptable?" Both men nodded. "Excellent. Now, as agreed, this is a traditional gladiator match. You may use any part of your body or any natural item within the arena as a weapon, such as logs or rocks. Do either of you have any questions?"

Kai and Rorik shook their heads in unison.

"Very well," Guri said. "Then let the match begin!!"

Easing forward, Kai kept his guard up and hopped on the balls of his feet. Rorik ambled forward, arms swinging and a huge smirk splitting his face in two. The crowd broke into cheers watching the two approach each other.

"Let's have a go, shall we?" Kai muttered under his breath. His gaze roamed over every bit of Rorik's body, searching for an opening. Dilating his pupils, Kai ignored the stinging behind his eyes and blinked.

That singular moment proved problematic. Kai's eyes bulged when he found himself cast in shadow with Rorik almost on top of him, right arm rearing back for a heavy hook.

How in Tapimor's hairy ass can someone that big move so fast?! Kai shouted in his mind.

Reacting on pure instinct, Kai lunged forward, ducking underneath the punch. A noticeable breeze ruffled his hair as the fist flew overhead. Spinning on his heel, Kai wound up and slammed a cross into Rorik's exposed cheek while the man was mid-turn.

Hopping back to put some distance between them, Kai stopped to catch his breath. His eyes refused to move from Rorik's still form. Then, a deep chuckle rumbled from the larger Norzen's chest, growing louder until it erupted into a full-grown belly laugh. Turning in place, he faced Kai with a toothy grin.

"Consider me impressed," Rorik taunted. "I actually felt that punch. Anyone else would've been knocked over. Pity it wasn't good enough against me."

Kai suppressed his shock at seeing Rorik's unruffled confidence. Other than some scuffing to the skin, his opponent looked undamaged. "You've gotta be bloody kidding me," he hissed. Kai's mane bristled as another throaty rumble came from Rorik.

"My turn," he growled.

Before Kai could react, Rorik charged. The taller man's eyes were rimmed in a familiar red, his arm cocking backwards. Kai shuffled backwards with a gasp, sidestepping to the right.

Is that a Frenzy Haze? Impossible!

Rorik seemed to predict the dodge, however, and threw another hook in the direction his body was moving. This one was quicker than the first and Kai threw up both arms in front of his face to block.

A loud thud echoed through the arena as Rorik's punch blasted Kai off his feet, sending him into a nearby boulder. The apothecary collapsed to the ground face-down, tremors of pain pulsing through his body. He let out a rumbling groan while struggling to his feet, pressing his knuckles into the soft dirt to push himself up.

"I suppose you were right about one thing," Rorik chortled. "You certainly have surprised me, son of Ulfrik. Few can take a direct punch from me and get back up, even with blocking."

Kai bit his tongue, ignoring the throbbing sensation permeating his whole body. That blow rang his bell a lot harder than he cared to admit.

"What in Nulyma...?" he mumbled. "Your eyes, it looked like a Frenzy Haze."

Rorik's eyebrow rose. "You noticed? You're the first to figure out the secret to my strength. It's a higher form of the Frenzy Haze where the user masters their emotions, making it more powerful but requiring intense focus."

Thinking back, Kai remembered the few instances where he felt more in control of his Frenzy Hazes, though his experience with the Haze was limited as a whole compared to other Norzen.

"Does it really increase your strength by that much?" Talking was taking a toll on his burning lungs, but Kai knew keeping Rorik distracted gave him needed time to catch his breath after that last punch. The extra knowledge he gained was simply a bonus.

"Indeed. I can tell you've had brushes with the mastered form in the past. It shows in how you carry yourself. Even after the Haze dissipates, your body doesn't easily forget the movements it makes while under the thrall. Why not let yourself go and release the Haze? You'll never defeat me otherwise."

Kai shivered. Memories of his prior Hazes pelted his mind, bringing a dark chill to his body. He hated the Haze's effects on him, leaving his body disjointed and fully out of his own control in most cases.

Even now, he still felt that tingle from the base of his neck, like a whisper echoing in his mind. Kai did his best to ignore the sensation ever since their last battle with Grimghast. While the Haze was instrumental in fending the beast off that day, he knew Orelia was the only reason he hadn't lost himself in the blinding torrent of rage from seeing Maple injured by Hemlocke.

He shook his head, clenching a tight fist. No matter what Rorik said, he'd win this without leaning on something as unreliable as the Frenzy Haze. A familiar coiling sensation spread through his arms, jarring him from his thoughts. His lips curved upwards, even as Rorik barreled towards him again with another barrage of punches.

He didn't need the Haze to win. Not when he still had a few *other* tricks hidden in his robes.

Fusette felt her confidence draining away the longer she watched. Every attack Kai launched at Rorik was brushed aside like a love tap, while her cousin was being tossed around with ease like a paddlepod ball. Her gaze flickered over to Osko on occasion, her frustration building as she saw the arrogant grin on his face.

"It appears your champion isn't quite as skilled as you thought he was, Your Grace," Osko jeered.

It infuriated her to bite her tongue, but Fusette wasn't sure what she could say in response. It was clear Rorik was a class above any opponent Kai had ever faced before, even if she couldn't figure out how that was possible. The warrior moved with a grace and speed more appropriate to someone half his size.

Osko's haughty attitude, however, proved no deterrent to either Maple or Orelia. "The fight isn't over until one of them gives up or passes out," the Aerivolk merchant reminded him.

Fusette watched as Maple ground her teeth through her words. The older woman's feathers looked distinctly ruffled as they watched Kai attempt to roll out of the way of another punch. Rorik spun in place fast enough to grab Kai by the leg and slam his back against a nearby tree.

"What in Nulyma is that bastard made of? Solid steel?" Teos snapped, his fingers curling hard over the arms of his chair and cracking the wood. Fusette wondered about that herself, seeing the hulking man brush off a kick Kai landed to his knee. Morgan looked not much better, clenching his jaw with a vibrating hiss rising from his chest.

She saw Orelia's eyes darting between Kai and Rorik, trying to figure out her husband's plan. On Orelia's other side, Ione was clutching the younger woman's arm in a firm grip while gaping in horror.

Fusette turned back and winced when Kai barely dodged another devastating right hook from Rorik. The punch struck a tree in the middle of its trunk, cracking the wood in twain and causing the tree to topple over with a sonorous crash. The crowd's deafening applause reached a crescendo, forcing Fusette and the other Norzen to flatten their ears in pain.

"D-did he just punch a tree in half?" Lucretia asked, shoulders slumped and mouth hanging open.

Yulia was watching the match with a mix of professional curiosity and concern. "Yes he did, and I don't want to consider the ramifications of a Norzen being capable of such a feat. I'd have trouble finding a Soltauri or Wasini capable of matching that, and pound for pound they're the only two tribes stronger than the Norzen."

Seated next to Yulia, Pelka and Hibbel both looked ready to be sick. Hibbel, in particular, turned a ghastly pale when Kai sidestepped the tree, only for Rorik to show up on his flank and backhand him in the cheek. To their amazement, Kai finally managed to deal visible damage as he flew backwards again, drawing a clawed hand across Rorik's forearm and leaving several bloody scratches.

Pelka bit her lip, seeing blood and spit fly from Kai's mouth when he landed hard on his back. "I must confess," she said, "I wasn't aware the Norzen of Livoria preferred settling diplomatic issues by beating each other to a bloody pulp."

"I'm pretty sure Sir Gravebane is the only one being turned into a bloody pulp," Hibbel commented, though he flinched back at Pelka's unamused stare.

From where she sat, Fusette felt more helpless than at any other point in her life, and she loathed the sensation. Sitting there, watching someone she cherished and trusted with her life get beaten down for wanting to save people, wrenched at her heart. It was like having an iron ball lodged in her chest with no way of removing it.

Glancing at Maple, the duchess leaned over to whisper in her ear, "You reckon we should start praying for a miracle? None of his attacks are working." Seeing the thin but determined smile on the merchant's lips helped bring some of her hope back.

"No need for that, quite yet. I can see it in his eyes, Fusette," Maple answered. "He hasn't given up yet, so neither will we."

"Besides," said Orelia, "Kai isn't one to keep beating a dead wiroch for no reason. I'd wager he's trying to find Rorik's weak spot."

A loud cackle rang from Osko, who cast a haughty sneer at the three women. "Rorik has no weak points, you stupid woman. That disgraceful excuse of a Norzen wouldn't stand a chance even if he had triple his current strength!"

Snorting, Maple wrapped a wing around Orelia's elbow and waggled a pinkie towards Osko, sending him into a sputtering fit. "I'm going to love the look on your face when our husband knocks your champion flat on his ass and makes you eat those words," she trilled. Despite the Aerivolk's confidence, Fusette couldn't help but wonder how Kai was going to turn *that* trick.

"What in holy Finyt is that?!" Ione cried out, pointing to the arena.

Everyone's eyes swung back to the battle, bulging at the sight before them.

Stumbling back to his feet, Kai wiped a dirty arm across his lips and spat a glob of blood and saliva to the dirt. He grew irritated at how ineffective his attacks were, but at least now he had a better idea of how to deal his opponent.

"I can't tell if you're the most stubborn man I've ever faced or the most foolish," Rorik said. The warrior barely looked winded as he advanced on Kai. "Anyone else would've surrendered by this point. You can't hide from me since I can simply sniff you out, and you have no way of outrunning or damaging me. Why keep fighting?"

Pain throbbed in so many places all over Kai's body. There was pain in places he didn't even know existed. Breathing was hard, as one of Rorik's earlier punches had struck his ribs and left at least one cracked.

"My lovely wives will be the first to tell you I can be more stubborn than a mule when it suits me. Besides, I'm not in the habit of surrendering to someone I'm perfectly capable of dumping on their ass."

Rorik stared. His trout-slapped expression made Kai want to laugh, but doing so would aggravate his rib, so he suppressed the urge.

"Perhaps I hit you in the head too hard," Rorik finally responded. "In case you've forgotten, you're losing, and badly. I shall order the match over to get you medical attention. You've clearly lost your senses."

A deep rumble echoed through the arena, originating from Kai's chest. "Oh, no you don't," the apothecary uttered. "We're done when I say we're done!"

Curling both hands into fists, Kai slammed his knuckles straight down, burying them in the dirt. The moment his fists made contact, streams of indigo dust erupted from his upper arms and shoulders, spreading across the arena. The thick cloud carried a fragrant grassy aroma, mixed with pepper and a scent reminiscent of beets.

Kai watched as Rorik stumbled backwards, his eyes turning bulbous as the cloud overcame them both. From the stands, he heard the crowd emitting confused gasps.

"What in holy Finyt is that?!" he heard lone shout, prompting a brief chuckle from Kai. His mirth was cut short when his battered rib pulsed.

Focusing his Timber, he felt the coiling sensation spread across his chest and down towards the injured bone. In moments, he felt a painful pressure on the rib before it subsided enough for him to move his body with minimal pain.

That should hold me together until I can finish this, Kai thought.

"What in Cuballa is this?" Rorik bellowed from inside the cloud. Kai could barely make out the warrior's large frame as a moving shadow in the dust.

Shifting his stance, Kai slipped around Rorik's flank. His smirk grew seeing the massive warrior flailing about in confusion.

He stopped when he heard the distinct sound of Rorik sniffing the air. "What the—? This smells like amaranth!"

Kai licked his lips and allowed his ears to swivel as he crept along. He admitted to questioning the pollen's usefulness when he first learned to wield it, as the amaranth masked his opponent from sight and smell as effectively as it did him upon expulsion.

However, he did discover a few bonuses to fusing so many plants inside his body, not the least of which was his eyesight adjusting to the pollen cloud's darkness with ease.

His eyes flashed, Rorik's shadow flickering amid the inky cloud. Kai positioned himself just behind and to the side of Rorik. Then, raising his left arm, he fired a vine from the wrist.

The thick tendril wrapped around the larger Norzen's ankle and knotted itself tight, prompting Rorik to spin in place while jerking the foot back.

"What the...?" he shouted.

Grasping the vine in his hand and coiling it around his wrist, Kai yanked as hard as he could. Rorik's foot flew upwards and sent the man face-first into the dirt. The apothecary felt a firm tug on the vine and spotted Rorik attempting to unknot it.

"Not so fast," he muttered. Kai grabbed the vine with his other hand and twisted his hips. Rorik cried out in shock when his body was lifted off the ground. The warrior's body may have been solidly built but that didn't translate to excessive weight beyond what his body's density already had, meaning Kai had little difficulty in swinging him around by the ankle like a lasso.

"Put me down, you fool!" Rorik exclaimed. "I'm gonna be sick!"

"Wish granted!" Kai shot back. His face split by a wide, toothy grin, he shifted the Origin flowing through his vine and loosened it enough to send Rorik spinning through the air.

The larger Norzen slammed into what Kai suspected was a tree, confirmed when the impact toppled the plant over with a deafening boom. The tree's collapse kicked up a gale of wind that dispersed the amaranth and revealed the arena to a stunned crowd.

Kai stood on shaky legs, the grin never leaving his face. Two dozen yards away, Rorik lay in a heap, dazed and with a noticeable lump forming on his temple where his head struck the tree.

After a few minutes, Rorik was able to stumble back to his feet. Nursing his head, he glanced over at Kai, eyes wide at seeing the vine draw back towards Kai and coiling around his forearm like an extension of his gauntlet.

Gobsmacked, Rorik stared at the vine before meeting Kai's unwavering gaze. The two stood frozen, their eyes matched in an unseen battle of wills. No one, not even in the crowd, dared to utter a breath.

Suddenly, Rorik threw back his head and laughed. Kai narrowed his eyes, wondering if his opponent was mocking him again.

"Well I'll be damned! You still got more fight in you than I imagined," the burly warrior chortled. Raising his arms and assuming a stance, Rorik cast a tilted smirk Kai's way. "Now let's see if you can keep it up."

"What in the sacred forests was that?" Guri asked, her mouth hanging open.

Fusette's chest felt warm, her confidence returning. Kai hadn't been very forthcoming in the past on what he could do with his Seeder magic, but it was obvious he managed to develop a few new tricks.

"That," said Maple, "is what happens when you brass Kai off."

"He's cheating!" Osko snarled. "There's no way a Norzen should be capable of such a trick."

The sound of a cleared throat brought everyone's eyes to Hibbel. "Actually, Headman Osko," the diplomat soothed, "Sir Gravebane's abilities are perfectly valid and legal in the context of this battle. Granted, they are exceedingly rare among Livorian faumen, but those techniques are derived from the natural energies of his body and Lady Guri did say the combatants could use *any* part of their body as a weapon."

It was clear this wasn't the answer Osko wanted, as the older Norzen's nostrils flared in rage. He spun towards Guri, who offered a single shrug.

"One would think your own confidence in your fighter is waning thin, Osko," Fusette teased, sending the man a cheeky smile.

Osko's jaw snapped shut. "Of course not," he spat. "Rorik still has the upper hand, and Ulfrik's son has already taken significant damage."

"He has a name, you arrogant twit," Orelia growled. Fusette saw the former priestess tighten her grip on the staff in her hands. The thought of watching Orelia club Osko about the head brought a bright smile to her face.

"I refuse to use that heretic's given name."

A sudden shout from Morgan startled the entire box. "What in hoarfrost kind of a cheap shot is that?!"

Everyone spun towards the arena, where Rorik and Kai charged each other. The larger Norzen threw a hand forward, sending a cloud of dirt into Kai's eyes.

Kai slid to a stop and wiped at his face, hissing in pain. Unfortunately, this left him open to a shoulder charge that took him off the ground. Rorik kept barreling forward, keeping an arm hooked around Kai's waist until reaching the arena's pond.

Grabbing Kai by the hair, Rorik pinned the smaller man under his boot while shoving Kai's head into the water, his face twisted into a manic grin and eyes burning red.

"That crazy bastard's lost it! He's going to drown him!" Teos roared, launching to his feet. The party scrambled to the box's edge. They ignored Osko's euphoric cackling in favor of shouting for Kai to fight back.

Maple and Orelia proved the loudest of the bunch by a long shot.

"Don't give up Kai!" Maple shrieked. "You can still beat him, I know you can!"

Orelia cupped both hands over her lips and shouted, "Hit him where it hurts, dear!"

To everyone's horror, Rorik opted to lift Kai up by the collar of his robes, holding him up with one hand and curling the other into a meaty fist. Fusette blanched at seeing Rorik turn and give the party a curved grin before turning his attention back to Kai.

"You put up an admirable fight, my friend. The kind that gets my blood running, even. But this is where I must finish things, I'm afraid," Rorik said, his voice heavy.

Chest heaving, Kai fought to remain conscious. Every breath left his chest burning and while the dirt Rorik had hit him with was washed out, the edges of his eyes still stung. Glancing at Rorik's wild grin, Kai suspected his opponent's hold on the Frenzy Haze wasn't as absolute as he suggested. He quickly rattled off the plants he remembered adding to his body.

Wisteria. Eldermary. Cexmeg. Citrial. Torp—wait, that's it! Kai thought.

The grim chuckle from Rorik's chest rumbled in Kai's ears. "Few have ever lasted so long against me in battle," he declared. "You may not be a full warrior yet, but I can respect you as a man, at least. Tell me, Kai Travaldi, do you have any final words to say before I end this and put you down for a long nap?"

Kai could feel his vision slipping in and out of darkness. Tightening his focus, he diverted some Timber to his cheeks. A wooly sensation erupted in his mouth. On instinct, he chewed. A sharp, tangy flavor burst over his tongue and he swallowed.

The apothecary gave his opponent a confident smile. "Just two: Good. Night!"

His vision cleared. A burst of energy surged through his body as the effects of the citrial he bloomed within his mouth took hold. Three sharp stings came from the space between the knuckles of his left hand, driving his eyesight into sharper focus.

With a defiant roar, Kai swung his left arm in a tight hook, landing a single blow into the side of Rorik's neck.

The wind swept over Kai's body as he hit the ground flat on his back hard enough to knock the air from his lungs. He heard Rorik emit a pained yelp. Glancing up, he saw the man clawing at his neck, where three deep puncture wounds oozed blood.

"What was—?" Rorik mumbled, his voice slurring. "What did you do?"

Rorik stumbled back, his body swaying. He looked to be having difficulty staying upright. His eyes widened when Kai lifted his fist, revealing three claw-like thorns jutting from between his knuckles, each covered in Rorik's blood.

"I already told you," Kai stated, "I'm not in the habit of surrendering to someone I know I can knock ass over kettle. Sweet dreams, Rorik."

The warrior's eyes were half-lidded as he pitched backwards. His body splayed over the arena floor and went completely still, rumbling snores rising from his chest.

CHAPTER XVII

S ilence reigned throughout the arena. The only sounds were the soft snores coming from Rorik. The crowd of Norzen looked on with astonishment, eyes wide and many with their mouths dangling open.

Struggling to hold himself upright, Kai stared up at the box and couldn't hold back a grin at the flabbergasted expression on Osko's face. Guri was frozen, pale and her fingers gripping the box's edge hard enough for the wood to visibly crack.

A sudden cacophony rose from the box as Fusette and the party burst into joyous applause. Maple and Orelia were hugging each other while jumping up and down. He saw hints of tears trailing down Ione's flushed cheeks, the tavern maiden clutching her heart.

Teos and Lucretia were more restrained in their revelry, flashing identical grins towards Kai. In contrast, Morgan was beating his cuirass with one fist and waving the other above his head, cheering as loud as he could.

"I believe that marks the end of the match," Fusette commented, casting a tilted smirk at Osko which made it clear she was enjoying the unrestrained horror on the headman's face. "Now then, Vice Commander, will you be announcing the result, or shall I do it for you?"

The duchess' comments proved enough to snap Osko out of his stunned state. "This is *bulskein*" Osko shouted. "What did he even do? That can't be legal!"

"As I mentioned before, sir," Hibbel said, "Sir Gravebane's abilities are natural and legal according to the stipulations of the match. None of what he did is considered cheating; he just happens to be the first Seeder to awaken within Livoria's borders."

Maple emitted a giddy chuckle. "I did warn you about what would happen. Besides, I'm sure Kai will be more than happy to explain once he has a chance to rest."

Flinching under Fusette's determined gaze, Guri raised her arm. "The match is over!" she cried out. "The winner, by knockout...is Kai Travaldi!"

The party hurried out of the box amid the mixed reactions of the crowd. Fusette's eyes swept over the stands, noticing many cheering in earnest while others remained silent, sending nervous glances in Osko's direction.

Kai stumbled to a fallen tree and sat down, groaning when his wives threw themselves into his arms.

"Easy, girls," he muttered. "I'm still a bit roughed up, ya know." Despite the pain spreading through his body, he reveled in the bliss their hugs gave him. Even Orelia's cool skin caused a level of warmth to bloom within his chest.

"I'm beginning to think you really enjoy making us worry," Maple whispered, planting a gentle kiss to his lips. "But you won, and that's what matters."

"Indeed. Now if only we can convince you to stop being so reckless with your own health," Orelia added while tucking her face into the crook of his neck.

Wrapping his arms around their waists, Kai drew the two close and gave each a peck on the cheek. Spotting movement near Rorik, he glanced over and saw Guri approaching the unconscious warrior. She knelt next to him and looked to be fighting back tears.

"He's not dead," the apothecary told her.

The older Norzen spun towards him, biting her lower lip. "What exactly did you *do* to him?" Guri demanded. "His body appears to be running a fever."

"Calm down. I can bring him around easily enough. Watch."

With Maple and Orelia supporting him by the shoulders, Kai staggered over to Rorik while accepting his satchel from Ione. Surrounded by the entire party, along with Guri and a small troop of guards, he took a knee next to the prone man. With a pained wince from the pressure it put on his legs, Kai pulled a single vial from the bag.

The elixir was a shimmering peach in color, with ground bits of dried herbs mixed in. Upon popping the cork off, an aroma of lemon mixed with grapes wafted from the vial.

"What is that?" Guri asked, her eyes twitching to the rapidly approaching Osko.

"The thorns I produced are from a bush called torpothorn, native to Galstein. While it's technically toxic, the worst it'll do to someone Rorik's size is cause rapid fatigue and a slight fever. The reason he fell asleep so fast is because heightened blood pressure will induce the symptoms more quickly. Considering what I've seen from him, I wouldn't be surprised if his body could flush the toxins naturally in a few hours.

"However, I'm going to go ahead and give him this elixir to wake him up now. It's made from a base of citrial balm, with sandsage and eldermary mixed in and steeped longer for higher potency."

Lifting Rorik's head, Kai gestured for Orelia to help pry the unconscious warrior's lips open, allowing him to tip the vial's contents into his mouth. He massaged Rorik's throat, making sure he swallowed before setting his head back down.

He allowed his friends to pull him back into a seated position. Reaching back into the satchel, he removed two more vials, one filled with a dark brown concoction and the other a common energy tonic colored in soft blue.

"What are those?" Fusette asked, watching Kai down the contents of both vials in unison.

He suppressed the urge to gag, taking a long swig from his canteen before answering. "The blue one is a standard energy tonic. It'll give me a brief energy boost, though I'll probably feel more tired than usual once the effect wears off. The other one is a tonic of fluxroot and a very tiny bit of emberona bud. Fluxroot is useful for boosting the body's natural healing factor, and the emberona enhances that by quite a bit."

"Fascinating," the duchess remarked. She gave Kai a roving glance and grinned, "but I *am* curious as to why you look ready to vomit."

"Because, milady," Kai shot back in a teasing tone, "fluxroot tastes atrocious on its own, and the emberona only amplifies it! It's what I would imagine a soup made from boiling unwashed undergarments and moldy cheese to taste like." Everyone around him flinched back in disgust at the description.

A soft groaning came from Rorik. The burly Norzen still looked woozy, wobbling to his feet and rising into an unsteady stance. He turned to Kai and gave a weary laugh.

"Damn...you really beat me, didn't you?" Rorik choked out. His eyes looked hazy and unfocused, but the cocky grin never left his face for even a moment.

Before Kai could react, the larger man clasped his hand in a firm grip and pulled the apothecary into an unexpected hug.

"I don't know how the blazes you pulled all that off," he continued, "but you did prove how much more I can grow. That was the first fight I've lost in years. Thank you."

Momentarily stunned by the sudden declaration, Kai could only return the gesture, pulling away enough to shake Rorik's hand.

"I can't claim full credit for that win," Kai admitted. "I didn't fight with everything I had for myself. I fought because my friends and family were depending on me."

Rorik paused. His dark grey eyes roamed Kai up and down, seeking any hesitation in his words. Finding none, the two men nodded in camaraderie.

"What are you doing, Rorik?" Osko questioned. The headman's eyes were narrowed and flashing silver in the sunlight.

The taller man looked down at Osko with a severe frown. "I am showing my opponent the respect he has earned through his victory. Speaking of...guards!"

The armored Norzen behind Guri all snapped the attention.

"Release the prisoners. As per the agreed-upon wager, the other fau-men shall be released."

"You have no authority to make that command!"

Osko let out a surprised squawk when Rorik picked him up by the collar of his tunic, much the same way he did to Kai earlier. "I am still Commander of the Guard, so I very much have such authority. Or are you suggesting we renounce our tribal honor so that you may renege on a legal wager?"

"P-put me down!" Osko demanded.

Snorting in the shorter Norzen's face, Rorik dropped him, a grim smile forming on his lips when the headman stumbled and fell backwards onto his butt. Kai raised an eyebrow at Rorik's actions. He was further surprised when Rorik bowed at the waist to him and Fusette.

"Even using my full strength, I'll confess I underestimated you and, in turn, didn't take our battle as seriously as I should have," said Rorik. "I appreciate you teaching me the importance of treating every battle as an important one. It appears I must also apologize for our headman's disgraceful behavior."

Turning to the guards, he nodded towards the platform where Maple's parents and the other faumen were still chained. A small squad of guards bustled to the platform, keys in hand, and began removing the shackles from their former prisoners.

Maple rushed off, drawing her parents and friend into a tight embrace the moment their restraints hit the ground as tears streamed from her eyes. "Oh thank the Saints, you're all okay!" the merchant sobbed.

Despite their weakened state, it was easy to see Cress and Willow were just as enthusiastic to hold their daughter. Willow was a full head shorter than Maple, yet didn't hesitate to pull the younger woman into a kneeling position while gripping with all her might.

"Maplyne!" Willow cried, not bothering to hide her tears cascading down her cheeks. Clove kneeled on Maple's other side, nestled under the merchant's arm. Cress said nothing but settled for embracing the three women at once. The group held each other in a pile of feathers.

"I can't believe it," Willow continued, pulling back and tilting Maple's head down for their eyes to meet. "When did my little chick get so big?"

Unable to control herself, Maple let out an amused snort. "I was thirteen when I left, Mama. I'd be a bit worried if I didn't grow a bit in all that time since."

Clove let out a giggle. "Sweet appleberries, Featherbolt," she commented. "You were already taller than me when you left. Now you're like a giant! But I wouldn't have you any other way."

"Featherbolt?" Kai inquired, his lips curving into a grin.

"Just a silly nickname, love," Maple answered. "She started calling me that the day after I got this scar. She evens calls me by it in her letters!"

Kai and Orelia chuckled but stayed back, the latter brushing away her own tears at the tender display. The apothecary could feel his younger wife's eyes on him, prompting him to take her hand with a firm squeeze. The rest of the party watched from a distance, though there wasn't a dry eye among them.

Rising to his feet, Cress ruffled Maple's hair while his own gaze shifted to Kai and Orelia. Kai straightened his posture, sensing the stony aura behind Cress' frown.

"It seems," the older man murmured, "quite a lot has happened since you left home, Maple. How did—?"

"Papa, don't." Maple turned on her father with ruffled feathers, a pinched frown, and her voice slipping back into its pronounced drawl. "I love ya, I truly do, but don't ya even think of going after my husband."

"I think I deserve to know how my little girl ended up married to a Norzen of all things. I know I joked about the idea the day you were exiled, but I never thought you'd actually do it! He didn't force you into this, did he?"

Rolling her eyes, Maple helped her mother to her feet and led them towards the party. "No, you dipwit. I swear, the day Kai does anything to deliberately harm an innocent, both moons will fall from the sky. I'll tell you how we met on our way back to the capital. Just...give him a chance.

Kai's a good man, finer than any I've ever met, and trust me when I say I've met my fair share traveling the realm since I left."

Cress looked ready to argue, but he let out a yelp when his wife gave his wing feathers a firm tug. "I'll keep your father in line, dear. I am curious though. Who is that young Vesikoi next to him?"

"That's Orelia, my sister wife."

Both parents gawked at their daughter. "Now I'm wondering just who this man is if he was allowed to breach one of the church's most sacred tenets twice," Willow said. Her pale face made it plain her own concerns on the matter.

Maple's grin grew wide as they reached the group. Kai stepped forward and offered his hand to Cress.

"It's a pleasure to meet you, sir," Kai said, suppressing a smirk at Cress' overt attempt to break his hand with a powerful grip. "Seems you're a lot healthier than expected, with a grip like that."

The older Aerivolk flinched when his daughter spun in place, her cheeks puffed out and flushed crimson.

"Papa!" Maple snapped.

Releasing Cress' hand, Kai chuckled and drew Maple into his chest, running his fingers through her hair. "Hush, honey," he whispered. "There's nothing wrong with your father worrying about you."

The gentle ministrations produced a throaty trill from the merchant, who cuddled deeper into Kai's embrace. "I know," she replied while nuzzling his mane, "but I don't want you two butting heads. We're supposed to be a family. All of us. And family is more important than all the gold and treasure in the world."

Cress and Willow froze at her words, their eyes flickering between the three younger adults.

"Maple," Cress muttered. His voice drew her eyes to him, a fresh set of tears prickling their edges. "Are you at least happy with the way things turned out?"

She nodded. "More than anything. I love him, Papa, and Orelia is like the sister I never had. Ever since I met Kai, I've made the most wonderful friends who have brought me nothing but joy. I really am happy, and I want you all to be happy with and for me."

Fusette approached the group, dragging the rest of the party behind her. The other captives inched closer as well, their eyes darting fearfully around them as the crowd looked on in curiosity.

"I'm so grateful to see you all free," Fusette said. "I suppose we'll have to load up on additional supplies after we finish things here, so that everyone might have food and drink for the return trip to the capital."

Willow led the captives in bowing low, many shaking with a mix of anxiety and exhaustion. "Your Grace," the woman fretted, "we must thank you for speaking up on our behalf and doing your utmost to free us."

Kai could see the captives were unsure of how else to proceed, given Fusette's ears and tails waved in the open for all to see.

The duchess released a tittering laugh, gesturing for everyone to rise. "Please, I'm hardly the one you should be thanking. After all, Kai is the one who secured your freedom. I simply cheered from the sidelines, same as anyone else here. I do have words for the two of you, however."

Cress and Willow's eyes widened when Fusette brought them into a hug of her own. "Y-your Grace?!" Cress stuttered.

"Hush now. I want to be the first to officially welcome you both to the family."

If anything, Fusette's words only made the pair more confused. "What?" Willow queried. "With all due respect, milady, what in the winds do you mean by that?"

Sharing a cheeky glance, Kai and Fusette broke into chuckles. "I suppose I never did publicly announce our connection," she said. "In honesty, Kai here happens to be a distant relation through my father's side and my last known blood relative besides my mother. And since your daughter happens to be married to him..."

The two blanched, the implication of Fusette's words being made clear. Willow looked ready to faint, her gaze shifting between her daughter and the duchess.

From the corner of his eye, Kai saw Osko arguing under his breath with Rorik. The guard leader leveled a deep scowl at the headman, pointing at the group and muttering obviously angry words.

"We may have a problem," Kai whispered to Fusette. He was so focused on the two, he failed to notice Guri approaching from behind, another older female Norzen following in her wake.

"Begging your pardon, Your Grace," Guri murmured, "but there's someone who wishes to speak with you." Fusette turned to face the two women, her eyes widening when she laid eyes on the vice commander's companion.

Kai placed a bracing palm against his cousin's back when she stepped backwards, asking her if she was okay.

The duchess gave a short nod, her gaze not leaving the woman. "Mother...?" Fusette whispered.

The newcomer broke out into tears, nodding and throwing herself at Fusette. Taking a closer look, Kai noticed the uncanny resemblance between the two. While Fusette's face had sharper lines she inherited from Duke Vonlo, she clearly had her mother's eye shade and dimpled cheeks, along with the same slender body shape.

"My baby," the woman breathed, tears streaming as she clung to Fusette as if she believed the younger woman would disappear if she let go.

Fusette proved unable to hold back her own tears, embracing her mother with a joyous smile. "Mother! I can't believe it. It's really you!"

"Of course it's me. Sweetheart, you have no idea how long I've wished for this day." Pulling back, the woman brushed Fusette's tears away and gave her an appraising glance. "I suppose I should have introduced myself first to make things proper. My name's Ingrid, and I work as a jeweler here in the city."

"Oh, Mother," Fusette chuckled. "There's no need to be so formal. I can't stand that stuffy etiquette nonsense. Of course, that might partly explain why Father was so cross with me for years. Then again, the only reason I recognized you is because he had your portrait hung in his chambers."

"Yes, your father…" Ingrid sighed, pulling Fusette into another hug. "I remember when he had that portrait commissioned. It was a chore, but before he left with you, Vonlo swore to come back for me after abdicating the throne to you when you were old enough. Sadly, the Blight prevented that from happening. We have much to catch up on, assuming of course you're agreeable."

"Of course!" Kai bit back a chuckle seeing his cousin jump up and down like a giddy teenager. "I must insist you return to the capital with the rest of us, at least for now. There's so much I want to share with you."

Rorik's booming voice rang from the box. "Your Grace!" the commander declared, jogging towards the group and dropping to one knee. Kai raised an eyebrow when Rorik took Fusette's hand and brushed his lips over her knuckles, provoking a searing blush from the monarch. "Allow me to escort you to the chancery so we might discuss your situation. With Kai's victory as your named champion, Duskmarsh is honor-bound to follow your command, regardless of Osko's wishes otherwise."

Fusette tilted her head in a demure nod. "Of course, Commander Rorik. We must discuss the particulars with due haste. And thank you for speaking on our behalf. Let us depart."

With that, the group fell into step behind Rorik and Guri, who led the way as the crowd dispersed, the former captives following at the rear. Osko trudged along to the side of his guard commanders, head dipped and a sneer covering his face.

Kai couldn't help but grin when the party congratulated him on his win. Ione and Morgan each wrapped an arm around the apothecary's shoulders, face-splitting smiles on their faces. At the same time, Teos and Lucretia both slugged him in the chest, chastising him for being so reckless. Judging by the smirks on their lips, though, Kai knew they were just worrying in their own way.

Pelka, Hibbel, and Yulia marched behind the party talking amongst themselves in excited tones, while Maple and Orelia peeled their friends off and tucked themselves under Kai's arms.

His eyes roamed over their growing entourage, filling Kai with hope. It seemed things were looking up, though he couldn't shake the itchy feeling in his mane that Osko had his own reasons for being so upset with Rorik's loss.

After returning to the chancery's audience chamber, Kai and the others accepted chairs from Rorik and the guards, taking a seat to rest while Osko resumed his place at the large desk. At the same time, Rorik pointed out the members of the city's ruling council taking their places.

The tables lining the outer edge of the chamber were filled with numerous Norzen. Kai noticed members of every walk of life accounted for in the seats; merchants, nobles, artisans, soldiers, craftsmen, and even the farmers and laborers all had at least one representative sitting amongst the council.

Fusette remained standing, squeezing Ingrid's hand before stepping forward and addressing Osko.

"Headman Osko, I think it's time we determined how much assistance Duskmarsh will provide in putting down this rebellion. I understand the concerns of you and this city's citizens. However, I want you to know that, with Parliament now disbanded until a special election can be held, I am able to ensure our tribe receives fair and impartial representation in not only Parliament, but the rest of the realm."

From his seated position, Kai let his eyes sweep over the room. Many of the council members nodded their heads with pleased smiles. Swiveling both ears, Kai heard several members muttering in small groups how long they've waited for a chance to be represented within Parliament.

He leaned over and tapped Rorik's shoulder. "Has Duskmarsh really not been given a voice in Parliament all these years?" he whispered in the warrior's ear.

Rorik chuckled. "Sadly, no. From what we know of the city's history, it was part of the agreement between Duke Tebalect and Erklaus when Duskmarsh was founded. Erklaus wanted more freedom for the Norzen in the face of overwhelming criticism against us due to the Desolation. In exchange for granting the city semi-autonomous status, Erklaus agreed to forfeit representation in Parliament. Only a royal decree sanctioned by the legislature could change that agreement."

"And with Parliament out of the picture..." Kai muttered, a sly grin on his face.

His attention was drawn back to Fusette, who stared as Osko rose from his chair and leaned forward, resting both palms on the desk.

"Your Grace, you can't honestly expect us to believe such drivel."

Kai was impressed at the headman's ability to ignore the angry complaints leveled at him by the rest of the council. "Silence!" Osko shouted in his hoarse voice. "The fact is, you abandoned us, Lady Fusette. You can't expect this city to simply roll over and bow to your whims after you bring that abomination in here and have him humiliate our city's beloved protector."

"Are you still sour about that?" Guri inquired, leaping to her feet. "Face it, Osko. Rorik lost the battle fair and square. Just because we haven't seen hard evidence of Sir Gravebane's abilities until now doesn't make him an abomination. If anything, it makes you look like the bloodists you love to bemoan about every day."

"You mistake your place, woman!" Osko snapped back.

Kai's fingers twitched towards his mace, wondering if he had the strength to prevent a brawl breaking out. The fluxroot was still repairing the extensive damage Rorik inflicted during the fight. Even knowing he won, Kai was willing to admit he may not have been so lucky without Timber flowing through his body.

"No, you mistake your place!" a new voice cried out. The party's gazes collectively shifted to a visibly pregnant woman on her feet on the left side of the chamber. Pointing at Guri, the woman continued, "My mother has worked herself to the bone to protect this city ever since I was a sprout and long before that, along with everyone else here. My own child will be born in the next few weeks and as a parent, I want nothing more than for my baby to grow up in a world where they won't be ridiculed or reviled simply because we are Norzen.

"We elected you as headman years ago because you promised to fight for our rights and freedoms. The Grand Duchess herself is now standing there, promising to bring us back to equal standing with the other tribes, and yet you're telling her to pound cobbles? Give us one good reason why we shouldn't toss you out on your ass!"

As the young woman's tirade went on, the rest of council shouted their agreement. Kai was impressed at how vocal the crowd was becoming, their booming rapport echoing off the chamber walls. His ears twitched, the tumultuous roar of the masses outside rattling his skull.

Kai peered at the chamber door, seeing it in constant motion with younger Norzen coming in and out. He guessed them to be messengers, taking word to the outside crowd on what was happening in the chancery. Thinking about it, Kai admitted it was a handy system that could be used once Parliament was reinstated.

Osko refused to back down, though, and flailed his arms about. "You want a reason for us to refuse this traitor's pleas? Very well! I am not putting this city in the hands of that inexperienced child because we've received a more reliable offer."

Kai's mind ground to a halt at Osko's words. *More reliable offer?*

"Should I have you arrested for possible treason, Osko?" Fusette warned, her eyes flashing and tails thrashing. "Duskmarsh may be semi-autonomous, but that does not give you leave to align the city with an outside party."

Pelka rose from her seat, addressing the council. "Did any of you know of this offer Osko is speaking of?" the diplomat asked. The entire council replied with a resounding negative. Kai's eyes landed on Osko, pinching together in a tight frown.

Now Fusette was in her element, stoking up the crowd as she demanded answers from the headman. "So, you've been sneaking around not just behind my back, but also the entire city you were trusted to care for. Perhaps it's time for a change in leadership, Osko. You have clearly shown a disregard for what leaders are meant to do."

"I've heard enough of your foolish platitudes, Lady Fusette. You know nothing of being a true leader. Compared to your father, you're nothing but a silly little girl playing pretend!"

Kai and his wives shot to their feet, the cool metal shaft of his mace slipping into his hand at once. "Say that again, you pompous pebblewit!" the apothecary growled.

"Oh please, you're hardly in a condition to fight. Besides, the agreement I've made will benefit all Norzen, not just those of us here in Duskmarsh."

A frigid chill ran through Kai's blood. He felt Maple and Orelia both clutching his arms, preventing him from charging the headman himself.

"Fusette," Kai said. The duchess responded with a curious glance, her fingers steepled together. "He needs to be brought back to the capital for questioning. Something about that comment is giving me the heebies."

With a grim nod, Fusette turned back to Osko and snapped her fingers.

"Commander Rorik." The burly warrior snapped to attention. "Place Headman Osko under arrest and secure him at once."

"You can't do that!" Osko roared, his voice turning hoarse as Rorik pulled both arms behind his back and bound them with chained shackles. "You dare try to suppress me for your own twisted means? The Norzen will only be ridiculed and beaten down further under your pathetic rule. If you arrest me, all you do is prove you're nothing but a tyrant, just as he said!"

The party stilled, Fusette's intense glower pinning Osko in place. "'He?' Who are you talking about?" she demanded.

"The one who offers our people a better way. A path to take back our pride and proper place in this wretched continent, above those who seek to trample us!"

Kai's hand clenched around the mace's shaft. "*Taen!*" he hissed. The chill in his bones deepened to the point even the warmth of his mane couldn't dampen it. There was only one person he knew who spoke of raising the Norzen to their 'proper place' in Alezon...

"And just who is supposed to be offering our tribe a better way?" Fusette pressed.

Before Osko could answer, the chamber door was thrown open with a thunderous bang, drawing the eyes of the entire room. Spinning in place, Kai raised his mace in a defensive stance.

His eyes bulged seeing a familiar habit-clad Soltauri stride into the chamber, flanked by a raven-haired woman in maid attire with two short blades clutched in her hands.

"Duarte," Lucretia whispered. Drawing her rapier, she rushed to the party's front.

Ione planted herself right beside the scholar, shield up and cutlass at the ready. "Mirabell," she said. Ione met the assassin's deadened gaze with grim determination, sliding into a relaxed stance.

Behind the two, a cloaked figure stepped between them, emitting a dismissive chuckle. Drawing back his hood, Hakan locked eyes with Kai and shook his head at the apothecary's battered state.

"Really now," Hakan jeered, "you sprouts look as though you've seen a ghost. Osko! Why didn't you inform your guests I was coming? Now everything feels so awkward."

Fusette stepped forward, head held high and hands clasped over her stomach. "Who are you? Are you the one trying to coax my people into insurrection?" she asked. She took another step, only to be pulled back by Maple.

"Stay behind us, Fusette," Kai commanded. A heavy rumble reverberated from the Exarch's chest, both of his tails straight as arrows.

The duchess clenched her jaw. She offered no resistance to Maple herding her behind the rest of the party.

"What's going on, Kai? Do you know that man? I do recognize the Soltauri, though; isn't he the one who attacked us at the Royal Archives in Runegard?"

He nodded. "You are correct, milady. As for the Norzen, he's the one we told you about: Hakan, the man responsible for orchestrating the Faumen War."

CHAPTER XVIII

K ai couldn't blame his cousin for the unbridled horror on her face when he revealed the identity of the Norzen in front of them. He was just as surprised as she was by the forge master's presence. It spoke of arrogance more extravagant than anything the prideful Norzen were infamous for. The council were all on their feet, staring between Osko and Hakan with equally aghast gapes.

The apothecary wondered if the main reason they weren't immediately siding with Hakan was due to Osko's foolishness in keeping his dealings with the other Norzen secret. Judging by the looks of anger on several, including Guri's daughter, it was obvious they didn't appreciate being disregarded.

"Kai, are you serious?" Fusette faltered. "Is that truly Hakan?"

He nodded, seeing her hands quaking and clutching the folds of her robes in an iron grip. To Kai's surprise, it wasn't fear he saw in the monarch's hardened stare.

It was fury.

Her soft grey eyes flared in the sunbeams drifting through the windows. The moment he noticed Fusette's muscles were tensing, he signaled Orelia with his hands. The former priestess encircled Fusette in her arms, stopping the duchess from charging towards the older Norzen as she clearly intended.

Hakan released a full-bellied laugh. "How cute, the duchess thinks she can fight at the men's table. Take my advice, little girl, and give up while I'm still feeling merciful. Your pet knight couldn't beat me before, and I doubt he can now in his current state."

"See what I mean, Lady Fusette," Osko piped up from the rear desk. "Master Hakan is more than capable of leading us to a Golden Age for our tribe. Think about it. We won't have to hide in the shadows or swamps anymore. The Norzen can finally attain true freedom and take our revenge on those who persecuted us!"

Shaking her head, Fusette let out an exasperated sigh. "And that is why you and Hakan are both morons," she said. "In order for true peace to be a reality, we cannot allow ourselves to be consumed by thoughts of vengeance and hatred."

The council members huddled into small groups amongst themselves, muttering in hushed whispers. Kai cast a stony glare towards Osko. He wasn't sure how long the headman had been in secret contact with Hakan, but he knew from experience the forge master preferred obedient puppets like Mirabell and Duarte over any potential equal.

"Osko," Kai called out. The headman returned his stare with a glimmer of curiosity. "Earlier today, you told me my parents were among the most respected members of your community, correct?"

Osko nodded. "That's correct," he said.

"Then let me ask you: Did this blighter bother telling you *he* was the one who murdered them?"

Before Kai could say anything else, Guri shot to her feet and released a furious roar. "What?!" she shouted. "Are you absolutely certain about that, Gravebane?"

Meeting Hakan's malicious sneer, Kai nodded. "I am. He admitted to it himself, and his family's goal has been to wipe out *all* of Cacovis' descendants, by any means necessary! That's why he arranged for this war in the first place."

The council erupted into a clamor. Many shook their fists at Hakan, who took the verbal abuse with an unflappable resolve. Guri hurried to plant herself in front of her daughter. The younger woman stared at Hakan in fear, allowing another member of council to usher her further back.

"Why have you come here, Hakan?" Fusette demanded. Kai glanced back, ensuring she wasn't attempting to step to the front of the party. In the rear, Hibbel and Pelka were herded among the council members on the right side of the chamber. Yulia stood at the end of the party, next to Teos and brandishing her spear.

Waving a dismissive hand, Hakan inspected his nails, not even bothering to look up and meet Fusette's eyes. "I came to cement the alliance of Duskmarsh with the rest of the Norzen under my command. The time has come for us to ascend to our rightful place, and you will not interfere. In fact, you being here saves me the trouble of having to drag you out of Whistlevale. I do love when my prey make things easier for me."

"If you think we're letting you get anywhere near Her Grace," Rorik announced, pushing past Kai to stand at the party's vanguard, "than you're not just a fool. You're an *arrogant* one."

Hakan released an exasperated sigh. "You would truly side with that traitorous woman over someone who only wishes to see our tribe achieve the greatness it has been denied for so long?"

Rorik's eyes narrowed, snapping his fingers and reaching out to take his greatsword from the guard bringing it forward. "The fact you seek to end the line of Cacovis despite being a Norzen yourself is heresy enough. Her Grace is right, though. We cannot achieve true peace without fighting the hatred your actions have spread through our realm."

"What a pity. I suppose if you won't follow me of your own free will, then I shall simply have to bring you to heel like a pathetic hound."

The council's fury flared at Hakan's words. All the men and even some women shouted at the guards to bring weapons. Osko tried raising his voice among the tumult, but a burly council member in a blacksmith's apron shoved the headman into his chair.

The forge master's attention shifted, locking on Kai. Hakan's eyes flickered to the apothecary's wrist, widening as he observed the two women flanking him.

"You know, boy," Hakan purred in a throaty growl, "I didn't need any additional reason to kill you, but I never would've imagined you capable of such a treachery against your own kind. I trust you're prepared for the consequences, because I'm going to enjoy seeing those two wenches ripped apart while you watch."

Kai's eyes flashed, Timber roiling beneath his skin. "Rorik?" he whispered.

The taller Norzen glanced down at him. "What is it?"

"I think I've got enough energy to get that bastard outside. Can I count on you to clean up the mess afterward?"

Rorik chuckled. "I was hoping you'd ask."

Turning to his friends, he gave Lucretia and Ione a tempered glance, gesturing to Hakan's companions with his eyes. The two nodded back, readying their weapons.

Maple gave one of his tails a firm tug. "Love, I hope you're not planning to do anything *else* stupid," she trilled in his ear.

"Of course not, honey, but we do need to take this outside where we'll have more room to maneuver."

"Don't worry, ma'am," Rorik offered, drawing the merchant's gaze upwards, "the city guard and I will handle the brunt of fighting that coward."

"Even though your city's headman wishes to ally with him?" Orelia asked.

Kai's spine trembled at the low baritone of Rorik's laugh. "Osko effectively forfeited his position in making an alliance with Hakan without even informing the council. The fact his supposed ally murdered a descendant of our city's beloved founder sealed both their fates."

"I really don't care for your silly strategizing," Hakan taunted, reaching up to push his spectacles further up his nose. "If you're that eager to die, let's get it over with."

Duarte and Mirabell slid into stances, their bodies tensing in preparation.

"Guardsmen, to arms!" Rorik shouted, twirling his sword. "Council members, please lead the non-combatants to the upper levels of the chancery. Guri, I want you to take some men, evacuate the plaza, and put the city on high alert."

"Yes sir!" Guri responded. "Will you be providing us a way past those bastards?"

Rolling his shoulders, Kai crossed both arms in front of his chest. "Leave that to me, Vice Commander," he growled. Leaning forward, the apothecary barked for the rest of the party to ready themselves.

A malevolent chuckle came from Hakan. "What exactly do you expect to—"

The forge master's voice caught in his throat when a cloud of amaranth erupted from Kai's shoulders, bathing the entire chamber. Lunging into the aromatic dust, Kai channeled Timber through both arms and head-butted Hakan square in the gut.

Hakan grunted at the blow, being taken off his feet and through the door into the second-floor parlor. Kai reached both hands behind his back, shooting a pair of vines out and wrapping them around Duarte and Mirabell's knees.

"Master!" Duarte yelled. "How did—woah!"

Gripping tight, Kai yanked both arms in an overhand rolling motion while retracting the vines. He felt the weight of his captives pulsing through his arm muscles, hauling them over his head. With a fanged grin, he unfurled the vines and heard a booming crash as the two were launched through the wall. Hakan soon followed when Kai slowed down, rearing back and blasting the forge master through the new hole with a boot to the chest.

Collapsing to one knee, Kai took several heavy breaths and felt a familiar warmth as Maple encircled him in her wings. He looked up to see Lucretia and Ione rush past him towards the stairs, Morgan and Teos on their heels.

A cooling sensation rushed over Kai's back. "Dear, can you please stop terrifying me?" Orelia asked, hooking her arm around his waist and helping him to his feet.

Rorik burst out laughing as he strode next to the trio. "It's been a while since I've seen anyone fight like that," he rumbled. "I wish even a quarter of my men fought with such a head for tactics! Now I don't feel quite so bad about having lost to you."

Before Kai could reply, he was stunned to see Rorik raise his sword overhead, emit a howling war cry, and jump *straight through* the hole to the plaza below!

Maple couldn't help but grin at Orelia. "I suppose we should count our blessings Kai isn't quite the battle maniac Rorik is," she said.

The trio made their way downstairs at a modest clip, being passed by several men from the council brandishing makeshift weapons. Once outside, they saw the town guards facing a squad of Norzen dressed in crimson armor. Rorik was pushing Hakan back towards the main bridge south of the chancery, their swords sending sparks into the air with every clash.

Glancing to the left, Kai saw Ione showcasing her improved skills in holding Mirabell off with Morgan's support. The tavern maid was swift footed, refusing to let her opponent get behind her and parrying Mirabell's kunai in the hope of driving her within range of Morgan's falchion. It was clear the assassin knew what the pair was trying to accomplish, as she pivoted away from each parry and started using the scrambling crowd and buildings to try and cover herself long enough to find an opening.

A growing weariness penetrating to his bones told Kai he wouldn't last much longer before he collapsed. He warned Maple to lead them somewhere more stable. The two women shared a knowing glance before hauling Kai to a nearby bench, away from the fighting but still close enough for Maple and Orelia to jump in and help.

On the other side of the mound from Ione and Morgan, Lucretia and Teos were doing well to keep Duarte at bay. Though smaller than the monk in both height and bulk, Teos' skill with his halberd left the other Soltauri infuriated with his inability to land even a glancing blow. At the same time, Lucretia took advantage of her former friend's growing agitation in copying Mirabell's hit-and-run tactics to land quick stabs in Duarte's blind spots.

"Why must we keep doing this, Duarte?" Lucretia pleaded, stepping back to avoid another two-handed swing from the Soltauri's massive axe.

Duarte snorted, pawing the ground with one hoof while pressing forward. "I told you before, Lu. I'm not the same person I once was."

"If that monster accomplishes his plan, the entire continent will fall to ruin!"

"I'm well aware of what fate awaits anyone not of the Norzen tribe," Duarte admitted, his gaze softening, "but I made my choice and must live with that, even if it means you and I shall forever be at odds."

Lucretia growled under her breath, wondering what it would take to break through the monk's stubborn pride.

Not being able to jump back into the fight and help was driving Kai out of his mind. Maple and Orelia held him back from attempting to take hold of his mace again.

"That's quite enough of that," Maple trilled, gripping Kai by the shoulders and holding him in place. His growing exhaustion proved a central factor in why the apothecary couldn't shrug her off, though a voice in the depths of his mind reminded him her actions were for his own benefit.

"But Maple—" he began, only to yelp when she tugged hard on his tails.

"No 'buts', love," the merchant muttered in a clipped tone. "I know you want to help, but I'm not letting you get yourself killed!"

"That goes double for me," Orelia reminded him, curling her arms around his neck while burying her face in his hair. "We are *not* losing you that easily."

A flash of green to the side caught Kai's attention, seeing Fusette come to a stop on Orelia's other side. She gave him a confident smile, followed by a short nod.

Around them, the town guard proved their formidability in driving Hakan's soldiers back. Over half the crimson-armored Norzen were already forced onto the southern bridge and the rest were retreating to the west.

Swinging his gaze to Rorik, he saw the burly Norzen still trading blows with Hakan. The warrior looked slower than he had shown in the arena, but the forge master was tiring more quickly, and Kai could see the burgeoning fury behind his grey eyes with each thrust Rorik deflected. A quick glance at the chancery revealed Osko at the front doors, watching the battle with a nervous expression.

"I suppose we should be thankful Osko bungled his plan so bad," Kai said. "I don't even want to imagine the trouble we'd have with Rorik as an enemy—"

His muttering was cut short when a familiar roar echoed through Duskmarsh, drowning out the sounds of battle. Everyone froze, many swinging their heads around in all directions searching for the source of the noise.

Kai's fur bristled at the sound, his face paling to a marble sheen. Beside him, he felt his wives' nails digging into his arm. The rest of the party broke off from their battles in an instant, backpedaling to the trio's position. Rorik was one of the few to not carry a look of fear, though he did retreat from his fight with Hakan as the forge master regrouped with his soldiers, Duarte and Mirabell once again at his flanks. Ione's entire body shook in terror, her chest heaving with every breath.

"*Taen!*" Kai swore, forcing himself to his feet. Maple gripped his arm to keep him steady, but she no longer fought to hold him down.

"You gotta be bloody kidding me," Teos growled, his own fur standing on end and tail thrashing about.

The sounds of horrified screams rose from the southern part of the city. From where he stood, Kai spotted hundreds of Norzen scattering among the mounds. The gondolas were filled in seconds, their pilots sending them across the water as fast as their strength would allow. At least a quarter of those unable to reach the boats opted to leap into the swamp directly, swimming for safety.

"Those folks had best hope that beastie don't feel like swimming after a snack," Morgan grumbled.

Fusette spun towards the sellsword with a worried glance. "What in Finyt are you talking about, Sir Morgan?" she asked. "What in Nixtral produced that unholy sound?"

"I think you're unfortunately about to find out, Fusette," Orelia answered. She rested a hand on Ione's shoulder, visibly calming the frightened woman.

A second roar reverberated through the air, causing Kai and many others to flatten their ears in pain. Near the bridge, Hakan broke out into booming laughter. Kai noticed Rorik looking at him curiously.

"Kai, it seems as though you lot know what this is. Let me tell you, the Norzen of Duskmarsh are hardly cowards. However, whatever made that horrendous roar has the entire city scurrying like mice. What are we up against?"

Releasing a heavy sigh, Kai popped his knuckles before resting a hand on his mace. "That beast and its handler are likely responsible for countless deaths since this war started. My friends and I have faced it as a group three times before today, though I first engaged it during the Battle of Mistport, before we all met. My entire Hunter squad was wiped out by that monster."

A heavy thump sounded every few seconds, faint but still loud enough for Kai's ears to detect, twitching with each step. His skin felt clammy despite his heart pumping blood through him with the intensity of a steam engine. Then, a shadow emerged from behind a building on the mound directly south of the chancery. Kai's hand formed a tight fist. Channeling Timber to his legs, he sensed the vibrations in the ground caused by each step of the approaching beast.

The apothecary heard Fusette's horrified gasp behind him when Grimghast reared its ugly head, stepping out from behind the building with Hemlocke and Obram perched atop its back.

"Sweet mother of Vadako," Fusette whispered. Her grey eyes bulged, taking an instinctive step backwards upon seeing the hulking monster. "Kai...are you telling me you've managed to survive *four* encounters with that monstrosity?"

Kai emitted an amused snort. "Trust me, I'm just as amazed I'm still alive as you are." His gaze met Grimghast's, the beast's singular eye widening in recognition as it stalked forward.

"What even *is* that thing?" Rorik asked. For the first time since meeting the burly warrior, Kai saw fear in his eyes. Jaw clenched and muscles tense, Rorik gestured for the rest of the town guard to spread out, barking at them to stay clear of Grimghast.

To everyone's surprise, it was the disgraced headman who staggered forward to answer Rorik's question. "Where in the voids of Abyssal did he acquire a lich bear?" Osko asked.

"A *what*?" Kai questioned, his head swinging towards Osko.

"The lich bear. It's an abomination of a creature. The stories say its body was corrupted by some sort of curse ages ago which is responsible for their ghastly appearance. I only know of it from an old acquaintance who encountered one during his travels overseas and lost his arm to it. To my knowledge, they're native to a single location: The Hollow Forest, found in the easternmost reaches of the Delkan Union."

Fusette clicked her tongue. "If I remember my geography lessons, Delkan is located on Uzura, the eastern continent."

Osko nodded. "Correct. The lich bear is a ferocious predator." The headman's eyes lingered on Kai. "I find it hard to imagine you could escape one so many times without losing a limb, at the very least."

Before Fusette could comment, Maple pointed an uchine at Osko's face. "I'll have you know I almost died to that monster, you incompetent pebblewit. Twice, in fact, if you count the poison made from its venom Hemlocke used on me. Take a good look at its scars; Kai is responsible for the vast majority of Grimghast's injuries, so don't you dare question his ability."

"Hemlocke! Obram!" Hakan shouted as Grimghast brought its riders onto the central mound. "You're both late. I was beginning to wonder if you two received my summons." Obram leapt from the beast's back, ignoring the menacing growl it emitted before dropping to its belly for Hemlocke to slide down.

"Apologies, Boss," Hemlocke demurred, offering a lackluster bow. "Nulla stopped at the gate for a little snack and getting her to hurry can be a pain, as you well know."

A deep rumble churned in Kai's chest. Compared to their fight on Tapimor's Crest, Hemlocke looked fatigued and his white feathers had lost much of their shine. Regardless, he could still see the manic gleam in the Aerivolk's eyes. It didn't matter if he was weaker than the last time they clashed.

Hemlocke was still dangerous, even without his vicious pet.

The other Norzen scrambled as far from Hakan's group as they could. Several more fleets of gondolas slid next to the mound, allowing the citizens to climb in. Even Hakan's own soldiers looked hesitant to step near Grimghast for fear of inviting a snap, many choosing to run towards the city gates in terror.

Rushing past the party, Osko threw himself to the ground in front of Hakan, prostrating himself in obvious fear. "Master," Osko whimpered, his body trembling, "how could you possibly control that beast? The lich bear is considered a being of death for a reason. They cannot simply be trained like a common boarhound!"

"You worry too much, Osko," said Hakan. "Hemlocke may have his flaws when it comes to personal usefulness, but his pet follows commands well enough and has proved rather useful in culling those who oppose me. I trust I won't have to count you among that number, will I, Osko?"

Refusing to take both eyes off Grimghast for too long, Kai's gaze flickered to the scowling Hemlocke, who stared at Hakan with ruffled feathers.

The headman's face turned a sickly porridge grey. "O-of course not, Master Hakan. I trust anyone working for you would be more than capable."

"I thought so. In fact, I think I should prove just how easily I can wield the power this creature will dispense at my command. Hemlocke?"

"Yes, Boss?"

Kai growled when he saw Hakan's gaze settle on Fusette, lips curved into a wicked smile. "Have your pet devour the Grand Duchess. It's high time we finally show these fools just who is in charge."

Reaching into his ratty tunic, Hemlocke drew his reed flute and raised it to his lips. "I couldn't agree more," he crowed.

A tremor of unease wracked Kai's spine at Hemlocke's look of unrepentant glee. It was a perfect match for the look he had when he poisoned Maple. Gripping his mace, Kai slid into a stance alongside the rest of the party. Rorik pushed Fusette behind him, bringing his greatsword to bear and roaring a challenge.

Closing his eyes, Hemlocke blew a string of melancholy notes which sent a chill throughout Kai's body. Grimghast's single eye blinked, shaking its head before releasing a bone-rattling growl. It bent at the knees, eyes focused forward. The entire city settled into an unnerving silence. Not a sound was heard, lest they draw Grimghast's attention.

Kai felt his Timber coil within him, ready to spring to life at a moment's notice.

Grimghast took a single step forward, causing the party to twitch. Behind it, Hemlocke smirked and blew another series of notes. The beast's ears wiggled for a moment before it *pounced*.

Everyone's eyes widened as a pain-filled scream shattered the quiet.

Chapter XIX

Kai's eyes bulged, his throat turning dry. It was impossible to tell whether he felt more stunned or horrified by the sight in front of him. He sensed movement in the corner of his vision, only to hear the unmistakable sound of someone retching into the swamp water below.

His mace was raised to chest height, though he made no move towards Grimghast. The beast stared back with blood dripping from its muzzle and a single arm dangling between its teeth.

The truly shocking part was that the limb belonged not to Fusette, as had been ordered, but rather to the screaming Hakan, who clutched at the ragged stump where his arm once was. The forge master stared at Hemlocke in open-mouthed horror, though the Aerivolk matched his gaze with the same malicious sneer.

"Hemlocke, you blithering simpleton!" Hakan bellowed, his teeth clenched together and hissing and pain. Blood spurted from the gaping wound and left a pool on the ground below. "What have you done? I thought you promised you had a handle on that insufferable creature!"

The foreboding chuckle coming from Hemlocke sent a fearful tremor down Kai's spine. In moments, the traitorous Aerivolk had erupted into full-blown cackling, his head thrown back in mirth.

"Y-you still think I'm loyal, Hakan? I can't tell if you're truly that vain or just stupid. I was *never* loyal to you, not for one bloody instant!"

Kai cast a sweeping gaze over the rest of the party, unsure of how to respond to this sudden shift among their enemies. He almost felt a pang of sympathy for the older Norzen, seeing the betrayed expression on his face.

"Why?" Hakan asked. "After everything I did for you, this is how you repay me? If it wasn't for me, you would've died in the alleys like a worthless tramp!"

"Obeying your orders only proved I traded one cage for another," snapped Hemlocke. "No more. Today, I achieve the true freedom I've searched for my entire life. And you...well, you'll make a fine start to the discord I shall sink this realm into."

Hakan snarled, backing away when he noticed Grimghast eyeing him with a ravenous hunger in its eye. "I've heard enough. You will pay for this treachery! Mirabell, kill him!"

Kai and his friends swung their eyes to Hakan's assassin, wondering if their enemies were about to save them a lot of trouble and destroy themselves. The apothecary was surprised, however, when Mirabell simply shook her head and turned away.

"Wait...w-what are you doing?" Hakan pleaded, his face sinking when the assassin ignored him. "I gave you an order, Mirabell! Obram, kill them both!"

The Risbado sellsword released a hearty chuckle. "Hakan, you should've seen this coming. Really now, allowing a *Norzen* of all things to stand at the top of a new order in Alezon? I'm hardly loyal to my tribe but I'd rather skin my own pelt than allow such a disgrace to occur. Besides, you already know I have a habit of turning on people when it suits me. You're just the next in a long line of betrayed 'masters.'"

Spinning to the last of his comrades, Hakan's face turned a sickly pale when he saw a look of defeat in Duarte's amber eyes. "Impossible. Not you too, Duarte. Please!"

Kai froze at the desperation in the forge master's voice, trying to process what was going on. Up till now, the Soltauri monk was almost fanatical in his devotion to Hakan. What in Finyt had happened since Havenfall to turn him down this path?

"Sorry, Boss," Hemlocke sneered with a crooked smile, "but it seems you're out of allies, out of options, and out of time. Nulla, my dear...kill him."

The Aerivolk blew a grim tune on his flute, one that cast a chill through Kai's tails. Maple and Orelia held his arms in a firmgrip, their nails digging into his forearms.

Hakan scrambled backwards, shrieking in terror while Grimghast bore down on him. Its venomous saliva dribbled to the dirt and shone in the midday sun. Spitting out a curse, Kai commanded everyone to fallback towards the chancery.

Hakan pushed himself to his feet and bolted after the party. However, he only managed three long strides before Grimghast lunged, his entire torso disappearing into the beast's mouth. Limbs flailing, Hakan emitted a muffled scream as Grimghast lifted him up and bit down hard.

The sound of crunching bones and splattering blood rang in Kai's ears, making him tremble. Fur standing on end, he turned and watched Hakan's body go limp just before Grimghast gripped the forge master's legs and tore him in half. Kai winced at the sight, unable to turn away from seeing the beast devour Hakan in only a few sickening gulps. He noticed the rest of the party watching alongside him, each with a disgusted look in their eyes. A firm tug on his robe drew his attention to Fusette, who returned his gaze with a grim expression.

"What now?" she asked. Despite her increased willingness to take charge in a crisis, she looked utterly lost.

If Kai was honest with himself, he had no idea how to answer. With Hakan out of the picture, the landscape of the entire war had shifted. Whether for better or worse, he wasn't certain yet.

Still, it didn't change the fact they remained in grave danger so long as Grimghast was anywhere nearby.

"Right now, we focus on staying alive and driving that monster and our enemies out of the city," he answered, lips set in a stony line. "Rorik!"

The warrior glanced at him, silently waiting.

"That thing can blend into its surroundings if given half a chance. We need every guardsman you have keeping the enemy busy. Have them focus on Duarte, Obram, and Mirabell."

"And what will the rest of us be doing?"

Kai stroked his mane, knowing his friends weren't going to like what he was about to say. "Teos, Morgan, Maple, and Orelia. I want all of you to back Rorik up and focus on Grimghast. You all know its weak points and how to drive it back. Ione and Yulia, I want you with Guri protecting Fusette, Hibbel, and Pelka from anyone who tries to get too close. Lucretia...you're with me. You've got quicker footwork than Morgan or Ione and better accuracy with your strikes, so I'd rather have you backing me up with how exhausted I am."

The scholar quirked an eyebrow at him. "I appreciate the compliment, but what shall we be doing?"

"We're going after Hemlocke."

Before Lucretia could reply, Grimghast let loose with a loud bellow. It pawed the ground while pacing, its bone-covered lower jaw dripping with Hakan's blood.

"Nulla," Hemlocke trilled, "kill them all!"

The Aerivolk blasted a series of notes on his flute before tucking it into his tunic. Pulling a small vial from his trousers, he took a minuscule sip of the contents before corking it and returning it to its pocket. His skin colored almost instantly, and his feathers returned to the glow Kai remembered from their battle outside Havenfall.

He growled. "Bloody Nulyma...he must have reserved some of the emberona elixir I made for him in Glimmerdale. It won't make him as strong as he was at Havenfall, but he'll still be plenty tough. You ready, Lucretia?"

Her mouth curved into a confident grin. "As ready as I will ever be," she said.

Nodding, Kai watched the others spread out to their assigned areas as he and Lucretia rushed forward to meet Hemlocke's charge.

After directing his men to surround Hemlocke's allies and pursue Hakan's fleeing soldiers, Maple watched Rorik lift a small pot from the ground and clanged it with his sword. The sharp ringing shifted Grimghast's gaze, the beast stalking forward with a bone-chilling growl. The merchant led the quartet alongside Rorik, each drawing their weapons.

"Good job, Rorik," Maple said, twirling her uchines. "This bugger has sensitive hearing, so loud noises will keep it off-balance. Its eyesight isn't as good, but it will still sniff you out if you get close enough."

The warrior nodded. "Thanks for the info, lass. That'll make this easier."

"Trust us," Teos growled while readying his halberd, "fighting Grimghast isn't easy in the slightest, no matter how much preparation you have. All it takes is one wrong move and it's over."

"I may not be at full strength, friend," Rorik replied, "but you'll be fine. I'll make sure of it."

As if to taunt the burly Norzen, Grimghast let loose a deafening roar before charging. Rorik met its attack, raising his blade and digging his heels in. Grimghast bit down on the flat edge of the sword, sparks flying as it pushed Rorik back. The warrior's eyes widened in shock when his body was forced back, unable to fully resist Grimghast's substantial weight.

"No bloody way," Rorik snarled.

Teos and Morgan ran around to Grimghast's sides, jabbing their weapons into its exposed side. At the same time, Maple and Orelia rushed behind the beast, each woman landing a solid strike to its hind legs.

Shrieking in pain at the wave of attacks, Grimghast lashed out with a hind leg that caught Maple in the ribs. The merchant squawked as the blow lifted her off the ground and sent her flying over the side of the mound and into the murky water. She sputtered, flailing her wings about in a desperate bid to stay afloat.

"Help!" she yelled.

Seeing the splash, Orelia swore and shouted to the others, "Keep it distracted! I'm going after Maple!" Sprinting for the edge of the mound, Orelia tossed her staff aside and dove head long into the swamp. Swimming towards her friend, she gestured to the nearest gondola, its pilot already pushing the boat in their direction.

Maple grew more frantic with each passing second. She could barely see through the splashing water. Her wings felt like iron anchors from being soaked through, and her talons barely produced enough force to keep her head above the water.

Before her head could sink into the murky depths again, she felt something hook around her waist and hold her up. A familiar voice urged her to hold tight. Blinking the water from her eyes, she met Orelia's concerned gaze and couldn't hold back a grateful smile from spreading across her lips.

"Ora, if we weren't in so much trouble right now, I'd kiss you!" Maple choked, turning her head to spit out some water that got in her mouth.

The former priestess giggled as the gondola stopped alongside them. Several hands reached into the water, hauling both women onto the boat. Maple broke out into a coughing fit, gulping down as much fresh air as she could. Using the side of the gondola to lift herself up, she glanced back towards the fighting.

To her surprise, Teos and Morgan were performing well, keeping just out of Grimghast's snapping distance and distracting it from focusing too hard on Rorik. The Norzen warrior took advantage of the diversions by chipping away at its bony armor with his sword. Kai shot her and Orelia a concerned look for a split second before turning back to Hemlocke when he let out a furious trill, Lucretia's rapier sliding across his shoulder.

Maple heard a pained hiss and looked over to see Orelia cradling her hand. "What happened?" she asked.

The former priestess opened her left hand to reveal a thin cut on the palm, blood slowly dripping from it onto the gondola deck. Her eyes shifted to the rough edges of the metal plating covering the gondola's hull.

"I think I cut my hand getting into the boat."

The gondolier, a younger Norzen, bowed his head. "My apologies, ma'am. The gondolas are armored to protect us from predators lurking in the swamp, and I'm afraid my boat's plating has been in need of filing for a few moons."

Orelia brushed off the man's apology and tore a small strip from her sleeve to wrap the wound. "No worries. Kai can fix this later. For now, get us back over there, please!"

The gondolier nodded, thrusting his rowing oar into the water and pushing the boat back towards the mound.

Kai wiped an arm across his brow, brushing the sweat from his eyes. Next to him, Lucretia looked winded, leaning forward with heaving gasps. Her cloak had several tears in it from the nails littering Hemlocke's staff and her rapier was buried point-first in the ground, being used to support her weight.

"How is he still so bloody strong?!" Lucretia snapped, taking a swig of water. Across from them, Hemlocke twirled his staff with a cocky smirk, his chest heaving.

Inhaling deep, Kai was on one knee and leaning on his mace. The apothecary scowled at their opponent. "That damned elixir is boosting his strength. I reckon we should consider ourselves lucky he doesn't have much left, or we'd be in even more trouble. As it is, he seems just as tired as us."

The traitor cackled with glee. "Looks like you two may have bitten off more than you can handle. I may be wearing down, but if you can't kill me now, I doubt you'll be able to do much to stop me from plunging this entire continent into chaos!"

Kai's eyes narrowed. What could he possibly mean by that? His gaze twitched to the rest of the battle, where Duarte's group was holding the city guard at bay with little difficulty. Ione and Yulia were back near the chancery, with Fusette directing the evacuation from the base of the stairs.

Rorik's group was being pushed back by Grimghast's stubborn advances, though Kai grinned when he saw the warrior land a solid hook to the beast's temple while Teos and Morgan distracted it, sending it staggering back. His grin quickly morphed into a grimace when Osko, seeing Grimghast backing away, took the opportunity to try bolting for the main bridge.

The headman only made it halfway before Grimghast spotted him and spun. Kai looked away, ignoring Hemlocke's malicious sneer and Osko's terror-filled screams as the beast pinned the older Norzen down and silenced him, via ripping his head off.

The sound of a boat bumping against the edge of the mound prickled Kai's ears. His eyes swung to Maple and Orelia scrambling out of the gondola and hurrying back towards him. He smiled, happy to see them safe, though he flinched back when Maple thumped him over the head.

"We're going to have a discussion tonight about pushing yourself too hard," the merchant intoned. Kai could only nod, knowing that arguing with either of them would only make things worse.

"As much as I would love to kill all of you now," Hemlocke snickered, "I think it'll be so much more delicious to see your hope die out along with this pathetic realm. Duarte!"

The monk glanced over at Hemlocke, grunting and shouting for a retreat. Grimghast swatted Rorik away and rumbled towards its master, ignoring Teos and Morgan's attempts to run their blades through its sides. Duarte's group broke off from their battle and followed the lumbering beast, though not before Mirabell rammed one of her kunai through a guardsman's throat and booted him into the swamp.

Hemlocke cast a leering grin at Kai while Grimghast rushed towards them. "With Hakan dealt with, I can get so much more accomplished. Don't worry though, Kai; I'll come find you when the end draws near. I suppose I should give you a parting gift. What say I stab the other one this time?" With a flick of the wrist, Hemlocke flung a dagger at Orelia.

"No!" Kai shouted, his eyes widening. He forced his body to move, throwing himself towards his wife. Seeing a shimmer of lavender on the blade, he already knew it was poisoned like the one Hemlocke used on Maple.

His arms wrapped around Orelia's waist as she lifted her arms. Letting out a pained cry, a flash of light enveloped the two. Kai hissed and contracted his pupils, trying to put himself between Orelia and the dagger. What he didn't expect was for a wet sensation to spread across his back. As the light dimmed, he turned his head and almost yelped in shock.

Orelia's left hand was glowing, encased within a soft blue orb of water. He raised a hand to reach out and touch the orb, only for Orelia to gasp and launch it. The orb struck Hemlocke's dagger like a cannonball, shattering the weapon and scattering its broken pieces backwards.

She can use Origin too?! Kai shouted in his mind, his eyes following the orb.

Eyes bulging, Hemlocke dove to the side. His dodge wasn't entirely effective as Orelia's unexpected attack caught him in the knee and sent the traitor spinning through the air to slam face-first onto the cobblestones.

"What in bloody—?" Hemlocke spat, staggering to his feet. He swore in his native Aerian when his injured leg crumpled beneath him, unable to support his weight. His gaze shifted to the stunned Kai, who stood protectively in front of his wives as Maple inspected Orelia's hands. "I swear to the void, I will *butcher* all three of you myself someday!"

Kai snarled and raised his arm, wincing at the pinch of firing several needle-like thorns from between his knuckles. Before they could hit, Grimghast lunged in front of Hemlocke, the thorns bouncing off its hide.

Duarte reached from his place on Grimghast's back and hauled Hemlocke up by the collar. The monk turned back, giving Lucretia a solemn frown, before patting the beast on the neck and sending it barreling back towards the southern gates.

"*Taen!*" Kai snapped, watching Grimghast vanish around the corner as swiftly as it arrived. He collapsed to his knees, feeling Maple's feathers and Orelia's arms encircling him in moments. He shivered at the soft trills the former emitted, letting their warmth spread through his body. Casting one last glance at where their enemies disappeared, he let himself melt into the embrace.

"I'm sorry if I worried you both," the apothecary murmured, "but I refuse to let either of you get hurt on my account again by that bastard." His arms reached up to caress their heads, threading calloused fingers through their hair. The sound of their heartbeats caused his ears to twitch and a sense of security to fill his chest. He still worried about what Hemlocke said before their sudden retreat, but for now all he cared about was having the most important people in his life tucked safely in his arms.

"It's okay," Maple whispered. "Thinking about it, I can't rightly be angry with you for what you did when I would've thrown myself in front of that blade first if my reflexes were better. What matters is that we're all safe."

"Kai!" Fusette called out. She led her crew towards the trio with Ione right on her heels and the allied delegates following along in a line. The duchess threw herself against the three, a gentle purr coming from her chest when Orelia wrapped an arm around her shoulders.

"Simply astonishing," Hibbel said as he approached the group. Kai saw the Vesikoi scholar's eager gaze on Orelia and bit back a growl. "Lady Orelia, how long have you been able to channel Mist like that?"

Her befuddled expression said everything about her thoughts on the question. "Hibbel, that was quite literally the first time I've ever done it! I *still* don't know how I did it! All I know is that, when I saw that dagger flying towards me, it felt like a raging river began flowing through my body. When I raised my arm, the river flowed straight to the cut on my hand and rushed out."

Hibbel drew a sheaf of parchment from his robe and began scribbling. "Fascinating. From what you've all explained so far, it seems high levels of stress were required to unlock your potential for harnessing Origin. Perhaps it's because you're the first Conjurers to arise in this part of Alezon in centuries. We've had Conjurers in Belomas for over seventy years, but most younglings with the potential these days develop their abilities as naturally as learning to walk."

From the other side, Rorik led Teos and Morgan back. The warrior's eyes landed on Kai with a confident smile. "Having faced it myself now, I don't know how you could survive that monster so many times. The fact you *have*, though, makes you a better warrior than I'll ever be."

"That's what I keep telling him!" Morgan crowed with a full-bellied laugh. "Our 'pothy has more stones than any mountain, that's for sure!"

Dropping to one knee, Rorik bowed to Fusette as the monarch stood. "Lady Fusette, I reckon with Osko dead, it falls to me to represent Duskmarsh. Now that the enemy has fled, shall we begin negotiations to join our fair city with your new alliance?"

Chapter XX

Once the city guard confirmed Grimghast's escape from Duskmarsh, via watching the beast's impressive leap from the city wall into the swamp as it swam south, Rorik ordered them to scatter, both to assess the damage and assist any injured.

His commands given, Rorik led Kai and the rest of the party back into the chancery building. Most of the council followed along, though Guri stayed closer to the back, tending to her daughter. Once everyone was in place and extra chairs brought in to allow everyone a place to sit, Rorik approached the party, Kai and Fusette standing in the lead, and dropped to one knee.

"Lady Fusette," the warrior said, "I must apologize for the danger you and your entourage were placed in today and beg your forgiveness. Thankfully, with Osko no longer a factor, we can now address the reason for your visit. With your permission, I'd like to submit a vote to the council to surrender Duskmarsh's autonomous status and take our place alongside the rest of Livoria."

Fusette nodded, stepping forward. "Commander Rorik, there is nothing to forgive. The events of today lay solely on Osko's shoulders along with Hakan, and their fates have already been sealed. Please feel free to conduct your business as needed."

It was then that Guri stood, her daughter standing up beside her. "There is no need, Your Grace. I must apologize for the way our guards and I treated your companions before. I was blind and ignorant of Osko's treachery due to the respect I held for his position, while you yourself were stifled by Parliament. I think I speak for everyone here when I say we stand with you. My daughter Saila is all I have left of my late husband. If there is any way our tribe can know true equality again before my grandchild is born, then I for one intend to stand on the front lines to ensure it happens."

The entire council broke into raucous applause at Guri's words. Kai's ears twitched at the noise, his tails coiling around Maple and Orelia's arms. Like a wave, every member of the council and even the ordinary citizens stood. Rorik barked out a command in what could only be the High Norzen tongue and everyone clapped a closed fist over their hearts in salute.

"Your Grace," Rorik intoned, bowing deep at the waist, "as our city's provisional leader, I hereby reaffirm our fealty to you and your cause. The Norzen of Duskmarsh shall defend you and this realm to the last."

Fusette returned the bow, cupping a hand to Rorik's cheek and bidding him to rise. "Thank you. While I'm not sad to see Hakan get his comeuppance, his untimely death is sure to throw the enemy's plans into chaos. It's bad enough the Liberators lost their top general at the Battle of Havenfall, but now with their financial backer gone, there's no telling how desperate they may become."

Kai cleared his throat, drawing the monarch's attention. "Fusette, I apologize if I'm speaking out of turn, but from what I saw during the battle today, it seems most of Hakan's minions are now taking their marching orders from Hemlocke. I'm not sure what the man's plan is, but he did mention something that has me worried."

Frowning, Fusette gestured for Kai to continue when a young man burst through the doors, gasping for air.

"Commander Rorik!" the man wheezed. "A large contingent of Galstan sailors, numbering at least a hundred, are approaching the southern gate!"

Orelia turned to glance at Yulia. "Did Father say anything to you about this, Captain Ruhl?"

The officer shook her head. "He said nothing of the sort. However, it's a gamble on whether it was his idea to follow us or Her Majesty's."

Rolling her eyes, Orelia chuckled. "Considering my presence? No, this is most assuredly Father's work, even if Her Majesty may have given the order. While I love the man, being overprotective tends to be among his more prominent flaws."

Rorik chuckled and gestured to the messenger, scribbling a short note on a piece of spare parchment. "Return to the gate at once with some guards and inform our guests we will allow an envoy of a dozen sailors to enter the city. The rest will have to camp in the field mounds outside the gate, which our guards will be more than happy to lead them to."

The messenger accepted the note and nodded, hurrying back outside with three guards in tow. The room settled into a tense silence. Fusette gazed at Kai as if to continue their earlier conversation, though he suspected she was waiting for the Galstan envoy to arrive before doing so. For now, he was content to sit with his family and wait.

A flash of movement in his peripheral vision had Kai glancing at Guri and Saila, approaching Fusette with the latter wobbling uneasily. He swiveled his ears towards the three.

"Your Grace," Saila said, offering a quick bow, "If I could have a moment of your time, do you truly believe we can overcome so many years of hatred towards our tribe by winning this war?"

Fusette gave the woman a kind smile before rising and helping her to sit. "I'm more than happy to speak with you, Saila. In fact, you bring up a legitimate concern, given the issues facing our people since even before Livoria's founding."

"Forgive me, milady," Guri spoke up, "but I read in the newsletters how you recently revealed the truth of your identity to the people in a public announcement. Were you not worried of the dangers?"

A soft giggle came from the monarch. "Why should I have been worried? I know our tribe has a reputation thanks to Cacovis, but I trusted the citizens to at least hear me out before doing anything dangerous. Besides, it helps I could give them a shining example to prove the Norzen are nowhere as bad as our reputation says."

Both women gave Fusette a curious glance. "What sort of example are you talking about, milady?"

With a smug grin, Fusette raised a finger towards Kai, who averted his eyes at once and tried focusing on the two pairs of hands threading through his mane. "I'm not sure what news has arrived from other newsletters across the realm, but Kai and his party are responsible for saving thousands of lives over the course of this war. Why do you think I named him my champion? In addition to his battle prowess, Kai has proven a steadfast dedication to protecting the innocent and his compassion is second to none. That's the sort of example Livoria needs to reach the peace and prosperity I envision for us all."

Even with his head turned, Kai could sense Guri's eyes on him, followed by an amused chuckle. "Hearing it from you, Your Grace, I would be tempted to convince Saila to name her child after Kai if it turns out to be a boy if she hadn't already decided on one."

Fusette's gaze shifted to Saila. "Oh? And what name did you choose?"

"Should the forests bless me with a son, I intend to name him Osvald," the young woman declared, "after his paternal grandfather."

The duchess nodded. "If I remember my High Norzen correctly, Osvald means 'blessed shield.' A fine name! Once we return to Whistlevale, I shall have an appropriate gift sent to commemorate the addition to your family."

Kai bit back a chuckle as both Saila and Guri flailed their arms, pleading with Fusette that she didn't need to make such a gesture for them.

A booming voice rang from outside the audience chamber. "Your Grace?! Orelia?!"

Glancing at his wife, Kai bit his lip at the exasperated expression on Orelia's face as she rolled her eyes again. She turned to Rorik and nodded. The warrior laughed when the doors flew open to reveal Ottoten in full military dress, marching at the head of a dozen sailors bedecked in Holy Navy white.

"Greetings, Admiral Basner," Fusette said. "I was unaware Her Majesty sent you to assist us. Did you happen to spot the enemy fleeing as you arrived?"

Ottoten's eyes narrowed. "The enemy?"

One of the sailors raised their hand from the rear of the group. "Admiral, I think she might be talking about that strange beast the scouts spotted swimming away from the city. They did say it appeared to have several people riding it."

"Wait, you mean *that* was the enemy?" Kai was impressed by the avalanche of curses coming from Ottoten's mouth when Fusette nodded.

"Father!" Orelia barked. Her rebuke brought the admiral's tirade to an immediate stop, his jaw snapping shut as he turned to see the severe glare his daughter was sending him.

"You know you look just like your mother when you do that, right?"

The compliment did nothing but cause Orelia's frown to deepen. "And do you believe Mother would appreciate the language you were just using? For Finyt's sake, Father, there are *children* standing in the parlor outside!"

Ottoten winced. "My apologies. You're right. I should've been more mindful of my surroundings. Wait..." His eyes drifted to Orelia's bandaged hand. With a heavy growl, he stomped forward and removed the torn cloth. The cut still leaked, though her rudimentary bandage had staunched much of the bleeding. "Orelia, what's this? How were you hurt?!"

"That beast knocked Maple into the swamp. You know as well as anyone how hard it is for Aerivolk to swim. I couldn't leave her there. My hand got cut climbing into a boat that came to help."

Kai tensed the moment Ottoten's glare swung towards him. "And where were *you* when this was going on?" the officer grumbled.

Anything else Ottoten could've said was cut short when Orelia used her good hand to lift her staff and thump the admiral over the head. "Don't you even think of blaming Kai for this. We already had this discussion and I will *not* revisit it! If anything, I should've been more careful, but I suppose some good did come of my injury."

"How could the fact you got hurt result in anything good?"

Before Orelia could answer, Hibbel stepped forward, a giddy smile splayed across his lips. "It appears, Admiral, your daughter is among the rare faumen in this part of Alezon capable of harnessing Origin. She fired a rather impressive water bomb towards that horrendous Aerivolk. You have every reason to be proud."

Spinning to face her, Ottoten's face lit up. "Well, I'll be damned," he mumbled. "Your mother always said you'd be something special, Ora, but it seems she didn't have a clue as to how true that statement would actually be."

"As fascinating as this topic is," Fusette interrupted, her gaze locking on Kai, "but we still need to discuss the issue of Hemlocke's usurpation. Kai, you mentioned he made some worrying comments during the fight. What did he say, and what are your thoughts?"

Stroking his mane, Kai ruminated over Hemlocke's declaration. "He said something about throwing the entire realm into chaos."

Teos snorted. "That traitorous bastard seems to thrive off discord. When he revealed his true colors, seeing how badly we were blindsided sent him into hysterics, like he was having the time of his life."

"Teos is right," Kai said. "I don't know what his overall goal is yet but I can tell you two things for certain. First, whatever his plan involves will be *bad*. He might be a demented monster, but he's never struck me as a liar. He wouldn't make such a claim unless he had the means to do so on hand. Second, it's going to be widespread. Hemlocke is determined to have the effects of whatever he does spread all over Livoria and possibly even Alezon, so his plan must hinge on something that can spread either quickly, silently, or both."

"That is disturbing," Lucretia piped up.

Fusette nodded. "Indeed. Unfortunately, we're currently on the back foot so long as we can't accurately determine what his ultimate plan is."

Kai chewed his lower lip, every interaction he'd had thus far with Hemlocke replaying in his mind. "Actually, I may have a rough idea on what he's up to."

Everyone's head twisted to him.

"How in the winds could you possibly guess what that toerag wants to do, 'pothy?" Morgan asked. "The man has clearly lost his plot! If there's one thing I've learned as a sellsword, it's that the crazy ones are the hardest to predict. It's what makes them so dangerous."

Rorik nodded, eyeing Morgan with a look of respect. "Your friend makes a valid point. Being lost in the haze of madness is far different from any Frenzy Haze. This Hemlocke will likely seek out unpredictable and destructive methods to disorient us."

"I can make a guess because, as much as it pains me to admit it, Hemlocke and I share some similarities."

A firm grip on Kai's shoulder caused his muscles to tense. His gaze flickered to Fusette, who stared at him with a curious expression. "What are you talking about? You and that man are nothing alike!"

He shook his head. "In most ways, you'd be correct. However, I remember Hemlocke saying he created the poison he used on Maple himself."

The merchant's hand slid into his hand, giving it a gentle squeeze that filled him with warmth.

"That suggests he has at minimum, a working knowledge of poisons and concoction preparation," Kai continued. "He was ready to use a similarly poisoned blade on Orelia when she stopped him with that water bomb. My guess is his plan will revolve around some sort of poison. Something he can spread quickly enough to infect swaths of people without much effort."

Pacing back and forth, Lucretia tapped her cheek while grumbling under her breath. Kai could see the tension in her hands as they alternated clenching open and shut. The short, choppy steps of her boots clicked against the wooden floor.

"As much as Morgan makes a good point on Hemlocke's madness, Kai brings up an equally valid counter. The man is no fool, that's for sure. The real question would be in how he plans on spreading such a poison."

"If he wants to spread it on a level capable of affecting the whole continent," Kai said, "then his best options are by spreading it in either liquid or gas form. Gas would offer a broader range but it's much harder to contain until he's ready to use it. No, my guess is he's planning to contaminate the water in the same way he did Glimmerdale. That means he'll likely stick close to the rivers."

"How can we deal with such a threat?" Fusette asked, her hands clenched into tight fists.

It was a worrying thought. Even with the rest of their allies assisting, the Royal Navy couldn't be everywhere and Livoria was famous worldwide for its abundance of rivers, giving Hemlocke plenty of potential opportunities. Hemlocke could attack via any point. Kai's blood chilled when he remembered the man's escape. If he had any toxic concoctions on hand, it wouldn't be outside the realm of possibility for the traitor to have spiked the swamp during his departure.

"Rorik, how many apothecaries do you have on hand in the city?" Kai demanded.

The warrior gave the room a sweeping glance before shrugging. "Maybe about ten or so of varying skill plus their apprentices. Why?"

"I suggest you have them inspect the surrounding swamplands to make sure Hemlocke didn't leave anything behind. Admiral Basner's men can likely show you his escape path. I doubt Duskmarsh gets its drinking water from the standing swamp filling the city, but all it takes is one dip in a contaminated pool to risk empoisoning if the water enters the mouth, nose, or ears."

Rorik and several council members swore.

"Damnation, you may be right about that," Rorik admitted while turning to Guri. "Get all the apothecaries together and do a sweep. Take as many samples as needed to make sure that bastard didn't infect the water.

Admiral, do we have your permission to have a few of your sailors escort us?"

Ottoten nodded. "Of course. It might take a day or two to finish the sweep, but it'll give our men time to rest and for you to make your preparations." The admiral pointed to three sailors and gestured for them to follow Guri.

Turning to Fusette, Kai stroked his mane. His lips were pursed as various scenarios played out in his mind. "Fusette, we may have to send out a slew of carrier hawks over the next day or two."

"I assume your suggestion will be to counter Hemlocke's actions on a scale as widespread as he wishes to take against us?"

He nodded. "Just so. We need to inform all the major cities across the realm of a potential attack. Their apothecaries must remain on guard and vigilant until we can defeat the enemy once and for all. The most important hawk will be to Saredi. With your signature and seal, he'll have the authority to muster the Royal Apothecaries and Exarchs to assist. We don't know for certain yet how Hemlocke will do this, so we have to be prepared for anything."

Fusette called for parchment and quill, asking Rorik if there were any spare scriveners available to transcribe her message. He gave a single nod and sent a small group of council members upstairs. Within minutes, a full dozen Norzen were shuffling into the chamber, their arms laden with parchment and boxes filled with inkwells and quills.

As the group set up a length of tables and arranged themselves in a line across from Fusette, Kai allowed himself to settle into a relaxed slump with Maple and Orelia at his sides. The rest of the party followed suit, everyone breathing a sigh of relief.

Kai made a half-hearted attempt to listen to Fusette's voice telling the scribes her message for the apothecaries of the realm. The echo of Hemlocke's words in his mind caused his fur to bristle with unease. They may not know exactly what his plan would entail, but they couldn't afford to sit back and wait for him to strike first.

Thinking of the potential damage of such a mistake was enough to chill him to the bone.

Chapter XXI

Agosti grumbled under his breath while watching the remnants of his army mill about the forest in haphazard groups. In the aftermath of fleeing the Marine Cavalry, the soldiers were exhausted and over half their supplies had been either left behind in the rush or used up by men desperate to sate the hunger and thirst gnawing at their bellies.

He found himself grateful for the Great Ardei. The river's expansive width made it easier for them to lose the Royalists after putting part of the forest to the torch. It served as enough of a distraction for the Liberators to find a bridge and reach the west side of the river before destroying it to prevent any immediate attempt to follow them.

Next to Agosti, Adalbard leaned against a large oak, muttering what he could only assume was a prayer. The aging priest's vestment was torn from the unforgiving march and his shoes looked to be holding themselves together by the thinnest of threads.

"Oi, priest!" Agosti snapped, drawing the older man's gaze. "You reckon we'll hear from that bastard anytime soon?"

"I assume you're talking about Razarr?" Adalbard asked, rolling his eyes.

The general's lips curled back. "Who do you think I'm talking about, you damned fool," he snarled. "Wasn't he supposed to be sending a new shipment of equipment and food? We're low enough as it is, and if we don't get anything soon, the men are gonna kill each other."

"Assuming you don't kill them first," the cleric mumbled in a whisper.

"You say something?" Agosti asked, his eyes narrowed as he slid a finger along the edge of his sword's sheath.

Adalbard shook his head, clearly not willing to provoke the volatile officer any more than he already was. Agosti knew the men feared his temper and wasn't above running a man through the gut if it got the others back in line. Still, he was also aware morale within the army was spiraling out of control and he needed to fix it before the Liberation Army tore itself apart from the inside.

"General Agosti," a wearied soldier gasped, approaching the pair from the bottom of the hill they sat on to overlook the rest of the army. On the man's soldier sat a ruffled carrier hawk and a bound scroll was clutched in one hand. "This hawk showed up a few minutes ago with a letter addressed to you."

Sneering at the soldier, Agosti snatched the scroll from his outstretched hand and unfurled it. His eyes roamed over the short missive, his eyes pinching together in frustration. Adalbard peered at the letter over the general's shoulder, one eyebrow quirking upwards.

"Is it from our wayward benefactor?" the priest asked. "The handwriting looks a bit different from the other letters we've seen."

"It looks like it is," Agosti answered, "and I reckon the fool probably has a bevy of servants to write things down for him. I never nailed him as someone willing to do such a mundane task himself if he could help it. Apparently, he wants us to break camp and start heading towards Whistlevale."

Adalbard's eyes widened. "The capital? I know we're already halfway there from Havenfall, but how does he expect us to make it the rest of the way without equipment or food."

"Says here a regiment of unmarked Corlatian soldiers is bringing our shipment with enough men to give us a fighting chance. They're also carrying more ammo for that improved cannon he sent us last time."

"The Shatterstar?" someone grumbled from behind. Agosti barely stopped himself from jumping at the sound of Medoro's voice, though Adalbard had no such discipline and backed away with a gasp of shock.

I need more sleep, Agosti muttered in his own mind. *That bastard never could've snuck up on me like that otherwise.*

Rather than pick a fight with the older officer, Agosti nodded. "That's right. He says he sent an updated design for the cannonballs to one of his forges near the border, where our backup grabbed them."

"Can we even trust that weapon unless Razarr comes to handle its use like last time?" Medoro pressed, his lips pinched in a thin line.

"It's a bloody cannon," Agosti snapped back. His gaze drifted to the group of carriages at the center of their forces, filled with specially carved pieces of wood and metal like those they assembled on Tapimor's Crest. "I reckon it works the same as any other once we piece it together, which shouldn't be too difficult if the new one is anything like the first. And as much as you like to complain, I know for a fact you're experienced in artillery use and the damn thing at least proved enough to wipe Havenfall off the map."

Agosti didn't trust Razarr or his minions as far as he could throw a bulwark deer, but he also knew their options were limited. This was their best, and likely *only*, chance at defeating the Royalists.

"So Razarr intends for us to do the heavy lifting," Adalbard said with a heavy sigh. "I shouldn't be surprised by it at this point. While I'm confident he and his lot will join us at Whistlevale, the men will not enjoy hearing this. If we want any hope of winning this war, we cannot have our soldiers giving up before the battle even starts."

Sharing identical grimaces, Agosti and Medoro watched the older man mutter under his breath while the former rubbed his knuckles in a circular motion. While Agosti appreciated Adalbard's glib tongue at times, he found the priest's penchant for verbalizing the army's shortcomings irksome at best.

"What do you suggest we do about it, Adalbard?" asked Medoro.

"Once our allies arrive, gather the men together at the base of the hill. I'm feeling rather inspired by Razarr's missive despite my frustration, or perhaps even *because* of it. Either way, I feel the winds urging me to keep the flames of our cause burning bright."

To Agosti's frustration, the Corlatians didn't arrive until late afternoon, as the sun dipped beneath the treetops. The regiment proved full of fresh volunteer recruits from the Federation filled more with enthusiasm and a hatred for faumen than practical combat experience. While Agosti would have preferred seasoned soldiers, he figured the newcomers would make adequate front-liners, if only to keep his legitimate veterans better rested once the fighting started again.

Nestled at the center of their group and given a wide berth was a single wiroch-drawn carriage, guarded by half a dozen well-armed veterans from the Federal Army. When Agosti questioned the regiment commander, the man informed him the carriage held three of Razarr's lekrite cannonballs.

The general snorted, hoping the new weapon could manage more than the single shot its predecessor fired before breaking apart.

As Adalbard requested, the Liberators and their new allies were herded into a large shifting mass filling the clearing at the hill's base. The priest himself stood atop a large rock jutting from the hillside and overlooking the throng. From his position off to the side, Agosti couldn't help thinking it looked like a long, grey crow's beak.

The priest smoothed out the creases in his vestment with an intense frown. Once he deemed the garment adequately presentable, Adalbard brandished his spiked staff in one hand with a flourish. The other hand raised a small warhorn to his wrinkled lips.

"My friends!" Adalbard cried out, the horn amplifying his voice enough to reach the farthest edges of the clearing. The soldiers settled into a tense calm, their eyes all focused on the former bishop.

"I know things have not gone so well for us since our great victory over the Royalist scum at Havenfall," he declared, prompting mutterings of agreement.

Agosti cast a sweeping gaze over the forest, searching for any sign of movement among the trees which might signal the enemy. Seeing none, he gave a stiff nod and returned his attention to the sermon.

"However, we must not allow these hardships to weaken our resolve. Only the weak surrender so easily to challenges, and I don't see a weak man among you! Does not Master Galen himself urge us in the holy Ventrominix to face life's challenges with a steady heart and steeled mind, so that we might taste the sweetness of victory?"

The crowd cheered, waving their weary arms in the air.

"The winds of change are in the air, my comrades! I know we are weary from constant marching. I know we are hungry. As you can see, our allies from Corlati have heard our plea for aid and answered the call. Together, we will rid our beautiful realm of the vile faumen menace."

More cheers erupted, followed by several torches being lit among the crowd. Agosti watched with a measure of respect. As useless as Adalbard was as a fighter, the priest remained a skilled orator and had a knack for whipping the soldiers into a frenzy, no matter how tired they were.

"The faumen have been a stain on this realm for far too long. With our allies at our side, we will finally cleanse Whistlevale of its sordid past and rebuild Livoria as a new realm. A prosperous one where those beasts know their place and serve their betters as they should've from the start. Even the royal family must pay for their lies and will be damned to the voids of Nulyma. The Grand Duchess herself is one of them! A filthy peltneck that dares to prop herself up as superior to those of us who are pure!"

The soldiers' cheers from before were nothing compared to the virulent clamor they raised at Adalbard's words. A tremor of concern slithered down Agosti's spine, hoping the Royalists were too far away to hear the ruckus. He could feel his hatred simmering in the depths of his chest. Hearing the old priest condemn the Norzen only reminded the general of his own burning rancor for the hellcats, and one in particular.

Adalbard rapped the bottom of his staff against the rock several times in quick succession. "We cannot allow this insult to the human tribe's purity go unanswered," he roared. "If we permit this atrocity to stand, who knows how far the beasts will be willing to go to stamp out humans. They may even try to force us out to turn Livoria into a realm solely for their own kind!"

The furor grew ever more intense, sending flocks of birds fleeing into the sky to escape the deafening tumult. Agosti glanced at Adalbard, now waving his staff in a flurry of motion as the collective army stamped their feet in tandem. It felt as though the joint stomping shook the entire forest with the vibrations Agosti sensed beneath his boots.

"Take heart, my friends," Adalbard declared while taking a drink from his canteen, "for while tonight we rest and prepare ourselves for the march, know that soon the bells of victory will ring and usher in a new era for Livoria. We will face the enemy to the last, we will show no quarter, and we will triumph!"

A bone-rattling applause erupted from the crowd. Agosti could see many of the men looking more refreshed than at any time since they left Havenfall. After some prompting from the senior officers, the army settled into a pensive quiet while enjoying their meager rations. Stepping next to the aging priest, Agosti chuckled.

"You never cease to impress me with how well you can light a fire in those boys," he said.

"I've worked hard for the skill, my friend," Adalbard replied. His lips were curved into a broad smile. "Besides, it helps our goals to keep them focused on the end prize. Whistlevale is only a few days away by march, though we may need to take longer to keep the Navy off our tails. So long as we evade them, we have a chance to end this and scatter those beasts to the winds as they deserve."

"You're not wrong. Listen, priest, I know we haven't gotten along the greatest, but you were right that we all share a common goal, and I reckon I let all the responsibility this damn rank saddled me with cloud my head. Once this is all over, if we're both still standing when it's said and done, I promise I'll put in a good word for whoever ends up in charge to have you named the new church's Archbishop. We never would've made it this far without you."

Agosti had to bite back a snicker at the dumbstruck look on Adalbard's face. While he would be the first to admit his temper often got the better of him, he was willing to own up when he botched something.

"I appreciate the vote of confidence, General Agosti," the priest muttered. "It would certainly prove a challenge for an old hawk like me, but if nothing else I can use the years I have left to reshape the church for the future we desire."

Nodding, Agosti bid Adalbard good night and left for his tent near the hilltop. The old codger was right about one thing: They had a long march ahead. Galen willing, though, they'd pull this crazy plan off and finally but that blasted duchess where she belonged.

Scattered to the winds as a cloud of dust!

Soon, General Doulterre, Agosti thought as he tried tuning out the muffled noises of the camp, *I'll pay that damn peltneck back for what he did to you.*

Chapter XXII

Nighttime in Duskmarsh was much more beautiful than Kai could've imagined. Despite the city's swampy location, the array of lanterns lining the streets and buildings illuminated the entire area in a vibrant glow. Swinging pinpricks of light dotted the water, marking the gondolas as they weaved their way through the mounds. The occasional hoot from an owl hidden within the surrounding cypress trees could be heard over the muffled conversations going on around them.

After their meeting with the council concluded, Fusette dismissed the party with an order to relax while she worked with Rorik on finalizing the preparations for half of Duskmarsh's defense battalion to accompany them back to Whistlevale. Kai was initially prepared to offer his own assistance, though Fusette saw his intentions right away and gave him a very firm command.

"You've been through two exhausting battles today," she had said. "At no point do I want to see you anywhere near this chancery until we're ready to depart. I told you all to relax, and I meant it. Get some rest and enjoy the sights. Treat your wives to a nice meal. By the winds, I don't much care what it is, so long as you do something that has nothing to do with *any* of your duties!"

Sufficiently reprimanded, Kai offered a contrite bow and allowed Maple and Orelia to guide him out of the chancery. Deciding to take his cousin's advice, he asked the locals for recommendations on a place to eat after napping for a few hours to rejuvenate himself. To his surprise, a fair number of residents agreed that a tiny meadhouse called the *Dapper Hat,* in the southwestern corner of the city, was the premier spot for a romantic night out. That, in turn, led to the three of them now standing in front of the tavern in question.

It had a quaint charm to it. A faceless wooden statue stood at the entrance, dressed in an eloquent waistcoat and trousers with a jaunty top hat tilted on its head that gave the place its name. The exterior was well maintained yet still had a rustic ambiance that reminded Kai of Havenfall and other small towns he'd visited on his travels. The interior was lively but not loud, a fact he was thankful for. He reached out and took his wives' hands.

"Shall we?" he asked.

Orelia rolled her eyes and leaned up to kiss his cheek before giving a nod. The trio stepped inside and were eagerly greeted by a young Norzen tavern maid in a flowing blue dirndl. Kai whispered a few words into the girl's twitching ears, which was followed by her leading them to a table on the far end of the meadhouse, away from prying eyes. Once seated, the tavern maid handed them a menu to peruse and took their order after they spent a few minutes deciding.

Seeing the girl saunter away, Maple gave Kai a teasing smile. "So how does it feel being ordered to actually take a break for once? I reckon we haven't had much time to rest since this whole damn war started."

From her place on Kai's other side, Orelia rested a hand on his, tracing her fingers over his knuckles with a pensive expression. "Mapes is right," she murmured. "Even when we weren't actively traveling, we still kept ourselves busy with training and whatever other duties Fusette or Saredi had us helping with. The closest we ever came to a true rest was the time we spent with your family in Havenfall and even then, we still had to worry about the Liberator attack."

Gazing down at the table, Kai couldn't help but focus on the minuscule scratches and dents in the wood while thinking about the truth in Orelia's statement. A heavy weight settled in his throat, his lips pulling taut in a deep frown.

It was obvious his companions were watching his reaction when Maple pinched his cheek, provoking a pained yelp from the apothecary.

"Don't you start," she trilled. "I can see it in your eyes. You're about to blame yourself for us not having time to rest and enjoy ourselves."

"But—" A new assault came at him from the other side before he could finish when Orelia's nails dug into his hand.

"Cut that line of thought right now. While that self-sacrificing nature of yours is appealing at times, right now it's proving a pain in my gills," she said.

Ears flattened against his scalp, Kai blushed with a timid nod. His chest erupted into a rumbling purr when both women brushed their lips against his cheeks, their noses nuzzling against his skin in silent joy. The three sat in the dim lighting, reveling in each other's presence as the tavern maid returned with their drinks. Kai thanked the girl and flipped her a silver before taking a long draw from the peach mead he ordered.

"Hmm," he thrummed, his eyes gazing into the frothy bubbles with a curved grin, "that's good. Some of the best mead I've ever had, actually."

The tavern maid's face bloomed with happiness. "I'll be sure to let the proprietor know," she assured him. "His wife is the meadmaker and does everything by hand from her brewery down the street."

Kai nodded, watching her venture off again while the trio enjoyed their drinks. Maple sipped at her own mead, smiling when Kai brushed his lips to catch a line of bubbles dribbling from the corner of her mouth.

"You're incorrigible," she murmured.

"Yet you love me anyway," he shot back, "even if I'll never understand how."

Orelia flicked him in the nose, producing a muffled yelp. "Hush, you. Do we really need to reason to love you when you treat us so well and work hard to keep us safe?"

"Yes, dear," Kai mumbled.

Before the three could descend into another round of affection, the maid sidled next to the table and dropped a trio of steaming plates in front of them. Licking their lips, they dug into the food with gusto. Another silver soon found its way into the maid's hands as Orelia and Maple gushed over the rack of bison ribs the three decided to share.

"So what do you reckon we should do after this war is all said and done?" Maple asked after tearing a strip of meat off one rib.

Kai gave her a sideways glance, a contemplative look on his face while he chewed. "All I know for certain," he said after gulping down his food, "is that I plan on retiring from anything combat-related. I'll remain an Exarch if Fusette wants me to, but I'd rather stick to a support role and just be a regular apothecary for the rest of my life."

"You won't hear any complaints from us," Orelia agreed. "I for one have had my share of worrying over you. No more fighting does sound wonderful, though. I will confess I'm intrigued by that idea you had before about me becoming a teacher. Do you really think I could do it?"

Maple rushed around the table and enveloped the younger woman in her wings. "Oh, I know you'd do a wonderful job," she exclaimed. "You have the perfect attitude for it. You've always been so patient and sweet with Tuvi."

The former priestess' cheeks flushed scarlet, returning Maple's hug with equal fervor. "Thank you," she whispered.

"Any time."

A familiar rough voice cut through the air, jolting them in their seats. "There you three are!" Guri called out, waving at the trio from a nearby window. "I was wondering where you wandered off to."

Clutching his heart, Kai took several calming breaths. "By the winds, Guri, you nearly scared the piss out of me. Is everything alright with Her Grace?"

"Oh pish, sorry about that," the older woman replied, breaking out into breathy chuckles. "Anyway, don't you fret none, young man. Lady Fusette is fine and I much doubt Rorik will let anything happen to her. I was, however, hoping to have a moment of your time if you don't mind."

Sharing a glance with his wives, Kai gave her a nod and allowed the guard to sit across from them, though she brushed off their offer of paying for a meal.

"I've already eaten, actually, though thank you for the consideration. The truth is, I came because I figured you might want to hear about your parents."

Kai's eyes widened, a torrent of conflicting thoughts and emotions colliding within him at once. Ever since he was a sprout, he'd hoped and fantasized of learning more about his birth parents. And now, here was someone who knew them willing to share their experiences and actually answer some of the questions plaguing him his entire life.

"Should we step away so you two can talk?" Maple asked, her hand resting on top of Kai's.

He shook his head, giving the two a demure gaze. "No," he whispered. "You're a part of this family too. If anything, I'd prefer you both be here in case..."

The apothecary shivered as Orelia's fingers threaded through his hair. She said nothing, only holding him close with her face buried in his neck. Maple soon copied the gesture on his other side. Kai gave Guri a timid grin and a slow nod.

To his surprise, the older woman only smirked.

"Astonishing," she grumbled in a good-natured tone. "You have no memories of the man whatsoever yet you're just as emotional as Ulfrik ever was."

Kai tilted his head and blinked, an act which sent Guri into a fresh peal of laughter. "Holy Cuballa," she gasped, clutching her ribs in mirth, "that head tilt is the same exact thing your mother did when she was confused!"

Maple and Orelia burst into giggles. "So what you're saying is Kai is definitely their son?" Orelia asked through her heaving gasps.

"Without a doubt," Guri said. "I was already certain enough just from how much Kai looks like Ulfrik, but this seals the whole thing with wax."

"So what were my parents really like?" Kai pressed, his eyes wide and full of hope.

"They...had a calming presence many in the city admired," Guri began. "Ulfrik was well respected due to his lineage but never let it define him. He liked to consider himself a simple man who needed only the simplest of comforts to enjoy life. Even then, there was a fire burning in his spirit that would come forth if he felt something threatened what was precious to him. His work was his greatest passion; it wasn't uncommon to find him sitting in front of his loom for an entire day just weaving tapestries or blankets and cloaks. The latter two, he and your mother would spend the entire harvest season handing out to the less fortunate in preparation for winter."

Kai sank back, the sensation of his wives' hands on his arms a mere afterthought. From the corner of his eyes, he did see them both casting knowing grins at him.

"And my mother?"

Guri's eyes glistened with fresh tears. "Frida was, without a doubt, the most compassionate soul you could imagine," she said. "There wasn't a soul in Duskmarsh with a bad thing to say about her, even though her family moved here from the Kingdom of Hilderic when she was a young sprout. As I mentioned, she and Ulfrik gave free clothes to those on hard times. She was only a simple scribe at the chancery yet also helped the priestesses at the orphanage and took time to teach both children and illiterate adults how to read and write."

Transfixed by the woman's words, Kai's thoughts raced with images of how his parents must have spent their days.

"They sound wonderful," he finally uttered, tears threatening to leak from the corner of his eyes. "I think we would have loved to know them."

"After what I've seen you do today, young man, I know for a fact they'd be proud of who you've become," Guri said. Her eyes glimmered with mischief as she gestured to Maple and Orelia. "I'd even be willing to wager they'd accept your ladies with open arms."

"If you don't mind us asking," Orelia piped up, "but how exactly did you know them so well?"

Guri burst into a full-bellied laugh. "Oh, that's easy. Frida and I knew each other from when we were sprouts, though I was a few years older. I first met her a few moons after her family arrived here, during the Spring Festival. As it was, she and I were up to some fun we weren't supposed to be having in our teen years. We snuck outside the city gates and were climbing a grove of cypress trees a few hundred yards from the wall when I slipped off and got a tail caught on a split branch. Ulfrik heard us shrieking up a storm after a giant gator started snapping at us. Frida kept trying to get me free but was so scared her fingers kept slipping. Your father, crazy fool that he was, jumped from tree to tree like a bat out of Abyssal and pulled me loose just as the gator knocked down the tree we were in.

"All three of us got lectured something fierce by Ulfrik's mother, your grandmother Perrinel, but it didn't change the fact he saved my life. Thanks to that incident, Ulfrik worked up the nerve to ask Frida for a courtship. Guess after nearly getting your nose snapped off by a gator, confessing to the girl you like ain't that scary. Still, I reckon both of them would be spitting nails at me for how I treated you before."

A grinning Maple pulled the guard into a tight hug. "All water under the bridge. We're on the same side now and that's what matters. Besides, you've given Kai a gift neither Orelia nor myself could ever hope to provide."

As much as Kai wanted to downplay Maple's words, he knew he couldn't. Without Guri, he doubted he ever would have heard the things he now knew about his birth parents. Part of him wondered how his life might have turned out if they had lived.

If Hakan hadn't let the grudge of his ancestors taint his heart with hatred.

"Do you truly think Kai's parents would have accepted us, even though we're of different tribes?" Orelia asked, her eyes downcast. Kai frowned seeing her despondent expression.

"Without a doubt," Guri assured her. "Ulfrik and Frida were known for promoting a hope for better relations between the tribes. The only reason Osko was even named headman over your father is because Ulfrik outright refused to put himself forward for it! Called it too much trouble. They would both be amazed, though, at how much progress you three are bringing to faumen relations in Livoria."

"I much doubt our relationship is quite so impressive," Kai replied, scratching the back of his head with a demure grin. "Impressively offensive, perhaps, to hear some people say it. All I know is, after all the time I've spent traveling with these two, it's impossible to imagine my life without them in it."

Raising his gaze to meet Guri's again, he was stunned by the shrewd smirk lining her face. It reminded him of his late adoptive father, Gaspard. The man often wore an identical smirk when he felt he knew more than whoever he was talking with. To Kai's never-ending frustration, it was often proven true.

"You truly are your parents' son. They felt much the same about each other as you do about those young ladies. Here's some advice from an old battlecat. Something Ulfrik always told me: Don't worry about the opinions of others when it comes to your own happiness. Live your life for your own benefit and never let anyone say how you're supposed to be happy. Only you can decide that."

Standing up, the older woman stretched out and gave Kai a reassuring pat on the back. She glanced at Maple and Orelia, offering a snappy salute before bidding the trio good night and slipping into the tavern's bustling crowd. Maple slid her wings around Kai's arm and rested her cheek on his shoulder, both eyes locked on where they last saw Guri.

"How does it feel, knowing a little bit more about your folks?" the merchant asked.

"It feels surreal, to be honest," Kai answered. "I'm happy to hear more about them, that much is obvious. It's just…"

"Just what?" Orelia prodded.

"I suppose in a way I needed to hear it from someone who knew them. At least now, some of the blanks have been filled. Questions I'd been asking myself for years. But now that I know these things, it frees me up to focus on something more important."

Seeing their questioning gazes sent a tremor through Kai's tails. His ears twitched and mane bristled as he leaned down to give each woman a kiss to their foreheads.

"Now I can set my eyes to the future. A future I intend to build with both of you at my side for the rest of our lives. For better or worse, we'll create something that's been budding since the day Ma and Da found me on the riverbank."

Maple's head tilted. "And what would that be, love?"

His fingers threaded through her feathers with an almost worshipful touch. Unable to contain his joy, Kai's face scrunched together in a blithe grin and whispered two words that tinted his partners' cheeks pink.

"A family, full of beautiful children borne of the two women I love more than anything."

Chapter XXIII

So this was the smell of death.

The rank stench of the air had Zelik, General of the Belomian United Tribal Forces, wondering what he and his men had stumbled upon. A Vesikoi from the coastal town of Dureca, he would admit to never encountering such a thing in almost thirty years of service. Even in seasons when noxious algae filled the shores near his home and illness struck the fishing grounds, nothing compared to the odor assaulting his nostrils in that moment.

The general's wiroch shifted as they gazed over the cliff at the encampment they chanced upon, the poor beast looking ready to faint. In truth, they almost passed it by completely following their assault on Shineford when one of his scouts spotted a plume of white smoke rising from behind a massive hill. The path leading between the hills to the south was partially blocked by a ramshackle gate which looked as though it had been built in a rush and torn halfway apart just as quickly. At first, Zelik believed the smoke to be from a camp of Liberators who'd abandoned Shineford after the attack. The Belomians were wholly unprepared, however, for what they found.

It was the remains of what appeared to be a labor camp, built into an abandoned quarry. Now, it was nothing but a graveyard. What surprised Zelik was the distinct lack of blood splattered across the dirt and rocks, suggesting it wasn't a battle that razed the camp's inhabitants.

At least, no battle like those he was used to drilling for.

Peering through their spyglasses, they saw bodies littering the ground, many wearing the Liberators' trademark ramshackle armor with a few

Norzen in ragged clothes dispersed among the masses. The only living creatures below were a horde of tree ferrets and rock mice weaving among the dead.

While some of the bodies leaked blood from their orifices, the only other markings were a bevy of broken blisters covering each corpse and streaks of black liquid staining the area around each blister. The marks sent a shiver down Zelik's spine. He was no apothecary, but it didn't take a healer's crest to know the camp had been stricken by some manner of disease.

After taking a long swig from his canteen, the general tore a strip of cloth from his undertunic and tied it over his mouth and nostrils. A quick signal to his deputy, a Norzen named Roni, had word spreading among the five hundred men who made up their vanguard to follow suit. Nausea swelled in the man's gut, making his face pinch in a disgusted frown before pouring some water over his gills to flush them of the putrid air. Zelik's eyes drifted down his armor, once a gleaming bronze though dulled considerably by the long march across Alezon, half expecting it to start eroding.

"What do you suppose happened here, sir?" Roni asked.

The man's tails bristled behind him while their soldiers peeked over the cliff's edge in disgust. Their eyes roamed over the scattered corpses in moon-eyed disbelief. Zelik couldn't blame them; Belomas hadn't marshaled the Tribal Forces for any major conflict in almost a hundred years, so there wasn't a single man in the army with practical combat experience. Seeing so much death had to be unnerving—

The sudden sound of someone retching in the massive crowd drew Zelik's lips into a thin frown. "Whatever it was, old friend," he answered, "I can assure you it wasn't a pleasant way to go."

Gazing into the eyes of the nearest corpse from the protection of his spyglass, Zelik was confident in his assessment, as the man's body and face were contorted in an expression that conveyed one thing: Pure, unrestrained agony.

"Where's Branek?" Zelik questioned, referring to the vanguard unit's apothecary.

"Right here, sir," a gentle voice responded.

The Vesikoi's eyes shifted, landing on an unassuming human male in his forties with a wiry frame, scraggly brown hair, and downturned blue eyes. Seeing the man sent a wave of relief through Zelik's mind. While he could be meek and demure most of the time, Branek was still among the best healers in Belomas and chosen personally by Chief Velibor to lead the brigade's apothecary platoon.

Sweeping an arm over the scene before them, Zelik asked, "What do you make of this? I'll confess I've never seen or heard of any illness that could take hold this quickly. We only left Shineford yesterday."

With a deft nod, Branek secured his scarf and took the offered spyglass to examine the nearest body. Zelik watched the healer work, a broad quill scribbling over parchment while annotating the body's condition and his observations. The rest of the men stayed back a safe distance, a precaution Zelik couldn't fault them for considering their lack of information.

As his good friend Ottoten Basner used to warn him, rushing into battle without adequate preparation was the surest way to get yourself killed without putting a bullet through your own skull.

After scratching a few more notes, Branek returned to Zelik and gazed at the senior officer with a stern frown.

"Well, General," he said. "I can tell you three things about the situation. First, these men aren't from the group we dislodged from Shineford. If anything, they've been dead for anywhere between three and five days already."

Zelik's eyebrow rose in confusion. "They're not? I suppose that means this was an established camp."

"Yes, sir. That was the second thing I figured out. Whatever the Liberation Army was doing here, it wasn't pleasant. Of the five bodies I can inspect well enough from here, four are carrying whips, and two or those have other items that could be used as torture implements. This was likely an internment or labor camp and judging by the lack of other faumen, I suspect it was specifically for Norzen."

The general's gaze drifted to his deputy, whose lips were set in a grim, deadened expression. "I see, and what is the third thing you determined?" A sinking sensation filled Zelik's belly at Branek's uneasy glance back at the rotting corpses.

"If my hypothesis is correct, we must leave this place at once and burn everything on the way out."

"What?" Roni snapped. His fur bristled and eyes narrowed at the apothecary. "While I care not one bit for these Liberator swine, to burn the bodies of these Norzen would be gravely disrespectful!"

"I understand your frustration, Roni, but I assure you I don't say this out of disrespect for your people. There aren't many afflictions mentioned in modern medical tomes that could wipe out a camp of this size in less than a week."

"What makes you think the disease worked *that* fast?" Zelik pressed.

"Think about it, sir. None of our scouts discovered anything like this before our entry into Livorian territory. What's more, I'm assuming the Grand Duchess didn't know of it either, otherwise she would have informed the Five Realms Council so Chief Velibor could brief us on the situation."

Zelik nodded, his lips curving into a smirk. "Thank you for your honesty, Branek. And Roni, you two have known each other since you were younglings, so what you said was harsh. You know Branek well enough that he'd never be so callous towards your tribe. How many times must I remind you not to let anger cloud your judgment?"

He was pleased when Roni mumbled a quiet apology to Branek and the two shared a brotherly embrace.

"Good. Now then, what do you think caused this, Branek?"

"That's just it, General. It feels like I've read about an illness that causes blisters such as these but for the love of the Rebirth, I can't remember what it was called! The name is on the tip of my tongue and yet it continues to elude me."

"Do you still believe we should burn the camp before leaving?"

Branek nodded. "Without a doubt, sir. Any illness that could cause this is either highly contagious, works obscenely fast, or both. And from what I've seen, I suspect it to be both. Burning everything will prevent the disease from spreading further. I also suggest the vanguard unit march separately from the rest of the brigade until we can be sure we haven't been infected ourselves. There's no telling how far the disease could carry in the air."

With a solemn nod, Zelik shouted for a cleric to chant a blessing. He raised his sword and turned back towards his men.

"Archers!" he bellowed. "Ready your bows and wrap your arrows in oil rags. I want this camp burned to the ground and nothing left behind! Feel free to loose at will once you're ready."

While the archers prepared themselves for their grim task, an elderly Wasini cleric slithered alongside Zelik's wiroch. The priest shook his head with a forlorn gaze and began chanting in his native Wasjet. The man's deep, resonant voice echoed throughout the camp, his words reverberating among the soldiers and prompting them to bow their heads in respect.

On Zelik's other side, Branek took out a new sheaf of parchment and begin scribbling once again. The general gazed down at the apothecary, eyes full of curiosity.

"What are you doing now?"

"Copying my observations and the symptoms on the bodies. I intend to send this to Chief Velibor and ask him to refer it to a member of Livoria's Royal Apothecaries. They might have an answer for what this is and, more importantly, how to treat it."

The ringing twang of bows interrupted the two, shifting their gazes to the volley of orange-tipped arrows soaring overhead, their flames flickering in the wind. Zelik's ears twitched, folding downwards to block out the missiles' sharp whistle. The arrows scattered throughout the camp, some striking the abandoned buildings and others digging into corpses. Within minutes, a wall of fire was spreading within the camp. Zelik took another swig from his canteen and urged his wiroch backwards, away from the searing heat.

"General," Roni muttered. "Take a look over there."

The Norzen raised a single finger, pointing towards a building at the far end of the camp. Taking the spyglass back from Branek, Zelik let out a confused hum at the large hole in the building's side.

"What in the crags could've done *that*?" Zelik asked.

"Judging by the beds inside," Branek mumbled, "I'd wager it was a prisoner barrack. I wonder if the Norzen they were keeping here attempted an escape. The cliff face does have claw-like markings just on the other side of the building."

"A sound theory. We can check for bodies on that side after verifying everything has burned."

Seeing the apothecary nod and amble over to Roni, Zelik soon lost himself in thought. Something about this whole situation gave him the heebies. They came into this expecting a drawn-out fight, only to find the work already done.

Was someone else attacking the Liberators as well? Or had the Liberators made a gamble on producing a new type of deadly weapon, only to be hoisted by their own noose? What frustrated him the most was having all these new questions and very little information to provide adequate answers. With any luck, Branek's missive to Whistlevale could help shine some light on the problem. Until then, they would advance slowly and keep an eye out for any other potential threats.

A grim chuckle escaped his lips as the inferno engulfed the camp in its entirety, the flames rising over ten yards into the sky in a flickering dance. The stifling heat forced him to pour more water over his rapidly drying skin and reminded him of a worrying fact.

If the situation was dire enough to push even the mild-mannered Branek into adopting a scorched dust strategy, then they were facing a threat with the potential to throw the entire war into chaos.

"Are you sure you don't want us to attack, Your Highness?"

With a spyglass pressed to one eye, Prince Mataga Aduleji grimaced as he stared at the town nestled between the hills; Galemore if he remembered correctly. His gaze flickered to his second-in-command—a wiry, grey-haired Soltauri woman wearing the typical silver crescents of an Imperial Army general on her epaulets—lingering on her face for a moment before he continued watching the inhabitants below with a stern eye. While Hihiru Nobarashi was a competent officer and warrior, she tended to be a tad hotheaded, though Mataga suspected that was part of why his father favored her.

"I understand your eagerness, General," he said, lowering the spyglass. "However, I can't help but think our enemy is in no condition to fight."

The officer blinked, tilting her head while her long ears fluttered in the wind. "With all due respect, what in hellfire do you mean by that, Sire? From the scouting reports we received on the march over, the Liberators have been growing more brazen ever since this damn war started and those sellswords we chased out this way have proven no better. Why would they just give up?"

"Take a look."

Gesturing for a nearby scout to hand Hihiru their spyglass, Mataga joined her in examining Galemore's defensive walls. While the rest of their brigade stood behind and below them, crowding around the base of the hill they were using as a vantage point, Mataga knew the enemy would likely spot them if they made any sort of concentrated effort to attack the town.

Then again, the Rodekan prince doubted they'd have to lift a single finger.

The few soldiers standing guard at the entry gates looked exhausted and uninterested in anything except their own troubles, though Mataga would admit he had no clue what those troubles could be. From what he *could* see, the soldiers' bodies were pale, and their faces flushed. They moved at a sluggish pace, as if their bodies were made of solid iron. Their weapons, long-barreled guns the likes of which Mataga had never seen before, dragged along the ground as the enemy soldiers didn't seem to have strength enough to lift them.

"By the Emperor," Hihiru gasped. Lowering her spyglass, her gaze locked on Mataga. "What's going on? They look as though they've been besieged for weeks! Did the Belomians already find this place and deal with it? Wait, that can't be it—"

Mataga shook his head. "Impossible," he murmured. "Zelik assured me his forces would move further south and liberate Shineford. No, General, this is something else."

The two shared a concerned look before casting a sweeping gaze over the rest of Galemore through their spyglasses. Despite its status as a provincial capital, the town looked almost deserted. Scattered individuals slumped along the streets, dragging their feet over the cobblestones. One elderly man tripped and toppled face-first to the ground. To Mataga's surprise, the man didn't bother attempting to rise. Either that, or the short fall had been enough to render him unconscious. Many others of all ages looked to be in similar conditions. Some leaned against buildings with a glazed look in their eyes. Others were walking along, scratching deep crimson rashes.

Out of the corner of his eye, Mataga was unnerved to notice Hihiru's entire body shivering. The grizzled woman was infamous for her refusal to flinch under the harshest of conditions; for her to react in such a way meant things were *very* wrong.

"I don't know what it is exactly," Hihiru said, "but something about this is giving me the collywobbles."

"I was afraid of that. Find an apothecary. I want them to make note of everything they see and send a copy to Father. He'll need to know about this."

"Understood, Your Highness." Before she could turn around to carry out Mataga's orders, Hihiru's eyes narrowed before raising her spyglass once more and pointing off to the west side of town. "Sir, what do you make of that?"

Mataga followed the woman's line of sight and spotted a group of people huddled around a fire. A small pile of brown objects lay just outside the group though on occasion one of the men nearest the pile would reach over and pluck one from the top of the mound. Adjusting the focus of his spyglass, the prince found that the small brown objects were dead tree ferrets. While common in Livoria's plentiful forests, the small rodents were rare in Rodekan's expansive plains and typically found only in the realm's sparse groves of hawkbane laurels along the northeastern coast.

His eyes widened when he realized the group was skinning the animals and cooking them over the fire. Looking at Hihiru's face, he noticed the blatant disgust in her eyes.

"I wasn't aware Livorians could grow desperate enough to use tree ferrets as food," she said.

"Is there something wrong with eating them?" Mataga asked. "Do they taste that awful?"

She shook her head. "It's not the taste that concerns me. My grandfather was an apothecary for the royal court and warned us never to consume rodents like ferrets or squirrels. They're known carriers of all manner of disease and some are even resistant to thorough cooking preparation. If those people have been eating such beasts for too long, they could be infected with anything!"

A bone-rattling chill spread through Mataga's body at Hihiru's words though now he felt more secure in his decision to not advance on the town. He didn't want to imagine the thought of disease running rampant through his own soldiers with the limited medicine they had on hand. He looked back and saw a young man wearing blue apothecary robes approaching.

"I was told you called for a 'pothy, Your Highness?" the man asked.

Mataga nodded and directed the man to observe the residents of Galemore for a while. "Once you have a sufficient list of symptoms," the prince said "we shall provide a copy to His Majesty. For now, we shall watch and wait before moving on."

The apothecary bowed low and assumed a seated position next to Hihiru. The general offered her spyglass to the healer who accepted with a gracious smile.

"Your Highness! General Nobarashi!"

The pair spun to see a wiroch-mounted scout rushing towards them. His eyes were wide and unblinking as he brought the large bird to a stop, its talons kicking up a small cloud of dust.

"What's the trouble, lieutenant?" Mataga asked, his gaze drifting to the man's rank for a split moment.

The man saluted before turning his mount and pointing to the south-west. "We discovered a large caravan of people camping out in the hills maybe a half-day's trek away. One of my Aerivolk scouts spotted a hunting party heading down a path leading through the hills and when we investigated, we found the caravan. They appear to have been there for quite some time."

The prince turned back to Galemore, stroking the faint stubble on his chin. A thin smile spread across his lips as his eyes swept over the town's near-empty streets.

"It appears we found the rest of Galemore's residents," Hihiru commented, an identical smile stretched over her face, teeth gleaming in the sunlight. "I wonder if perhaps they decided it was better to flee the town than submit to the Liberators."

"We won't know unless we see for ourselves. Rally the troops, General. Once our apothecary compiles his notes, we'll take a jaunt to this caravan and get some answers. They might even be able to tell us where those wayward sellswords scuttled off to, though my instincts are telling me they might be marching towards Whistlevale."

CHAPTER XXIV

After three days in Duskmarsh following the battle against Hakan and his treacherous band, Kai found himself pining for the quiet of the forest as he sat in a chair on one side of the chancery's audience chamber, Maple and Orelia flanking his sides with the rest of the party surrounding them.

While the city was more hospitable with Rorik's ascension to interim headman, a position the warrior admitted he couldn't wait to hand off to someone else, Kai felt he was under just as much scrutiny here as he was in Whistlevale. Everywhere he and his family went, the locals gazed at them with an odd mixture of doubt, respect, and curiosity. In his heart, he didn't blame them, as he knew he and his wives made for an odd grouping. That didn't mean, however, that he enjoyed having a bunch of strangers gawk at them!

At least Rorik provided the party with free rooms at an inn in the quiet part of the city. Kai knew the girls appreciated that gesture most of all, as Maple and Orelia made good on their promise during the trek there and invoked their wifely privileges every night since their arrival. Multiple times, even, which made Kai thankful for the stamina built up through years of Hunter training.

In fact, beginning the morning after the battle, Kai found himself training with Rorik to further build his strength and stamina. The larger Norzen's brutal training regimen was nothing if not effective, as Kai's Timber combined with his stores of fluxroot afforded him an enhanced healing factor he made use of to build muscle much quicker than he would have otherwise been capable of. Improvement that would normally take weeks or even moons was showing itself after only a few days.

Once Fusette confirmed the Duskmarsh contingent's preparations were complete, relief flooded his body. While the capital was louder than he liked, it was still familiar. It also soothed him that, with their new allies, they stood a better chance at ending the war before the Liberators could cause irreparable damage to Livoria.

"Your Grace," Guri said, strolling into the chamber while waving a pair of bound scrolls in one hand, "these missives arrived for you at the city hawkery this morning."

Fusette thanked the older woman and accepted the scrolls with a quick bow. Retaking her seat, she unfurled the first one and leaned back to read.

From their spot on the head table's left side, Kai saw her face shift through several expressions in rapid order. Confusion, relief, then worry. The duchess bit her lip and set the first letter aside before opening its companion. Her reaction to the second scroll filled Kai's belly with unease, seeing the open-mouthed horror on Fusette's face. He shared a look with Maple and Orelia, which spread through the rest of the party.

Pushing himself to his feet, he approached the head table and stooped to one knee. Lifting his head, he spotted Rorik staring at her with pinched eyebrows and lips set in a narrow frown. The look reminded Kai of Saredi when the Vesikoi noble was in one of his overly fretful moods, so much so that the apothecary wondered for a fleeting moment if the Lord Chamberlain had followed them.

"What has you so worried?" he inquired.

Her gaze met his, sending a frigid chill crackling down his spine and through to the tips of his tails. Her pupils were contracted to pinpricks, mouth agape as one shaking hand rose to cover it. Kai's worry only grew; he'd never seen Fusette in such a state before.

"Kai," she breathed at last. Her quivering hand, the parchment still clutched in its grip, reached out to him. "I...I'd prefer your professional medical opinion on the contents of this missive. It's from Emperor Kabuji, concerning two separate incidents the Imperial Army and Tribal Forces discovered while scattering the Liberators."

Kai's face pinched inward. What in Nixtral had their allies found? Anything requiring a professional opinion from an apothecary couldn't be good. He accepted the parchment and read at a slow pace.

The emperor proved much more eloquent on parchment than his overbearing and crass demeanor from the Five Realms Council suggested. His words were succinct, calculated, and meaningful. Kai gazed over the descriptions he and Chief Velibor received from their respective brigades. A dark painting formed in the apothecary's mind, his breath hitching as he reviewed the list of symptoms provided by the healers in both incidents. His mind raced with a niggling thought that he'd seen these symptoms somewhere before.

Damn it all, Kai thought, *why is this so familiar? I know I've read about this because I've never encountered any ailments with the dark blisters they're—wait!*

His eyes bulged while spinning towards his satchel. Kai plucked a pile of parchments from within. Setting Kabuji's letter on one side of the table, he spread out the ones from the satchel and reviewed them with a critical stare. The words blended together, producing a minor ache in his temple.

Then, some familiar words jumped out at him. Cross-referencing the documents with the letter, Kai's unease twisted in his gut, growing and transforming into a well of horror. His fingers trembled, scrunching the parchment together as the full magnitude of what the letter's contents suggested weighed him down.

"He wouldn't have dared..." Kai muttered.

He shifted his focus back to Fusette, who stared back with a pleading expression.

"Is...Is it really—?" she asked.

The temptation to deny it—to give her a false sense of hope—was there, of that there was no doubt. Knowing what he did of his cousin's history, the mere thought of admitting the truth out loud was enough to leave Kai's throat drier than the vast deserts of Ruquall, the western continent.

Yet at the same time, the thought of lying to Fusette rankled his core. She trusted him enough to ask his opinion as a healer and give her the truth, no matter how vile it may have been. To ignore that trust and break his oath was an act he couldn't go through with, no matter how great the temptation. That the idea even ventured into his mind left a bitter taste in his mouth. Instead, he readied himself and gave a solemn nod.

"It appears Hemlocke's plan is even more disgusting than I could have imagined. I know that craven bastard said he wished to drive the land into chaos, but this is beyond the pale."

Lucretia took a step forward, a fearful Ione holding her back by the arm. "What is it?" she pressed. "What is he planning to do?"

"Hemlocke isn't attacking through a traditional poison. He's begun recreating the events of nine years ago, intending to infect all of Livoria with the Black Tear Blight."

The entire chamber erupted into a furor. Fusette's face turned porcelain white, her eyes sunken. Rorik's skin darkened and Kai saw the telltale crimson ring of the Frenzy Haze around the edges of his eyes. The rest of Duskmarsh's council glanced about with fearful expressions while the Galstans, Ottoten especially, looked apoplectic.

"Has that monster lost his mind?" Ottoten whispered, Kai's ears twitching forward to catch the mumbled statement. "That disease sent all of Alezon into a panic the last time despite being restricted to only Livoria. Galstein even closed all of its borders for the first time since Livoria gained its independence. The truly terrifying thing is that relatively few people died compared to other Blight outbreaks—maybe around ten thousand deaths were officially recorded, though we suspect there were much more."

"If you want my opinion," Kai said, "we won't be able to stop him without working together. I don't know for certain how he's been spreading the Blight—and it's clear he *has* just from the reports sent in by our allies—but what I do know is we need to nip this in the bud before Hemlocke can spread it wide enough to make containment impossible."

"How exactly do you propose we do that?" Rorik asked. "If we don't know how he's spreading it, what can we do to stop it?"

Fusette stepped forward. "Rorik's question brings up a major concern," she said, drawing a light blush from the warrior. "To this day, our knowledge of the Blight is underwhelming. All we can guess is that it spreads through the air like similar diseases. I'm worried our comrades may have unknowingly walked into Hemlocke's trap. But why would he attack his own allies?"

Standing at the front of the party, Lucretia shook her head. "The Liberators and Hemlocke's party are allies of convenience—nothing more, nothing less. Remember, the Liberators despise all faumen, not just the Norzen. When you consider that, it doesn't surprise me Hemlocke would turn on them before they can do the same to him."

"Then there's the fact Hemlocke thrives on death and destruction," Morgan brought up. "He and Obram seem to be cut from the same cloth in that manner. From the brief time I knew him, Obram was always a bit battle hungry and even admitted he's not above backstabbing his so-called 'allies' to save his own skin. Chances are he's providing Hemlocke military tactics to carry out his plan and may have even been the one to suggest going after the Libbies first to test their ideas out."

Kai nodded while laying out the Blight reports he received from Saredi before they left. "You may be onto something. I started researching the last Blight outbreak after Saredi told me about it, and part of me thinks it spreads through multiple means."

"Holy Finyt, I hope that doesn't mean what I think it does," Ione gasped.

"I'm afraid so," Kai replied with a grim expression. "I'd wager he started the infection through one method and is allowing it to spread naturally via other mediums to cover up how he did it."

"Then what do we do?" Fusette asked. "I refuse to allow that horrific disease to take root in this realm again. Not after it killed my father and so many others the last time!"

Kai frowned, his eyes drifting across the old reports and flickering back to Kabuji's missive. He knew there had to be a hidden trick to Hemlocke's plan. While the traitor relished the damage his actions did, he was also slicker than fresh lard and wouldn't be so overt in causing destruction unless he was there to personally gloat about it.

But how was he doing it?

"We need to return to Whistlevale as soon as possible," Kai finally declared. "Rorik, if it's not too much trouble, we also need to make use of several carrier hawks."

Rorik bowed, stunning the apothecary for a brief moment.

"I freely admit this is beyond my understanding," he confessed, giving the rest of the council an exhausted smile. "Just as our city stands ready to fight for Her Grace, all of Duskmarsh's assets are yours to command, Kai. Just tell us what you need."

Kai's gaze shifted to Fusette, a silent question on his lips. She nodded at once, her face set in resolute determination. Beckoning his party to join him and turning to Rorik, he laid out a bare parchment and asked the scribes nearby to copy his orders down.

"First of all," he explained, "we need to warn the Tribal Forces and Imperial Army of the danger they're in. Send missives at once to General Zelik and Prince Mataga and have them quarantine anyone who got close to the infected. Any apothecaries they have on hand need to mix the strongest antibacterial concoctions they can. Until we acquire a suitable amplifier, I'd suggest a mix of clove, garlic, honey, and coneflower.

"Next, send a message to Saredi and have him muster the Royal Apothecaries to ready every single healer this realm has available. If Hemlocke wants to cause death on such a massive scale, it's only fitting we respond with a defense equally as vast."

"How will we figure out how Hemlocke spread the Blight?" Orelia asked, her ears wiggling as she rubbed her arm with an apprehensive grimace.

Kai waved the reports in one hand. He forced himself to smile at her, despite the niggling worry lining his stomach. "I plan to comb through these while we head back. They might hold a clue suggesting how the last outbreak started so suddenly. From what I've read, the realm was hit without much warning. Perhaps Hemlocke figured out the trick and wants to recreate it on a larger scale."

With a clap of her hands, Fusette caught everyone's attention. Nodding to Kai, she strode forward and ensured all eyes were on her before speaking.

"This sounds like the best plan we have available to us at this moment," she said. "I expect all of you to put forth your best efforts to ensure the health and safety of our people. We can no longer look at ourselves according to our tribes. All of us, no matter if you're fullblood or mixblood, human or faumen, are in this together. Rorik, ensure your men are rested and well-equipped. We leave for Whistlevale at first light."

"Consider it done, Your Grace."

Chapter XXV

Following four days of travel, Kai was surprised by the efficiency with which Rorik led the Norzen battalion as they neared Whistlevale.

It was clear the soldiers respected their leader. Each one accomplished their assigned duties with an energetic glee Kai only saw in a few career soldiers, such as Admiral Larimanz. The Duskmarsh contingent took overall responsibility for the caravan's defense, which allowed Kai more time to review the pile of medical reports Saredi acquired in search of a hint to Hemlocke's plan.

As for the caravan itself, it gained a few new members upon departure. Kai wasn't surprised in the least when Fusette's mother, Ingrid, joined them for the return journey. It filled him with joy seeing the relief in Fusette's eyes as she and her mother spent their time in the carriage with Yulia, Pelka, and Hibbel each taking turns at the driver's box, making up for lost time. Along with the other freed faumen, Cress and Willow were sticking close to their daughter and Clove, using Kai's and Orelia's wirochs to ride alongside Maple to talk with her more easily. Even after spending time with them in Duskmarsh following their release, Kai couldn't help purring at how happy Maple looked being able to hug her parents and friend while talking outside of letters.

Rorik stuck to the front of the vanguard, eyes sweeping over the fields in search of potential threats. However, Kai could also see the warrior's gaze drifting back to the carriage every so often. He chuckled, wondering if Rorik realized how obvious he was.

He leaned over to whisper in Orelia's ear, "You think I can get away with giving Rorik the 'hurt her and I kill you' talk since Duke Vonlo isn't here to do it himself?"

She slapped a hand over her mouth to muffle her giggling, lest the subject of their discussion overhear them.

"Perhaps. You *are* Fusette's only surviving male relative after all. And considering what you did to him in the arena, he'd probably know to take you seriously."

A flash of movement from the carriage drew Kai's attention to Fusette poking her head through the window. Her hair fluttered in the wind, partially concealing her eyes as she waved him over. Giving Orelia a smile, he strolled over and left her to fall back and talk with her father, who they had both seen watching them with a discerning eye for much of the trip.

"How long do you believe it will be until we arrive at Whistlevale?" she asked.

Kai pursed his lips, pulling a map from a side pocket on his satchel. Glancing about the area for notable markers, he drew a single finger along the parchment before clicking his tongue.

"If we keep our current pace, we should arrive tomorrow. In fact, we'll probably be able to see Ballad's End by the time we make camp tonight."

"How wonderful! While I'm grateful we've accomplished what we set out to do, I'll admit I love knowing home is within reach."

Kai's ears twitched, swiveling towards the front where he heard a growing ruckus. He narrowed his eyes, gesturing for Fusette to tuck her head back into the carriage. After signaling Orelia, he whispered for her to warn the other women and bring the rest of the caravan to a stop before shifting to the other side of the carriage and tapping Morgan and Teos on the shoulder.

"There's something going on at the front," he murmured. "You boys feeling in the mood to back Rorik up and be responsible bodyguards?"

Morgan burst into a full-bellied laugh. "Since when have you ever known me to be responsible, 'pothy?" he asked.

"Never," Kai shot back, giving the sellsword a playful punch to the elbow.

Teos' lips curved into a toothy grin. "If you two didn't look so different, I'd wonder if you were long-lost brothers with the way you act."

"I'll take that as compliment," Morgan retorted, sticking his tongue out.

Sharing a hearty laugh, the three men marched to the front of the fifty Norzen soldiers serving as the caravan's vanguard. Kai wasn't sure what was going on but whatever it was brought the entire platoon to a halt. Once they were twenty yards away, Kai could more clearly see a second group opposite the Norzen, his ears picking up heated words coming from both sides. He was relieved to see no one had deemed it necessary to draw a sword yet, which let him hold out hope it was simply a disagreement with a merchant company over the number of people traversing the main road. His ears twitched as Teos and Morgan focused more on each other in a bantering argument, swiveling forward when he heard Rorik's voice booming from the front of the group.

"Listen here, you scamps," the warrior bellowed, "this caravan is transporting important cargo, so I'm afraid you'll need to step aside and let us pass!"

One of the men opposite Rorik, a Vesikoi with red and white mottled skin, wearing grungy clothes and a battered tricorne hat atop his head, chuckled. The man's thick, stringy beard wobbled as his body shook with mirth.

"Ye think we were born yesterday, sir?" he asked. "One o' my boys already spotted the royal carriage after ye left the swamps. We know ye got the Grand Duchess back there, and we wanna have a word with her."

Kai's hopes sank when the ring of Rorik's greatsword leaving its scabbard echoed in the air. The Vesikoi drew a sailor's cutlass in response, a wide grin on his face.

"Not a chance," Rorik challenged, bringing his weapon into a defensive stance. "Her Grace has important duties she must attend to back in Whistlevale. We don't have time to cater to the whims of a pack of vagrants."

Rolling his eyes, Kai tapped Morgan on the shoulder and ordered him to inform Fusette of what was going on. As the sellsword scampered off, Teos gave him a befuddled look.

"Why send Morgan of all people to go fetch her?" he queried.

"Two reasons. First, I trust Morgan enough to know he'll do what I ask, even if he may get distracted along the way. Second, you know how he gets when he's feeling bored and a fight breaks out. I'd rather keep him farther away with Rorik trying to draw these folks into a brawl."

Teos nodded. "Can't argue with you there. We haven't had an actual fight since the scrap against Hemlocke's group. I should've figured he'd start feeling anxious."

Giving Morgan one last fleeting glance, they ambled forward to disperse the argument. Kai noticed most of the Vesikoi's band, many wearing wide-brimmed hats and thin cloaks that concealed their identities, standing back with hands resting on their swords, ready to draw at a moment's notice.

"What seems to be the trouble, Rorik?" Kai asked. The warrior turned and met his stern gaze. To the apothecary's relief, Rorik understood the unspoken request and stepped back, sheathing his blade.

"Apologies for the delay, Kai," he responded, "but, as you can see, these travelers are blocking the road and are demanding an audience with Her Grace."

Kai's attention shifted to the Vesikoi, perhaps a head taller than himself, who looked down at him with a sneer. Another glance backwards revealed Teos mixed in among Rorik's soldiers, though his greater height made him stand out against the smaller faumen. The smuggler stared at the man with an intense frown, one hand resting on his hip and the other stroking his beard.

"You seem a little on the scrawny side to be bossing around someone as big as he is," the stranger said.

To Kai's amusement, Rorik gave a hearty chuckle and responded, "Don't let his size fool you, *sir*. I can assure you he's even more dangerous than I am. I learned the hard way. Now, why should we waste Lady Fusette's time by permitting you to speak with her?"

"We have information on those Libbie bastards she might find useful, so we wanted to engage in parlay to offer it up in exchange."

The apothecary's eyes narrowed. "In exchange for what?" he asked.

"We'd rather discuss that with Her Grace, if you don't mind."

"Wait a tic," another of the strangers mumbled, pushing the brim of his hat up to reveal a lanky Soltauri with long horns that curved downwards behind his head. "I-is that you, Teos?"

Kai froze, his gaze shifting back towards his friend. Teos' mouth dropped open as he pushed his way to the front. The Vesikoi and his entire group stepped backwards in unison, a bevy of gasps coming from them. With a piercing glare, Teos stomped forward and towered over the Vesikoi, yanking the man's hat off. The two smirked at each other.

"Well, I'll be damned," Teos exclaimed. "I thought you looked familiar! What are you doing all the way out here, Hans?"

Emitting a hitched gasp, Kai's eyes widened.

Hans, he thought. *As in Captain Hans, leader of the pirate crew Teos used to be a member of?*

The Vesikoi burst into raucous laughter. "I don't believe this! I ain't seen your scraggly hide in ages, Teos! Did the smuggling business finally dry up and you decided to go straight instead of coming back?"

Teos, to Kai's shock, flushed red at the verbal jab.

"Shut it, Hans," he groused while giving the pirate a shove backwards. "I just found me a crew that needs me more than you lot ever would."

Hans took the push in jest and stroked his beard with a thoughtful expression. "Is that so? Well, I'm happy for ya, sprout. Still, it'd really help us out if you could let these dipwits know we need to speak to Her Grace. I know we ain't the most respectable folk out there, but the Libbies are on the move and we'd like to parlay."

Nudging Teos' arm with an elbow, Kai gave the taller faumen a nod. He signaled for Rorik to have his troops stand down while he mounted a spare wiroch and turned it around to canter back to the royal carriage.

Fusette was already waiting, her head poking from the window and a curious look in her eyes as Kai approached.

"What seems to be the problem?" she asked.

"Turns out we've come across the pirate crew Teos was a part of in his wild youth," Kai answered, trying not to laugh at Hibbel's paling face. "They've requested an official audience with you for parlay to offer up information on the Libbies."

"Have they explained what they want in exchange for their information?"

"They said they'd prefer to explain that to you directly, but if I were a gambling man...I'd wager they're seeking some amount of leniency for their illicit activities."

With a single nod, Fusette opened the door and stepped out despite Hibbel and Yulia's protests. Kai dismounted his wiroch and assisted the duchess in taking his place in the saddle. Gripping the reins, Kai led the bird and its new rider back towards the front. From his vantage point, the apothecary could see Rorik's men and the pirates standing opposite each other on the side while maintaining an alert stance as Teos conversed with Hans.

"Your Grace!" Hans cheered, waving to Fusette with a friendly grin. "It's such an honor to be in your lovely presence!"

Kai glanced up at his cousin, seeing her with an amused smirk. She greeted the pirate leader with a respectful bow while keeping a safe distance.

"I understand you wish to parlay, Captain Hans," Fusette said while tugging on her sleeve. "Perhaps it's best we cut right to the quick. What are you seeking in exchange for whatever information you're hiding under that rather dashing hat?"

A deep belly laugh burst from Hans' gut at the compliment, one hand tilting the tricorne forward in a roguish manner.

"I like you, Your Grace!" Hans crowed. "Straight and to the point. I'll be honest: I'd like a pardon for all the ruckus we've caused, at the very least for my crew. If I need to sit in the gaol in recompense, I'm perfectly fine with that. I've lived a damned long life and reckon I've made my bed. Just...have some mercy on my crew, if you please."

Fusette's gaze pivoted to Kai, who gave a subtle smirk. Her head spun to the other side to look at Teos, who was busy leveling a disappointed frown at the elderly Vesikoi. Coughing into her hand, she gave a slight bow before speaking.

"Captain Hans, I will confess I've kept track of your exploits since I first heard of you back when my father was on the throne. One thing I distinctly remember from the reports I read is that you're well known for attacking primarily noble districts. May I ask why that is? Do you have a grudge against the nobility?"

"Shucks, milady, it ain't nothing so serious as that. I just feel like the nobles can at least afford to part with some of their marks. See, I came from a family of fishermen. It's what my pa taught me and his pa taught him, going back as far as we can remember. But we never had much money, and after I took up the pirating business, I swore to never take from people who already had little to give. Sometimes we even share our loot with the slum districts in towns we pass by if they really need it. A lot of other crews call me a soft-hearted fop for running things that way, but at least it lets me have a little bit of honor in a business where most folks haven't got a lick of it to speak of."

Kai and Fusette shared a look before giving Teos another glance.

"I suppose I can see where Teos gets his generous nature from," Fusette muttered. Her smile widened as she took Hans' wrinkled hand in her own with a hearty shake. "Assuming your information turns out to be useful, I see no reason why we can't come to an agreement. However, if I issue a pardon, I need your solemn oath that you and your crew will give up pirating and take on more respectable ventures."

Hans nodded and slapped an open hand to his forehead in salute, palm facing outward. "If that's what it takes to keep my crew out of shackles, I'll do it with a smile on my face. As you can see, Your Grace, a good chunk of us are faumen, so we've got a damned good reason for wanting to see those Libbies get thumped. The truth is we spotted them headed north at a slow clip a couple days ago. I think they might be making a play for Whistlevale."

Kai's eyes narrowed. "*Taen*," he swore, "and here I was hoping we'd have a little more time to get things ready before the Libbies made their move. How long do you think we have?"

Glancing back at his crew, Hans scratched at his beard and twirled the stringy hair around one finger. "From what I saw, they was being chased by a Navy fleet at the time which is why we abandoned our ship and rushed inland, but I figure they might reach the capital by the end of the moon at the speed they was going and the way they were dashing all haphazard all over the place. Of course, that depends on whether the fleet runs them down first."

"Then we don't have much time before the enemy reaches the capital," Fusette said. Her eyes pinched together in a frown as she clutched at the reins in her hands. "Captain Hans, I thank you for this information. I'm willing to provide a full pardon for you and your crew. However, I'd also like to ask for your help in the coming battle. While I *could* make it a direct order, I know your crew has a lot at stake trying to face the Liberators directly given how many of you are faumen."

Hans held up an open palm, stopping Fusette's plea from going any further.

"Your Grace," he said, "I think I speak for the whole crew when I say we'd be honored to fight with you and send those Libbie bastards to the bottom of the Great Ardei where they belong."

The pirates burst into cheers at their captain's words. Swords were drawn and waved in the air, while several raised their flintlocks into the air and fired celebratory rounds into the surrounding forest.

Kai watched with a curious gaze as Fusette, with Rorik by her side, instructed Hans to sail ahead to Whistlevale with a hastily written letter of passage stamped with her seal. The pirate took the offered parchment with a reverent bow before leading his crew back down the trail.

Casting another glance at Teos, the apothecary nudged his friend with an elbow. "Be honest. How likely is it they follow Fusette's instructions?" Kai asked.

"I'd wager a ship on it," Teos answered with abroad grin stretching from ear to ear. "Hans may be a pirate, but he's also a man of his word and the crew respects him enough to follow him into Nulyma if he ordered it. If he says the crew will fight then by the winds, they'll fight to the last with everything they have."

Fusette steered her wiroch back to Kai wearing a smile identical to the one on Teos' face. "I'm starting to feel really good about our chances," she told the two men. Her entire body was quaking in excitement, both ears fluttering in the summer breeze.

"Don't get too overconfident, Fusette," Kai warned. "Things may be looking up with the alliance taking shape, but we still need to think of a counter to Hemlocke's plan. If it's really what I suspect, you know better than most just what we're facing."

Despite his warning, Kai could see the undaunted fire blazing in his cousin's eyes. It was clear she wouldn't let the potential danger dampen her spirit and desire to see the war ended. Clenching a fist a this side, he swore to come up with a way to stop Hemlocke, one way or another. His pride as an apothecary would accept no less.

Besides...after reading the medical reports Saredi acquired for him in more detail, thinking of what would happen to Livoria should the Black Tear Blight be allowed to run rampant again was too bloodcurdling to consider.

Chapter XXVI

Kai felt an odd sense of insignificance growing in his belly. In the days following their return to Whistlevale, the capital remained in constant motion, both within and outside the Royal Palace. Just that morning, an entourage of soldiers from the newly recognized Buxlow Republic arrived, with their commander riding in the most unusual contraption the apothecary had ever laid eyes on.

The new arrivals dubbed the device a 'steam carriage' and, oddly enough, it was an apt description. It looked for all purposes like a standard wiroch-drawn carriage with the roof replaced by a fabric bonnet fastened in a manner allowing it to be raised and lowered. A heavy steam engine was affixed to the carriage's rear, the boiler emitting puffs of white smoke every few seconds while it produced a rumble that reminded Kai of a stampeding herd of bison.

Once the Buxlow contingent was assigned a resting plot outside the city walls, Fusette decided to host a planning stage in the palace's war room. The moment Kai set foot inside, he was reminded of two things.

First, Livoria had enjoyed the comforts of peace for a deceitfully long time. Second, Parliament had proven to be more of a distraction to Fusette during the Faumen War than they should've.

The expansive room, situated on the top floor of the Royal Palace, was covered in a thin layer of dust suggesting it was cleaned only on rare occasions. A massive table three yards square was the centerpiece, hidden beneath a leather tarp. Saredi whipped the cover off with a snap of the wrists, sending a cloud of dust into the air and revealing a map of the duchy stretched across the entirety of the table.

"Perhaps once this mess is over, we can have our military forces conduct training drills together," Kabuji murmured as the leaders led their entourages into the room while a squad of maids bustled about armed with feather dusters and brooms. The Rodekan emperor's eyes surveyed the room with a hint of disappointment.

Kai saw Fusette notice the man's expression and, without wavering, replied, "That sounds like a wonderful idea, Your Majesty. Despite the Navy's ability to meet the Liberators on equal footing thus far, I'll admit additional training is in order to ensure something like this doesn't happen again."

"Don't make too many promises yet, Fusette," Isolde reminded the younger monarch, her lips pursed in a thin line. "After all, the war isn't over."

Taking his place behind Fusette with Saredi on her other side, Kai watched the rest of the party settle in behind him. The other leaders arranged their groups in a similar manner, with Pelka, Yulia, and Hibbel returning to their respective leaders after thanking Fusette for the opportunity to join the expedition. Kai's gaze swept over the room, the sheer magnitude of what he was witnessing threatening to overwhelm him.

As far as he remembered from his history lessons as a boy, an alliance of this size and scope hadn't been seen since the early days of Nixtralian civilization, when warring clans across the four continents banded together to overpower their myriad rivals. Outside of Fusette's inner circle, around the table stood the representatives from each of Livoria's allies plus additional factions within the realm itself who had pledged themselves to the Royalist cause—Verona representing the Hunter Corps, the interim Highmaster of the Citadel, Rorik representing Duskmarsh, Captain Hans standing for his crew, and lastly Jaco, head of the Royal Apothecaries.

While Kai's hope of seeing victory grew seeing the amount of support Livoria had at its back, his Hunter training and worry about Hemlocke's plan tempered it with a healthy dose of pragmatism.

Any Hunter worth their vest knew wounded beasts were often the most dangerous, and the traitorous Aerivolk and his allies had more than enough accumulated wounds to make them *extremely* so.

"Thank you, everyone, for coming," Fusette started. Everyone nodded in reply, though Kai swore he saw a look of unmistakable pride in Ottoten as the admiral watched from behind Isolde. "First, I'd like to thank Emperor Kabuji and Chief Velibor for the progress their forces have made. As of the most recent reports, we suspect we've freed most of the enemy's prisoner camps and at least three quarters of western Livoria is back under alliance control."

The mentioned leaders offered gracious nods, Kabuji sporting his trademark grin.

"However, thanks to information from Captain Hans," she continued, motioning to the pirate leader who tilted his hat, "we know the enemy is at last attempting to march on Whistlevale. Worse, scouts from the Marine Cavalry have reported a new variant of Hakan's cannon, the Shatterstar, among their forces."

The aura of the room darkened. The reminder of Havenfall's destruction only served to remind everyone of the fate awaiting them should they fail. Kai clenched his fists, ignoring the pain of his own claws biting deep into his palms. The cold pain thrumming in his chest was more than enough to divert his attention from the blood leaking from between his fingers. It wasn't until Maple took hold of him and pried the fist open, dabbing the bloody cuts with a damp cloth. His eyes met hers, full of shame but offering a mumbled thanks as she tended to him with her tilted smile.

"We'll need to do something about that beastly weapon," Isolde said.

Gideon let out a pained groan. "From what our forge masters told me, the Shatterstar has a ludicrous range, much greater than any artillery we have. If the Liberators wanted, they could set it at a safe distance and simply obliterate us before our forces can get in range to strike back."

His mane bristling, Kai scowled at the map in front of him while Maple and Orelia stroked his tails. "Then," he mumbled, "our best option is to simply strike at them before they get close enough to hit the capital."

All eyes swerved to the apothecary.

"Are you suggesting our combined forces leave the safety of Whistlevale's walls and attack the enemy head on?" Gideon asked. "That will leave us completely open to attack if they know we're coming! And I assure you...they'll see us marching across those open plains."

"What point do the walls serve if that lekrite cannonball clears them and vaporizes the city?" Kai shot back, causing the Buxlowian president's mouth to snap shut. "The walls won't do a damn thing against a weapon like that. If anything, they'll just serve as a tomb for anyone not reduced to dust."

Kai smirked and leaned over the map, inspecting it with a critical gaze. "That's why we set ourselves up before they have a chance to see us coming. Look." Tracing a clawed finger along the parchment, he tapped a specific point at the plains' far side.

A chuckle rang from Lucretia, pulling everyone's eyes to her. "I should not be surprised to see such a plan from you. You intend to ambush them at Ballad's End."

The alliance erupted into confused mumbling. "What's the point of that?" Velibor asked. "Those hills might offer some level of concealment, but the enemy could still spot us if they send scouts ahead and wipe us out with the Shatterstar."

"That's the beauty of it," Fusette explained, her lips curving into a broad smile. "Ballad's End used to be a Wasini enclave before even the Desolation Wars. It wasn't until Berelmir conquered the region that the Wasini were driven out, but the intricate cliffs and cavern system they built remain. Hiding our forces inside will provide more than adequate protection and are close enough to reach in a few hours' march."

"Well I'll be damned," Hans said, scratching his head. "I've sailed the rivers 'round those hills for years, and not once had a clue there were caves in 'em!"

"The entrances are hidden quite well. I doubt the enemy knows they exist, so Kai's plan has potential. Plus, Ballad's End is far enough away from Whistlevale I doubt even the Shatterstar could cover the distance, which means the people will stay safe."

The crowd's excitement grew as several other voices offered their own suggestions on how to set up the ambush. Maple and Orelia curled against Kai's sides and whispered how proud they were of him for coming up with the idea. He gazed down with a nervous smile, threading his fingers through their hair while his heart pounded in his chest. He knew the plan was solid. It was more a matter of getting into position before the Liberators got too close to Ballad's End.

More worrying was the fact that the Shatterstar wasn't even the biggest threat facing them.

"I wouldn't celebrate too soon," Kai murmured. His tails tingled seeing everyone's eyes on him once more. "Your Majesty and Chief Velibor. I'd like to thank you for sharing the reports you received from your forces while we were in Duskmarsh."

Kabuji chuckled. "Think nothing of it, Gravebane. We're all working towards the same goals. Are you sure you're okay, though? You look even more pale than usual."

"Emperor Kabuji is right," Velibor added, his eyes pinched in concern. "Have you been getting enough rest, Sir Gravebane? The last thing we need is you pitching over in a dead faint."

The apothecary grimaced, sharing a look with Fusette. "I assume from the missives we received that your commanders didn't tell you exactly what it was they found?" Kai asked. Both men shook their heads, admitting the reports they got from Zelik and Mataga only offered descriptions of their discoveries with a vague warning.

Jaco, crossed his arms over his broad chest with a scowl. The grizzled Soltauri was one of the few senior apothecaries Kai held deep respect for, having gone over the head of the guild master to approve his apprenticeship to Geraldo years ago.

"I never had a chance to inspect these reports myself, so I'm just as blind as the rest of us. Saredi and I did receive the hawk from Lady Fusette ordering us to call up the Royal Apothecaries and Exarchs for a massive operation. Do you have any suspicions, Gravebane?" Jaco pressed.

The expectant eyes of everyone in the room filled Kai with dread. He glanced at Fusette, who stood frozen, staring at the map with unblinking eyes. The only hint she was still alive was the quickening rise and fall of her chest. Seeing her in such a state of distress proved too much, offering Kai a stark reminder of what they faced and how his cousin was already affected by it. He flew into a stream of virulent curses that had his partners stepping back in shock and everyone else staring with fear and confusion.

"Sir Gravebane!" Lady Bidelga shrieked. "What on Nixtral possessed you to use such uncouth language in front of our guests?" The minister turned to the paling Fusette and bowed deeply. "Your Grace, I warned you of—"

"Silence, Bidelga." The woman's mouth clamped shut, her gaze bulbous at the biting tone in Fusette's cracked voice. "Kai...tell them. They deserve to know the truth."

"What truth? What in sodding hellfire is going on that has you two spitting nails like this?" Kabuji asked. For once, the jovial ruler's smile was gone, replaced by grim apprehension.

"As reported upon our return, we encountered the Liberator's backer, Hakan, while in Duskmarsh," Kai said. "During the fight, one of his minions led a mutiny: A sickly Aerivolk I've been acquainted with since the start of the war named Hemlocke."

Gideon sighed in visible relief. "So Hakan was deposed? That's wonderful news!"

The president froze at the frosty scowl Kai gave him. "I wouldn't be so sure about that. At least we knew what Hakan was after. Hemlocke is an unpredictable madman who desires to throw the entire continent into chaos. If the reports from both your forces are accurate, then it seems my worst fears are true. Hemlocke is attempting to cause a resurgence of the Black Tear Blight."

A dank chill settled over the room. Each of the leaders clutched the table to steady themselves, while the rest of the crowd turned a sickly green.

"Gravebane," Isolde whispered, her knuckles marble-white from gripping the table edge hard enough to crack her fingernails, "for the love of the Saints, please tell me this is some twisted joke."

"I'm afraid he's not joking, Isolde," Fusette confirmed. The duchess' eyes leaked fresh tears as her teeth ground together. Saredi laid a comforting hand on her quaking shoulder. "Kai told me after reading the reports he suspected this Hemlocke of desiring to bring back the Blight. Considering his history with the man and his recent study of the specifics concerning the last outbreak, I was inclined to believe him while remaining hopeful. Sadly, it appears my hope was for naught."

The entire room bowed their heads in solemn respect.

"Lady Fusette," Ione murmured, stepping next to the younger woman and taking her hand. To Bidelga's visible horror, Ione cradled Fusette close and recited a heartfelt prayer while the latter sobbed. Kai said nothing but offered his friend a grateful nod. It came as no surprise when Fusette's fingers clenched around Ione's dirndl while struggling to remain standing, her sniffles echoing in the chamber's somber air.

It was Jaco who broke the uneasy silence. "I would have been content to never hear of that disgusting illness again for eternity," the aged apothecary groused. "What sort of madness would cause someone to willingly spread something so terrifying?"

Kai met the other healer's eyes and bit back the shadow of guilt eating at his core. "Pray you never meet the man face to face. Hemlocke may look frail, but he's a lethal opponent and is determined to sow the seeds of death wherever he goes," Kai said. "I'd prefer to sit back and let whatever illness he suffers from kill him before he becomes more of a problem than he already is."

"Speak for yourself, love," Maple trilled. "I still owe that bastard a good plucking for what he did to me."

"Mapes, as much as I'd love to see you rip each of Hemlocke's feathers out and shove them down his throat, you won't be going anywhere near him by yourself," Orelia quipped.

"Agreed," Kai growled. "You already know wherever he is, *Grimghast* likely won't be too far away."

"Wait, Grimghast?" Kabuji piped up with a befuddled expression. "When did we start talking about old horror tales from when I was a youngling?" Kai cursed himself for realizing they forgot to brief the leaders on all the details of their journey.

"If I may, Your Majesty, that horror tale as you call it is a lot more real than I'd like it to be," Pelka spoke up. "Every one of us who went to Duskmarsh saw it and trust me when I say that compared to how frightening the old stories are, it's much more terrifying up close."

Isolde and Velibor turned to Yulia and Hibbel, respectively, both of whom nodded with obvious fear in their eyes.

"It may look like a mangy old bear," Teos added, "but damned if it isn't tougher than stone and a pain to kill. It sunk my boat while we were trekking to Runegard last year. We even tied an anchor to its leg to sink it in the river and it still won't die!"

"Forget about Grimghast for now," Kai cut in, though he winced at Kabuji's stern frown, letting him know the emperor would expect nothing less than a full account later. "The most pressing matter right now is countering the Blight."

Jaco shook his head. "Gravebane, the Blight isn't like any disease you've ever treated before. It's not something you just whip up a tonic for. We still don't know how it spreads so fast and if your suspicions are on the copper, the enemy has already begun seeding it within Livoria. Bloody Nulyma, this could be worse than the outbreak nine years ago. We just don't have the resources to fight it with the war taking our focus!"

"Is there a specific treatment that's been considered effective?" Kai asked. "I did include a recommendation for a generic antibacterial concoction in Fusette's missive.

"It's a start, but such a treatment can only do so much. If there *is* an actual cure for the Blight, none of the apothecary guilds on Alezon have seen fit to share. As it stands, the best we came up with last time was a tonic of black garlic, kettlebore, and emberona, though it was most effective when given in the early stages of infection. The frustrating thing is our emberona reserves have been depleted by the war effort."

Kai nearly jumped when Orelia spoke up at his side, her fingers sliding up his arm. "What about whorled everoak?" she asked. "Could that possibly be used to replace the emberona?"

In all the years he'd known the man, Kai couldn't remember ever seeing Jaco rendered speechless. The old Soltauri's jaw moved up and down in an amusing manner, though no words came out. After a few minutes, Saredi rolled his eyes and reached over, giving Jaco a firm pinch that provoked a strangled yelp from the other man.

"Th-that might actually work," Jaco finally announced. "While the concoction's makeup would require adjustment accounting for the differences between everoak and emberona, it would certainly be better than our other options at this point."

Isolde turned to Velibor, her eyes pleading. "Velibor, how swiftly would you be able to have enough everoak delivered?"

The Aerivolk elder shook his head and replied that, even if they had enough everoak harvested to meet the demand, moving such a large amount across the continent would take almost half a year. The budding hope which had been building from the moment Orelia put forward her idea deflated all at once.

"Jaco, be honest," Fusette said, wiping her tears and pulling away from Ione, "how much everoak would we need to mount a full recovery effort across Livoria?"

"For an operation of that magnitude, Your Grace..." Jaco said, "we'd need at least a full ton of material. A fully mature tree would provide a sufficient amount, but—"

"Use ours."

"...I beg your pardon, milady?"

Kai bit his lip. If Fusette looked any more putout, he wouldn't have been surprised to see her imitating one of Saredi's infamous lectures.

"Perhaps I should have Kai inspect your ears, Jaco. While I would have preferred it to be our last resort, I said we will be making use of the whorled everoak from the garden beneath the palace."

"What in Cadell's sacred name?" Morgan choked. The sellsword emitted a hacking cough as Teos thumped him between the shoulder blades. "Ya mean to tell me you've had one of those bloody healing trees sitting under us the whole time?"

Kai shrugged. "It's an open secret among apothecaries that the royal family owns one of the few mature everoaks outside the Highlands. As far as I know, though, only the Royal Apothecaries are permitted to use ingredients from it, with some exceptions."

He was surprised to see Jaco staring at Fusette in unbridled horror. "Your Grace," Jaco said, "you can't possibly be suggesting we tear down one of our realm's most important medicinal resources for the sake of one task. I understand your distress and the situation we're in, but that tree took generations to reach its current size!"

"Jaco, I say this with all the respect in the world for you, but that tree means absolutely *nothing* if it isn't used to save lives. I know how vital the everoak has been to your research into developing new medicines, but if we don't act fast we could be looking at one of the worst disasters in Nixtralian history! You know as well as I do how destructive the Blight is. If we don't stop it now, the number of lives lost in the Faumen War will look like a drop in the bucket in comparison."

Eyes scanning the room, Kai could see the rising tensions. Bidelga looked as equally aghast as Jaco, her face looking like polished marble. He could sympathize with Jaco's frustration. The palace's everoak was responsible for the creation of several breakthrough concoctions over the past two hundred years, including energy tonics, so to lose it would be a devastating blow.

However, he also knew Fusette had a point in saying all that progress could be made worthless if the Blight was allowed to run rampant. And given his research into the illness, he had no doubt in the Blight's ability to lay the entire continent low.

"I agree with Fusette," he said at last. Once again, his fur stood on end as everyone's eyes turned to him. "It's not something I like seeing done but our circumstances are dire. If harvesting our everoak will allow us to defend against Hemlocke's plan, then my professional opinion is we do it."

"I suppose it's a good thing that's not your decision to make," Jaco grumbled. "I'll admit you have talent in the healing arts, Gravebane, but you still need a few years to temper that skill with wisdom and experience."

"It may not be his decision, Jaco," Fusette intoned, her voice dropping to a low rumble echoing through the chamber, "but I trust Kai's skills as a healer as much as yours. My duty is to the people, and if harvesting that tree will prevent our realm from being desecrated by those who would see us brought to ruin, then by the winds I will see it done!"

Jaco bit his lip but nodded in supplication, dropping to a knee. Kai frowned, scratching at the itch in his mane. Seeing the older healer so despondent sent queasy tremors down his tails and he wished he could think of something to say. He was saved the trouble when Velibor spoke up, his gravelly voice almost too soft to hear.

"Lady Fusette," Velibor said, "to make such a sacrifice for the sake of your people is the epitome of what it means to be a leader. I think everyone would agree that Vonlo would be delirious with pride at seeing how you've grown. As a sign of good faith, once peace has been restored, the Belomas Highlands will be glad to offer a small grove of young but mature whorled everoaks to Livoria."

It surprised no one when Jaco bowed repeatedly to the aging Aerivolk blubbering words of gratitude for the offer, tears dripping to the floor. With one hand resting on her heart, Isolde stepped forward and drew Velibor into a hug.

"My friend, that sounds like a wonderful idea!" Isolde said.

Fusette offered a curtsy with flushed cheeks and a timid smile. "Chief Velibor, you have no idea how much that would mean to us. If I may ask, though, how do you plan to move an entire grove of mature trees such a distance without harming them?"

The Belomian elder replied with a confident smirk. "We have our methods. After all, the Highlands has had access to Conjurers for quite some time, and our Seeders are more than equipped to handle such a task. While the younger trees won't be as potent as the one you currently have, having access to an entire grove should provide you more materials in the future."

"The Grand Duchy of Livoria thanks you, Chief. Now then...Jaco, I expect you to gather the remaining members of the Royal Apothecaries here in the palace. Once that tree has been harvested and you've developed a new tonic, we'll be making use of carrier hawks to send it to our allies and apothecaries throughout the realm. I leave this in your capable hands."

"It shall be done, milady. May I make use of Gravebane's services for the time being?"

Kai's mane tingled at the brazen leer his cousin was sending his way. "Unfortunately I must decline that request," Fusette purred, "as Kai will be serving a vital role I can't entrust to anyone else."

Eyes swiveled around the chamber in confusion until Isolde broke the silence. "What role will that be, exactly?" she asked, her voice trembling. Fusette responded with a wink and mischievous smirk that sent tingles down Kai's spine.

"Where would the fun be if I simply told you? You'll all see soon enough."

Chapter XXVII

The moment Kai woke up, he could feel in his bones the day would be significant. Doing a mental tally, he let out a groan and sat up with a stretch.

That's right, he thought, *it's the 24th of Regemond. That means...*

A gentle moan on his left brought his gaze to Orelia, her dusky skin glowing in the morning sun peeking through their window. Her eyes fluttered open, locking on him with a toothy grin stretched across her face. She rolled over, exposing bare shoulders while wrapping both arms around Kai's chest and nuzzling her cheek into his mane.

On his other side, Maple emitted a prolonged chirp as she sat up and stretched. She looked unbothered in the slightest when the blanket fell away to reveal her nude form. Kai blushed, but didn't divert his gaze while watching her ruffle her wings and scratch the base of her dorsal feathers with half-lidded eyes.

"Morning, you two," Kai whispered, wrapping one arm around Orelia while tracing the fingers of his other hand up Maple's back from her tail feathers to between her shoulder blades.

The apothecary wasn't disappointed to see Maple shiver under his caress before turning on him. Her violet eyes flashed with cheeky resolve.

"You did that on purpose," Maple trilled, a sultry smirk slipping into place as her hands moved under the covers.

"So what if I did?" Kai retorted. He fought to keep a straight face when both women began exploring with eager fingers. "As much as I'd love a repeat of last night, we should get ready. Fusette said she had big plans for today. I shouldn't be surprised though. It *is* her birthday, after all."

Maple's eyes lit up with recognition. "That's right! I almost forgot about that," she exclaimed.

"What do you reckon she's planning?" Orelia asked. "I heard her scribbling away in her study last night when we passed by on our way to bed."

"Whatever it is, Archbishop Jovanni is in on it. He was snickering to himself when I passed him in the halls yesterday."

The three partners shared confused glances, though Kai's fur bristled when Orelia's cool touch reached the base of his tails, eliciting a throaty purr.

"Dang it, woman, you know that's one of my weak spots..."

"Oh, I know, darling," Orelia replied and used her other hand to push Kai onto his back. "Whatever Fusette has planned can wait, though. You started this, so don't complain when we want you to fulfill your husbandly duties."

Kai blinked. "Do I look like I'm complaining?"

As the two clambered on top of him with matching grins, Kai muttered a silent prayer to Cacovis that nobody would need them for at least the next hour.

When the trio finally emerged from their bedroom and staggered into the dining hall for breakfast with the rest of the party, it didn't escape their notice how Fusette eyed them with a cocky smirk while one of the palace blacksmiths exited the room from the other end. A quick inquiry to Ione informed Kai the rest of the leaders were enjoying the morning meal in their own camps.

"Seems like you three had fun," the duchess teased, her tails twitching in the open air. A young seamstress stood behind her, jotting down meticulous notes with a look of intense focus while taking measurements as Fusette ate. Kai's head tilted in confusion. After a few more seconds, the woman bowed to Fusette and rushed from the room, leaving through the same door the blacksmith had taken just before.

"Jealous?" Maple snarked back, the merchant's face curved into a saucy smile.

Kai fought to control his blush when Fusette's lips refused to move. "Of the act, perhaps," she finally answered, "but there's nothing wrong with being a healthy woman."

"Must you speak of such things at the table?" Lucretia snapped. The scholar was clearly trying to focus on her food rather than the lurid conversation, though it didn't seem to be working.

To nobody's surprise, Morgan burst into one of his full-bellied laughs and hammered a fist on the table. Kai was impressed at his friend's ability to carry on without choking on the grilled salmon constituting his meal. On the sellsword's other side, Ione and Teos shared an exasperated expression.

"How do you even know what they were up to anyway?" Ione asked, her cheeks darkening to a deep crimson.

Fusette's grin widened further, revealing a pair of glinting fangs. "I happened to pass their bedroom on the way. It wasn't exactly hard to guess from the noise those two were making," she explained while pointing an accusatory finger at Maple and Orelia.

In unison, both women stuck their tongues out at the monarch, ignoring Saredi leveling a piercing frown at them from the other end of the table the entire time. Kai bit his own tongue and tapped his partners on the chin, diverting their attention.

"Before we all forget our manners," Kai said, "let me wish you a happy birthday, Your Grace." The apothecary's words jolted the rest of the room's occupants from the previous conversation and incited a round of congratulations from everyone.

"Thank you for the blessings, my friends," Fusette responded. Her cheeks were dusted with a light pink tinge as her eyes surveyed the room. "However, you know how I feel about you using such formal talk when it's only us."

"Perhaps," Kai answered, "but even if we're family, my mother would box my ears if I didn't show proper respect for such a special occasion."

"Gravebane is correct, Your Grace," Saredi piped in while shooting Kai a gracious smile that almost rocked the apothecary from his seat. "It's not every day you turn 27. Allow us to at least offer our respects in this small manner. Besides, you already know the Archbishop has some grand celebration hidden beneath that pompous mitre."

Kai's head tilted once again. "Wait, so Jovanni isn't part of the plans you told me about yesterday?"

Fusette's body quaked with mirth. "By the winds, no. If I know Jovanni, he's gathering people to put together a festival or the like to celebrate the day. My plans involve the last report we received from Larimanz."

"The one saying the Libbies will reach Ballad's End by tonight?" Ione asked.

"Yes. I've tasked the city guard with spreading word of an important announcement I must make before the battle begins. This time, however, I intend to host it in the market square. Everyone should be in place before lunch."

The firm resolution with which she spoke gave Kai pause. He wasn't sure what type of plot she was concocting, but he was determined to support her in any way if it meant ending this wretched war once and for all.

Following breakfast, Kai offered to assist Fusette with her preparations for the upcoming announcement. However, he was rebuffed at once as his cousin told him to take the next few hours to relax with the party. He could see the tension in her pinched cheeks as she gave the order. With the shadow of battle hanging over them, the message was clear as the cloudless sky above the palace.

"Spend time with your friends," Fusette murmured to him in private before departing for her chambers. "Who knows what will happen once the fighting begins."

Rather than follow the command blindly, Kai gave his partners a peck on the cheek before rushing off. When he returned less than ten minutes later, the party cast curious glances to which he only responded with a smile and promise to explain following Fusette's assembly.

"What do you suppose Lady Fusette wants to speak about?" Lucretia asked as the seven friends exited the dining hall.

"Who knows?" Morgan quipped, using a small hook from his belt to pick out a fish bone between his teeth. He flicked the offending bone away to Lucretia's obvious disgust. "All I can say is my belly's all fired up for this fight!"

Kai dug an elbow into the mixblood's chest. "Let's not get carried away. Remember, we have a chance to finally end this once and for all. We can't let our guard down because the enemy is on their last legs and we allies have ready to stand with us."

"You worry too much, 'pothy. Just so we're clear, if that mangy bastard Obram shows up, I'm gonna put his furry ass in the dirt once and for all. It'll be easy as—"

"Don't you dare finish that sentence," Kai warned, his grey eyes flashing silver.

The others glanced at the apothecary with worry. "What in the winds is eating you?" Teos asked. His eyes drifted to Maple and Orelia, both of whom shrugged.

Kai refused to take his gaze off Morgan, the fur of his tails puffed out. "Sorry," he mumbled at last. "I just don't any of us getting complacent. That's how you get yourself killed. Trust me, I know, and there's no telling what those bastards have waiting for us."

Stunning everyone, Ione strode past Maple and Orelia and drew Kai into a warm embrace. No words were shared between the two, though it was clear Kai needed it as his body quaked in the older woman's arms. Unable to find his voice, he could only nod. Thinking of his old squad still hurt at times, especially knowing complacency was what ultimately led to their fate. Regardless, he knew they wouldn't want him moping at a time like this. Not with so much on the line. A small voice, almost imperceptible, whispered in his ear reminding him to focus on what was important. Within moments, he felt two more pairs of arms wrapping around him.

"We'll be fine," Maple assured him while standing on the tips of her talons to give Kai's ear an affectionate nibble.

"That goes for *all* of us," Orelia added, giving the others a stern look until they nodded in agreement. "Now, let's get ourselves presentable and not worry about the war unless needed. We don't want to look anything but our best for the assembly, after all."

A sense of familiarity washed over Kai as he looked out at the crowd. The sea of expectant eyes gazing at them on the hurriedly built platform in the square's center sent a tremble down his back. His eyes swept over the area. The other leaders and their delegations took up the far side on his right with Isolde in the point position. Hanblum and Ottoten stood beside her, the former's ebony feathers gleaming in the sun just as brightly as the resplendent white of the admiral's uniform.

Near the platform's rear were Dewthorn, Burnsong, and Swiftlock. All three met Kai's inquisitive stare with serious nods. At the front edge opposite the leaders were Saredi and Bidelga. The minister twiddled her thumbs while sweeping her eyes over the area. Saredi looked unflappable as ever, his suit just as crisp as Ottoten's with a simple longsword strapped to his belt. Kai's eyes narrowed when he realized the notable absence among their number.

Where was Fusette?

The soft clink of metal coming from behind prickled Kai's ears. He turned just enough to glance at the crowd behind the platform clearing a path for a single figure, dilating his pupils. The extra brightness in his peripheral vision stung, but it gave him a clear view of a sight that nearly sent the apothecary reeling in shock.

Fusette stepped onto the platform, her entire body brimming with confidence. The familiar chartreuse gown was gone, replaced with a cobalt silk tunic and rugged brown pants. Wrapped around her waist was a woolen skirt lined with bison fur trim and holes cut at the rear to allow her tails free movement. A fitted steel cuirass was fastened over her upper torso with a shining emerald embedded over her heart. As she strode past, Kai saw the royal family's seal on the cuirass' back in green filigree and one of the new blunderbusses strapped across her back. Steel cuisses covering the front of her thighs were visible under the skirt, the metal clanking against a small buckler hanging from her belt. Lastly, her formal flats were supplanted by thick, calf-length boots also trimmed in fur up top and lined with metal studs along the upper.

The most shocking item was the polished spear clutched in her left hand—a partizan as tall as she was with its head plated in silver and triangular protrusions jutting from the head's base at a slight curve. The central spearhead had a honed edge and a thin crimson ribbon tied at the top of the shaft, fluttering in the breeze.

Scanning the landing, Kai could see he wasn't the only one stunned by Fusette's new attire. The other leaders stared agog, their expressions ranging from Isolde's concern to the blatant pride shining in Kabuji's face. Saredi, however, looked apoplectic.

"Your Grace," the Lord Chamberlain hissed. From his reddening cheeks, it was clear he was fighting back an urge to bellow like an angered bison. "What in the sacred winds are you wearing? For that matter, is that your *father's* lance? Why does it look like that? I don't remember it being quite so...polished. It looks almost brand new!"

"For your information, Saredi, Cacovis' journal described this as the traditional battle garb of the ancient Norzen culture, stemming from the tribe's origins in the south-central forests of Feswili. I'll explain the rest later. For now, I expect you to remain silent. Now then, I suppose I shall get this started before I lose my nerve."

Marching past with head held high, Fusette met Kai's gaze and flashed him a warm smile. Kai couldn't help grinning as he fell into step beside and just behind his cousin, following her to the edge. His ears twitched, hearing a cacophony of baffled mutterings from the surrounding crowd.

A fair number of onlookers pointed at Fusette and even at this distance, Kai saw the confusion in their eyes. Near the front of the mass, he spotted numerous scriveners from the newsletters, their quills and parchment ready to move at a moment's notice.

"Thank you, everyone, for being here on this momentous day," Fusette boomed, her voice carrying over the masses. Everyone stilled, their gazes pinned to the monarch. "I stand before you today for many reasons. First, let me say I'm well aware of Archbishop Jovanni's cheeky plan for a surprise celebration of my birthday."

A wave of snickers pulsed through the crowd, their volume increasing when someone pointed out the blushing Jovanni standing at the base of the platform. Dozens of well wishes arose from the din and Kai even spotted some children on their parents' shoulders, waving flags embroidered with the royal family's emblem. His heart thrummed with anxiety seeing several among the crowd watching with grim scowls.

"Yes, yes, thank you very much for your kindness," Fusette continued. Tears trickled down her cheek, prompting Kai to reach over and brush them away. She shot him a grateful smile. "I know today is supposed to be a day of joy and festivities. However, I would be remiss if I didn't inform you the Liberation Army is on its way."

An oppressive tension blanketed the plaza as the crowd muttered among themselves. One scrivener at the front shouted, "What of the rumors we've heard concerning a massive weapon the Liberators possess that can destroy a city?"

The tension gave way to a growing terror in the throng, with multiple groups jostling each other in an effort to move towards the plaza exit. Fusette raised both hands, palms out, and gestured for calm.

"I'm afraid those rumors are well-founded. The enemy has a cannon dubbed the Shatterstar, a variant of the same one used to destroy Havenfall. I want to assure you all that we do not intend to idly sit by and allow the Liberators to march on our beautiful city without a response."

"What can you possibly do against such a weapon?" another scrivener pressed.

Fusette's eyes glowed. "Alone, nothing. As you see, though, our realm is *not* alone. Our fellow Alezonians have come to offer aid in our hour of need. While the bulk of the Royal Navy faces the enemy across Livoria, the Marine Cavalry Fleet is hounding the Liberation Army's main force as we speak. As they drive our foes north, our allies and the Whistlevale city guard shall stop the enemy advance at Ballad's End. And that leads me into my attire, something I'm sure many of you are wondering about."

Multitudes of nodding heads shifted throughout the crowd. Kai risked glancing over at Saredi, who chewed on his clenched fist while his body swayed side to side.

"Many of you standing here remember my father, Duke Vonlo. To the average Livorian, I understand he was a stern man who brooked no foolishness in public and was infamous for his temper. To me, though, he was just my Papa. He wasn't afraid to do foolish things in private to make me laugh when I had a bad day. When I struggled to understand something he did his best to explain, even if looking back it was clear he had no clue either."

The crowd burst into amused snickers.

"The point is," Fusette pressed, fresh tears leaking down her cheeks, "he was a loving and caring father and leader who was wrenched from us far too soon. Thanks to Gravebane here, we suspect a rogue ally of the Liberators of wishing to bring back the Black Tear Blight, the very illness that took not only my father, but many of your own friends and family."

A shadowy pall fell over the plaza. Kai could see the horror in the people's eyes, many clutching at each other as if afraid their loved ones would disappear if they let go.

"M-milady," the first scrivener stammered, his quill slipping from his fingers in shock, "what can we do? Several of our contacts out west sent us hawk post with concerns of illness spreading among the smaller villages. Could it possibly be...?"

Fusette nodded. "I would not be surprised if the Blight has already begun taking root in those regions. All is not lost, though, my friends. Thanks to the combined efforts of Gravebane and Jaco, along with the

Royal Apothecaries, we have developed a new medical elixir which will hopefully prove more effective against the Blight. Our intent is to scatter this elixir across the realm and beat the disease back before it spreads too deep. We will also be posting instructions throughout the realm letting you know what you can do to shield yourself and your families from illness. As for the rogue responsible, we have reason to believe he's entrenched near the enemy army.

"With that said, I refuse to stand by and watch from afar as the people of Livoria fight for everything they hold sacred. In wishing to make us relive the horrors of the Blight, these bastards have declared war on not only our realm, but myself personally. Thus, *I* will be leading our forces into battle, with Gravebane serving as my deputy commander!"

The crowd erupted into a tumult unlike anything Kai had ever seen before. The scriveners' quills flew across the parchment while the crowds behind lashed out with pleas for Fusette to reconsider her decision. The uproar forced him to fold his ears down before the noise rendered him deaf. To the side, Saredi's face paled to a point Kai worried the man might pass out from the shock.

"Everyone, settle down!" Fusette bellowed. The crowd stilled in moments, many of the adults gazing at her in shock.

Kai suppressed a chuckle when his ears picked up one gruff old man behind the scriveners muttering, "She's Vonlo's daughter, alright."

Eyes blazing with determination, Fusette rapped her spear on the floor three times. "I feel your worries, and appreciate it with every fiber of my being. However, let me tell you something. My father would never have stood back and cowered in the palace with such a grave danger facing our people. As his daughter, I can do no less than see to it with my own hands that this rogue and everything he stands for is defeated. Regardless of how my fate is determined after this battle, if I am to be remembered for anything as Grand Duchess, I'd rather be known as someone cut of the same cloth as someone I hold deep respect for: My ancestor, Lady Cacovis."

A wave of gasps rose from the crowd.

"Like her, I intend to fight for what's precious to me: All of you, who I care for as deeply as if you were my own blood. Cacovis gave her life to protect her sons and the innocent souls who suffered under Berelmir's tyrannical rule, and now I'm prepared to do the same in defense of everyone on this continent. Our allies stand with us because we desire the same thing. To see an Alezon where people are allowed to love who they wish regardless of physical differences. Where an individual is judged not by their looks, but by their actions and character. We must stand united against such unrestrained animosity, otherwise we will assuredly lose everything we cherish."

To Kai's surprise, the crowd exploded into raucous applause after several tense seconds of silence. Banners waved through the air. Fists were waved alongside shouts of support. On the landing, Kai saw the other leaders offering their own gentle applause. Velibor and Gideon looked on with blossoming respect, while Kabuji had a grin so wide it split his face in half. Isolde marched forward and drew the younger monarch into a crushing hug.

"If your father could see you now," Isolde whispered, pulling back and gazing at Fusette in clear pride. "I daresay the man would be torn between praising you or locking you in your room until the fighting was done."

Shaking her head, Fusette buried her face in the older woman's chest. "He would have no one to blame but himself. He taught me everything I know, after all."

The two women shared a cheeky grin before giggling amongst themselves and turning to face the others, led by Kabuji.

"Fusette, you may be the youngest among our number," the Rodekan emperor said, "but you speak with the wisdom and passion of someone three times your age."

"Well, Father always said the crown was such a heavy burden it turned his hair grey. I reckon the added weight of war made me realize I can either find a way to stand strong or be crushed beneath it."

"You ain't lifting that crown alone, little lady," Kabuji assured her. "Each of us here is ready to end this. I don't know about the rest of our group, but I for one will be fighting right alongside you!"

"Your Majesty!" Pelka snapped. "Aren't you getting a little old to be swinging a weapon?"

"Hellfire, Pelka, ya know I ain't the kind of man to sit on my ass when things get rough! I may be 46, but that doesn't make me too old to do what needs done!"

A hearty chuckle rang from Velibor and Gideon. "Kabuji speaks the truth, Miss Pelka," the Belomian chief interjected. "It's as Fusette said. We must stand together, no matter the cost. I may be past my prime, but Gideon and I will direct the city's defenses while you face the enemy on the field."

"Indeed," Isolde said, "and I will be right there with you as well, my friend. I may not be a fighter, but let it be said no Queen of Galstein has ever backed down from a fight where freedom was at stake."

Kai watched as Fusette was surrounded by her peers, each offering heartfelt congratulations for her speech. By the time she escaped from the circle they formed around her, her tunic was rumpled and her hair and ears had a distinct scruffy look. He smirked, laughing when her eyes landed on him, cheeks puffed in a childish pout. Together, he gestured for the party to head back into the palace.

"Even my own family laughs at my misfortune," Fusette bemoaned, leaning back with a hand raised to her forehead in an exaggerated dramatic pose.

"Oh hush," Kai mumbled, "you know they do it because they like and respect you. What say we enjoy some lunch before it's time to begin the march? I arranged a little something special for you."

Before Fusette could answer, Saredi set himself in front of her with a familiar frown. "Your Grace," he said, "as your advisor I must question this decision. You don't know how to fight!"

Without warning, Fusette twirled the lance with a speed and grace that left everyone present flummoxed. The metal spearhead gleamed in the lantern light, a palpable breeze formed with each sweeping motion. Kai couldn't help being impressed, though his eyes bulged when he saw her come to a sudden stop, the tip of the weapon's center blade pointed just beneath Saredi's chin. The rest of the party gaped.

"I'm not the same little girl who took the throne grieving my father's death, Saredi Bastion," Fusette declared. "It took me years of practice during the rare moments you weren't hovering over me, but I'm quite confident in my skills. I've made my decision and will stand by it. The way I see things, everyone here has three choices. You can either lead me, follow me, or *get out of my bloody way.* Which will you choose?"

Mouth hanging open, Kai blinked at the uproarious laughter ringing from the Vesikoi's mouth.

"Sweet Luopari!" Saredi groaned, eyes wrenched shut with what Kai could've sworn were tears trickling down his cheek. But that was impossible. Right? "It's like seeing your father back from the grave. Very well. It's obvious I can't change your mind, so I shall simply have to go along to make sure you stay out of trouble."

Fusette said nothing. She only smiled and patted Saredi on the arm before turning back to Kai.

"Now that we've cleared that up, you said you had something for me, Kai?"

Leading the leaders and Saredi into the throne room, Kai was pleased by Fusette's surprised gasp to see the pathway to the throne lined with tables of food. She spun towards him and pinched his ear just hard enough to grab his attention.

"Kai," she purred with a leonine grin, "what is this? I thought I told you I didn't want a huge celebration."

The apothecary's grin didn't waver as he gripped her wrist to free his twitching ear. "Perhaps, but this is as small as I could make it. I've already instructed the guards to turn anyone away unless it's an emergency. You're always fond of saying you don't like the hullabaloo people make around your birthday, so I thought you might prefer something a little more intimate. A small party for friends and family only."

Raising one hand, Kai snapped his fingers. A small crowd of familiar faces poured out of the rear hall leading to Fusette's chambers—Rorik, Guri, Ingrid, Verona, Serafina, Tuvi, Cress, Willow, Clove, Pelka, Hibbel, Yulia, Ottoten, and Hanblum all stepped forward and took turns offering the duchess heartfelt congratulations. Fusette's eyes filled with tears as she thanked everyone for being there. Spinning in place, she sprinted and threw herself against Kai, the taller Norzen catching her in a soothing hug.

"Thank you," Fusette mumbled.

Smiling at his partners, Kai threaded his fingers through Fusette's ebony locks. "No need to thank me for anything," he replied. "That's what family does. We take care of one another, no matter how different we may look."

"He's right," Morgan said, pouring himself a stein of mead from one of the barrels occupying a nearby table. "It don't matter a lick that most of us don't share a drop of blood. We're family all the same. Some people think the word stops at blood kin, but if there's one thing I learned from 'pothy, it's that *true family* runs deeper than that."

A round of murmured agreement echoed from the rest of the group. Clapping her hands together, Fusette demanded everyone enjoy the food. With that, the crowd split off into smaller groups. Kai was pleased to see Maple and Orelia's families chatting eagerly with his mother and sister. His eyebrows cocked upwards seeing Rorik approach Fusette with a heavy blush painting the warrior's face, a small bundle in his hands haphazardly wrapped in cloth. He couldn't see the contents when Fusette opened it, though he had a clear view of her timid giggle in response, followed by her raising herself up to brush her lips against Rorik's crimson cheek.

Grinning to himself, Kai shook his head and watched Fusette spin around to rush towards him. Her blush was readily apparent, a shy smile on her lips as she cradled the bundle in her arms. Glancing down, the apothecary smirked seeing a bouquet of red and purple tulips, their petals shimmering in the early afternoon sun.

"Should I give Rorik a warning of what will happen if he hurts you?" Kai offered, laughing when Fusette slugged him in the shoulder with her free hand.

"Don't you dare," she growled. "I think it was rather sweet. Besides, you and I both know I'm not getting any younger."

"So long as he makes you happy, that's what matters most."

"Kai, what makes me happy is knowing the people I love and care about are safe. It goes beyond just being Grand Duchess and wanting to protect the people out of a sense of duty. I have my mother back, this is true, but you... you're the last connection I have to my father, no matter how distant. Once the fighting starts, I want you to promise me you won't take any reckless risks."

"Fusette..." Kai started, only for her to jab a finger into his mane.

"Promise me! Our relation may be distant, but since discovering the truth, you've become the brother I always wished I had. I...I can't lose you, Kai, any more than Maple or Orelia could."

"Your Grace," Saredi interrupted while strolling over with Hibbel and Pelka in tow, the Norzen diplomat ogling Fusette's attire with a proud glimmer in her eye, "I feel we deserve that explanation now. What did you do to Lord Vonlo's lance?"

Fusette peered at the partizan, still clutched in one hand and gleaming in the sunbeams. "I honestly don't know. I grabbed it from the grand hall and it started glowing before turning into its current form. I also felt an odd warmth along my arm and *this* appeared!" The duchess twisted her arm to reveal a strange black mark infused into her wrist. Formed of thick, flowing lines that reminded Kai of High Norzen script, the mark looked vaguely like a single wing with feathers splayed outward.

A sharp gasp came from Hibbel. "Mother of Origin..." the scholar muttered with bulging eyes, "could the ancient legends be true?"

Kai's gaze swung to Hibbel, the obvious question on his lips, when the door to the throne room burst open. An older, grey-haired Wasini man slithered in, a glitter emitting from his scarlet scales and an excited grin stretched tight across his weather-beaten face. An elongated bundle wrapped in cloth was cradled in his arms.

"Master Mica," Fusette said, tilting her head to the side as Kai performed the exact same action, "I believe the staff were told not to disturb us unless it was an emergency."

Mica had the decency to look abashed. "I apologize, milady," he mumbled, "but I recently completed a project I've been working on for Sir Gravebane since his return from Havenfall and wanted to present it before the battle begins."

Kai's eyes shone with curiosity, twitching to the bundle Mica held out towards him. Taking it from the blacksmith, he unwrapped it to expose a gleaming flanged mace. It was identical to his current weapon with the exception of the metal being a dusky shade of blue. Kai found himself mesmerized by the mace's detail and generous heft.

"I don't recognize this metal," Kai finally said. "Even through the wrap, the sturdiness feels like tungsten, but the color's off and it's nowhere near as heavy."

"It's a new type of metal we discovered in the mountains outside Shiverhill shortly before the war started," Mica explained. "We decided to name it eorium because the color looks eerily like Eoria's surface when held under bright light. Sadly, it's taken us this long just to figure out how to properly work it. It requires a delicate temperature balance while shaping or it becomes brittle. If done properly, though, it appears to be harder than steel. This mace is the first project we've completed without any cracking issues. I'd be honored if you give it a few test swings, Sir Gravebane."

Wearing a broad grin, Kai nodded and curled his left hand around the cool metal shaft. Without provocation, the mace burst into a blinding light that elicited a shocked yelp from Kai and everyone nearby. The metal quickly shifted from cool to warm in his hand, a similar heat blooming within his palm.

"Kai!" Fusette shouted. The room's occupants spun to face the apothecary, shielding their eyes until the light dimmed to a less blinding level. Kai briefly considered dropping the mace out of shock, yet a gentle voice in the back of his mind told him to maintain his grip. That it would be worth the minuscule pain.

After a few moments, the shine dispersed completely. Kai blinked the spots from his eyes and gazed down, his breath hitching. The mace had transformed, its simplistic design gone completely. Each flange extending from the shaft was shaped like a curved axe head, their blades honed to a fine silver edge that popped against the weapon's dusky blue tone. The shaft itself was now covered in an intricate imprint of leafy vines highlighted in bright green encircling it from top to bottom. Along one side of the shaft, a line of flowing runes he recognized as High Norzen script was inscribed.

His gaze narrowed at the sight of a mark similar to Fusette's now branded on the back of his hand. Formed of the same swirling lines as his cousin's mark, it was drawn into the distinctive wide petals and elongated pistils of an emberona flower.

A quick glance at Hibbel told Kai the Vesikoi scholar looked ready to have a fit. What surprised him was seeing Pelka with an identical flummoxed expression on her face. "How?" Pelka whispered. "I-I'd heard the stories as a youngling, but I never could've imagined seeing one in the flesh, never mind *two*."

"What stories?" Fusette demanded. Her free hand rested on her hip while she pinned the other Norzen in place with a perplexed frown. "You and Hibbel obviously know something about all this, so out with it, if you please!"

Pelka tucked her head between her shrugged shoulders with a timid smile. "I suppose the old tales may not have been passed down on this side of Alezon following the Desolation Wars," she answered. "To put it simply, milady, there are ancient legends that speak of individuals given unique marks by the will of Origin itself, chosen for some greater purpose."

"The will of Origin?" Fusette parroted.

"Chosen?" Kai added. His eyes drifted back to the mark on his hand, a sinking feeling spreading through his gut.

It was Hibbel who raised his hands in a placating manner. "Please remain calm. Keep in mind, these are only stories passed down among the tribes for centuries. Many are considered nothing but tall tales for children. We have no conclusive evidence that Origin is responsible for this phenomenon. I'm sure there's a reasonable explanation for this."

"Hibbel," Fusette purred, her lips curling back to reveal shimmering fangs, "how else would you explain these strange markings? While I'm no scholar, I certainly have never heard of anything that could cause something like this. Being formed of magic wouldn't be too far outside the realm of possibility, given what we've learned of Origin in the past moon."

"Uh," the scholar hummed with eyes shifting about to stare at anything except Fusette's leonine grin, "the thing is, I can't explain it, milady. According to the legends, these chosen individuals typically only appear every few hundred years. I suppose if the legends are in fact true, then we really shouldn't be surprised to see both of you among their number."

"What does that mean?" Saredi interjected, his piercing gaze promising retribution if Hibbel's answer wasn't to his liking.

"One of the reasons Lady Cacovis is so well regarded in the Highlands is because there are rumors she herself bore a mark similar to the ones on you and Gravebane. While there hasn't been confirmation, it's been hinted among faumen scholars that the tattoo mentioned to be on Master Galen's chest was *also* such a mark, an oddity considering the fact he was human."

The room erupted into a clamor, Kai and Fusette's eyes bulging widest of all. The two stared at each other, unsure of what to make of this newest clue to their ancestor's life. A quick look at Lucretia had her shaking her head, admitting nothing of the sort was mentioned in Cacovis' journal.

"If this is true," Guri said, "then it's only proper the Norzen tribe's new champions have their weapons granted names befitting the status. May I take a look, Lady Fusette?"

Nodding, Fusette handed her spear to the older Norzen, who inspected it closely. Her eyes roamed over the weapon with a critical intensity, fingers sliding along the freshly polished shaft. After a few moments, she gave it a brief twirl and swung it in a wide arch. The silver blade shone in the sunbeams, casting a brilliant flash with each swing.

"This lance is the most balanced I've ever seen," Guri appraised. "And the blade is such a beautiful color. With your approval, milady, I'd like to dub it Frimanir. In the High Norzen tongue, it roughly translates as 'Freedom Cast in Moonlight.'"

Fusette's cheeks glowed. "That sounds like a lovely name, Guri," she replied. "I'm quite honored."

Giving the monarch a respectful nod, Guri turned towards Kai, who turned his new mace with a deft flip and offered the shaft to her. She grasped the handle and took it with a startled shout, the weapon's heft proving too much as it struck the ground with a sonorous boom and left a small crater in the polished stone floor. Kai noticed her muscles tense as she attempted to lift the mace to no avail. After a few more seconds of trying, she eyed the line of script on the shaft and stepped back while gesturing for Kai to take it, eyes bulging when he lifted the mace over one shoulder with ease.

"Impressive," said Guri. "It seems your training with Rorik is showing results. It's not often one comes across a weapon such as that. All I can say in this moment is: Not just anyone can wield that mace. Given what I've seen and know of you, I feel the name Mimilrun would be perfect. It means 'Star of Wisdom.' You also share a personal connection, as it was the name Frida wished to give you had you been born a girl."

Face beaming, Kai clutched Guri's hand in a firm shake. "Thank you," he murmured. "Knowing that, it helps me feel like my parents are just a little bit closer now."

Once Kai slid Mimilrun into the loop on his belt, Fusette tugged the blunderbuss from her shoulder and shoved it against his chest.

"As interesting as this is, we can discuss the deeper implications after defeating the Liberators. For now, I want you to take this," she commanded, her eyes firm and unyielding. "I know as a Hunter, you're not in the habit of using firearms, but the smiths gave me a demonstration after our return and I'd feel much better if you had it."

Kai took the gun with a nervous touch, his eyes roaming over it. A second weight pulled on his belt moments later, drawing his attention to the pouch of what could only be iron balls Fusette tied into place.

"Are you sure you don't want to take it yourself?" Kai pleaded.

Fusette shook her head with a tilted grin. "Turns out I'm a horrid shot," she confessed. "The smiths let me fire a few rounds and promptly chased me out before I, in their words, 'put more holes in the kiln than Bruzian cheese.' Just promise me you'll use it if the need arises."

A deep laugh rumbled from Kai's chest. Staring at Fusette's pleading eyes, he finally nodded, murmuring a whispered promise before slipping the weapon's strap over one shoulder. The relief in her face was palpable. He saw Maple and Orelia striding over with their families and ruffled Fusette's hair, watching her ears flutter under his fingers.

"Thank you, Kai. I pray to Cacovis you won't need to use that thing, but you never know with how war can be." The duchess beckoned Saredi over and, clasping a hand to the Vesikoi's shoulder, gave him a solemn nod. "Have the guards spread the word. Once our meal is done, we break camp and march for Ballad's End."

Chapter XXVIII

In the setting sun's faded light, the hills of Ballad's End loomed over the Liberation Army with all the solemnity of a magistrate passing judgment. The soldiers trudged about at a snail's crawl, their faces sunken and bodies slouched forward. Many looked half-starved and all of them were covered in dirt with a variety of scratches littering their exposed skin. Their camp, hastily erected and filled with tents just as ramshackle as their armor, reeked of sweat and the faint iron tang of blood.

A frustrated scream reverberated through the air, jolting many from their thoughts. Frightened eyes swerved towards the base of the nearest hill where a large tent in noticeably better condition stood, tilting to one side. Inside, Agosti slammed his fists on the table where he and the rest of his officers were conferring on a plan of attack.

"What do you mean we can't attack tonight?" Agosti demanded, his eyes glimmering in the candlelight while the Medoro stared from across the table with a stony glare. "The capital is finally within our grasp, and you're saying we need to wait?"

"Agosti, I understand your frustration but you cannot allow your desire for revenge to make you act like a blithering fool. Well...more of one than you already are," Medoro countered, ignoring the searing glare coming from the other man. "Our army is in no condition to march another step, and to be perfectly frank, I can't blame them. The Marine Cavalry has been running us ragged since we ransacked Brightwise. I'll admit your plan to draw their attention with a diverted scouting company was impressive, but they'll realize our duplicity soon enough. When that happens, they'll run us to ground if the men are too exhausted to even swing their swords."

Agosti clenched his jaw, the desire to throw a punch at his deputy growing by the moment. His eyes flickered towards the open entrance of the tent, where he saw their soldiers stumbling as they walked. The sight only served to feed his rage. As much as he hated admitting to it, Medoro was right. In its current state, the Liberation Army wouldn't be able to put up a fight against a brigade of infants, much less the Royal Navy.

"Very well," he grumbled, "we'll pack it in and rest here for the night. Have the quartermasters divvy out the remainder of the rations. We'll be eating like kings once we surprise the Royalists tomorrow."

"What makes you so sure they don't already know we're coming?"

Agosti's thoughts drifted to their trump weapon, nestled in a small pass near the top of the hill they were camped under. "We're between the Marine Cavalry and Whistlevale and haven't seen a single carrier hawk. Chances are they have no clue. Even if they did, what could they hope to accomplish against the Shatterstar? So long as we have that cannon, we can wipe out the Royalists from a safe distance and reap the benefits afterward."

Seated directly behind Agosti, Adalbard leaned on his staff and regarded the map with a pinched frown. "How will we loot the capital if we end up destroying it in the process?" the disgraced bishop asked.

"I'm actually glad you asked that, priest. My plan is to get us close enough to launch our cannonball *over* the city itself. The Royal Palace is near the seaport, correct? Well, if we hit the ocean relatively close to the palace, we should be able to minimize damage to the city itself. That way we can loot what we need from the locals until we can establish a new government to replace the monarchy."

Everyone in the tent stared at the bellicose general in abject shock. Medoro's mouth hung open while many of the other officers slumped back in their seats. Adalbard almost slipped, leaning too hard on his weapon before catching himself.

"Th-that's actually not a bad plan, General," Medoro muttered, perusing the map of Whistlevale in front of him and tracing the palace's location with an armored finger. "If we get close enough without alerting the Royalists, we may be able to pull it off. The major trouble will be keeping them occupied as we cross the open plains past Ballad's End. For that, we'll need some sort of distraction."

"Did somebody call for a distraction?" a malicious voice trilled.

Agosti leapt back with a curse, spinning around to find himself staring at a grinning Hemlocke. Behind him stood the rest of Razarr's beastly retinue, though the general couldn't help noticing the forge master's absence. That damned faumen who struck him before, Obram, was also missing for some reason.

"Has anyone ever told you you're creepy as Nulyma?" Agosti growled, refusing to take his eyes off the diminutive Aerivolk. He still couldn't shake the feeling of danger Hemlocke emitted, as if he were staring into the eyes of a predator.

No, Agosti thought, *the real predator is that beastie he always keeps nearby. Now that I think about it, where—*

A clamor rose from outside the tent. Agosti's gaze shifted to the tent flap long enough to confirm Grimghast ambling among his soldiers and sending them into a right panic, though the beast made no gesture to attack anyone. He locked eyes with Hemlocke, fingers twitching towards his sword.

To his surprise, the sickly faumen only burst into laughter. "They tell me that quite often, actually," Hemlocke answered with a congenial smile. "Then again, I suppose folks have good reason. I do try to encourage such a view when it suits me."

"Where's your master?" Medoro inquired.

"I'm afraid he ran into a whole new set of problems while in Duskmarsh. Suffice to say, he won't be joining us for the battle. I do have authority to negotiate with you in his name, however. How confident are you in being able to destroy the enemy?"

Refusing to relax his arm, inching subtly downward, Agosti shrugged. "If you can draw the Royalists' attention for about two hours once we start crossing the plains, wiping out the palace will be the simple part. Give us a few more minutes after that and we can launch a second cannonball right on the enemy's heads. I reckon I shouldn't need to warn you to make sure you're well clear of 'em when that happens."

Hemlocke burst into a trilling cackle. "My good man, don't forget I was at Havenfall alongside most of you. I know exactly what that contraption can do."

A young soldier burst into the tent, his eyes widening at the sight of Hemlocke's group. He skirted around them and rushed to Agosti, slapping a fist to his cuirass in salute. "Begging your pardon, General, but we have a few companies of sellswords approaching camp from the west. Should we rally the men to defensive positions?"

"Don't bother," Mirabell piped up in a flat tone. "Those are the men Master Razarr hired to assist you. If nothing else, they should also be able to make an effective distraction themselves once the fighting starts."

Agosti nodded, eyeing the woman with a critical eye. Something about her unnerved him, though not to the extent Hemlocke did. Looking again, he realized it was the deadened expression in her eyes. Soulless and empty, like a doll. The last time he saw eyes like that was back when he was groveling under Bloodbeard's boot. Thinking of those days sent a shiver of mixed emotion racing down his spine. Anger, pity, and a healthy amount of fear. He didn't want to think of what the woman experienced to gain eyes like that.

"Those sellswords might actually be enough to help us pull this off," Medoro commented. "Supposing we send half to the rear to handle the Marine Cavalry, that would let us divert more resources to taking Whistl-evale. Once the Grand Duchess is dead, the rest should fall like dominos. Even the great Admiral Larimanz will lose the will to fight if we show him the results of his failure."

"What if the other realms get involved?" Adalbard questioned. "I've been keeping track of the newsletters, and apparently Livoria's called a summit of the Five Realms Council. We'll be wiped out if all of Alezon converges on us!"

Hemlocke emitting a dark, foreboding chuckle. "You worry too much, old man," he said. "The only realm you may have issues with is Galstein, who sent a single fleet to provide support. If the others try sending their forces over the border, they'll be unfortunate enough to stumble into a lovely trap I've laid across the western lands with assistance from your comrades."

Agosti's eyes narrowed. While it wasn't a stretch to assume Razarr procured assistance for such a task from the remainder of the Liberator forces out west, given his status as their financier—shoddy as his assistance was—any trap laid by the Aerivolk in front of him had to be unnaturally repugnant. The very air around him reeked of death in a way that made Bloodbeard look like a virginal saint, as ridiculous as it sounded given the actions which earned him that epithet.

The thought alone was enough to give him pause and question the sanity of allying himself to such a creature.

"Very well. We don't have much choice but to put some faith in whatever you did. For now, we focus on the task ahead. I'll lead some men to do a final check on the Shatterstar. Medoro, I want you to arrange space for the sellswords. Make sure they're placed where they'll be most useful. As for you…" Agosti cast a suspicious leer at Hemlocke, "try to keep that pet of yours under control until we're ready to depart. We meet back here at daybreak to signal the march."

Leading a small platoon up the hill, Agosti wondered, not for the first time, if the burden of command was more than he could handle. He wouldn't say he'd *never* dreamed of being in charge. That would be a bald-faced lie. The reality of the position, however, had him questioning every decision he'd made in life to get him to this point.

At least now I know why ol' Bloodbeard was such a cranky bastard, Agosti thought chuckling to himself. *Responsibility is a royal pain in the ass!*

The sound of cheering jarred him from his thoughts. He turned his head to glance back towards the camp. Adalbard was leading the men in one of his bombastic sermons. Behind the priest lay a small group of faumen captives they acquired from a village passed on the march. Agosti suppressed a smirk, knowing Adalbard would soon delve into one of his favorite pastimes and allow the soldiers to take the beasts apart piece by piece. The bishop had an unnecessary flair for the dramatic but his hatred of the faumen ran as deep as Agosti's, something the general could appreciate despite Adalbard's relative uselessness in everything else.

He turned back to the path and spotted a familiar group of bushes, tramped down as if crushed by something. Gesturing for the others to follow, Agosti led them down a dirt trail leading around to the other side. After a short walk, they came to a cliff jutting out behind the hill at the end of a steep incline. The craggy protrusions seen from the path had an ominous look in the darkness, the jagged stones hinted at by the moons floating overhead.

Tucked away amid a grove of dusk pines, their dark teal needles shimmering in the moonlight, sat a cavern. Inside, the Shatterstar loomed over them. The barrel, once polished, was covered in a thin layer of grime and debris from the surrounding woods.

"General," one soldier mumbled while circling around the device, "is there a specific reason you had us make this thing so dirty? What if it doesn't fire properly?"

"That's why we only wiped down the outer metal parts," Agosti answered. He leveled an irritated glare at the young man but restrained himself from raising his voice. "If the enemy's smart enough to send any forward scouts, we don't want them to find where we hid this thing. If polished, the metal would shine in any kind of light at the right angle. The dirt and leaves will prevent that."

The soldiers all stared at Agosti in admiration. He snorted and strode forward, checking inside the heavy metal crates behind the weapon. A breath of relief escaped his lips when he saw three lekrite cannonballs, each securely fastened and smothered in cloth covers, straw, and an abundance of wool.

Best treat these with more care than a sleeping infant. Considering what just one of these things did to Havenfall, I don't even want to imagine the destruction if all three were to blow at the same time...

A shiver ran down Agosti's spine at the thought. Seeing the other soldiers finishing their inspection of the Shatterstar itself, he shut the lid and secured the locks on each side. Given how securely they were nestled inside, Agosti doubted anything short of dropping a mountain on the crate would disturb the cannonballs. With a silent gesture of his hands, the general led them back down the trail towards camp. The closer they got, the louder the ruckus from Adalbard's sermon, indicating they'd likely moved on to the main event. Seeing the men gazing at him expectantly, he rolled his eyes and nodded. As they rushed off, Agosti felt a tremor in his bones. He may have been a hard ass, but he knew better than to deny the troops their fun.

For some of them, this would be their last chance to indulge in such activities.

"You're late, Obram."

Several hills over, Obram emerged from the trees atop an exhausted wiroch as Hemlocke watched Duarte scowl through his spyglass at Adalbard's revelry in the center of the Liberator's camp. While he cared not a whit for his allies' screaming victims, he knew the monk still harbored such sentimental thoughts despite his best efforts to hide them.

Such foolish notions were a superfluous disadvantage to saddle oneself with.

"Sorry if I couldn't remember which hill you decided to camp out on," Obram demurred with a mocking tone, dropping from his mount and filling a bowl of water for it from the leather sack dangling from his saddlebag. Once the beast was content with its refreshment, Obram jerked a thumb in a general northerly direction. "I've been running around these overgrown rock stumps since mid-afternoon."

"Did you at least learn anything useful after being gone all day?" Hemlocke asked while leaning against Grimghast and threading his fingers through its fur as it slept.

A dark grin spread over the Risbado's lips. "Now that you mention it, I think you'll love this. Turns out the Royalists are marching this way to try and get the drop on the Liberators before they can get close enough to destroy the capital. No clue when they'll get here, but I reckon it'll be before noon tomorrow. Even better, it looks like you brassed off a lot of people, Hemlocke. The Grand Duchess *herself* is going to be leading the Royalists!"

The sudden news jarred Hemlocke for a moment, though he was quick to recover with a grin to match Obram's sliding into place.

"Oh that's beautiful," Hemlocke murmured, his shoulders quivering. "I do love it when my enemies make things easier for me. If the duchess is stepping onto the battlefield, then I'd be willing to bet the royal treasury Kai and his wenches will be with her. I can finally finish that bastard and pay all three of them back for the damage they've done to my precious Nulla."

"Didn't that boy run you through back at Havenfall?" Obram asked. "I thought you'd be more pissed about that."

"Obram, look at me." Standing up, Hemlocke spread his wings and allowed his body to relax into a weary slump. His feathers were dull and frayed to the point they looked ready to fall out. His chest rose at an erratic pace. The rattle of his ragged breathing sounded more bestial than anything human. "This body is on its last legs, I'm afraid. I had a good run, but I'll be lucky if I make it to the end of the next moon.

"In all my years, Nulla has been the closest I ever had to a friend. So to see her return with new scars after every run in with that blasted Norzen was like a knife in my heart. I intend to end his wretched life, after I make him watch Nulla devour his females, of course. I have enough of Kai's elixir remaining to give me the strength I need. If I can do that, I'll be content to watch from Nulyma as the Black Tear Blight tears this continent apart."

Mirabell encircled her arms around Hemlocke, easing him back down while Grimghast eyed her with its beady crimson eye. She offered a respectful nod to the beast before stroking its cheek with a tender touch.

"We'll help you accomplish your goal," the assassin whispered. "One way or another. None of us have anyone or anything to return to. If I may ask, though, how do you plan to spread the Blight further without the Royalists finding out?"

Rather than speak, Hemlocke smirked and pointed towards a pile of crates nestled in a crevice dug into the side of the hill. A series of high-pitched squeaks rose from the crates every few seconds and, even in the dark, the shadows of tiny, clawed paws emerged from the gap between the slats, scratching at the wood.

"Those fools still have no clue how the Blight is spread, a fact I plan on taking full advantage of," Hemlocke bragged, fighting the urge to cackle. "Infecting the Royalists will be simple once they enter the woods here. After all, who would suspect the vessel of their destruction to be something so small, common, and unassumingly cute?"

CHAPTER XXIX

Kai scanned the area with nervous anticipation. With Velibor and Gideon remaining in Whistlevale to lead the capital's last line of defense alongside Bidelga, Fusette stood in the center of the command group at the army's center flanked by Kabuji and Saredi while Isolde rode atop a wiroch next to them. Kai and his party were lined up on Saredi's other side to the left of Fusette while Ottoten and Yulia stood by Kabuji with Captain Hans, Rorik, and several other senior officers. Hans' crew encircled the command group, each armed with a single cutlass and pistol shifting as they walked.

The air around the allied army was thick. Oppressive. Even as the sun began its slow ascent above the horizon, the troops were veiled in the shadows of the cavernous hills and trees surrounding them. They marched through the hills at a steady pace, their chainmail armor making a soft clink with each step that was drowned out by the clop of boots striking the ground in unison. For a moment, Kai worried the Liberators might hear their approach, though a quick scan of the otherwise quiet hills suggested the enemy remained tucked away in their tents.

"Are the troops ready?" Fusette asked.

Her cuirass and Frimanir shimmered in the sparse sunlight, while her ebony hair was tied into two long, thin braids. Kai tilted his head and cast a sweeping gaze over the gathered troops. Every group waved brilliantly colored banners and wore the distinctive armor of their homelands, but each group stood tall and proud together, all facing the hill to the west, where the scouting reports said the Liberation Army was encamped.

"It would appear so, Your Grace," Saredi answered, his fingers tracing the edge of his sword's scabbard. "The latest hawks we received said that the Rodekan and Belomian armies are closing in from the west and southwest, respectively. Please try to stick close to me once the fighting starts. The last thing we need is you running off and getting injured or captured by the enemy."

"I will go where I'm needed, Saredi, but thank you for watching out for me. Now then, our main goal will be to crush the enemy's command tent and capture their leaders. If possible, inform the troops to keep an eye out for Hemlocke and his group. There's no telling where they could be hiding and given what we know, he's the most dangerous piece on the enemy side of the field."

Taking a deep breath, Kai rapped a knuckle against the barrel of the blunderbuss strapped to his back. The weapon's weight felt unnatural against his back and made the march more tiring than it should have. Still, Fusette ordered him to carry it, thus he would do so.

"Allow us to worry about Hemlocke," he declared. The rest of the party nodded in unison. "If I know him, he won't hide himself directly among the Libbies. No, they'll be somewhere close enough to strike at our blind spot when we least expect it. Regardless, I'd like to give you some support just in case he tries switching things up. Teos!" The smuggler tipped his hat in recognition. "You alright with backing up Saredi as Her Grace's personal bodyguard?"

Teos' lips curved into a broad grin. "It'd be a pleasure. Besides, it'll be nice to work with Hans and the rest of the crew again." The former pirates almost let out a ringing cheer until their captain leveled a warning glare at them.

"We're glad to have you, Sir Teos," Fusette replied reaching out to grip the Soltauri's hand in a firm shake. "Do you have any idea where to start searching? Our scouts haven't had any luck in tracking them down."

Swiveling his head side to side, Kai stepped to the edge of a nearby cliff. He tilted his head up and took several deep inhalations. The aromatic scent of the pines calmed his thrumming heart, while he could detect the familiar aroma of his partners behind him. His lips settled in a thin line. He inhaled again. This time, he picked out the metal polish used to clean everyone's armor. The musky tang of the morning dew. Then...

Kai's eyes flew open. His ears swerved to his left, away from where the army was facing, followed by the rest of his head. Guiding a flow of Timber upwards, he fought down a wince as the sounds of the army became more pronounced. Tuning out as much as he could, he angled his ears and listened. After a few moments, he heard it—the familiar ragged breathing that haunted him at night. He sniffed again. There it was. A sharp, iron-filled odor mixed with decay and ammonia that he'd memorized by heart.

"I found them," Kai declared. "Or at the very least, I found Hemlocke. I'd say he's one, maybe two hills over."

Moon-eyed, Fusette goggled at him with a look of wonder. Kabuji and Isolde held equally stunned expressions. "How could you possibly know that?" Fusette inquired.

Memories of his squad rose to the forefront of Kai's mind, drawing a pinched scowl from the apothecary. "Grimghast," he growled. "After facing it so many times, I'll never forget the sound of that monster's breathing, or the rank stench it gives off, no matter how faint. I may not be able to tell exactly where they are, but at least I have a solid estimation."

"Spoken like a true Hunter. Very well. I'll leave you to it, cousin. Just do me a favor and try not to get yourself killed."

"Trust me," Kai replied with a confident grin. "I have too much at stake to let that beast get the better of me now. Alright, everyone. Let's do this."

"Gravebane," a throaty voice called from behind. Kai looked back and saw Dewthorn, Burnsong, and Swiftlock all standing at attention, their fists clasped to their hearts in salute. "If any of you find yourself struggling, remember your training. Each of you on your own are strong enough to compete with the best the Exarchs have to offer. Now give 'em Nulyma."

Offering the older knight a solemn nod, Kai led the rest of his party down the opposite path heading further east. Glancing back, he saw Fusette stare after them with her lance raised. The spearhead shone in the morning sun peeking between the hilltops. Beside her, Saredi and the other two leaders offered salutes of their own. Smiling in appreciation, Kai turned back to see his friends staring with resolute determination.

A heavy weight settled in Kai's chest, his mane prickling in anticipation. After all this time, one way or another, accounts would be settled. There was no way to know how the dice would roll when they found Hemlocke, but he was prepared to see it through to the bitter end. It was the least he could do to respect his squad's memory. The six tromped through the mossy grass, their eyes looking to the hills beyond where their self-inflicted destiny awaited.

As they reached the bottom of the hill and merged onto the path leading through to the next, they heard Fusette's voice resonate through the air. Birds were sent scattering into the sky and various critters along the forest floor darted for safety at the duchess' war cry.

"For freedom, my friends! Attack!"

Agosti stood alone in his command tent, wondering why the rest of his officers were so late. He peeked through the flaps and grimaced, spotting Medoro and Adalbard ambling towards the tent looking exhausted.

"I thought I told you to be here at daybreak," the general growled, "and where are the others?"

Medoro responded with a dismissive snort. "Those damned sellswords insisted on making a ruckus half the night. Nothing we said could quiet them down. Worse still, I overheard a few of them bragging how they were promised the royal treasury as payment for their presence here today. You'll have to excuse me if I'm a tad irritable today."

A well of rage swelled in Agosti's gut. *There's only one person who could've made those jackals a promise like that.*

"If I ever get my hands on Razarr, I'll rip his spine out through his ass."

A hearty chuckle rose from Medoro. "For once, Valdis, you and I can agree on something. Considering the situation, part of me wonders if—"

The two were interrupted when a bloodcurdling sound echoed among the hills. From where he stood, Agosti noticed several men poking their heads out from their tents, gazing about in a delirious stupor. He spun towards the north, his eyes bulbous.

"Am I imagining things or did that sound like a woman shouting her bloody head off? What in Nulyma is a *woman* doing out here?"

Medoro swore. "That voice...Valdis, you dipwit, that's not just any woman. That's the Grand Duchess!"

Behind the two officers, Adalbard's face turned a sickly pale. "T-the Grand Duchess?" he stammered. "But that's impossible. That would mean—"

The ground itself vibrated under the men's feet. Adalbard stumbled backwards, landing on his rump. A low rumble grew in intensity with each passing second. More and more soldiers emerged from their tents, many scratching their heads and questioning each other. Agosti tuned out their ramblings and focused on the sounds further away. His frown deepened as the rumble awakening them grew louder. A second sound accompanied it, one that sent a bone-numbing chill through his entire body.

The clank of metal and shouts of enraged men.

Frozen in place, Agosti watched in horror as the hills themselves appeared to move, a roiling mass surging towards them. He pulled the spyglass from his belt and peered through it, cursing when he recognized the armor of the Whistlevale city guard adorned by the center mass. What concerned him more were the other groups wearing distinctly foreign armor, among them the pristine white of the Galstan Holy Navy.

"Damn it to bloody Nulyma!" Agosti screeched. "The enemy is already here, you incompetent dipwits! Get up and fight!"

The general's furious roar spurred the Liberators to action. They scrambled to don their own armor and retrieve their weapons. The rapport of muskets rang out in response. What left Agosti speechless seconds later was seeing half of his soldiers abandoning their tents and bolting half-naked for the presumed safety of the woods. He quickly spotted Medoro among their number, rushing into the trees with several soldiers in pursuit.

"What are you doing? Get back here, you cowards!"

Shrieks resounded through the hills as the alliance reached the camp's edge. The sound of enemy pistols firing back pierced Agosti's ears, along with a deafening boom that sounded unlike anything he knew of. Looking through his spyglass again, he noticed some of the city guardsmen carrying bulky firearms with a flared muzzle.

What in the name of Galen are those?

Agosti got his horrific answer moments later when a Royalist sailor advanced on a Liberator and aimed the massive gun at his opponent's chest. The weapon belched a flash of fire and metal, sending Agosti stumbling back after seeing the Liberator's body torn apart in an explosion of gore by a mass of iron pellets.

Biting his lip, Agosti knew there was only one way to get their men back in fighting spirit. "Oi, priest! We could really use one of your serm—"

The general's voice died in his throat at the sight of Adalbard scurrying onto a nearby wiroch and spurring it into a full run. The bishop flew past, his mount carrying him to the southeast towards where he saw Hemlocke's group leaving the night before. Fists shaking, Agosti leaned back and expressed his frustration in the only way he knew.

"Fuck!"

Casting a forlorn gaze towards the battle, Agosti saw just as many men attempting to mount a defense as were fleeing into the trees. The same feminine roar from before stopped him cold, drawing his eyes towards its source. Peering through the spyglass, he saw the Grand Duchess in the thick of the fight, twirling an ornate lance with a level of skill he would've found impressive from a woman...were it not for the feline ears atop her head and twin tails lashing behind her. Beside her, he spotted that winds-be-damned Soltauri from Hans' crew, Teos if he remembered correctly, sweeping his halberd and cutting down multiple Liberators at once with each strike.

"That damned Razarr was telling the truth," Agosti growled. He wasn't sure how trustworthy the forge master was, given his duplicity in providing less than pristine equipment to their cause. At the very least, it appeared the man wasn't yanking his chain when he claimed the Grand Duchess herself was a peltneck.

Tightening his grip on his sword, he spat out a string of curses before rushing down the path Adalbard took moments before, towards where the Shatterstar lay. If they were going to lose this battle, then at least he'd make sure the enemy died with them.

He failed to notice the pair of eyes tracking him as he ran headlong into the forest.

The silence of the woods cast an ominous pall that made the morning summer air feel much colder than it was.

With each step through the grass, Kai was reminded of his first encounter with Grimghast. His eyes darting in every direction, watching for any sign of movement. The others marched behind him, each with their weapons drawn and surveying the trees as critically as he was. The path they followed upwards was empty and mostly reclaimed by nature. The only reason they spotted it was Lucretia guiding them with a map detailing every pathway weaving through Ballad's End.

"It's way too quiet," Ione murmured, her shield raised and cutlass pointed at the ground in a relaxed pose. "I don't know about the rest of you, but it's giving me the heebies."

"That just means Grimghast is somewhere nearby," Kai reminded her. "I've only ever seen it like this when something on the level of a Great Beast is in the area, and there hasn't been a bulwark deer sighting in these hills for years."

Maple nodded, nudging a shoulder against Kai's arm. "He's right. It was the same way when we ran into that deer back in Grantide. Keep your eyes peeled and reflexes sharp, everyone."

"Wait," Orelia said, bringing the party to a stop. "Does anyone else hear something?"

Frowning, Kai swiveled his ears. It only took a second to determine what she was talking about—the familiar sound of a wiroch's talons stomping through the dirt at a full sprint. It was accompanied by another sound. Heavy, ragged breathing and the indistinct muttering of a hoarse voice.

"There's someone here," Kai said. His eyes searched the path below, widening when he saw a wiroch rushing along. What stunned him most was the identity of the rider. He let out a rumbling growl from his chest, pointing out the figure and none too surprised to hear his wife hiss beside him.

"Adalbard!" Orelia snapped. Her hands clenched tight around her staff, a visible tear running down her cheek. Kai reached over to brush the tear away, his fingers drifting down to take her hand in a gentle squeeze.

The apothecary sighed and glanced at his friends. "Looks like we're taking a detour. After everything that bastard has done, we can't allow Adalbard to escape."

Lucretia smirked and waved him off. "You three can go. I know Orelia needs the closure more than any of us. Ione, Morgan, and I will continue upwards and try to locate Hemlocke from the top of this hill."

"I'd rather we not split up," Kai retorted. He was left speechless when Lucretia gripped him by the mane and yanked him down, her piercing gaze pinning him in place.

The scholar's lips curved into a haughty grin. "Go. Ione has the warhorn, so if we need help, you will know before anyone else. I promise the three of us will be fine. As Dewthorn said, we trained for this."

As much as he wanted to argue the point, Kai knew Lucretia could be more stubborn than him when she wanted. Instead, he offered a single nod and signaled Orelia to lead the way. The Vesikoi rushed off with Maple on her heels. Kai whispered a hurried prayer for the others to stay safe, an action copied by Ione, before bolting after the two women.

Orelia weaved through the trees with the same practiced ease Kai remembered seeing back in Faith Hollow. If she felt the sting of low-hanging branches scratching her arms and leaving thin cuts in her shirt's sleeves, she didn't acknowledge it. She moved like a woman possessed, her staff brushing aside smaller branches while ducking and swerving around those too big to move. The entire time, Kai could see Orelia's gaze never wavering from the fleeing priest.

Adalbard's mount took a sudden turn and starting cantering up a path which would take him past the trio. At a glance, it was clear the bishop wasn't paying attention to where his wiroch was going; his eyes remained fixated on the path behind him while the forest flew past at a blurring pace.

Stopping at a boulder laying on a plateau next to the path, Orelia waited as Kai and Maple sidled next to her. Before Kai could ask what her plan was, Orelia let loose a bellow of rage.

"Adalbard!"

The bishop's head snapped forward in an instant, his eyes widening at the sight of the former priestess. The wiroch he rode squawked at the sudden noise and jerked to the side. Adalbard's lack of awareness left him open to the low hanging branch his mount ducked to avoid.

Kai winced at the audible smack resounding through the woods when Adalbard noticed the branch too late, his face slamming into it at top riding speed. The force of the impact pitched the bishop from his wiroch, sending him tumbling to the dirt and his mitre blowing away in the wind while the bird continued scampering away. He looked at Maple and signaled with his hands, the two splitting up to swerve around Adalbard's opposite side before he could recover.

"Oh, my head," Adalbard moaned. He rubbed his balding pate with a pinched expression, slowing rising.

"That headache will soon be the least of your worries," Orelia snapped. She leapt from the rock and strode forward, rapping her staff to the dirt with each step. Kai and Maple remained in place, arms crossed over their chests and their weapons sheathed.

Adalbard returned Orelia's glare, his eyes flickering to her companions. "I suppose it was too much to pray that damned Aerivolk and his pet would finish you off," he grumbled. "Three on one is hardly a fair shake, though. What happened to all that blathering you used to spew about justice, Sister Orelia?"

Kai met his partner's gaze and offered a smile, nodding to the unspoken question passing between them. Orelia smiled back before directing a piercing scowl at Adalbard.

"They won't be interfering in this, *Your Excellency*," Orelia said, drawling the honorific in a biting, sarcastic tone. "This is between you and me. Their only job will be to make sure you don't try to scarper off and avoid your judgment."

Despite wanting to keep out of the fight, Kai kept a sharp eye on Adalbard's motions. Should the disgraced priest try escaping, he wanted to be ready to block. Memories of their last encounter in the royal archives, of the fear in Tuvi's eyes when the priest held her hostage, churned a bubbling fire in Kai's chest. Clenching his fist, he leaned against a tree and let his ears swivel in place, searching for unusual sounds.

"You have the gall to assume you can judge me?!" Adalbard roared. He brandished his staff with lips drawn tight in fury. "Only the Wind Saints are allowed to judge a man of my station and breeding. I should've turned you away the day you darkened the doorsteps of Stahl Granz."

Orelia snorted. "You claim your actions serve the church, yet all I see is a murderous beast using the Wind Saints' names to excuse your bigoted views. I have no doubt Master Galen would break your neck himself if he were alive and saw your deeds."

"Shut your filthy mouth! A beast like you knows nothing!"

"I know you seem to be protesting a little too strongly," Orelia quipped, her smile widening. "Don't like being called out for the disgusting creature you really are?"

"The only creatures I see are the three of you. Now begone!"

A gleam of silver darting from Adalbard's robe was the only warning Orelia got as he lunged with a hidden dagger. The blade's serrated edge gave it a wicked appearance, its hilt fashioned into the shape of a wolf's head and a prominent blood groove forged along the serration. Kai's visage darkened at the liquid sheen on the blade's cutting edge.

"Watch yourself, Ora!" Kai warned. "That blade is poisoned!"

Orelia eyed the dagger with a brief look of concern. Shaking her head, she twirled her staff and knocked Adalbard's own aside when he thrust its spiked head towards her. The two circled one another like wary predators, each searching for an opening.

Emitting a heaving growl, Adalbard rushed forward with a downward slash. Orelia ducked behind a tree, leaving the blade to tear splinters of bark free when it flew across the trunk. She lifted a boot to Adalbard's ribs and pushed the bishop backwards. He skidded across the ground with a grunt.

Scrambling to his feet, Adalbard scuttled behind a tree. Kai and Maple smirked and circled around in case he wanted to make an escape attempt. To their surprise, he only looked to be catching his breath.

"Don't get overconfident, Sister," Adalbard gasped. "Your luck will run out soon enough. Then you'll suffer the same fate as those accursed brats you were so fond of."

Gritting his teeth, Kai searched Orelia's gaze for the anger that often surfaced when the orphans of Stahl Granz were mentioned. However, what he saw was grim acceptance, her lips set in a pursed line and clutching her staff in an iron grip.

"You truly are pathetic," Orelia said. Marching towards the tree her opponent was hidden behind, twigs snapped under her boots and her breathing grew heavier. More focused. "There is no greater oppression than to harm others under the banners of law and faith and in the name of false justice. The lives you've taken cannot plead for justice. Thus, it falls to me to ensure their souls can know peace!"

Emitting a strangled roar, Adalbard rushed from his hiding place and charged. Swinging the dagger with the ferocity of a rabid beast, the priest pushed Orelia back. She parried the blade with surprising ease, though Adalbard's fury seemed to fuel a speed that defied his age. Every deflection failed to open the man's defenses, his movements too tight for Orelia to counter. Taking another step back, Orelia cursed when her heel struck a large rock that sent her tumbling onto her back.

Adalbard leapt on top of her, abandoning his staff in favor of trying to drive his dagger with both hands into Orelia's breast. A loud clang echoed through the forest as her staff's plated head stopped the blade cold.

"I warned you, stupid wench," Adalbard growled. "The Wind Saints will protect me, just as they have throughout this damned war. Once I'm done with you, I'll slaughter the rest of your abominable family as an offer to the new order!"

Orelia's face darkened. "Let's see the Saints protect you from this!"

With a wide grin, Orelia launched her knee upwards. An ominous thud rang among the trees, accompanied by the sound of tearing fabric and a strained hiss. Kai and Maple stood transfixed, the latter's hands covering her mouth while Kai's face pinched inward in phantom pain. Orelia's knee lay buried in Adalbard's groin, the priest's face turning a pasty white with his mouth hanging open. The impact shifted her staff just enough for the dagger to slide past and graze her left upper arm.

Snorting, Orelia shoved Adalbard off. She saw Kai moving towards her, his hand reaching into his satchel. He skidded to a stop when she shook her head and held an open palm out, kicking the dropped dagger away at the same time. Adalbard hit the dirt in a fetal position, cradling his broken crotch. His eyes, filled with rage, rose to meet Orelia's while he moaned in pain.

"At least I still cut you," he snarled. "That poison doesn't have any known antidote and will probably kill you within the hour. Best say good-bye to your family."

The priest's delirious glee withered to fear when Orelia only smirked. Reaching up, she tore a hole in the sleeve of her shirt to reveal a thin steel rerebrace covering the upper arm and gleaming in the sparse sun. Kai's face brightened, a sense of pride swelling up within his breast.

"I had a feeling at least one of you would carry a poisoned weapon, given Hemlocke's love for them," Orelia said, "so I decided to hide some light armor under my clothes. It's not a perfect defense, but it worked well enough. The Wind Saints are dead and gone, Adalbard, and prayers can only do so much beyond offering comfort. The only one who can protect you is yourself."

Mouth twisted in terror, Adalbard scuttled away and tried to push himself into a run. Orelia pulled the pistol she received from her father and aimed low, fired a single shot into the disgraced bishop's knee and sent him sprawling backwards screaming in pain. She grabbed him by the collar and hauled Adalbard to his feet, letting her staff fall to the ground. Pulling the sash from his vestment, she wrapped it around the struggling priest's neck and wrenched her arms outward. The cloth's length gave her plenty of slack to plant a boot on the man's back and slam him belly first back on the dirt, drawing the sash tighter. Adalbard choked, trying in vain to pull himself free but unable to overcome Orelia's superior strength. His cheeks shifted to a pastel red, darkening as Orelia pulled back harder. The priest's arms flailed, seeking anything to cut the sash loose. The red gave way to a dark indigo, Adalbard's desperate pleas growing softer. Kai and Maple looked on in silence, neither moving to assist.

After a few more minutes passed, Adalbard went limp, his arms flopping to the ground. Eyes rolled to the back of his head, mouth hanging open as Orelia relaxed her hold and allowed his head to rest against the mossy grass. She massaged her worn hands and gave the corpse one final glare before tromping back to where her family waited.

Kai enveloped Orelia in his arms as she collapsed against him, sobbing. Maple joined the hug, wrapping her arms around the other woman and humming a lullaby.

"You did it, Ora," Maple whispered. "That bastard got what he deserved."

Orelia nodded, letting out soft sniffles while Kai brushed her tears away. "What matters is the children can rest easy in Finyt now. Kai, Maple...would you mind praying with me?"

"Of course," Kai answered, brushing his lips over her forehead.

Together, the three settled in the shade of a nearby sun birch nestled among the dusk pines, its white bark shining against its neighbors. Clasping their hands together, Orelia gazed upwards and released a weary sigh.

"Honorable Wind Saints, hear our prayer," she murmured. "May the souls of those lost to us find peace in the gardens of Finyt. May their surviving loved ones find the strength to continue living and honor their memories. And may your virtues shield and guide us in forging a world where vitriol such as what we fight against cannot take root. In this, we humbly ask of you from the depths of our spirits. *Zephyrus ulme.*"

"*Zephyrus ulme,*" Kai and Maple mimicked. While not commonly used anymore, the phrase was a remnant of Centric's linguistic predecessor, Meluvian. Roughly translated, it meant 'winds of love,' if Kai remembered his church history correctly.

Rising to their feet, the trio left Adalbard where he lay and doubled back towards where their friends continued on. Kai's ears twitched, turning to the sides. The sounds of battle further back pounded in his ears, giving him a slight headache. Adjusting their position, he inhaled deep.

It was faint, but he detected Grimghast's distinct odor a little to the northeast. Gesturing in that direction, he led his partners through the trees. With Maple and Orelia tucked against his sides as they walked, he let memories of their first meeting with Tuvi and the other orphans of Stahl Granz flutter through his mind. While they couldn't bring the lost children back, he was glad to see Orelia bring justice to their killer and offer their spirits some measure of peace in the hereafter.

Cacovis, please watch over the others until we catch up, Kai prayed.

CHAPTER XXX

"I hope you have a good reason for leading us away from the battle, Sir Teos."

A ball of unease settled in Fusette's gut. She and the rest of Hans' crew slinked through the forests of Ballad's End after Teos, who looked to be searching for something with all the intensity of a miner seeking precious metal.

Or *someone*, now that she thought about it.

"I apologize if my actions seem reckless, Fusette," Teos responded, "but I saw a Liberator officer leaving this way and I'm certain it's not because he wanted to stop for tea and biscuits."

Fusette suppressed the laugh threatening to bubble out at the remark. Teos liked to present himself as seriously as Lucretia most of the time, but then he would say something to remind her he could be quite witty and endearing when he wished. They marched off the beaten path, sneaking uphill amid the shadows of the towering pines. Their scent calmed Fusette's nerves, giving her a sense of peace even as the sounds of the fight raged behind them. She knew Saredi was going to have a lecture for the ages when he caught up with them, but she decided it would be worth it.

"This ain't like you, Teos," Hans said from his place behind Fusette. The older pirate carried a battered cutlass, worn and chipped from years of heavy use. "You wouldn't abandon the main fight to go after one piddling officer. You recognized him, didn't you?"

"Aye," Teos answered. He turned back to give Hans a grim frown. "Remember Agosti? Bloodbeard's first mate back when I was with the crew?"

The older pirate hissed a curse. "Sodding Nulyma! The officer we're chasing is Valdis Agosti? Shucks, that explains why you're so keen to run him down."

The unease in Fusette's belly worsened. In the short time she'd known him, she couldn't remember Hans reacting with such vitriol. "Who is this man? I assume you lot have a history with him," she asked.

Teos released a sigh and tapped the stub where his horn used to be. "He's the dipwit who broke my horn off. He's also the one who ambushed us on the trip to Havenfall and it turns out he still keeps my horn as a damned trophy." A wave of horrified gasps rang through the crew. "Most importantly, he's got a wallop of a mad-on for the Norzen. It's rather funny seeing him go ballistic every time he sees Kai."

Rolling her eyes, Fusette tapped Frimanir's shaft against the ground. "Oh, he's going to *love* seeing me, then," she proclaimed in a haughty tone. The duchess flipped her curled hair back with a melodramatic flair, allowing her ears and tails to flutter in the breeze. The crew burst into snickers, though Teos looked ready to explode judging by the dark crimson tint in his puffed out cheeks as he held back his laughter.

"Look alive, lads and lassies," Hans warned, raising a long finger. "I think we found him."

Fusette dropped to her knees behind a tree, watching the others do the same. A sudden weight was pushed against her chest. Blinking, she looked down to see a pistol with the hammer cocked back and ready to fire. Her eyes rose to glance at the pirate who handed it to her, a blonde Wasini woman with a finger-length scar on her left cheek. She peered out from her hiding place to see a single man in Liberator uniform with shoddy plate armor stomping down the path above them. Using a spyglass, she saw what looked like an admiral's brass stars adorning his epaulets. His sword was the only item on his person that appeared to be in good condition.

The man's face was twisted in anger, his rounded cheeks scarlet with sweat dripping along his skin.

"Hans," Teos whispered. "Do you think you can pin him at this angle?"

"Easy enough," the captain answered, drawing a gleaming pistol from his belt. "You sure you don't wanna do the honors yourself?"

"You know I'm a clod with a gun," Teos said. "Besides, if we can put him down without him noticing, it'll save us some trouble. If you miss the shot and he figures out we're here, *then* I'll deal with him myself. Considering how much he hates the faumen, though, he wouldn't abandon the battle without a reason. No, I think he's trying to get to that damned cannon."

The unease Fusette felt grew and shifted at Teos' words. Writhing and bubbling like a boiling cauldron, it morphed into a mass of righteous fury. While she didn't experience Havenfall's destruction the same way Kai's party did, she still had to read the reports of the aftermath. She couldn't imagine the pain her cousin went through, seeing the only home he'd ever known obliterated in a flash, though she had a fair idea given her conversations with Maple and Orelia.

"If that truly is his goal," she said, "then it would be in our best interest to stop him before he reaches it. Take your shot, Hans."

The Vesikoi nodded, raising his pistol and taking careful aim. Fusette held her breath, eyes locked on the retreating Liberator. She clamped her hands over her ears, folding them down just before the pistol went off with a deafening crack.

To the group's surprise, Agosti threw himself behind a tree in that instant, leaving Hans' bullet to zoom past and slap into a tree trunk further up.

"Damn it!" Hans swore.

Agosti's cackling laughter echoed through the trees. "You idiots didn't think you'd kill me that easily, did you?" he boasted. "I suspected some-one was following me out here but I never would've guessed it'd be you, Hans. How's it feel to subject yourself to the whims of a peltneck, ya old rockfish?"

"It's a damn sight better than having to take orders from yer ugly mug!" Hans shot back. "Not that you'd have let us join anyway."

Fusette moved to step out from behind the tree, only for Teos to grip her arm and shake his head. She met the smuggler's gaze and gave a hesitant nod. Settling onto her knees, she watched him rise and trudge up the hill towards Agosti.

"You'd best give up now," Teos said. "We have you outnumbered."

"I have better things to do than waste my time with you," Agosti snapped. Reaching into the pouch at his waist, he removed two objects that brought Teos to a halt: a stonehood bomb and a sparkstone.

"What in bleeding Nulyma is that?" Hans asked. "A bomb?" The rest of the crew mumbled in confusion while glancing amongst themselves.

Teos tightened his grip on his halberd. "Careful, everyone. That particular bomb has stonehood pollen inside," he warned.

"Lovely," Hans said, "just what we needed. Now if only the pissant would drop it on his own foot after he lights it, we'd be good as gold."

Teos froze. Fusette fought another round of giggles as he turned to his former captain, mouth hanging open.

"Hans, you're a genius!"

The older faumen blinked and glanced at Teos in brazen confusion. "I am? News to me. Here I always thought I was just a drunken ol' fish!"

The hiss of a crackling fuse resounded through the woods, drawing everyone's eyes to Agosti. He reeled his arm back and launched the bomb, aiming for Teos. Muttering a curse, he spun his halberd and gripped the shaft with both hands.

"Old man, remember how we used to make a game of using the hand nets to fling a paddlepod ball around the deck and try to catch it?" Teos asked. Hans threaded a finger through his beard, a befuddled expression on his face.

"Aye. We still do that whenever we need to blow off some steam. Why?"

"Watch this."

The bomb spun in air, its fuse shining amid the shadows cast by the canopy overhead. From behind the tree, Fusette watched it descend towards Teos, her eyes widening as he broadened his stance and kept his eyes on the small explosive. At first, she wondered if his plan was to smack the bomb back towards Agosti using his weapon as a makeshift bat. Part of her felt such an idea was unnecessarily dangerous, as the impact could potentially set the bomb off the moment he struck it.

Instead, she was stunned when Teos swung the weapon forward at a much slower speed than expected, its blade facing the ground. The halberd slowed as the bomb approached. Just as the explosive reached him, Teos eased off with a gentle touch, allowing it to push the halberd back. She watched the smuggler juggle the bomb with his halberd's blade, a broad grin stretched from ear to ear.

"Hey, Agosti...catch!"

Tightening his grip, Teos threw an expert swing and lobbed the bomb back into the air. Towards the moon-eyed Agosti.

"You son of a—!"

Whatever Teos was the son of never quite escaped the Liberator's lips before his own bomb exploded just short of reaching him. The ensuing blast tore out a chunk of ground under Agosti's feet, bringing part of the path crashing down and dragging the furious officer with it.

A cloud of dust enveloped the area, leaving Fusette unable to see. She could make out a darker patch of dust, likely the stonehood pollen, where the bomb had exploded moments ago. Within minutes, however, the dust dispersed to reveal Agosti lying in a heap atop a pile of broken stone and covered in dirt. She bit back a gasp when he coughed and staggered to his feet with only a few new scuffs adorning his body.

He's quite durable for a human, Fusette thought.

"That does it," Agosti growled. "This time, I'm gonna snap off your other horn and use it to carve your damned heart out!"

Hans and the rest of the crew jeered, drawing their weapons and stepping forward. To Fusette's shock, Teos blocked them from rushing the prone officer.

"Remember what I said earlier?" Teos said. "I'll handle him. Besides, I kinda prefer it this way now that I think of it."

Agosti snorted. "You think you'll be able to pay me back for breaking your horn? I'm not the same man I was back when we scuffled on the Great Ardei."

"Unfortunately for you," Teos retorted, "neither am I. And I could care less about avenging my horn, though I'll admit I hated you for years because of it. If anything, losing it taught me more than I realized. Like valuing what's truly important in life."

Twirling his halberd, Teos assumed an open stance, keeping the blade low to the ground. The two men circled each other while Hans and the crew spread out to surround them, forming an impromptu arena. Agosti's sword gleamed in the broken sunbeams. Teos pawed the ground with one hoof, his droopy ears fluttering among the breeze.

Agosti shifted a foot forward and lunged. Teos eyed the sword flashing through the air towards him, swinging his halberd to parry the sudden strike. The smuggler winced, blinking away the sparks from their clash. He pushed Agosti back and sent the other man careening into a tree.

"Not bad," Agosti said, spitting a glob of saliva onto the ground. "You're a fair bit quicker than I remember."

Teos said nothing. Fusette watched in amazement as his eyes narrowed while shifting his stance with a grace she never would've expected from the gruff smuggler. Hans and the crew looked equally thunderstruck by his dance-like movements. Teos took a deep breath and struck the moment he exhaled.

"Gah!"

Agosti dove aside as Teos' halberd bit into the tree, sending shards of bark flying. The Liberator snarled and lashed out again. This time, he let out a cry of joy when his sword grazed Teos' rib cage. What he didn't expect was for Teos to yank his weapon free, brushing the blow aside with the shaft before raising a hoof and delivering a devastating sidekick to Agosti's chest.

"Teos!" Hans shouted. He took a step forward but froze when Teos turned and leveled a searing glare at the older man.

"I'm fine," he growled. Pressing a hand to the shallow cut, he frowned. "It was worth it to kick that bastard's ribs in."

"I ain't dead yet," Agosti replied, rising to his feet yet again.

Every instinct in Fusette's mind screamed to take the pistol and aim for Agosti while the man's back was facing her. However, not only did her heart know Teos would feel insulted if she stepped in on his behalf mid-fight, she also doubted her ability to land a killing shot.

The two men weaved forward and back, their weapons sending sparks everywhere with every clash. Teos took a moment to wipe the sweat from his brow, cursing when Agosti took advantage and slashed at his exposed leg. A clump of fur was cleaved free, fluttering away. Teos was unable to back away quickly enough, however. Agosti reached forward with his free hand and gripped the smuggler's tail, yanking hard. Teos roared in pain and dropped to his knees, his halberd clattering to the ground. Around them, Hans and his crew turned the air blue with their profanity.

'Hah!" Agosti crowed, his lips curved into a sinister smile. "You damn goats can't stand having your tails pulled, can you? Looks like I win. Now to gut you like the beast you are while your friends watch."

Seeing Teos' face pinched in agony tore at Fusette's heartstrings. She watched Hans draw his own cutlass and prepare to charge. Teos, even through the pain, shook his head at the older faumen, stopping Hans in his tracks. The shouts and slurs flung by the crew faded to dull background noise in Fusette's head. Her entire focus was on Teos, whose strength seemed to have been sapped from his body. Gritting her teeth, she made her decision.

Lady Vadako, please let him forgive me for my foolishness.

Stepping out from behind the tree, the duchess took a deep breath and let loose a roar of anger that froze everyone in the vicinity. "Unhand him this instant!" Fusette demanded, allowing her ears and tails to stand tall.

Agosti spun to face her, his face paling. "It's you," he whispered. Fusette could see the terror in Teos' eyes at her appearance, but she refused to falter. Her eyes met Agosti's and the Liberator licked his lips in blatant glee as he moved to attack.

Unfortunately, his desire to kill Fusette distracted him enough that his hold on Teos' tail slackened.

The smuggler breathed a sigh of relief, though when his head lifted, Fusette noticed the scarlet ring of the Frenzy Haze around his eyes. Before Agosti could take two steps towards the duchess, Teos snarled and swung the halberd back, embedding its pointed blade in Agosti's kidney.

With a pained gurgle, Agosti slouched forward clutching at Teos' halberd, trying to forcibly remove it. He was taken off his feet when Teos lifted up and slammed the general on his back. Leaves and dirt flew into the air from the impact, gliding back down as Teos pressed a hoof on Agosti's chest, pinning him to the ground.

"Your Grace, why did you reveal yourself instead of staying safe?" Teos asked, his eyes gazing at the young monarch in confusion.

Fusette grinned. "First of all, what have I told you about being formal with me? Second, if I wanted to stay safe, I would've simply done as Saredi wished and barricaded myself in the palace. I came here to make a difference, Teos, and that includes defending my friends."

Eyes wide, Teos shook in place. "Lady Fusette...," he mumbled.

"Damn you, you peltneck bitch!" Agosti screamed. He pounded a fist against Teos' leg, though all it did was prompt the Soltauri to lean more weight on that leg, increasing the pressure on Agosti's chest.

"Such a filthy mouth," Fusette murmured. She stepped forward and used her lance to send Agosti's sword flying with a flick of the wrist. "I suppose Kai has heard that odious slur from your lips more times than he cares to count. Tell me, Mr. Agosti, what drives such unrelenting hatred? What have my people done to you to deserve the unwarranted malevolence you've expressed for so long?"

"What does it matter?" Agosti spat. "You hellcats are nothing but beasts, even more than the rest of them. Why else would Cacovis destroy everything the way she did? You say my hatred is unwarranted, but it's because you Norzen have proven you're nothing but a worthless stain on this world. One that deserves to be wiped out!"

Fusette shook her head. "And this is why the true history will be taught once this is all said and done. I doubt I can change the heart of someone as bitter as you. Even if I could, your crimes in this war are too numerous and atrocious to warrant redemption."

"So that's it?" Agosti said with a cocky smirk. "Gonna have your pet goat finish me off as punishment for my supposed crimes against you monsters?"

"Actually..."

Before anyone could react, Fusette drew the pistol she was handed earlier and aimed. The brief lessons she received at the palace flashed through her mind. Taking a deep breath, she held steady and pulled the trigger.

A sharp crack rent the air and splotches of dark crimson splattered across the dirt. Agosti's head snapped to the side, a long gash torn into the side of his neck. Teos gaped at the thunderstruck woman as she gave him a sheepish grin and tossed the pistol back to the Wasini who gave it to her. Before anyone could speak, she lowered Frimanir's pointed blade and rammed it into Agosti's heart. The man gagged, releasing a bloody gurgle before his head lolled back with empty eyes. Meeting everyone's stunned expressions, she grinned and spoke directly to Agosti's corpse.

"Why would I waste my friend's energy after the pain you inflicted when I'm perfectly capable of passing judgment myself?"

Sensing everyone's eyes on her, she peered at Teos and gave a nervous chuckle. "Umm...I meant to do that," said Fusette in a shaky, hesitant tone.

Teos burst into laughter, leaning against the nearest tree. Hans and his crew followed suit, several of them rolling in the grass in hysterics. The sight of them reveling in their small victory filled Fusette's heart with warmth and hope that the rest of the battle would pass easily.

The short blast of a warhorn boomed behind them, sending everyone scrambling to face where the sound had come from. Fusette's heart pounded in her chest like a drum, her pupils dilating and darting in search of the one who produced the sudden sound. A familiar voice reverberated through the forest moments later.

"Sodding Dolmaru," a crisp, low voice rang, "is that you, Your Grace?"

To Fusette's pleasant surprise, the voice was followed by a broad-chested figure slinking through the trees. A Wasini man in full Royal Navy battle armor appeared, an admiral's stars adorning his shoulders and a throng of sailors marching in step behind him, each bathed in a thin layer of dirt. His neck-length sandy brown hair was shaggier and greyer than she remembered and covered in sticks and leaves. It was relieving to see his amber eyes still so full of life.

"Well I'll be," Fusette said, "it's good to see you again after so long, Admiral Larimanz."

CHAPTER XXXI

Lucretia led the way through the forests, her overcloak rustling against each branch they passed by on the way. Behind her, Morgan and Ione kept pace while swiveling their heads every few seconds. The trio's weapons were all drawn and pointed at the ground, ready to move at a moment's notice. The dead silence continued permeating the area, sending a tremor of fear down the scholar's neck. Glancing upwards, she felt a since of calm upon realizing they were close to the summit. It would be difficult for their enemies to get the drop on them, so long as they had the high ground, and the hill's craggy, bald peak appeared empty, suggesting Hemlocke and his cohorts were hidden among the trees further down.

"I will be most thankful when this is all said and done," Lucretia whispered. "In fact, if we live through this, I hope to return to Runegard and never leave the city walls unless absolutely necessary."

"Don't you say such things," Ione reprimanded. "We're all gonna make it out of here. I refuse to believe otherwise."

A dry twig snapped under Lucretia's boot, causing the three friends to freeze in place. Their eyes darted about, searching for movement. They saw nothing, releasing a collective breath before moving on.

The shifting winds around them provided the only music to their advance, producing a soft whistle that both calmed and worried Lucretia. Part of her worry stemmed from the unnatural nature of the silence. Knowing that Grimghast was somewhere in the vicinity was bad enough. The thought of possibly facing the beast without Kai's support was blood-chilling.

Suddenly, the sound of raucous laughter shattered the quiet. Beside her, Lucretia sensed Morgan's body tensing in anger. A quick glance saw his hand tightening around the hilt of his falchion.

"Obram," the sellsword growled under his breath.

"Do not even think of rushing off on your own," Lucretia ordered. Her eyes shimmered as she gripped Morgan by his habit and pulled his face level with hers. "I know we have not had the smoothest of relationships, but Ione is right. We will make it through this, so long as we work together. That means not being as reckless as you usually are."

A wave of relief rushed through her when she saw his body visibly relax. "Aye, yer right as usual," Morgan said. "Thanks for stopping me before I ran off half-nocked. That bastard just rattles my scales, is all."

"I am aware," Lucretia replied, "now stay down and keep quiet."

The trio slinked through the trees. The laughter grew louder the further they descended on the path leading to the hill's other side. Lucretia kept a firm grip on her rapier, palms slick with sweat. Even in the shade of the pines around them, the air was warm and thick with moisture from the morning dew. She unclasped her overcoat, letting it flutter open to let more of the cool breeze brush over her skin.

Passing a thick grove of trees halfway down the hill, Lucretia spotted a cliff ahead. Obram's laughter seemed to be coming from beyond it. Glancing at her companions, she tilted her head towards the cliff. They nodded and, raising their weapons, inched forward to duck behind a cluster of cypress trees at the cliff's edge.

"How was I supposed to know the damn Royalists would attack this soon?" Obram brayed, his deep chuckles reverberating over the hill. "Why are you even getting your pantaloons all scrunched up? It's not like it matters anyway. Wasn't Hemlocke's plan to wipe out the Liberators and everyone else in one swoop anyway? We should be fine so long as we stick to the plan."

Lucretia frowned. Peering down, she saw Obram leaning against the rocky wall with his sword on a small, upturned crate next to him. Across from him stood Mirabell and Duarte, the former glaring daggers at the

Risbado while fingering her kunai. Duarte stood silent at the other edge of the cliff they were camping on. She turned and saw both Ione and Morgan eyeing the group with pinched scowls.

"How can you be so uncaring about everything?" Mirabell snapped. In a rare show of emotion, her face was twisted in a smoldering glare. "Hemlocke's entire plot hinges on opening those crates while the Royalists and Liberators are all occupied. Why do you think he and Nulla rushed off the way they did? Having the attack start this early was not part of the plan and could ruin *everything*. It'll be even worse if the Royalist Army finds us because of your incessant laughing!"

Lucretia's frown deepened. What crates? And why were they so important?

"If I didn't know any better, I'd think you were doubting our ability to get the job done," Obram fired back. "What do you think, Duarte? You've been pretty damn quiet since ol' Featherbrain scuttled off."

"What I think is of no consequence," Duarte answered. Lucretia felt a twinge of sorrow in her chest at the monk's lifeless tone. "I should've known better than to trust Hemlocke when he convinced me of the insanity in Razarr's plan. That man's words are as poisoned as the blade he hides in his wing."

Mirabell gave her kunai a menacing wave towards Duarte. "If it wasn't for Hemlocke, you'd still be groveling under Razarr's boot heel as I was," she said. "I know he saved you from the slave houses, but it doesn't change the fact he treated us worse than vermin."

"I'm curious about something," Obram said. His fingers threaded through his bushy tail as he cast a dubious look towards Duarte. "You served under that man for most of your life. Are you seriously telling me you had no idea he was Norzen?"

"I suspected he wasn't what he presented himself as," Duarte admitted, his eyes downcast. "The only person I'm sure who knew the full truth of it was Mirabell, if only because of Razarr's...relations with her, and she certainly never mentioned it to me."

"Of course not," Mirabell confirmed. "Do you really think that bastard would have allowed me to mention such a thing to anyone without his approval? No, he warned me that if I ever breathed a word of his identity to anyone, he wouldn't give me the mercy of a quick death. In fact, he promised I'd beg for death for over a moon before putting me out of my misery."

Lucretia crinkled her nose. While hearing such a thing was repulsive, at least now she understood the reasoning behind Mirabell's strange behavior. She glanced at her companions and saw Ione staring at the woman with a solemn expression.

"Well, I guess my curiosity's been sated," Obram said. "Now comes the tricky part. What should we do with the gaggle of spies watching us?"

"Wait, what?" Duarte snapped, spinning around in confusion.

"Oh, you noticed them too, Obram?" Mirabell quipped. "And here I thought you weren't paying attention." The assassin stared upward and traced her tongue along the edge of a kunai. "You can come out now. Unless you'd prefer us to drag you out before we kill you."

Suppressing a groan, Lucretia gave the others a nod before they stepped out from their hiding place.

"Well I'll be damned," Obram cackled, lifting his sword and giving it a twirl. "It's my ol' friend Morgan, and he even brought some lovely company for me to enjoy. Where's the rest of your band?"

Shooting Morgan a warning glance, Lucretia brandished her rapier towards the Risbado. "I could ask the same about your companions," she shot back, "though I suppose it does not matter much. Hemlocke and that vile beast of his will simply be dealt with after we settle things with the three of you."

"You needed your whole party to handle us last time. I doubt you can do much without that Norzen Hemlocke is so desperate to kill," Mirabell said. She clutched her kunai and hooked a finger through the rings to secure them while slipping into a stance.

The trio shared a determined glance and nodded, sliding down the incline and coming to a stop across from their opponents.

Ione raised her shield and regarded Mirabell with astern glower. "We're not the same people you faced back at Havenfall, or even Duskmarsh. With the Saints as our witness, we'll put an end to Hemlocke's plot before the day is done."

Pulling his axe from where it was buried into the ground, Duarte said nothing but ambled between Obram and Mirabell with a grim frown in place. He and Lucretia stared at one another, silent understanding passing between them. Next to her, Morgan's chest was rising erratically, his breathing uneven as he fingered the tip of his weapon while eyeing Obram with unrestrained anger.

"Remember what you were taught, Morgan," Lucretia ordered, drawing a surprised stare from the mixblood. "For once, try to rein in that confidence of yours."

Morgan gave a stiff nod. "Aye. Thanks for the advice, lass."

"I've heard enough," Obram said. "Shut up and fight!"

Raising his sword, the Risbado let loose a howling war cry and charged. Morgan planted his boots and brushed the women aside, telling them to spread out. The two sellswords met in a clash of sparks, though Morgan's stance held firm. He pushed back, sending Obram skidding away. Obram licked his lips with a malicious grin stretching from ear to ear. He charged again, thrusting his broadsword forward in a fencing motion. The moment Morgan parried the blow, Obram pushed off his back foot and slammed his shoulder into the mixblood's chest. Both men tumbled to the dirt. Pinned down with Obram's knees buried in his gut, Morgan held his falchion in front of his face to block his former commander's overhead slash.

"You're not getting out of this one, old man," Obram wheezed, choking on his own laughter.

Morgan groaned, his cheeks caked in dirt with sweat beginning to slide down his face. "You ever thought of cutting back on the food, fat ass? Get off!" Cocking a fist back as far as he could, he threw a quick jab into Obram's nose.

A loud crunch sounded out. Obram reeled back to cradle his bleeding face with his weapon hand while the other kept a firm hold on Morgan's cuirass. Taking advantage of the reprieve, Morgan pulled one leg back and kicked the other man off. The sharp crack of broken metal rang as Morgan's cuirass was pulled free and Obram landed on his back with an audible thud.

As the two men battled it out, Ione swatted aside a slash from Mirabell's kunai, the small blade ringing off her shield. Mirabell darted about, seemingly at random, while throwing lightning quick strikes. Every blow pinged against the heater shield as Ione pivoted in place to keep Mirabell in her sights.

"You're reflexes are sharper," Mirabell noted, leaping back to keep some space between them.

Ione stood firm, her cutlass tucked against her side. "I had some wonderful teachers. At least now I'm certain I can stand against you on even ground."

"Even ground? You? Silly woman, I was trained to kill hardened warriors over years of grueling pain and effort. It was the one good thing I received from Hakan. What makes you think you can stand up to me?"

"I may not have your experience, but I have faith in what I was taught and will let that guide me."

Mirabell snorted, a dismissive smile on her lips. "Faith is such a foolish notion. I used to think much the same as you. Then Razarr showed me faith means absolutely nothing. I prayed for so long for the Saints to save me from him, yet I remained a slave to that monster, forced to do his bidding on pain of death."

"And yet you're free now," Ione pressed. "Why not simply leave after Hemlocke killed Razarr?" The two eyed each other with nervous glances. Mirabell charged again, thrusting her blade against the shield and using her weight to shove Ione backwards.

"You wouldn't understand," Mirabell replied in a forlorn tone.

Near the cliff edge, Lucretia and Duarte faced one another with solemn stares. The scholar glanced at her rapier before meeting her former friend's gaze once more.

"We do not have to do this, Duarte," she implored, a single tear sliding down her cheek. "If you lay down your weapon, I am willing to plead with the Grand Duchess for leniency on your behalf."

Duarte shook his head. "I'm afraid I'm too far gone for any sort of forgiveness, Lu," he answered. "Ever since Duskmarsh, I've had much time to think. The truth is my hands are stained with the blood of many innocents. Even if I were to surrender and be given a fair trial, I'd be sentenced to execution for the horrors I've done in Razarr's name. I have nothing left but to see this through to the end, come what may."

Biting her lip, Lucretia nodded. "Very well. If that is your decision, I will do what I must and stop you before any more innocent lives are taken."

Raising their weapons in respectful salute, the two assumed ready stances and charged. Duarte swung his axe in a horizontal strike, intending to cleave Lucretia in two. She dropped into a slide, letting the blade fly overhead. Focusing on a single point, she thrust her rapier at Duarte's exposed rib cage. She was surprised when he twisted his body aside, her attack only grazing him and slicing a hole in his dirt-covered habit. Seeing him raise his free hand to backhand her, she rolled away and put some distance between them before scrambling to her feet.

This will be more difficult than I imagined, Lucretia thought, her mind awash in memories of the past. The pair raised their weapons in defensive stances and inched forward. She truly had no desire to kill the monk. However, it was either that or roll over and die, something she had no intention of doing when her friends depended on her.

Fusette knew if Saredi could see her now, he'd be one step short of suffering heart failure. She found herself not really caring, though, as she encircled her arms around the stunned Larimanz in a familial embrace.

"Your Grace," Larimanz choked out, "whatever happened to decorum? You know if Bidelga or Saredi saw you, they'd have a fit. Also, I see you've, uh, let your hair out, so to speak."

The duchess snorted, tightening her grip on his neck. "I haven't seen you in person since before this damn war started, Waveweaver, so right now decorum can kiss my fluffy ass."

Behind her, Teos erupted into a booming laugh. "See what we've had to deal with, Admiral? I swear she's more of a handful than Kai sometimes."

"She's certainly more open than her father about it. Vonlo could be a bit stuffy in public because he always felt he had to put on airs due to his position."

"Pish to that," Fusette declared. She rolled her eyes while Hans and his crew crowed with laughter behind Teos. "It's wonderful to see you again, Larimanz. I trust the Marine Cavalry has already joined the fight?"

"With gusto, Your Grace. Apparently your surprise caught the enemy with their trousers down. Quite literally, in fact. I saw dozens of Liberators fleeing from atop an outcropping south of here, all dressed in solely their undergarments!"

Fusette burst into giggles, bent over at the waist. Teos had no such restraint and brayed in hysterics, hammering a fist against a nearby tree.

A familiar baritone voice rose over the clamor. "Really now, milady, must you make such a scene in the open? And we had to scour the entire area after you and Sir Teos wandered off," Saredi whined as he rode into view on a wiroch. Following him was Rorik and a small platoon of Norzen soldiers.

"You really should learn to relax, Saredi," Fusette answered. "From what I've seen, the battle seems to be going well in our favor. The enemy is on the run and their general is now facing his judgment in Nulyma as we speak. All that should be left is to clean up the mess and ensure this

Hemlocke fellow is captured or killed before we can call it a resounding victory."

"Then we'd best start looking," Rorik said, "before he scarpers away like a—"

A low rumble echoed across the hills, cutting Rorik off and growing louder with each second. Fusette froze, sensing the ground vibrating under her boots. A cacophony of terrified shrieks and yells carried through the trees, intensifying as the vibrations turned to the land itself shifting beneath them. Fusette detected movement in her peripheral vision, turning her gaze skyward. Her mouth hung open. The hills themselves appeared to be moving, some side to side and others straight downward.

"What in the sacred winds...?" she muttered.

Then, the ground jerked under her feet. Fusette swore under her breath, kept from pitching forward onto her face by Rorik catching her with one arm around her waist. She glanced up at the warrior, her cheeks reddening.

"Thank you, Rorik," she said, steadying herself.

"I think we'd best evacuate, Your Grace," Larimanz warned.

The moment the words left his lips, a deafening boom shook Ballad's End. Fusette's vision swam as everything in sight wobbled like glassware on an unsteady table. The cries rising from further down the hill and the next one over sent a chill down her tails. Her eyes widened when another rumble coursed through the ground, sending clouds of dust and flocks of birds skyward. The dust cleared after a few moments, revealing a mass of rock, dirt, and trees disappearing into a widening black abyss. More horrifying was the hordes of flailing bodies from both sides disappearing into the void.

"L-Larimanz," Fusette stammered, "what's happening?"

"*Keki*!" Larimanz swore in what the duchess recognized as Wasjek. "Everyone, run! It's a sinkhole!"

A blast from a warhorn rattled Fusette's skull, her ears folding down to muffle the sound. She gazed towards where the sound came from to see a mass of soldiers waving the banner of the Rodekan Imperial Army marching across one of the adjacent hills. They appeared to be chasing another group with no identifying markers or banners. The Rodekans stumbled to a stop as the vibrating ground knocked them off balance. To a man, they reversed course and backed away as the hills around the other group descended into the widening hole.

"Stay close, Your Grace," Saredi cautioned, hooking an arm around Fusette's elbow and guiding her away from the chaos.

Another curse from Larimanz stopped the pair short. "Damnation," he growled. "Look there!"

Fusette took the offered spyglass and peered in the direction of the admiral's pointed finger. Her eyes bulged at seeing the massive cannon being hauled across one of the hills just beginning to sink. A small band of soldiers carried up the rear dragging a metal crate on a wiroch-drawn cart.

"That's the Shatterstar?" she whispered. "Wait, isn't that Vice Admiral Medoro?"

Larimanz plucked the spyglass back and scanned the area around the cannon. Seeing one of his former subordinates leading the squad of Liberators surrounding the Shatterstar sent him into a fresh wave of curses.

"Damn it all, we need to get out of here before they turn that blasted thing on us. If I remember right, Medoro started out in the Navy as an artillery cannoneer, so he'll know how to aim the Shatterstar with damn good accuracy."

"Uh, Waveweaver," Fusette stuttered, "I don't think we have to worry about the cannon any longer considering where they are. Also, where are the cannonballs that thing was supposed to use?"

The Royalist entourage watched in horror as the Liberators and their weapon shuddered amid the strengthening quake. Several visceral cracks formed along the hillside, first in front of Medoro's squad cutting off their advance, then another behind them preventing any escape. Fusette wanted nothing more than to turn away but forced herself to continue watching. The hill shifted downward, a low thud echoing through the air before it dropped, carrying Medoro, the Shatterstar, and everything else into the dark abyss.

"May Cacovis guide them on their final journey," Fusette murmured, prompting a wave of agreement from the others. "Come, let's get out of here before something else goes wrong."

Medoro screamed in frustration as he plummeted through the darkness. The light from the surface grew smaller with each second. Another Liberator shrieked in panic beside him while the Shatterstar and the crate containing its cannonballs tumbled among the falling stones. The cannon itself tilted sideways away from them, drifting towards the wall while knocking the crate aside. With a thunderous crash, the Shatterstar struck the wall and fell a bit further before exploding on the crags.

The wind rushed past, stinging his eyes. Further below, Medoro saw something moving. Pinching his eyes half-shut, he couldn't make out the amorphous object until the distinctive sound of splashing reached his ears. A larger stone struck the water, sending a wave upward. Growling under his breath, Medoro reached over and grabbed the hapless soldier next to him, dragging the man beneath him.

"S-sir?" the soldier stammered, meeting Medoro's malicious sneer. "What are—?"

Anything else the man was going to say halted when his back hit a protruding rock. Blood sprayed from his mouth, getting into Medoro's eyes as he struck the dead man's body and bounced off into the open air.

Moments later, Medoro's body hit the icy cold water. His eyes flew open and a stinging prickle spread throughout his body. Flailing about, he swam in what he hoped was an upwards direction. To his relief, his head breached the water after a few powerful strokes and he gulped down a breath of air. Around him, gravel and larger stones slapped against the surface. He paddled to the nearest rock and pulled himself up. His body shivered in the biting chill. The light from above shone more brightly, the sinkhole above them growing in size. Scanning the now shimmering water, Medoro frowned.

An underground lake, he thought. *I wonder how long this has been here without anyone knowing about it?*

A sharp reflection in the air caught his attention. Glancing up, Medoro spotted the metal crate tumbling against several other large boulders of dirt and rock before striking the water with a thud. He winced, expecting the crate's contents to explode. To his surprise, the crate only bobbed on the water for a few seconds before sinking below the surface. Medoro released a bated breath, trying to discern a path out of the cavern. His mind went blank when the light overhead vanished. His eyes shifted upwards to see a massive chunk of rock and dirt plunging towards the lake. With a single, forlorn look towards the spot where the crate sank moments before, the man said the only thing he could think of.

"Damn you, Agosti."

The last thing Medoro knew as the mass hit the water, and the crate, was a blinding flash and searing heat.

Fusette followed behind the Marine Cavalry and the rest of her entourage through the woods at a determined pace. Swallowing a lungful of air, she urged everyone to retreat to safety. The mass inched forward, crossing over a broad cliff and entering a path leading around the hill. Teos and Saredi flanked her sides with Admiral Larimanz and Rorik bringing up the rear. The cries and shouts of the Liberators had faded to nothingness following their plunge, though the ground under their feet continued to shift and rumble with every step.

"When we get back home," Fusette huffed, resting her palm against a tree to steady herself, "I plan on taking a week-long nap and the first person to disturb me will receive a boot to their skull."

Larimanz chortled. "Running about in the field is a bit tiring, isn't it, Your Grace?" he questioned, his laughter intensifying at the unamused frown on her face.

"Admiral, do me a favor and shut your—"

An ear-shattering explosion interrupted her, staggering the entire hill they were on and bowling the entire group over in an entangled mass of bodies. Fusette's eyes swung about, gasping when the rumble of the sinkhole grew louder and all of Ballad's End seemed to ripple. A cloud of ash and dust spewed from the sinkhole, enshrouding the hills in a heavy blanket of shade as the sun was completed shielded from their eyes.

The ground jolted again. Much like the breaks that surrounded Medoro earlier, new cracks shot towards the group, stopping just beneath their location. Fusette wished to breathe a sigh of relief but restrained herself, feeling the dirt move under her feet. She looked up and met Teos' eyes, the smuggler's lips pinched inward in a nervous glower.

"Listen up, everyone," Teos commanded, "I want you all to start moving across to the other side of the hill. Slowly. The less we disturb the ground, the more likely we are to walk out of here."

Before anyone could follow through on the order, the hill itself shook. The cliff behind them snapped free and began its descent. Saredi swore, belting out a command to run. No one needed telling twice as the entire group rushed to escape in case more of the hill followed suit.

Fusette sprinted after them, only to trip over a crack in the dirt and drop onto her face. Spitting out a bit of loose grass, she pushed herself up when the ground jolted again. This time, the bit of ground behind her broke off and sank into the void. Swinging her arms, the duchess struggled to regain her balance and tipped over.

"Help!" Fusette shouted.

She felt a powerful grip envelope her waist, clutching tight before her sudden fall came to an equally abrupt stop. Her head and legs snapped downward while her hands sought any sort of purchase in the open air. The cool, smooth sensation of scales against her fingers registered in Fusette's mind after a brief panic. Opening her eyes, she saw Admiral Larimanz's warm grin shining down at her.

The new edge of the hill lay about three yards above Larimanz, his hands holding fast to the broken wall. Below them lay an open expanse of black. Gazing into it sent a tremor of fear through Fusette's core. Her body quivered while grasping at Larimanz's tail wrapped around her as desperately as she could. A loud cry from above broke her concentration on the sinkhole.

"No!" Saredi's voice rang out. "Bloody Nulyma, she can't be gone!"

She heard Teos speak next, a repeating thump accompanied by falling dirt and grass suggesting he was punching the ground. "Damn it all! How could we let this happen? Oh, merciful Vadako... Kai's gonna *kill* us when he finds out."

Fusette snorted.

She was stunned when Saredi continued on. "You don't understand, Teos...*I* was ultimately responsible for her safety! Not only due to my position, but I swore to Duke Vonlo personally I'd protect her! Because of my inadequacy, the last member of the Ardei family is dead. How can I look her father in the eyes if I meet him in Finyt?" While she couldn't see Saredi's face, her ears twitched at the unmistakable sound of sobbing coming from the Lord Chamberlain.

Blinking back her tears, she rolled her eyes and shouted, "Oi, quit your bellyaching, Saredi, I'm just fine!"

Staring upwards, she heard cries of shock and scratching against the dirt. Seconds later, the gaping faces of Saredi, Teos, and Rorik all stared down at her. Several sailors braved the edge as well, their moon-eyed expressions peering down.

"Y-your Grace?" Rorik gasped. "You're still alive!"

"Quite so. Would you boys terribly mind tossing us a rope?" Fusette asked with a nervous chuckle. "I reckon Waveweaver will be getting tired before long."

A sharp crack rent the air. Fusette's breath hitched seeing the rock Larimanz clung to crumbling under his grip. The admiral shot her a quick glance and shaky grin.

"I think we're already out of time, Your Grace," Larimanz mumbled. "I know I didn't get to be here to help with the troubles you faced, but I've kept up with the newsletters and it's clear Saredi and Gravebane provided you a good base to weather the storm from. Your father would be so proud. I'll be sure to tell him everything."

Fusette's heart sank. "Wait, what are you saying, Larimanz? I know you're not thinking what I think you're thinking!"

"Young lady, you still have a long and prosperous reign ahead of you. You may not realize it, but Livoria *needs* you to guide it to a new age. As for me? This old war snake has done what was needed. If I can die fulfilling my duty, that's enough for me."

"Waveweaver, by the Saints, don't you dare!"

With a cocky smirk, Larimanz swung his tail as Fusette struck her closed fists against it. Turning to look up at the others, he threw his entire body weight into snapping his tail up like a whip, uncoiling Fusette and sending her airborne. Rorik and Teos hooked their arms under her armpits even as she kicked and screamed.

The stone shattered under Larimanz's shifting bulk. Fusette cried out, trying to pull free and reach for the admiral as he plummeted towards the empty void. Despite obviously knowing what was coming, Larimanz looked at peace. His eyes held no fear, only acceptance. He offered Fusette a tired smile and raised his closed fist in salute before vanishing amid the shadows.

"No!" Fusette shrieked.

Rorik and Teos pulled her onto stable ground, collapsing onto their backs. The sailors hit the ground on their knees, tears in their eyes. Fusette pulled against the two pairs of hands securing her. Giving up the struggle, she threw herself against Rorik's chest, wailing into his mane. The warrior looked taken aback, his cheeks darkening to a deep crimson. He saw Teos quirk an eyebrow at him before encircling his arms around Fusette's back.

Saredi remained kneeling at the cliff edge, staring into the sinkhole in abject astonishment. When he finally turned back and spotted Fusette cradled against Rorik's sturdy form, he blanched. "Sir Rorik, what in the winds are you doing?"

Feeling the warrior stiffen against her, Fusette sighed in relief when he answered, "Whatever Lady Fusette needs of me."

"Thank you, Rorik," she hiccupped.

Steeling herself, she tilted her head and rose to her feet, brushing her lips against the larger Norzen's cheek. Her sudden affection drew a choked gasp from Rorik that seemed unnatural compared to his broad physique. Teos smirked when Fusette turned her gaze on him and leveled a warning stare at the Soltauri.

"Don't you say a thing," Fusette said. She was about to continue but froze when a soft, wispy voice echoed in her mind, warning her of danger. Her eyes flickered to the mark on her arm, its dark form contrasting against her pale skin.

Hibbel and Pelka said the ones who bear these marks gain them through the will of Origin. Could that voice possibly be...

A booming roar resounded across the hills, sending flocks of birds into the sky. Fusette spun in Rorik's arms, her eyes bulging. In the corner of her vision, she saw Saredi paling while Teos looked ready to spit nails.

She recognized that roar, having heard it back in Duskmarsh.

"What in the Saints' great names was that?" Saredi asked, his hands trembling against his sword's hilt.

"Grimghast," Fusette growled. Peeling herself away from Rorik and giving the warrior a wistful smile, she turned to address the group. "Everyone! I know we've only just lost Admiral Larimanz, but we shall have time to grieve later. Those of you who wish to rejoin the allied forces in routing the Liberation Army, I give you full leave to do so. For those seeking a greater challenge, the beast which created that horrid sound is somewhere on these hills. Gravebane is moving to intercept it and the mastermind of a plot to spread the Black Tear Blight."

A wave of gasps rose from many among the Marine Cavalry. "I intend to be there when Gravebane puts these monsters down. Anyone who wants to join me, get in line and let's go!"

Everyone broke out into cheers. Before her eyes, Fusette watched as the group split itself into two groups. She was briefly surprised when Hans and his crew declared themselves among those wishing to fight the Liberators, though she couldn't fault them for the choice, given what was at stake for them. Half of the Marine Cavalry joined the former pirates and Fusette wished them luck as they sidled down the path. Coming to a fork, they turned to the left, heading north towards the remnants of battle. Giving one last, furtive stare at the enormous chasm splitting Ballad's End in two, Fusette clasped a fist to her chest in salute.

"Thank you, Waveweaver," she murmured.

Raising the same fist, Fusette bellowed a war cry and sprinted down the path until taking the right fork. Teos, Saredi, and Rorik charged alongside her, followed by the remainder of the Marine Cavalry with their armor clanking.

Kai, Fusette thought, *I swear to the winds, you better be alive when I get there.*

Chapter XXXII

The iron stench of blood drifted across Kai's nostrils. His muscles pulsed with each step, ears twitching from the thrumming of his partners' heartbeats pounding beside him. The chill from Mimilrun's shaft contrasted starkly from the warm sunlight against his fur and skin. Strapped over his back, the blunderbuss rested between his shoulders with its muzzle pointed at the ground. Maple's feathers brushed against his arm, bringing his gaze to her violet eyes. On his other side, Orelia quivered with one hand resting against the small of his back just above the base of his tails.

"How close do you think we are?" Maple asked.

"Not too far, I'd reckon," Kai answered. "There's blood in the air. That thing has fed recently."

Orelia's shaking intensified. "Would it be too much to hope it ate a Liberator instead of any of ours?" she wondered.

Kai shook his head. "At this point, there's no way to be sure. Hemlocke seems ready to kill anyone who gets close enough, regardless of what side they fight for. He's essentially created a third force in the war, dedicated solely to sowing chaos."

"Wait," Maple said. Her ear feathers fluttered, tilting up and down as she scrutinized something up ahead. "What's that?"

Frowning, Kai swiveled his own ears, pointing them forward. It was faint, but he heard the clang of metal against metal coming from further up ahead, along with the shadows of something moving among the trees. His own grip on his weapon tightened.

"Sounds like the others found our wayward targets. Let's hurry."

The trio bustled through the woods, weaving between the pines. Obram's abrasive laughter cut through the air like a gunshot, sending a tingle down Kai's tails. His first instinct was to rush forward and help his friends. He stopped short, however, when a familiar growl prickled his ears from a different direction. He held both arms out, stopping Maple and Orelia in their tracks. He could sense their confused stares boring into him but his entire focus was centered on a side path leading further up the hill.

"Up there," Kai said, pointing with his mace.

He led them along the path, taking care not to disturb the leaves and twigs underfoot too much. The ladies' grips on his arms tightened, their fingers digging into tense muscle. Before long, Hemlocke's rattling cackle reached their ears, interspersed with a hacking cough. They peered through the trees and spotted the two, looking down at where Kai assumed the rest of their friends were fighting. Several yards away, several wooden crates sat buried under a haphazard mass of leaves, dirt, and branches to hide it from view.

Kai glared at the boxes. Whatever Hemlocke had stowed within them, he was confident it wasn't anything good.

"Just a little while longer, Nulla, my dear," Hemlocke whispered in a loving tone. "Once we locate Kai and his wenches, you'll be allowed to feast to your heart's desire, instead of the paltry snack I brought you before."

A wave of nausea swept through Kai's gut at how ecstatic Hemlocke sounded at the prospect. Part of him wondered how he could have missed the traitorous man's true self for as long as he did. His gaze twitched down to the mark on his left hand, many questions still fluttering through his mind. He peered at his partners and squeezed their hands. His eyes widened when one of his tails brushed against a low hanging branch and sent a tawny sparrow flapping into the canopy.

Grimghast emitted a confused chuff. Kai's body froze seeing its head turn towards them halfway. He rubbed his thumbs over the women's hands, the sweat greasing their palms allowing the fingers to glide effortlessly over their skin.

"It's just a stupid bird, Nulla," Hemlocke muttered. "Focus. I suppose if we can't find them, perhaps they'll show up if we start torturing the others."

The trio watched their quarry peek through a battered spyglass, face twisted in a befuddled scowl. As he searched, Grimghast stretched itself out to its full length, pawing at the ground while pacing around Hemlocke. Kai released a nervous breath through his nose. He quickly regretted it, however, when the beast's ears twitched before its beady eye spun and landed on him. Grimghast's lips curled back with a snarl. The beast's sudden vexation drew Hemlocke's attention as well, his head turning in their direction.

"*Taen.*"

Hemlocke growled. "W-what the?! How did you...?" he sputtered while reaching for his reed flute.

"Maple!"

"On it, love!" Extending one arm towards Hemlocke, she snapped her fingers and fired a tiny bullet of compressed Breeze at her fellow Aerivolk. Unprepared, Hemlocke swore when the attack struck his flute and shattered it. He staggered back with a vehement trill, clutching his left arm. Kai smirked seeing a stream of blood dribbling down the limb from where a large splinter pierced him.

"Apparently I've been too complacent with you," Hemlocke growled. "A mistake I intend to rectify at once. Nulla, kill them!"

He whistled a haunting tune that sent chills across Kai's body. Grimghast narrowed its eye at them and prepared to pounce, letting loose with a bloodcurdling roar. Stepping in front of his wives, Kai met Grimghast's stare as Timber coiled within him. The beast stalked forward, emitting puffs of condensed air in the morning chill.

"Surely you're not planning to fight Nulla alone?" Hemlocke taunted. "You don't have that overpowered Frenzy Haze to save you again, and I much doubt you can control the little vine trick you used on me before! Wait...I take it back. I want to see this."

Kai suppressed the urge to smirk. Instead, he rolled his shoulders while eyeing Grimghast. Slipping into a stance, he bobbed Mimilrun in one hand as the other curled into a fist. Thick tendrils wriggled within him in a circular motion, their movement visible through his shifting skin. The silence was broken only by Grimghast's heavy breathing and the occasional snort coming from Kai's nostrils.

In a flash of gleaming teeth, Grimghast launched itself through the air. Maple and Orelia darted out of the way, circling around at a wide arc. Kai stood his ground, feeling his Timber flare to life. Extending his right arm, three thick vines burst from the wrist and wrapped themselves around Grimghast's front legs and neck.

Hemlocke's eyes bulged. "How in the void...?"

Yanking down, Kai slammed Grimghast belly-first into the dirt. The apothecary was surprised at the ease with which he could manipulate his opponent, making him wonder just how much his strength improved from Rorik's training. The beast was stunned by the unexpected move, leaving it open for Kai to rush forward and hammer Mimilrun into the armored plate protecting its shoulder. The weapon's curved flanges generated a loud crunch upon impact, crushing the plate and scattering bone shards about as Grimghast roared in pain.

Don't give it a chance to rest, Kai told himself. *Disorient, attack, and repeat!*

Grimghast reared back, slicing through the vines with its claws. Kai rushed in close and threw an uppercut into the beast's jaw plate, snapping the head upwards and giving him an opening to slam his shoulder into Grimghast's belly. The blow sent them careening over the side of the cliff. Kai grabbed a fistful of fur and held tight, sliding down the rocky crags atop Grimghast before they crashed on the plateau below.

"I swear that bastard will pay," Hemlocke snarled. He drew his staff and peered over the cliff edge, readying himself to jump.

"Oi! Aren't you forgetting something?" Maple's trilling voice drawled behind him.

Hemlocke's eyes widened as he spun around in time for Maple to crash into him with Orelia perched on the smaller woman's back. Maple's talons stretched out, one clasping onto Hemlocke's waist and the other holding the wrist clutching his staff. Plummeting through the air, the two Aerivolk struggled in a clash of flapping wings and sharp talons. Orelia was pitched from Maple's back, hitting the dirt in a controlled roll, when Hemlocke planted his talons on the merchant's stomach and pushed back. The claws tore gashes in Maple's vest, revealing a thin, bison leather undershirt.

Drawing her uchines, Maple assumed a defensive stance and planted herself between Hemlocke and Orelia. "Ora, keep me covered in case that bastard tries any of his usual tricks," she commanded.

"You sure about that, Mapes?" Orelia asked. "I'm still able to fight."

"I appreciate the offer, but I owe this dipwit an ass kicking for Glimmerdale."

Hemlocke snickered, his lips curled into a vicious sneer as he downed the remains of Kai's emberona elixir. "Your precious Kai couldn't kill me outright in either of the times we faced each other. What makes you think you'll do any better?"

Maple scowled and scraped her talons across the dirt while inching forward. "As much as I love him, I know Kai still thinks of when you two first met. Even if it's in the depths of his mind, those memories keep him from using his full strength against you. I don't have such memories stopping me from tearing your feathers out and shoving them *up your ass!*"

Ione batted aside another strike from Mirabell's kunai. The younger woman proved persistent in her attacks, keeping the tavern maid on her toes with every dash. Not for the first time since the fight began, she thanked her lucky stars the Shieldbearer Corps pushed her to carry a full heater instead of the small buckler she initially preferred. While much heavier, her training taught her to use the shield as a pivot to manipulate her movements and deflect attacks from quicker opponents.

"You can't hide behind that damned shield forever," Mirabell snapped. "I reckon it's not exactly as light as a feather. You'll tire at some point."

"So long as I have something worth protecting, my faith will give me the strength to continue," Ione shot back. Her eyes narrowed and flashed towards where Kai had crashed to the ground atop Grimghast with Maple and Orelia following close behind. She twirled her cutlass in time to parry a backhanded slash. "Perhaps if you had the same, it could heal you of the scars Hakan's treatment left on your spirit."

"I have nothing of the sort," Mirabell confessed. "When Hakan found me, my family had recently been killed in a fire. I let myself be bewitched by his lies and promises to save me. In reality, all I did was trade one horror for something worse. Why do you think I was so eager to join Hemlocke's rebellion?"

A sharp clang resounded in the air, sparks flying between the two women with each clash. Similar sounds of battle arose throughout the cliff, interspersed with groans, swears, and the occasional growl from Grimghast. Mirabell lunged forward, thrusting her kunai at Ione's heart. The tavern maid deflected the blow, knocking Mirabell off balance. Dropping her cutlass, Ione pressed her thumb against the button on her glove. A sharp click resounded as a small dagger with tooth-like protrusions along the dull edge shot into her hand. With a smooth motion honed by constant practice, Ione caught the kunai's blade between the dagger's teeth and twisted. Mirabell's eyes widened when her weapon was wrenched from her hand, leaving her open to Ione slamming her shield into the assassin's chest and sending her sprawling onto her back.

"Did it never cross your mind that Hemlocke might not be who you think he is?" Ione asked. Dropping the dagger, she kicked her cutlass back up into her hand and pointed it at Mirabell's breast. The pair stared at one another, their chests heaving.

Mirabell wiped an arm over her sweaty brow. "My skills as an assassin are all I have left. Hemlocke promised me the freedom and love I so desperately craved if I helped him put that bastard down once and for all. Seeing that beast devour Hakan was probably the closest I've felt to true happiness since my childhood. Because of that, I'd do anything to make Hemlocke's plan come true."

A loud, braying cackle froze both women in their tracks. They turned to see Hemlocke eyeing Mirabell with a haughty smirk. Across from the traitor, Maple and Orelia watched with curious but alert gazes, their weapons held at the ready.

"Y-you really believed all that tripe?" Hemlocke crowed with glee. "I can't tell if you're just that gullible or if you're stupider than I thought."

Mirabell's mouth dropped open in shock, her lip quivering. "Wait, what do you mean? You promised to take care of me until the end!"

"So you *are* simply that stupid. The only reason I even said any of that nonsense was because you served a purpose—or to be more precise, your skills did. Now that my plan is about to come to fruition, I have no use for you anymore."

Ione watched a wave of varying emotions flicker across Mirabell's face. Doubt, shock, fear, sadness, and fury. The tavern maid's heart pulsed with empathy as memories of her own husband and his disappearance flashed before her eyes. Mirabell collapsed to her knees, tears cascading down her crimson cheeks. Off to the side, Ione spotted Duarte and Lucretia watching the exchange with identical surly frowns. Further back, near the camp, Morgan and Obram continued fighting without either taking their eyes off the other.

"I trusted you!" Mirabell screamed at last. Her tears drifted across the air with each wild flail of her head. "I-I'll kill you myself!"

To Ione's shock, the assassin ignored her completely and, rising to her feet, launched herself at Hemlocke after snatching her dropped kunai from the dirt. Weapon held in a reverse grip, Mirabell spun on one heel and aimed the blade at the Aerivolk's neck. Hemlocke swung his staff, batting the kunai away and sidestepping Mirabell's follow-up strike. He emitted a cackling trill, twirling his weapon with ease. Despite Mirabell's skill, Ione could see her attacks were wild and frantic, while every swing of Hemlocke's nail-riddled staff was precise, adding fresh cuts to her pale skin.

"You have some stones to turn on me, girl," Hemlocke chuckled. "Seems like you're a little winded, too. Did failing to kill that woman wear you out that much?" When Mirabell lunged forward, intending to drive her kunai into his heart, he gripped her wrist with his free hand and stopped the attack cold.

Mirabell struggled against Hemlocke's iron grip, chest heaving as she pulled back to no avail. Ione stood frozen, watching him allow the assassin to lead him back—towards the cliff—while maintaining his hold. Letting out a frustrated howl, Mirabell swung her other kunai at his face and lost her grip when he punctured her forearm with his weapon's nails. The kunai tumbled through the air and clattered to a stop at Ione's feet.

Eye's gleaming with malice, Hemlocke leaned forward and met Mirabell's furious glare with a confident smirk. "It's rather pathetic, how you thought I actually cared enough to waste my time on you. You may have suffered some in your life but compared to mine, you practically lived in luxury. The only thing that makes me feel alive is making others know the anguish I've been plagued with my whole life."

Mirabell ground her teeth. To Ione's surprise, she dropped the kunai from her hand still locked in Hemlocke's grip. Then, she lashed out and struck the ring on its pommel with a kick, launching it back towards the Aerivolk's face. His eyes widened. Jerking his head sideways, a splatter of blood sprayed across the ground. Hemlocke dropped his staff to clutch at his face, lifting his hand to reveal a gash at the edge of his right eye.

"You," Hemlocke breathed, his eyes narrowing into pinpricks. "I'll admit, you almost caught me by surprise there. Very well. If you're so eager to be free, then let me grant your wish."

Without another word, Hemlocke released his grip on Mirabell's hand the moment she pulled back again. Shifted off-balance, she stumbled back and teetered at the cliff's edge with a fearful expression.

Ione gasped, rushing forward as Hemlocke lifted a leg and slammed his talon into Mirabell's chest, pitching her over the edge before stalking back towards a horrified Maple. Dropping her shield, Ione reached for Mirabell's outstretched hand. The tips of their fingers brushed together, the assassin slipping out of reach with a terrified expression.

The two stared at each other, Mirabell's eyes leaking fresh tears. With a strangled cry, she plummeted through the air swinging her arms in a desperate bid for something to slow her descent. Ione could only stare in horror as Mirabell's attempts proved futile and she hit the craggy stones a hundred yards below with a sickening crunch. Blood sprayed across the ground, pooling under the assassin's broken body in a crimson stain Ione could see even at such a distance.

"Such a pathetic excuse of a woman," Hemlocke mumbled, threading a hand through his dirty white hair. His talons scraped along the dirt, shifting the gravel. "I may not have had the same training she got from that wretch Hakan, but I never needed it. I always had an inherent talent for spreading pain and suffering."

Ione gripped her cutlass tight and stepped forward, twigs cracking under her boot, only to hear Maple bark, "Stand down, Ione! Don't worry. I'll give this asshole an extra special kick in the tail feathers for you."

"I'm going to enjoy watching that confidence melt away before I gut you," Hemlocke trilled, his feathers ruffling as his signature haunting cackle echoed throughout the cliff.

Twirling her uchines, Maple ruffled her own feathers before spreading her lips in a toothy grin. "Let's see ya put your marks where your mouth is. You may have a talent for killing, but *I* at least have something worth fighting for and that gives me a strength you'd never hope of matching."

Chapter XXXIII

Sweat dripped down Morgan's brow, chest heaving with every swing of his falchion. Obram looked similarly winded, the Risbado's fur covered in a mix of sweat, blood, and dirt. Their blades collided again and again, neither giving an inch. Hopping back, Morgan led his opponent closer to the trees while parrying Obram's strikes. The rising sun peeked through the hills, causing Morgan to flinch and raise an arm to shield his eyes.

"You've improved," Obram muttered. Bouncing on the balls on his feet, he sidestepped to the left, then to right. "I figured that battered old body of yours would've given out by now."

Morgan chuffed. "I've been doing this a lot longer than you have, pup," he snickered. "Besides, it helps that I got my ass beat like a drum constantly while training. You'd be surprised how much that teaches you what *not* to do."

Obram's lips curled into a snarl. Rushing in, he thrust his broadsword towards Morgan's chest. He got a painful surprise when Morgan lifted his weapon, angling it to reflect the sun into Obram's face. The Risbado slid to a stop, shouting in pain as he clutched his eyes. Morgan pivoted and hammered Obram's armored kidney with a solid kick. The strike forced Obram backwards, pitching him onto his back as his sword clattered away.

Emitting a victorious shout, Morgan charged and thrust his blade towards Obram's head. The falchion struck nothing but dirt when Obram rolled to the side, sweeping his foot in an arc to knock Morgan's legs out from under him.

"You didn't think you'd be able to beat me *that* easily, did you?" Obram taunted, rising to his feet with a cocky smirk. Kicking his sword into his hand, he gave it a twirl.

"Ya can't blame a man for hoping," Morgan quipped, a tilted grin on his face as he staggered back up.

The two circled each other. Morgan's eyes drifted further back to where he saw Kai wrestling with Grimghast and surprisingly holding his own. Closer was Lucretia ducking and spinning around Duarte's axe while landing precise stabs with her rapier. Returning his gaze to Obram, Morgan tightened his grip before taking a calming breath. Remembering everything he and Teos learned from Dewthorn, Morgan forced himself to relax. He loosened his grip again on the falchion and got control of his breathing.

"What's the matter, Morgan?" Obram cooed in an infantile tone, his glee clear as day behind the honeyed words. "Finally realize you and your friends won't live to see the next sunrise?"

"You ain't half as smart as you wish if you think we're just gonna roll over and die," Morgan retorted. "No matter what happens, we're a family and will watch each other's backs to the end."

Steadying himself, the Wasini mixblood tensed his muscles for a single moment before dashing forward. He saw the shock in Obram's eyes as he closed in on the traitorous sellsword in a flash. His blade arced in an upwards slash, intending to cleave his opponent in twain from the hip. Morgan bit back a curse when Obram brought his sword up just in time to deflect the strike, though he grinned when his blade still bit into the left side of Obram's ribs as he backed away, drawing rivulets of fresh blood.

Morgan's gaze followed Obram's backpedaling form as he continued his assault. His sword felt almost lighter in his hand, cutting through the air with ease. There was a glimmer of what could only be fear in Obram's eyes. Morgan's renewed attacks were lightning-quick, producing flashes of light in the morning sun with every clang.

"I've had enough of this," Obram muttered under his breath.

Stepping into another thrust, Morgan overextended and felt his body lean off-balance when Obram darted sideways. In that split second,

Obram surprised him with a brutal haymaker to the jaw. Morgan's teeth snapped together. The sudden shift in momentum sent him sprawling to the dirt. On instinct, he rolled onto his back and raised his sword to block the inevitable follow-up strike he knew was coming.

None came.

Blinking, Morgan lifted his head and erupted into a string of swears when he spotted Obram fleeing with the fur of his bushy tail standing on end. "Oi," he barked, "get back here, ya filthy coward!"

Ducking under another of Duarte's slashes, Lucretia launched a probing thrust into his ribs, tearing a hole in his habit. The monk's lack of heavy armor didn't seem to bother him, however, as his bulk offered a natural resistance to her rapier's stabs. The two darted around each other, exchanging attacks that ultimately proved ineffective. For every hack and slash Lucretia avoided, every one of her strikes was brushed off like mosquito bites. Gritting her teeth, the wind rushed around Lucretia when Duarte finally swatted her aside with a backhand from his muscular arm and sent her flying.

Why must we continue to fight like this? Lucretia thought, the breath knocked from her lungs as her back struck the cliff.

She knew in her heart she needed to kill her former friend, yet two things held her back. First, a tiny voice fluttering in the winds warned her to stay her hand, whispering that the Duarte she knew as a child may still be reawakened. More practical was the fear she lacked the skill and strength needed to land a killing blow to Duarte's neck or heart. The fact he towered over her by almost a yard combined with his body's dense muscles meant she would have to get creative if she wanted to win.

"Duarte, this is pointless," Lucretia said, staggering to her feet. "I know you are better than this. What happened to the sweet boy who wanted nothing more than to join the Navy and protect people?"

"Time changes people, Lu," Duarte answered. His gaze drifted to stare at the ground, his body shivering. "I'm not the same boy I was when we were little. I know I've made bad choices, yet I only did what I felt was necessary given the horrors people like Nerod forced me into."

Lucretia scoffed. "You still have choices," she countered. "I know you're not stupid. Your past will continue to haunt you, so long as you allow it. You can alter the course of your future by making better choices in the present. It's not too late. For Dolmaru's sake, look at me! I swore up and down from the day I arrived at the Citadel I'd never trust a Norzen. Yet here I am, fighting alongside at least *two* who have proven to me not everything is solely black and white"

Dumbstruck, Duarte stared at Lucretia, his axe lowering until its blade rested against the dirt. The scholar offered a nervous smile, brushing her ponytail back. Duarte's gaze turned to the weapon in his hands. His cheeks hollowed, a forlorn groan rumbling from his throat.

Out of nowhere, Lucretia heard Morgan bellow, "Oi, get back here, ya filthy coward!" Her head twisted to see Obram barreling towards her and Duarte with a manic smile on his lips and Morgan in furious pursuit.

"Duarte!" Obram shouted. "What the blazes are you waiting for? Kill that stupid wench and help me!"

The monk's befuddled gaze rose to meet his comrade's scowl. "Is the mighty Obram actually *running* from a fight?" Duarte asked.

"Never mind that, just kill her! You know you're in too deep. Do the deed already so we can finish these bastards and get out of here!"

Duarte turned back to Lucretia. She saw the emotional war waging in his mind. The unsure stance and loosened hold on his weapon. His downcast expression. The quaking of his body.

"I will handle this as I see fit, Obram," Duarte finally responded. "You have no authority to give me orders, especially as the only one who held that authority is dead."

Obram skidded to a stop, forgetting about Morgan as he stared at Duarte, utterly stupefied. "Don't you dare tell me you've gone soft," the sellsword growled.

Duarte hesitated. His eyes flickered to Lucretia, unable to speak.

"So it's true," Obram continued. "After all the people you've killed, you falter at the thought of ending one stupid bitch?"

"You have bronze baubles to say that to my face," Duarte rumbled. His eyes narrowed and jaw tightened, a single hoof pawing the ground.

Behind the group, Morgan reeled his arms back mid-charge, swinging his falchion towards Obram's neck with a bellow of rage. Lucretia bit back a curse when Obram dashed sideways, lashing out to grab Morgan by the habit and shoving him aside. The mixblood's tunic was ripped open as he ducked into a roll, putting himself upright again in one fluid motion.

"Fine," Obram snapped, "if you won't kill her, I'll save you the trouble and do it myself!"

Stalking forward, Obram smashed a backhanded fist into Duarte's cheek. The monk spun and hit the dirt face first in a cloud of dust. An inhuman growl rose from the Risbado, shaking his head while his face twisted into a deranged, toothy smile stretching from ear to ear.

Lucretia swore and backed away, brandishing her rapier. She didn't need her scholar's crest to see Obram had murder in his eyes. Biting her lip, she parried Obram's frenzied attacks as best as she could. His blows were so powerful, though, her very bones rattled with each hit. A sharp tingling spread from her wrist down her forearm.

Damn it all, Lucretia thought, *I cannot take many more of these strikes before I lose my grip. Even my fingers are going numb!*

Dodging to the left, she evaded a downward slash and found herself amidst the dangling branches of a cypress growing from the hillside above. Stepping back, she felt cold stone against her shoulders as Obram closed in. Lucretia grit her teeth and lunged. She smirked when her blade struck true, leaving a wide gash in Obram's exposed neck on the right side. To her horror, though, the rabid grin never left his face.

"It'll take a lot more than that to make me feel pain, darling," he cooed. His voice dripped with a mixture of malice and arrogance. It filled Lucretia's chest with a sick, rotting sensation that gave her the chills.

Her breath hitched when Obram gripped her rapier with one hand and tore it from her grip, casting it aside. The sound of her friends' alarmed shouts rang like thudding bells in the background, her entire focus centered on the approaching Risbado. Lucretia glanced sideways, searching for an escape route. Her thoughts ground to a halt when Obram wrapped his fingers around her throat. Behind Obram, she saw Duarte staring fish-mouthed, his eyes flaring with anger and fear.

"This is the end for you, love," Obram cackled while angling his sword towards her heart. "Say hello to Hakan for me in whatever you Livorians call your hell."

Lucretia's heart pounded in her chest, nails clawing at Obram's outstretched arm. She wanted to search more for any method of forcing him to relinquish his crushing grip, yet her eyes refused to move from the gleaming sword about to pierce her breast.

Heavy footfalls echoed in her ears, accompanied by skittering gravel. Obram's blade thrust forward, sending her mind into a blind panic. Lucretia choked against his grip in a desperate struggle. Her vision swam, the sword's keen edge morphing into a shapeless cloud. Then, a familiar voice roared.

"Lucretia!"

A second silver mass appeared from nowhere, slamming into Obram's arm and sending a spray of crimson through the air. At the same time, a heavy weight pushed on her body, ripping her from the Risbado's hand and tearing her overcloak away at once. Obram released a pained bellow and Lucretia saw the fury blazing in his eyes as her back hit the cliff face, the sudden pain bringing her vision back into sharp clarity.

A dull thump reverberated in Lucretia's ears, followed by a warm wetness splattering over her face and chest. Her eyes stared ahead, shaking within her skull. Obram's broadsword was pointed at her heart, coated in a liberal varnish of steaming blood. She couldn't breathe, her chest tightening as if crushed under the weight of a nobletusk bison. An audible gulp sounded and she let her gaze travel upwards. The sword protruded from the middle of a broad, muscular back covered in glittering scales and topped by a head of scruffy blonde hair with a face bearing the same cheeky grin that never failed to rankle her patience.

Morgan.

CHAPTER XXXIV

Lucretia stood frozen, her eyes locked on the thin line of blood dribbling from the corner of Morgan's mouth. His pointed canines poked out from between quivering lips as a weak chuckle escaped his throat.

"What the hoarfrost are you looking so surprised for?" Morgan asked.

On Morgan's other side, Obram stared at his former comrade in shock. Morgan's falchion was buried in the top of his sword arm, though it only cut a third of the way through before stopping against his radius bone. Blood streamed from the wound, dripping against the dirt.

"You!" Obram snarled. "Why would you—?"

The Risbado was cut off by Morgan grinning wide and throwing himself forward in a brutal headbutt. Obram was launched backwards, getting entangled in a mass of cypress branches and vines while yanking the sword from Morgan's chest with a nauseating squelch. Morgan winced, releasing an agonizing groan before tipping forward. The movement jarred Lucretia from her thoughts, driving her to rush forward and catch Morgan around the waist. His weight nearly dragged her down with him, though she turned him in time for his side to hit the ground rather than his face. Lucretia brushed Morgan's dusty bangs away from his face, her lip trembling.

"Why?" she pressed. "Why would you do such a thing?"

Morgan's lips curved into a weak smile. "Why wouldn't I? You lot would do the same for me in a pinch—well, maybe not you."

Lucretia blinked, fresh tears streaking down her face. "You truly are an idiot," she muttered. "Of course I would. I know we always butt heads over foolish things, but you are still my friend."

A brilliant glimmer flashed through Morgan's eyes at the scholar's words. "Really? Tha's nice to hear," he murmured, coughing up a fresh splotch of blood.

Ignoring the new stains on her blouse, Lucretia searched the cliff and frowned, seeing Kai busy holding Grimghast at bay. "Damn it to Nulyma. We need Kai here *now*."

A firm pressure settled over her hand, drawing her attention to Morgan's fingers wrapped around her own. "Lass, we both know 'pothy ain't gonna make it in time," he said. "Not with that monster keeping him busy. I just wish...I could've lived long enough to see the beastie taken down."

"Silence," Lucretia commanded. "Control your breathing and try not to talk. I refuse to let you die here."

Morgan grinned. "I know you're smarter than that. I can see the truth in your eyes." He coughed up another round of blood, his free hand pressing against the bleeding wound. "Sorry I couldn't beat that bastard Obram. I'm just making things tougher on you."

Lucretia heard a horrified gasp as Ione rushed over, dropping to her knees and cradling the wounded sellsword's head in her lap. The sounds of battle continued ringing around them, including a worried shout from Kai, though loudest was Obram's agitated cursing in his attempts to free himself of the cypress.

"By the winds," Ione whispered, tears dribbling down her face.

"You lasses shouldn't cry so much. Mam always said if you do it long enough, your pretty faces will get stuck like that."

Lucretia snorted, her mouth tilting upwards at an angle. "Of all the times you decide to get flirty, it has to be when you are knocking on Cacovis' door?"

"At least I made you smile, didn't I?" Morgan snickered, lifting a finger to brush the corner of Lucretia's lips. His perpetual smile refused to waver even as his breathing weakened. "Don't feel too bad for me. At least I died protecting the people who matter most. Tell 'pothy something for me, would ya? Let him know...he was the best brother an old snake could've asked for."

Lucretia's eyes widened. Morgan gave her a sad, wistful smile before leaning his head back against Ione's legs. His eyes closed and the hand clutching his wound limply slid to the ground. Lucretia pressed a hand to his chest, praying with all her might.

There was no heartbeat.

"No," Ione murmured. Her head shook, the tears falling without end. Lucretia was no better, weeping as she beat against Morgan's chest with both fists.

"Wake up," Lucretia growled, her tears dripping onto the man's cheeks. "Wake up, wake up, I said WAKE UP, damn you!"

A low, rumbling chuckle echoed within the cypress branches. Both women raised their heads to watch Obram crowing with laughter while still fighting to free himself.

"How sad," the Risbado taunted. "At least one of you bastards is finally dead. Now if only I can...ah ha!"

Sliding his boot into the dirt underneath his sword, Obram kicked it upwards and gripped the blade with one hand. He strained against the mass of vines and branches holding him still until his other hand caught hold of the weapon's hilt. With a morbid grin, he lifted his arm and drew the blade across the vines, slicing through them with ease. Free once again, Obram stalked towards the pair with tongue hanging out and a vicious grin on his lips.

Lucretia glared at the sellsword and planted herself in front of Ione, still clutching Morgan's body. "I do not give a whit if you *are* stronger than me," she intoned. "I refuse to let you harm anymore of my friends!"

"Lovely speech, darling," Obram snickered, "though I'd love to see how you plan on stopping me. You're not exactly strong enough for me to be concerned about."

"If I were you," a dulcet baritone thundered behind Obram, "I'd be more concerned about this!"

To Lucretia's unbridled shock, a dark shape darted around the Risbado, who twirled with wide eyes just in time to be struck across the face by the flat side of Duarte's axe, the blade grazing against his cheek and leaving a thin cut oozing fresh blood. Obram was sent flying, spinning in mid-air before crashing amid a cloud of dust. Lucretia turned to Duarte, her mouth agape.

"D-Duarte," she stammered, "why would you...?"

"I must apologize for being such a craven coward," the monk answered, giving his old friend a nervous grin. "Because of my indecision, your friend lost his life. Seeing you prepared to face Obram anyway after what he did, knowing what the likely result would be...well, there was a reason I always admired you, Lu, even when we were sprouts."

Lucretia stumbled back as if struck, her cheeks tinting to a dark pink. A hacking cough came from the cloud of dust as Obram emerged, face contorted in a furious snarl.

"You have the audacity to betray me after everything we did to free you?" Obram roared, his fur standing on end.

Duarte stood his ground and responded with a sly, cheeky smirk. "You're hardly one to talk, considering the betrayals you've boasted about leaving in your wake. All I did was follow your upstanding example," he countered.

An undignified snort bubbled from between Lucretia's lips. Her hand flew to her mouth in a vain attempt to smother the wave of giggles. Obram remained stock still, flabbergasted by Duarte's carefree retort. Lucretia watched the Soltauri slide into a battle stance, both hands clutching his axe's shaft and resting the blade on the ground.

"Just for that," Obram said, "I'll make you watch me skin those women alive. After I break all your limbs, of course."

A booming growl echoed from Duarte. "Is that so? Then I dare you to prove it, you perfidious mongrel."

"I have no clue what the hell 'perfidious' means," Obram grumbled, "but I'm pretty sure you just insulted me again, so now I'm gonna have to hack your baubles off for good measure."

"Hack this," Duarte said before stepping into a wide swing.

Obram met the blow with his own sword, the two colliding in a shrill clang that pierced Lucretia's ears. She and Ione dragged Morgan back, leaning his corpse against the cypress' trunk. Lucretia sent a quick glance towards where Kai and Maple were busy with their own fights. Grimghast would let out a pained roar with every blow Kai struck against its armored hide. All the while, the beast had trouble keeping up with the apothecary's erratic movements as he kept it disoriented by drawing a sharpened claw over his weapon's flanges, producing a discordant screech. Nearby, Maple was holding Hemlocke at bay with surprising ease. Burnsong's training shined through in the merchant's acrobatic dodging and enhanced grace. The traitor was growing visibly frustrated, his fangs bared as Maple deflected his staff once more and jabbed an uchine at his wing. The sharp blade sliced through one of Hemlocke's feathers and sent the lower half fluttering to the ground.

A distressed yelp drew her attention back to Duarte. His shoulder was stained crimson, blood soaking through his torn habit. Obram looked not much better. Several new cuts adorned his face and neck, while a scarlet splotch grew on his left upper thigh. Both men gasped for breath. It astounded her the two were able to damage each other so much in such a short amount of time, at least until they charged one another again. Seeing them swinging wildly made it crystal clear they were both preferring an offense-centered approach to the fight, using the bare minimum of defense to keep themselves from getting killed.

Now I'm certain Duarte was holding back against me, Lucretia thought.

Her eyes widened when Obram spun on one heel, evading an overhand cleave from Duarte and moving to separate the Soltauri's arm from his shoulder. He choked in shock when Duarte grabbed the blade open-handed, the steel biting into his palm. Grinning wide, Duarte copied Morgan's earlier tactic in rearing his head back to bash his forehead into Obram's in a fierce headbutt that sent the Risbado reeling.

"What are we supposed to do?" Ione asked, her lip quivering.

While Lucretia took pride in her studious nature, she had to admit she was at a loss for how to help Duarte. Obram was a class of warrior unlike any she'd faced before, which made Morgan's ability to go head to head with him more impressive. Falling to her knees, Lucretia's hands clenched into tight fists, fingers curling around a mass of loose dirt.

"Ouch," she hissed, drawing her hand to her breast. Her gaze wavered over the cluster of fresh cuts she got in her fight with Duarte. The wounds, while small, stung horribly even after brushing away the dirt. A hitched breath escaped her lips when her eyes landed on the swollen skin around the cuts.

"Ione," Lucretia said. The tavern maid met her curious scrutiny, tilting her head. "You have food in your pack, right?"

Ione nodded. "Yes," she drawled, "though I hardly think this is the proper time to ask for a snack."

Rolling her eyes, Lucretia snapped, "That is not what I meant. What kinds of foods do you have? Any fruits tucked away in there?"

"Well..." Ione answered, "I do have some lemonberries I was holding for Morgan. He told me once he likes snacks with a bit of sourness." She reached into her pack and revealed a handful of the fragrant fruits, their bright yellow skin shimmering in the sparse sunbeams. Looking up, she flinched back at the sharkish grin on Lucretia's face.

"Perfect."

She plucked the berries from her friend's open palm. Rising to her feet, she bolted towards the fighting men, gripping the fruit hard enough to feel the skin give under her fingers. Her rapier clattered to the ground, abandoned in her rush.

"Oi! Obram!" Lucretia shouted.

Duarte and Obram paused mid-swing, their weapons hanging in the air as they turned towards the furious scholar. Lucretia's neck erupted in goosebumps at the cold laugh coming from Obram. Every step towards the maniacal sellsword felt heavy, as if her legs were made of cast iron.

"Are you truly so eager to join Morgan in the void?" Obram inquired with an upturned smile. "I didn't realize he meant so much to you. Be sure to tell him how much of a failure you are when you see him."

Before Lucretia could react, Obram dashed within her guard and wrapped his free hand around her throat again. Her muscles clenched on instinct, the berries in her right hand crushed to a juicy pulp.

Obram's sneering face drew close, his pointed nose a fraction of an inch from her own. His heavy breaths passed over her nostrils, filled with the odor of under-cooked meat, blood, and ale. The noxious cocktail of scents would have made Lucretia gag, were it not for the calloused hand cutting off her airway.

"Let her go!" Duarte bellowed, rumbling towards the two with axe drawing back.

A sudden rush of wind stung Lucretia's eyes, whipping her hair around with every twirl Obram made while evading Duarte's lumbering swings with a cackle.

"You're looking a touch slow, Duarte," Obram teased. "I guess all that blood loss is finally getting to you."

Lucretia decided to take full advantage of Obram's distraction. Hooking her left hand under his wrist, the scholar pushed upward hard while pulling away with all her strength. A ragged yelp tore from her throat when Obram's claws scraped along her neck. She saw his head snap around to her, eyes blazing.

"Dinner time!" Lucretia wheezed, lips curved in a mischievous grin. She opened her palm, colored in pale yellow, and gave Obram a ringing slap to the open gash at the edge of his left eye.

The Risbado's hands flew to his face as he staggered back in a caterwauling fit, dropping Lucretia to the ground with a thump. Duarte stood flabbergasted when Obram's hands peeled back to reveal globs of berry mash stuck to the side of his face. His body quaked, though whether it was from rage or pain Lucretia didn't know. Nor could she bring herself to care.

"What the hoarfrost did you do to me?" Obram demanded.

"Aww, you dislike lemonberries?" Lucretia fired back. "Normally I would say they are healthy for you, but this might be the rare exception where fruit can be quite fatal."

Obram growled, "You insufferable witch…wait, all this does is sting—what do you mean it's fatal?"

Shink!

"*That* is what I meant," Lucretia deadpanned.

A pleased hum rang from her mouth as Obram's face froze in stupefied confusion before his head slid free of his body at the neck. Duarte stood behind him, arms extended in clear follow through of another wide-arced swing. Hands twitching, Duarte fumbled his axe and let it hit the ground in a dull thud at the same time Obram's corpse did the same.

"I am glad you made that swing when you did," Lucretia whined, "because I doubt I could have given you a second opening. Good job, Duarte. You beat him."

The monk's eyes rolled. "*We* beat him, Lu. I'm not sure I could've killed that bastard on my own with all these injuries I sustained fighting both him *and* you."

"Regardless of the semantics, he is no longer a threat. You are now truly free to live your life however you wish."

The two stared at one another, though Lucretia could recognize the melancholy weight in her old friend's gaze. Duarte picked his axe off the ground and strolled past her, ignoring the unspoken questions buzzing in her eyes. He came to a stop at the edge of the cliff, gazing out at the rolling hills. Lucretia sidled next to him and let out a muffled gasp drowned out by the sound of clashing battle continuing on the other side of the plateau. The sun peeked through the hills, covering Ballad's End in a warm glow. The explosion from earlier rocked the entire area to the point that swaths of trees even on the hills farther away had toppled over like a pile of matchsticks, leaving patches of bare grass and uprooted dirt with logs splayed across the ground.

"It looks beautiful," Lucretia said, tears brimming at the edge of her eyes, "I only wish Morgan were still alive to see this."

Duarte's grip on his weapon tightened. "Lu, I must apologize for several things, first of which for not stepping in earlier. I hesitated, and an honorable man died for it."

Shaking her head, Lucretia replied, "Do not blame yourself. Morgan had his faults and could be crass, but I will be the first to admit he was a man of honor and displayed a loyalty to our family that would rival even Edeval's."

She heard a deep chuckle from Duarte. "You would truly put him on par with the Saint of Loyalty himself? That's high praise coming from you."

"Indeed. You said you wanted to apologize for other things. I hope you are not planning to spend the rest of the day bemoaning every little thing you think you did to offend me. All that matters to me is that you have come to your senses and begun taking steps to atone for your past choices. Besides, we still need to help Kai and Maple."

"About that..."

Eyes narrowing, Lucretia craned her neck towards Duarte. He was ogling his axe with a somber expression. It was impossible to tell what exactly the Soltauri was thinking, but a frigid chill spread through Lucretia's chest the longer she watched. Something about his actions unnerved her.

Then, without warning, Duarte twirled his weapon around, with the shaft pointed outwards. Lucretia could only watch in mesmerized horror as his mouth twisted into a resolute smirk before ramming the axe's pointed spike into his own stomach.

"Duarte!" Lucretia screamed.

From the cypress, her eyes flickered to Ione who carried a similar aghast expression with one hand covering her mouth and the other clutching Morgan's torn habit in a claw-like grip. Lucretia tore her attention from her friend and turned back to Duarte. The moment she stepped towards him, however, the monk growled and took a step back, inching towards the same cliff Mirabell fell from earlier.

"What are you thinking?" Lucretia demanded. She skidded to a stop seeing him lean precariously over the cliff edge, arms spread to keep her balance. "Have we not seen enough people die today who did not need to?"

"Lu, Obram may have been a pissant of the highest order but he was right about one thing. I was already in this too deep well before I decided to help you. We both know I have too much blood on my hands. Call me a coward if you wish, but even if I worked to make amends for what I've done, that stain will always follow no matter what. I know my death won't bring back all the innocents I killed on Razarr's orders. Still, my hope is that this will at least let their spirits know peace at last."

Lucretia shook her head, sending a wave of fresh tears flying through the air. "And so you simply decided on this without thinking of how it would affect me," she sobbed. "I thought we were friends!"

"Lucretia Dineri, you and Rialta were the best friends I ever had. Still, I knew I couldn't give you a chance to change my mind about this or you'd actually pull it off. You always were the most persuasive of the three of us. At least this way I can die with my head held high, knowing I could reclaim even the tiniest fragment of my honor."

"Damn you, Duarte," Lucretia said, "I already lost one friend in this fight. Do not tell me I have to lose another."

"You still have plenty of friends to watch over you, Lu. I only hope that, when you think of me in the future, you'll try to remember the better days when we were kids. Goodbye, my friend."

In the moment it took Lucretia to blink, she let out a hitched gasp when Duarte flung himself over the side of the cliff. The shock of it kept Lucretia frozen, her legs unwilling to move. It wasn't until an ominous thud echoed from below that she found the strength to take a step forward. Taking a quick peek over the edge, she flinched and looked away from the grisly sight of Duarte laying scant yards from Mirabell, a dark stain spreading around him.

"Is he…?" Ione asked with an uneasy frown.

Lucretia nodded. "He is. Surviving a fall onto those stones from this height would be next to impossible. The one saving grace is the impact likely killed him at once, so I doubt he felt much pain other than from stabbing himself."

Turning on one heel, the scholar observed Obram's corpse with a baleful glare. She strode towards where the Risbado's detached head had rolled and scoffed. Anger swelled in her chest, roiling under her skin like a cauldron of boiling stew. She bit her lip and, emitting a howl of rage, reared one leg back to punt Obram's head across the plateau. A sputtering laugh from Ione brought a tiny smile to Lucretia's lips.

"Sweet Luopari, I should probably scold you for showing disrespect to the dead like that," Ione muttered, "though I find myself not caring, considering what that ghastly man did."

"Then we are both in agreement," Lucretia replied. "I must confess that felt quite good. Perhaps I should do it again." The two women laughed, though their mirth was interrupted by the ring of Maple's uchine pinging off Hemlocke's staff. Easing herself from beneath Morgan's head, Ione rested the sellsword's body on the ground before retrieving her cutlass and shield.

"We'd best go see if Maple needs some help," Ione said. Lucretia nodded and snapped her own rapier from where it lay. The two bolted across the plateau, ready to assist in whatever way they were needed.

The fight wouldn't be over, after all, until Hemlocke and his ghastly beast followed their allies to the voids of Nulyma for the pain they caused.

Chapter XXXV

White-hot rage pulsed through Kai's veins. Every nerve from his neck down to his fingers and toes wanted nothing more than to rush to Morgan's aid after seeing his friend skewered by Obram's broadsword. Unfortunately, Grimghast was proving as frustrating as ever and left him with no room to break away from the fight.

His vines were proving unable to hold Grimghast in place for more than a few seconds. Its claws tore through the plants with ease, preventing him from distracting it long enough to reach Morgan. Even more vexing was how the monster's intelligence was on full display with a remarkable ability to adapt to his battle tactics. Kai's normal methods of disorienting Grimghast through loud noises proved useless when it began anticipating when he was about to draw his claws over Mimilrun's flanges, covering its own ears with its paws before charging.

If this thing weren't so maddening and dangerous, I'd suggest it be studied to see just how smart it really *is,* Kai thought when Mimilrun bounced off Grimghast's armor once more, putting another crack in the bony rib plates.

His eyes widened when a pair of loud wails pierced his ears. He swung his gaze to where Lucretia and Ione were crying over Morgan's prone body. The sellsword wasn't moving. An icy chill slithered down to the tips of his tails.

"No," he whispered.

Kai paid for his moment of inattention when Grimghast swatted him in the chest with an open paw. The blow picked him off his feet and sent him crashing into the craggy wall. With the air knocked from his lungs, he collapsed to his hands and knees, wheezing.

"Kai!" Orelia shrieked.

His partner's shrill cry snapped him to attention, Timber flaring to life inside his chest. A coiling tingle spread across his back while a pulse of energy surged through his eyes and ears, sharpening his senses at once.

The sharp ring of Hemlocke's braying trill grated his extra-sensitive ears, though Kai refused to take his eyes off Grimghast again while hauling himself to his feet.

"What a shame," said Hemlocke, his mouth twisted in a venomous leer. "It seems as though you've failed another one, Kai. Tell me, which one hurt the worst? Losing your squad, your village, or that oafish chimera?"

A vibrating trill emanated from Maple. "You shut your damn mouth," she warned in a low, frosty tone. "I've met all manner of assholes since my hometown exiled me, but I'll confess none had the same callous disdain for life that you do."

"Why would I waste time searching for any purpose in the suffering my life has been filled with?" Hemlocke snapped. "The way I see it, if I had to be forced through years of anguish and pain, then the rest of the world deserves to suffer with me."

With only a muffled grunt as warning, Grimghast pounced towards Kai, forcing the apothecary to roll away from its jagged claws. Gripping Mimilrun in both hands, Kai spun on one heel and landed a blow to the beast's hip. A sickening crack echoed followed by a horrid shriek. He let a small grin settle on his lips while darting around Grimghast from behind, allowing him to keep one ear swiveled towards Maple.

The merchant ruffled her feathers, the stony glare on her face drawing a chuckle from Hemlocke. Both Aerivolk scraped their talons along the ground in anticipation though Hemlocke's posture was much looser, even dismissive.

Maple peered at Orelia, ascertaining the younger woman's position. Rocks skittered across the ground when Hemlocke rushed towards her, preparing to club her over the head with his staff. The merchant's lips shifted into a confident smirk when she sidestepped the blow and launched an upwards slash of her own. She let out a victorious shout when Hemlocke stumbled away, one hand grabbing the new slash mark crossing his left cheek from the chin to his ear.

"You're beginning to grate on my last nerve, girl," Hemlocke hissed. "How are you proving so frustrating?"

"Good," Maple sniped back with a tilted grin. "Means I'm doing my job."

She raised her hand and launched an orb of compressed wind from her palm. The blast's recoil snapped her arm back, causing the orb to fly too far right and miss Hemlocke completely, smashing into the wall and creating a smokescreen of dust and crushed gravel. Muttering a flurry of curses under her breath, a throbbing wave of fatigue spread through both her arms. Maple fought to ignore the sensation and thrust both arrows towards her opponent's chest.

Twirling his staff, Hemlocke parried the uchines and shoved her away, skittering back to put some distance between them. His mouth slipped into a pensive sneer. Maple fought the urge to chase after him, though cursed when the traitor clambered up a tree and began hopping from branch to branch.

"Oi! Where in the winds do you think you're going?" Maple screeched.

A wave of confusion swept through her feathers when Hemlocke halted at the pathway above them, letting loose a maniacal cackle. Beckoning Orelia over, Maple motioned for her to follow when they lost sight of Hemlocke seconds before the distinctive crack of broken wood resounded from above. Amplifying their befuddlement was the chittering sound that followed.

Why do I have a bad feeling about this? Maple wondered. Her dorsal feathers tingled with anxiety. The bushes along the path's edge rustled. Both women readied themselves into stances, only to blanch when a pack of tree ferrets burst from the leaves.

"Wait...ferrets?" Orelia questioned, her ears wiggling up and down.

"*Taen!*" Kai shouted while dodging Grimghast's fanged maw. "Stay away from those things, girls—they must be how Hemlocke is planning to spread the Blight!"

The pair's eyes bulged as they scrambled back. Overhead, Hemlocke's cackling grew more obnoxious. "You always *were* frustratingly quick to figure things out, Kai," he said, "but yes, these little critters will be the vessels that bring this entire continent to its knees! The ticks I laced them with will spread to other animals, which will then spread the Blight to anyone who gets too close!"

"Damn it!" Orelia swore. The Vesikoi's grip on her staff grew so tight, her knuckles shifted to a ghastly pale sheen.

The ferrets scattered among the trees, their chattering squeaks the only evidence of their continued presence until even those faded to silence. Maple's body quivered as her mind produced gruesome images of what could happen if the ferrets were allowed to roam freely.

"Orelia," Maple said, "go help out Ione and Lucretia, then once y'all are done, find Fusette to warn her about the ferrets. We can't let even one of them escape!"

"Mapes, I can't leave you like this on your own."

"It wasn't a request, Ora! Don't worry about me—so long as I can keep up with him until that elixir wears off, we've still got a chance."

Hemlocke guffawed. "You're oddly confident for someone all the way down there. What's to stop me from disappearing as easily as those ferrets did?"

Instead of answering the hysterical Aerivolk, Maple grinned and aimed her arm once more. Using her left hand as a brace, she fired another wind orb at Hemlocke. This time, it struck true and exploded against his chest. He flew upwards until his back struck an overhead branch. He collapsed to the ground a precarious distance from the edge, causing his attempt to roll over to send him tumbling down to the plateau with a pained groan the moment his back slammed into the dirt. Maple and Orelia cheered, cleaving to each other in a celebratory embrace.

"That's it," Hemlocke growled, his chest expanding with each heavy breath. "You're pissed me off for the last time. Nulla!"

Kai leaned back, letting Grimghast's paw pass over him. His lungs burned from the constant dodging, though he took solace in the fact Grimghast looked to be tiring as well. Dashing sideways, he scooped up a small pebble from the ground and flung it into Grimghast's eye, sending the creature into a bellowing rage. The apothecary's face morphed into a toothy smile as he leapt onto Grimghast's back and smashed Mimilrun between its shoulder blades in an overhand strike.

Grimghast pitched forward and shook itself side to side, roaring in pain. Kai was unable to maintain his hold on its back and was thrown off, rolling along the ground. Spitting some dirt out, he peered up to see Grimghast advancing towards him with hunger in its eyes. Before it covered half the distance between them, Hemlocke's voice cut through the air and brought it to a halt.

"Nulla!"

A sharp whistle emanated from the Aerivolk in a strange, melodic tune. Kai locked his gaze on the beast, searching for any hints of what its handler's wordless command truly was. To his surprise, Grimghast let out a low chuff before turning away from him, beginning to scale the cliff. Terrified understanding bloomed over Kai's face.

Hemlocke was ordering it to escape!

"I don't think so!" Kai roared, firing a vine from his wrist and encircling it around Grimghast's hind ankle. Giving a harsh yank, he pulled it free of the rocks and brought it crashing back down with a boom. Grimghast twisted its neck around to level a menacing glare at the apothecary.

Another series of clicks and whistles came from Hemlocke. "Nulla, it's time," he crooned. "Finish that bastard so you can complete our mission."

Once again, Kai bit back a growl seeing Grimghast shred his vine with little effort. It pushed itself onto its hind legs, towering over Kai with lustrous saliva dribbling from its jaw. Then, to Kai's horror, the air around the beast shimmered in a familiar wavy pattern. Before his very eyes, he watched as his opponent appeared to melt out of existence, its body completely disappearing. Somehow, Grimghast had learned to use its blending ability while in the midst of battle.

Oh, baubles and berries, that's not good...

CHAPTER XXXVI

A bone-chilling frost crept through Kai's body despite the warm air. The telltale prickle of his fur standing on end was worsened by his heart pounding like a drum within his chest. His head swiveled back and forth, searching for Grimghast. Waves of panic pulsed through his mind when his gaze swept over the ground. The lack of recent rain meant the ground was bone dry. Finding Grimghast through the paw prints it typically left behind would be difficult.

While he scrambled to think of how to locate the beast, a heavy weight collided with his chest. The air was knocked from his lungs as he rolled away, covering half the distance between where he started and where Maple battled Hemlocke. The strap holding the blunderbuss to his back snapped under the strain, the gun clattering away. A familiar voice rang from the other side of the plateau.

"Kai!" Lucretia shouted as she and Ione barreled towards him.

He stifled a groan and pushed himself onto his knees before halting the scholar's advance. "Stay back!" Kai commanded, bringing the two women to a halt. "Lucretia, I need you and Ione to find Fusette. Warn her about the ferrets and to spread the word among the alliance. We'll handle these two!"

"You've lost your kettle!" Ione replied. "How are you going to fight that thing if you can't even see it?"

As much as Kai hated admitting it, he knew the tavern maid had a point. Grimghast's blending wasn't perfect, but it was more than sufficient to throw him off guard. His gaze drifted to Ione, only for his blood to freeze in terror.

It was faint, but the air in front of Ione *moved* in a familiar pattern. Pumping Timber into his legs, Kai blasted forward as if shot from a cannon. He angled his shoulder at the shimmering spot and grinned when he crashed into solid flesh. Grimghast slid across the ground with a pained roar, its body melting back into view.

Ione and Lucretia backed away moon eyed, tightening their grip on their weapons. Kai snapped his fingers, gesturing for them to run. To his relief, they did exactly that, tearing down the path as fast as their legs could carry them. Seeing them disappear among the trees filled Kai with relief.

A rumbling growl drew his eyes back to Grimghast. It rose up once more, its beady eye piercing through him as if staring straight into his spirit. Licking his lips, Kai readied himself. Grimghast paced back and forth in front of him, its tongue lolling in the open air with puffs of condensed air escaping its maw with every breath. The air around its body shimmered again, though moments later it stopped, unable to reproduce its vanishing ability. Kai slid one foot back to brace himself as his tails coiled behind him. His eyes swept over the beast, scanning for even the slightest movement. The moment Grimghast's legs tensed beneath its lanky body, Kai grit his teeth in preparation.

Grimghast lunged, mouth open wide in an attempt to bite the apothecary in half. Venomous saliva dripped to the dirt, reflecting the sunlight. Before it could reach him, Kai ducked into its guard and reached up to grab a fistful of the beast's muzzle. With an infusion of Timber, his muscles pulsated with power as he yanked down and slammed Grimghast to the ground on its head. A wave of pain and fatigue rattled his nerves, jarring him from the intense focus his mind had settled into.

Taen, Kai thought, *I must be using too much Timber. My body's losing strength faster than I can replenish it!*"

A low chuff from below was all the warning Kai had before his entire gut flared in pain. Grimghast's gangly elbow dug into his stomach, pushing him back. Both hands clutched at his throbbing abs, leaving him vulnerable long enough for the beast to snatch him in its paw and lift him off the ground. The wind rushed over Kai's skin, his feet dangling haplessly in the air. He had no time to consider what was happening when his back struck dirt with a solid thud. Mimilrun bounced away in a cloud of gravel.

Forcing his eyes open through the pain, Kai thrust his leg up and caught Grimghast in the lower jaw with his boot. Unphased by the blow, Grimghast pressed its paw on Kai's chest, leaning in to pin him under its substantial weight. Kai pushed against the massive paw in a futile effort to free himself, his muscles throbbing with pain. Staring into Grimghast's eye, he emitted a disgusted groan as globs of saliva splattered on his face and shoulders. Grimghast's head lunged down, intending to snap him in twain. With a defiant roar, Kai raised his arms and grasped the beast by its jaws. He fought to ignore the stinging of Grimghast's dagger-like teeth digging into his palms and fingers. A familiar, sharp tingle vibrated through the various cuts on his exposed skin where the saliva pooled. Maple and Orelia's screams set off a bevy of anxious jitters that spread from his neck, arcing down his spine until reaching his arms and legs.

When this is all over, I'm gonna be in so much trouble with those two...

Hemlocke's vile trill brought a perturbed frown to his face. "Looks like it's over, girls. All that's left is to see what kills your precious husband first: Nulla, or her venom."

Glancing over, he saw Maple staring at him in fear. Her lips were parted in a terrified gasp while leaking tears from her reddening eyes. To his surprise, it was Orelia who was staring with renewed confidence. Her mouth was tilted in a cheeky smirk. The former priestess simply gave him a nod before grabbing Maple by the wrist.

"Kai will be fine, Mapes," she declared. "Just focus on kicking that traitorous bastard's ass and don't let him get in your head!" The sudden statement jolted Maple from her thoughts, bringing her attention back to Orelia with a baffled expression, one eyebrow quirked upwards.

"How stupid are you?" Hemlocke gloated, eyes furrowed. "The lich bear's venom is one of the most potent on Nixtral! There's no way that bastard will survive being envenomed with so much without taking an antidote in the next few minutes."

Orelia's smirk elongated into a sharkish grin, her teeth gleaming. "What would Kai need an antidote for?" she said. "He's imbibed so much of that thing's venom since their first encounter on his own, he's almost fully immune to its effects!"

Were he not struggling to keep Grimghast from devouring him, Kai would have laughed at the fish-slapped gape on Hemlocke's face at Orelia's words. He wasn't sure what was funnier: The Aerivolk's expression, or the sputtering babble of nonsensical words currently spewing from his mouth.

"Damn it all!" Hemlocke roared. "How are the three of you such a bloody pain in my tail feathers? What is it going to take to finally *kill* you?"

Kai's vision turned hazy with rage, the prickling under his skin growing stronger with each second. Grimghast pushed harder against his hands, carrying him across the ground until his shoulders met the rocky cliff leading to the upper path. A sharp pinch erupted in his knuckles where a set of torpothorn thorns emerged. Kai threw a hook into the side of Grimghast's head, wincing when the thorns snapped off against the bony plate protecting the beast's lower jaw. His gaze flickered to where Maple slid back into a fighting stance in time to meet Hemlocke's charge.

The traitor's strength looked to be ebbing at last, his strikes unable to push Maple backwards the way they did before. Her uchines sparked against the nails in Hemlocke's staff, snapping one off that grazed her cheek as it flew past.

With a feral leer, Hemlocke ducked under Maple's next thrust and reached for her throat with his free hand. Maple's eyes widened, a short gasp escaping her lips. She stumbled back just enough to evade his sharpened nails, though not enough to prevent him wrapping a slender finger around the pendant dangling from her neck. Kai's breath caught in his throat when Hemlocke yanked back, tearing his mother's pendant away. Undeterred, Hemlocke pressed his advantage and lashed out with a second swipe of his hand. He let out a shrill yelp when Orelia appeared from behind Maple, smacking the offending claws away with her staff. Hemlocke's raging glare spun to the former priestess, who met the odious look with unyielding determination. He swung his staff towards Orelia, who backed away only to lose her own pendant when it was cut loose by the jagged nails.

"I thought I told you to stay back, Ora!" Maple snapped. Her arms encircled the other woman in a restraining embrace as they put some distance between themselves and their opponent.

"No," Orelia retorted, her grin never fading, "you asked me to watch your back, and I don't give a damn how much you want to kick his ass on your own. I'm not losing the closest thing I've ever had to a sister to this deceitful coward."

"You have nerve calling me a coward," Hemlocke said. He swung the pendants back and forth by their torn cords, eyeing them with a contemplative sneer. "Though I suppose it won't matter much once I kill you both. These are rather pretty little pendants, aren't they? Oh well, you won't be needing them where you're going."

Kai gasped when Hemlocke flicked his wrist, sending the pendants slicing through the air towards him. The glass orbs smashed against the craggy wall above Kai's head, the shattered glass glittering like stars in the sunbeams as the pieces came to rest beside him. The piercing crack produced by the pendants' impact jarred Grimghast for a moment, its head rearing back and giving Kai a needed respite. He only had time to catch his breath for a moment before it lunged again. This time, Kai leaned back and raised both legs, catching Grimghast's jaw with his boots. The extra strength in his legs allowed him to keep them outstretched, holding the beast back. Glancing to the side, he saw Mimilrun shining just out of arm's reach. He extended his arm, straining with all he had to reach the shaft while continuing to push against Grimghast's ravenous maw. Unfortunately, no matter how hard he tried, the weapon was too far away. Flinching in pain, he extended a vine from his wrist and slithered it towards Mimilrun's shaft. His agitation swelled when Grimghast saw what he was doing and, releasing what sounded suspiciously like a grumbling laugh, sliced the vine in twain before sliding a paw along the ground to bat the mace even further away.

Damn it to Nulyma, he bemoaned, *it's gonna take a miracle for me to get out of this one.*

His ears prickled, twisting towards the staccato thump of rushing footsteps. His eyes drifted to Maple, who was now pushing Hemlocke back closer to the plateau's edge. He was stunned by the familiar thin ring of crimson around the rim of her eyes, her furious trills resounding in the air. His shock grew when a familiar voice rang in his ears.

"Merciful Galen, Kai!" Fusette cried out. Behind the duchess stood Lucretia and Ione, along with her entire entourage. Her eyes were bulbous, the entire group frozen in place watching Kai's struggle.

He let out a chuff, his lungs burning. "Stay back, Fusette!" he bellowed. "Actually, can one of you do me a favor and grab my mace? My legs can't hold out much longer!"

"I'll do ya one better," Fusette answered before rushing off. Saredi shouted at her to come back, though the stormy glare she leveled at him stopped the Vesikoi from attempting to follow.

Further back, he spotted Maple continue pushing Hemlocke inch by inch towards the edge. With an enraged shriek, she spun on one heel, slashing an uchine towards the other Aerivolk's chest. Her eyes widened when he raised his staff and took a short hop just before her weapon clashed with his. The impact carried him in an arc, switching their positions. Hemlocke pushed off, his grin growing to manic proportions while thrusting his staff in an attempt to shove Maple over the edge instead. His smile transformed to a vicious snarl as Orelia rushed between them and thrust the rounded head of her cudgel straight into his gut.

Hemlocke staggered back, coughing and wheezing. "This doesn't make sense. How are you two even more of a pain in my tail than your damnable husband?" he gasped, one hand pressed to the tender muscle. Hemlocke's cheeks puffed out, his chest shifting. "The elixir shouldn't be wearing off this soon! My calculations said I should still have a few more minutes of strength left!"

"You wanna know why we're so strong?" Orelia shouted, the sudden response drawing Hemlocke's attention to her. "It's because you made the mistake of threatening our future with the man we love. Ready to nail him to the wall, Mapes?"

Maple curled her fingers together, a gentle white glow enveloping her hand. "I've been ready," she murmured. A powerful gale encircled the two women, picking up dust and rocks and swirling them around the pair in a miniature tornado.

Kai's entire body burned, his muscles screaming in pain as Grimghast refused to relent. He was grateful for the beast's furious, singular focus on trying to swallow him whole, as it seemed to have forgotten it could snatch him in its paws. He reached into his robe pocket and pulled out a vial filled with a pungent brown liquid.

"Let's see how you like this," Kai said.

Popping the cork free, he flung the vial of fluxroot extract into Grimghast's cavernous mouth. The effect was immediate, as Grimghast reeled back with hacking coughs. Its eye dilated to an enormous size, saliva and extract dribbling from its mouth and coating the dirt in a viscous slime. Moments later, the beast leaned forward and retched, the contents of its stomach splashing across the ground.

Kai scrambled back to his feet. Searching for Fusette, he called for his weapon. The duchess' grin stretched from ear to ear as she heaved a long, cloth-wrapped object towards him. Kai erupted into sputtering confusion when an unfamiliar weight landed in his outstretched arms. The cloth fell away to reveal the blunderbuss, its polished barrel reflecting the sun's rays. His hand reached for the pouch of iron balls he'd tied to his waist only to grasp empty air.

"*Taen,*" Kai muttered, "how does she expect me to use this thing without—"

Sliding his foot back to turn back towards Grimghast, a soft tinkle rang in Kai's ears. He glanced down, spotting the shattered remnants of Maple and Orelia's pendants. A muffled gasp escaped his lips. Grimghast's rumbling growl snapped Kai from his thoughts. Seeing the beast recovering from the fluxroot, he dropped to his knees and scooped the broken shards and handfuls of gravel into the blunderbuss' barrel. The moment he glanced up, Grimghast released a blood-curdling roar and charged. Kai clenched his fist, swinging his arm in a wide arc. His hand opened, flinging a cloud of dust and glass chips into Grimghast's eyes. It skidded to a stop, flailing its head and clawing at its eyes.

"This ends now!" Kai bellowed, seating the blunderbuss against his shoulder.

"Couldn't have said it better myself, love," Maple said. The winds whipped the merchant's hair and vest about, coalescing into a gleaming sphere of energy above her palm. Orelia stood beside her, a matching cobalt orb of water condensing in her hands.

The energy produced by the two orbs crackled with power, filling the air with waves of energy. Kai's fur stood on end as the charged air sent a tingle through his entire body. His grip on the blunderbuss loosened, so transfixed was he on the beautiful sight of his wives raising their arms in tandem to aim at Hemlocke's chest.

"Hemlocke Desmort," Maple said, "the trials you suffered in your life were terrible, yet you still could have made something of yourself. Instead, you chose to kill and spread suffering as a sick form of revenge against the world. Now Nulyma will judge you according to those choices."

"Stupid woman," Hemlocke snapped, "this fight isn't over. I answer to no one!" The traitor raised his weapon and took a single step forward when he froze in place. Eyes bulging, he stared at the two women in horror as his body seemed to tighten all at once.

"Why can't I move?" Hemlocke gasped.

Kai thrust his arm out, feeling the familiar pinch of his vines bursting forward. The thick ropes coiled around Hemlocke's waist and shoulders, drawing taut and eliciting a stunned yelp from the Aerivolk. His head spun to Kai, their gazes meeting.

"May Cacovis guide you on your final journey," Maple and Orelia intoned, their eyes flashing with steely determination.

In unison, the pair released their attacks in a deafening boom, the magical orbs spiraling towards Hemlocke. His eyes bulged, a strangled shriek of defiance rising from his throat. The elemental bombs struck him in tandem, exploding against his chest in a storm of wind and mist.

Hemlocke was blasted towards Kai, blood spraying from between his clenched lips. A familiar growl caught Kai's attention, his head whipping back to see Grimghast advancing at an awkward gait with its eye shut. The beast sniffed the air before lunging forward with its jaws opened wide. Lips curling into a smug grin, Kai stepped back and swung his arm, pulling the vines back to let him guide Hemlocke's airborne form directly into his pet. The two collided in a dull thud, Hemlocke trying to push away only to be snatched up by Grimghast's dagger-like claws encircling his torso.

"Nulla, what are you...?" Hemlocke questioned, freezing when he noticed her damaged ears and bloodshot eye. "Wait, stop!"

Kai raked his claws across the mace once more, producing a shrill tone that drowned out Hemlocke's shouts. The traitor cried out as Grimghast grabbed his legs with its other paw, holding him in place. With a ravenous roar, the monster crushed Hemlocke's waist with its jaws. A sickening crunch filled the air, blood splattering over the ground. Kai forced himself to watch as Grimghast tore its handler in twain, his insides spilling into the beast's open gullet. Within moments Hemlocke's body was devoured, the only evidence of its presence being a few dusty white feathers and a crimson stain in the dirt at Grimghast's feet.

Kai's body tensed when Grimghast faced him again. Its nostrils flared, a heavy growl rumbling from its chest. The blunderbuss' bulk felt unnatural in his hands, weighing his arms down as if it were made from solid iron rather than steel and wood. Grimghast leapt forward, sending Kai staggering away as his friends and allies shouted in alarm. His heel thumped against an exposed root and he pitched backwards onto his rump. Grimghast barreled into him with the force of a rampaging bison. Planting his feet into its chest, Kai pushed back as hard as he could.

Pain erupted in his side. Emitting an agonizing howl, Kai's gaze drifted for a split moment to see one of Grimghast's claws slicing the edge of his torso just beneath his ribs. Blood leaked from the wound in a crimson river.

"Damn it, Kai, *shoot!*" Maple's voice cried out, breaking through the pain.

Gritting his teeth, Kai lifted the blunderbuss. The faces of his squad mates drifted through his mind, as if cheering him on. Calvino's hearty, jovial laugh. Faust's silent but expressive bemusement. Marko's boisterous guffaws and flirtatious grin. A single tear slid down Kai's face.

"This is for you, boys," he whispered. Kai waited for Grimghast to thrust its head forward in another snap, then jammed the blunderbuss' muzzle into its open mouth. Eyes blazing, he pulled the trigger.

An explosive boom battered Kai's ears, forcing him to flatten them against his skull as the weight pinning him to the ground lifted in an instant. Grimghast's head snapped backwards with crimson mist and chunks of brain matter cascading through the air. The beast toppled sideways, its body spasming and twitching for several seconds before falling still.

Hands quaking, Kai dropped the blunderbuss. One hand tightened into a fist while the other clutched his injured side. His instincts reminded him to be wary as he approached Grimghast's body. A cynical voice in the back of his mind breathed that no amount of fluxroot could heal the damage that single shot left in its wake.

"I-Is it dead?" Fusette asked, creeping forward and brushing off Saredi's attempts to hold her back.

Kai stepped around to Grimghast's head, fresh torpothorn spikes jutting from between his knuckles. He released a heavy sigh noting the melon-sized hole in its skull.

"I think I can safely say it's dead," Kai confirmed. "If getting its brains blown out and scattered to the eight winds isn't enough to kill it, I'll eat my robes. Right before it eats me, most likely."

A wave of raucous applause tore through the crowd. Fusette launched herself at Kai, wrapping her arms around his neck and nearly knocking him off his feet. The moment he steadied himself, two more bodies crashed into him—Maple and Orelia proved more than enough to send the quartet collapsing to the ground in a pile.

"I knew you could do it!" Maple squealed. Her violet eyes glowed with a mix of relief and joy. Kai blushed when her lips mashed against his in a searing kiss. In seconds, he was pulled free from Maple's ardor only for Orelia to take her place. His grip on them tightened. "The word is being spread across the alliance with orders to burn every tree ferret we come across for the foreseeable future. In fact, I've already had Saredi call for the Hunter Corps to break away from the fighting to take the lead on that mission. The little buggers might be hard to find around here for a while once the Corps is done with them, but it'll be worth it."

"And the Blight?"

"I weaved several Royal Apothecaries in with the alliance forces. Thanks to our everoak, they managed to produce more than enough elixir to hold off the Blight in the chance the ferrets infect anyone ."

Elation bloomed over Kai's face. Grimghast and Hemlocke were no more, along with their allies. The Liberation Army would likely be wiped out or captured before the sun reached its zenith. His eyes drifted to Morgan, where several Livorian sailors were wrapping the sellsword's body in an ivory shroud and preparing him for movement. He limped towards the group, one hand on his wound. The sailors looked at each other with nervous expressions when Kai stood over Morgan's body and placed his free hand on the man's chest.

"Damn it, Morgan," he grumbled, unable to hold back the tears sliding down his cheeks. "May Cacovis guide you on your final journey, my brother."

As much as seeing his friend's corpse filled him with pain and remorse, a tiny voice in his mind reminded him that Morgan would want him to keep marching forward. With that in mind, he resolved to ensure the man's sacrifice was given its proper dues.

For the first time since Mistport, a sense of calm permeated his being.

They were safe at last.

Chapter XXXVII

In all the times he'd been there since his Branding, Kai had never seen Whistlevale so full of life. With the sun beginning to dip beneath the far horizon, the streets were overflowing with joyous people of all ages, nationalities, and tribes. Brightly hued banners, flags, and ribbons waved through the air in a sea of vivid colors. A variety of sights, sounds, and scents assaulted Kai's senses all at once, originating from the gaggle of fresh food and people singing and dancing to the tune of numerous instruments from across Alezon. To the apothecary's surprise, even the Norzen contingent from Duskmarsh was reveling in the festivities and being welcomed with open arms.

Marching at a slow pace beside Fusette as she rode down Main Street into the palace plaza with Maple and Orelia on his arms, Kai was left speechless by the waves of praise being showered on the party. The sheer magnitude of it all kept his attention diverted from the bandaged wound Grimghast left under his ribs. Glancing backwards, he emitted an amused chuckle seeing Ione overwhelmed by it all. Teos and Lucretia gave off an aloof poise, though Kai could see the minuscule smiles and tiny hint of blushes on their cheeks while the people rained applause on them.

On Fusette's other side, Saredi and Rorik marched with a regal grace. Both men were covered in dirt with their armor dented and scuffed, though were otherwise mostly unharmed. Behind them came the rest of the Alezonian leaders and their entourages, Kabuji leading the way with a broad smile stretched over his lips and his son Mataga at his side looking embarrassed. Even Gideon looked relieved, a thin smirk on his face.

Bringing up the rear was a squad of sailors carrying Grimghast's corpse, its limbs splayed out and bound to a pair of thick poles. Kai couldn't blame the shock and fear in the faces of those close enough to see the beast. The crowds seemed eager to give Grimghast a wide berth, even when it was clear the creature was dead.

Fusette lead the procession into the plaza with a determined expression. The crowds bundled together at the entryway, pouring through the opening like a river. Kai flashed a gracious smile to his wives, thankful for their arms hooked around him as they trudged up the steps. Once everyone reached the palace landing, Fusette spun and faced the crowd. Kai's own face furrowed at the traces of fresh wrinkles spreading across the duchess' face. Accepting a warhorn from Rorik, Fusette brought it to her lips and spoke with an authority that sent tremors through Kai's mane.

"Citizens and honored guests," she began, "it is with great joy and relief that we return to you all. I am pleased to announce that the Liberation Army has been utterly routed. Rejoice and calm your fears, for the Faumen War is officially over!"

The crowd burst into raucous applause, whistling and waving their banners. Dilating his pupils, Kai could see the looks of unrestrained glee in the people's faces. His gaze shifted to the bottom of the stairs, where his mother and sister stared with toothy grins.

Gesturing for the masses to settle, Fusette continued, "This is indeed wonderful news. First of all, I want to extend the utmost gratitude to our friends and allies from across Alezon. Without their aid, this war could've taken countless more lives than it already has. For that, the Grand Duchy of Livoria owes you all a debt I'm not sure can ever be repaid."

Stepping forward, Isolde rested a firm hand on Fusette's shoulder while accepting the warhorn from the younger monarch. "Livoria owes no debt, especially not to Galstein," she declared. "If anything, this war has taught us we all have a long road ahead to ensure such a calamity does not spread elsewhere in our beautiful continent. If such vitriol could fester within a realm many would agree is historically the most peaceful among us, then it proves we must all do our part to promote a doctrine of love and understanding."

Kabuji released a booming laugh, clapping Fusette on her other shoulder. The rambunctious emperor needed no warhorn to project his voice. "Couldn't have put it better myself!" Kabuji brayed. "I'm sure I speak for everyone on this landing when I say we couldn't be prouder of the leader you've become, Fusette. I knew your father from when we were young, and I doubt Vonlo could've handled this war with the grace and dignity you have."

Rather than offer their own remarks, Velibor and Gideon opted to bow at the waist, nodding their heads in respect. Kai bit his lip, trying not to chuckle at the tears flowing from Fusette's eyes.

"Thank you so much, all of you. My fervent hope is we're seeing the birth of an alliance for the ages. One that will defend and honor the people's hopes for many years."

The crowd burst into renewed cheers.

Fusette's smile burned brighter as she faced Kai before speaking into the warhorn again. "As I'm sure many of you now know, Sir Gravebane and his party have proven themselves an instrumental key to our victory today. This may come as a shock to many of you but I've recently discovered that Gravebane is, in truth, a distant relation through my father's family. Thus, I am proud to publicly declare House Travaldi as a full branch of the Royal House of Ardei!"

For the briefest of moments, the crowd was stunned into silence. Kai gulped, his wives' arms hooked around his elbows being the only thing stopping him from shrinking away into the foyer behind them. Then, just as suddenly as they quieted, the entire throng burst into approbation. The Norzen proved the loudest of the lot, their whistles and roars of pride drowning out everyone around them.

"It is my hope you will all treat Graveb—no, *Prince* Kai, and his family with the same respect and courtesy you do me. Assuming, of course, you all wish for me to remain as Grand Duchess..."

The entire palace shook from the ear-shattering chorus of cheers reverberating from the crowd. Banners and flags rippled like a tide, their colors shining in the diminishing sunbeams.

Fusette emitted a giggle, one hand over her mouth in a dainty limp. "It appears you've made your opinions quite well known on *that* matter," she chortled. "If that is your will, then I will happily serve until the end of my days."

Her face sank into a forlorn frown. "However," she continued, "it saddens me to confess that many good lives were lost during the battle. For one, I wouldn't be standing here now if not for Admiral Larimanz. He gave his life to save me when a sinkhole opened in Ballad's End, swallowing many souls from both sides. In addition, Morgan Cauzet, a member of Kai's own party, sacrificed himself to protect one of their number."

Giving her cousin a sad smile amid the torrent of horrified gasps coming from below, Fusette held the warhorn towards him. "I know this is rather sudden, Kai, but I feel it would be more appropriate if you said a few words about Morgan. After all, you knew him far better than I ever did."

Kai stared at the horn, his stomach feeling as though the bottom had fallen out. He found himself unable to breathe, his hands turning clammy and muscles locked in place. The apothecary was snapped from his terrified state when Orelia's smooth fingers traced a line across his jawline, inching down his neck.

"You can do this," the former priestess murmured. "I'm certain Morgan wouldn't want anyone else to give his memory the respect it deserves."

Swallowing his fear, Kai reached out to take the warhorn and gazed out at the expectant masses. He took a calming breath, relishing the touch of his wives' hands on his back, and spoke.

"Morgan Cauzet," he said, "was a man of many talents, not all of them good or appropriate. I'll be the first to admit he could be a right pain in the tails when he wanted. Morgan tended to be crass, lewd, and had table manners that could make a drunken ape look like a member of high nobility."

A wave of laughter rang throughout the crowd, drawing a smile from Kai's lips. "But I'll also be the first to tell you he was a warrior of the highest caliber and one of the most passionate men you could meet. He was brave, selfless, and above all else, a loyal friend who could've given Edeval a run for his coin. For all his faults, Morgan was a man you could count on when the scales were stacked against you. He may have been from Corlati, but he was more of a patriot to his family and beliefs than to any national flag."

Kai's breath hitched, unable to stop the flood of tears now trickling down his cheeks. "Morgan was...he was my brother in everything but blood. The word 'family' runs deeper than any amount of blood ever could. Morgan and the rest of my friends standing before you are living proof of that. We don't agree on everything, but when it came down to it, we watched each other's backs and faced every trial Nulyma sent our way. As a family.

"Therefore, I'd like to propose a call in remembrance of not only Morgan and Admiral Larimanz, but *everyone* whose lives were snuffed out before their time." Lowering the warhorn, Kai raised a single fist into air.

"To a bright future filled with love, hope, and justice!"

The throng echoed the sentiment in earnest. Kai could see many displaying tears of their own. He blushed when Maple and Orelia kissed his cheeks, their lips gliding over his skin in a tender caress.

"That was beautiful, love," Maple said.

Fusette nodded. "Thank you, Kai," she praised. Sweeping her arm towards the crowd. "In celebration of the war's end and in honor of the fallen, I hereby declare this day, the final day of Regemond, shall henceforth be celebrated as Remembrance Day."

A cheeky grin slipped onto Fusette's face, making Kai wonder just what was going through her mind. He was surprised when she gestured for the rest of the party to step forward. "As I mentioned before," the duchess pressed on, "Kai and his friends contributed so much to our victory whether through tactics, research, or actual combat, that I fear we may have even lost the war without them. Therefore, I am hereby Branding each of them as Exarch Knights in recognition of their service to the realm."

Kai stumbled, though his reaction paled in comparison to his friends, each of whom wore expression of shock mixed with befuddlement and a hint of fear. Ione, in particular, looked ready to fall away in a dead faint. Behind Fusette, Saredi cradled his head in his hands with a look that made it clear he had no idea this was coming. Rorik's head was tilted, a blank stare on his face, while the leaders were all leaning on each other in their mirth.

"This is a decision I've been considering for some time now," Fusette confessed, "so much so that I have already selected your Brands and had your service watches commissioned. Yes, even Morgan's. Since our first meeting as a group back in Runegard, you seven have proven yourselves time and again as not only ardent defenders of the people, but dear friends who've given the world a shining example of what family truly is. Saredi, my scepter."

The Lord Chamberlain gave a single nod, snapping his fingers towards a maidservant standing near the entryway. To Saredi's confusion, she rushed forward with scepter already in hand, handing it to the baffled Vesikoi with a deep bow.

Saredi's eyes pinned Fusette in place. "This scene seems rather familiar, Your Grace," he said, his voice clipped. "I feel we went through this same dance when you Branded Gravebane. You had this planned before we even left, didn't you?"

Another giggle rang from the duchess' throat, accompanying a saucy smirk on her lips. "I can neither confirm nor deny such a thing, Lord Bastion," Fusette retorted.

Shaking his head, Saredi muttered, "Saints preserve me."

Fusette accepted the scepter, a simple brass rod with an octahedral diamond head decorated in varying colors of stained glass, with a broad smile and took several steps before spinning to face Kai's party. "Well then, shall we begin the official ceremony? Since there are so many, this will be a tad different from the traditional Branding. I feel it will be smoother to anoint each of you first before I give you the oath of service collectively. Now, all of you except for Kai, step forward please."

A bubble of laughter welled up in Kai's chest at his friends' gobsmacked faces. Maple and Orelia's faces erupted into matching crimson flushes as they lead the group in front of Fusette. He could see their eyes flickering towards the crowd, which had gone surprisingly quiet in that moment. Fusette stepped in front of Maple before twirling the scepter with a flourish.

"My friends," Fusette boomed, "in recognition of your acts of service in defense of Livoria and in accordance with the powers granted me by the Livorian Codex, I hereby anoint each of you as members of the Order of Exarch Knights. As such, you will be expected to uphold the laws of our realm and be guiding lights to the people. You must be willing to listen to the needs of those who seek your help and embody the Eight Paths of Virtue in all actions. Do you believe yourselves capable of fulfilling this duty?"

"Yes, Your Grace," the five responded in unison.

"Excellent." Fusette tapped Maple on both shoulders with the scepter. "Maplyne Travaldi, thank you for taking care of my cousin and being there to give us the cold, hard truth when we needed it. Your frank honesty is a breath of fresh air after all the duplicity I dealt with on the Parliament floor." The entire party broke out into suppressed chuckles. "I've had the pleasure of speaking with your parents and a certain Miss Clove several times since our return from Duskmarsh. Your old friend informed me of a certain nickname she gave you upon your departure from Shiverhill, inspired by the events that gave you that scar..."

Maple let out a drawn out groan, one hand pressing against her side where her scar peeked out from under her vest.

"By the winds, are you serious?" she whined. "I swear, if I ever see Clove again, I'll yank her tail feathers for saddling me with that silly name!"

Biting her lip, Fusette snickered. "I'll have you know I happen to like it. You should wear that badge with pride. From now on, you will be known as Featherbolt."

Sending a quick glance to the foot of the stairs, Kai spotted Cress and Willow laughing among themselves with Clove hiding directly behind them bent over in hysterics.

The ceremony continued as Fusette sidestepped in front of Orelia. "Orelia Travaldi," the duchess continued, "in all the time I've known you, you've proven yourself a champion of hope and justice. Where Maple can be a flexible purveyor of mischief when she sets her mind to it, you are the sturdy voice of reason your family can rely on. Thus, I am honored to offer you a Brand that symbolizes that role: Hopebearer."

Glistening tears trickled down Orelia's cheeks, her knees buckling in a sudden curtsy. "Thank you, Fusette. I love it," she said. Off to the side, Kai saw Ottoten holding back his own tears with a hand cupped over his mouth. The monarch drew Orelia into a sisterly embrace.

Next, Fusette moved to Ione, who still looked prepared to pass out. "Ione Rasina, of all the people I've ever met, few can match your unwavering faith and love. In spite of the trials you've faced, you ultimately never allowed the darkness to push you over the edge and remained the same gentle soul you've always been. That takes a level of willpower I find inspiring and you've served as a warm, motherly rock for those dearest to you. In honor of that hidden strength, I hereby name you Hearthfawn."

Fusette's words proved too much for Ione, sending her into gracious sobs. As with Orelia, Fusette offered the tavern maid a warm hug, something she was more than willing to return with open arms.

Moments later, Kai bit back a laugh when Teos snapped to attention with the crispness of a veteran sailor the instant Fusette drifted in front of him. "Teos, if there were ever a living embodiment of virtue and generosity, I believe I'm staring him in the eyes. While you were on the wrong side of the law for much of your life, it's obvious you held onto your morals and helped those in need in your own unique way. Your knowledge and skill in navigating our realm's rivers ensured the success of so many of your family's adventures. With that in mind, I grant you the Brand of Riverseer."

Teos removed his battered hat and dipped his head. "I shall try to live up to your faith in me, Lady Fusette. Just don't expect me to start parading around as stiffly as our mutual friend, the Lord Chamberlain."

Saredi's offended, "Oi!" sent ripples of laughter through everyone on the landing. Kai chewed his lip, seeing a surprising level of warmth in the older Vesikoi's slanted smirk. At last, Fusette shuffled to the side and stared a somber Lucretia in the eyes.

"Lucretia Dineri," Fusette said, "your dedication to your trade is unlike any I've witnessed. I must offer you the deepest of gratitude, both as Grand Duchess for the service you've performed during this war, and yet also as a woman searching for true family. When my father passed and I proved unable to visit Duskmarsh to see my mother, I worried I would remain alone and trapped within the duties of my throne. Because of you, I discovered a family I never knew existed as well as the hidden truths of my ancestry. Thus, thank you for proving to the world that the power of knowledge is greatest when wielded in the hands of the righteous. In dedication of these efforts, I give you the name Lorekeeper."

Bowing low, Lucretia's lips curved into a rare bright smile, her teeth shining in the early evening sun. "I am grateful for this honor, Your Grace. Thanks to you and Kai, I feel the shadows of my past are at last drifting away. I only wish that—"

The scholar's voice cracked before breaking down into sobs. Ione reached over and encircled an arm around her distraught friend's shoulder. Fusette gave a solemn nod. "I know," she whispered before facing the party as a group.

"That, in turn, brings me to Morgan Cauzet. As Kai mentioned, he was a splendid warrior and loyal friend without equal. I still remember his silly jokes and unorthodox humor with fondness. Morgan was proof of our ability to care for others and form bonds in spite of seemingly insurmountable differences. In recognition of his strength, both in body and spirit, I am happy to give him the posthumous Brand of Titanscale."

Stepping forward, Kai dropped to one knee in supplication. "Thank you, Lady Fusette. I'm glad to accept the honor in his name, though we all know Morgan would be proud to accept it himself if he were still with us."

"Certainly," Fusette replied. "As Exarchs, you will all be expected to serve the people in whatever capacity necessary. That being said, I'm already aware of your party's intention to retire from active combat, is that right?"

The party nodded in tandem, relieved smiles on each of their faces.

"That is indeed correct, Your Grace," Lucretia said. "While I cannot speak for the others, I am eager to return to the Citadel to resume my research into the faumen languages and translating their native works."

Fusette clenched her hand around the shaft of her spear. "While it is hard to see you step back in this manner, I can also empathize. If anyone has earned a life of peace in all this, it's you lot. All I can say is thank you for your service and I hope you'll still be open to accepting support missions should I need you."

Teos burst into laughter. "Of course, milady! We'll always be there to give you a hand when you need it. It's the least we could do."

"Excellent!" Fusette exclaimed. "First of all, what have I told you all about being overly proper with me?" The group bowed their heads with nervous grins at the admonishment. "Next, as one final gift, I'd like to bestow your party with a new title. Each of you have proven prime examples of the Paths of Virtue, in word *and* deed. So much so that it reminds me of the stories we grew up learning of Windbringer history."

Kai's eyes narrowed slightly, his hands gripping Maple and Orelia's tight. What was she planning now?

Raising Frimanir up and slamming its shaft on the cold stone, Fusette continued, "Thus, in honor of the heroism you've all displayed in saving Livoria and promoting the ideals of peace and cooperation, I hereby dub you all as the Seven Harmonies—the Wind Saints of our generation!"

The entire party arched back with moon-eyed stares while the crowd exploded into thunderous applause. The noise sent waves of pain pulsing through Kai's ears. Where before the cheering seemed to shake the palace, now the apothecary wouldn't have been surprised if the entire city were vibrating from the force of the acclaim they were hearing. Thousands of feet stomped the ground in unison with shouts of affirmation and gratitude filled the air. It took the combined efforts of the city guard and Fusette producing another blast on her warhorn to bring the audience's noise level to a manageable level again.

"I'm sure everyone is happy and eager to help rebuild our beautiful realm," Fusette pressed on. A twinge of concern ruffled Kai's mane seeing the look of exhaustion on her face. She looked to be leaning on her spear with each passing second. "However, you should know I and the rest of the new Grand Alezonian Alliance will be working together to restructure things in a manner that will, hopefully, prevent something like this from happening again. Now, I release you all back to your normal business. Please cooperate with the Navy, city guardsmen, and any other government officials as they work on helping those of you visiting from outside the city in returning to your homes. Good day to you all!"

The crowd let loose with a gentle yet still booming applause. Fusette released a heavy sigh and whispered to Saredi. Kai's ears twitched, hearing her instruct the Lord Chamberlain to attend to the other leaders and work on preparing a schedule for her. Casting a weary eye towards Kai, the duchess gestured for him and the rest of the newly named Harmonies to follow.

"Are you alright, Fusette?" Maple asked once the group entered the throne room and watched the monarch collapse in her throne.

Fusette's gaze drifted to the merchant. "I shall be fine," she murmured. "Eventually, anyway. My main concern will be reorganizing the nobility in the wake of this war. My father was right when he told me not to let them have too much leeway and that came back to bite us in several instances."

"Why not do away with the nobility entirely?" Orelia suggested, leaning on her staff with a curious expression.

It was Lucretia who refuted the idea with a shake of her head. "While it would be an effective solution, the nobility is far too ingrained to simply get rid of in one swoop," she explained. "A more probable method would be to redistribute some of their authority elsewhere, possibly with the guilds or even creating a new faction of Parliament formed entirely of elected representatives from every province."

Kai chuckled at the way his cousin's eyes lit up with glee. "That's a wonderful idea, Lucretia!" Fusette exclaimed. "Why not also promote some new blood to the nobility, as well? I could select individuals who have exhibited meritorious service and can provide a more...grounded model for the entrenched nobles to follow as an example of what is expected from someone of their rank. For starters, I need to select four new Margraves to handle the realm's largest provinces as Kendela was the only one who didn't defect to the Liberators, for obvious reasons, and we all know what happened to *him*."

The group nodded in waves. "That would definitely help," Kai replied. "The real question would be who to promote. We've been so busy with the war, I haven't met too many folks long enough to gauge whether they'd be appropriate for the role."

Raising his eyes, Kai felt a distinct chill ripple down his spine. Fusette was staring at him with a leonine grin he recognized when she was planning some form of mischief.

"I happen to be staring at a prime candidate right this moment," she said.

"Wait, *me*?!" Kai squawked, his tails going ramrod straight with fur on end. "Have you lost your kettle, Fusette? I'm not noble material!"

Beside him, his wives burst into amused titters. "I don't know," Maple trilled, "she may have a point. If anyone could teach those pompous nobles the proper way to act, you'd be the perfect example to follow."

Kai gulped. "Are you saying you think I should do it?" he asked.

A soft, cool hand cupped his chin and turned him to face Orelia. The young Vesikoi's head was tilted and a wistful smile danced across her lips.

"I don't think Fusette would be suggesting it unless she believed in you," she said. "It might not be an easy job to take, but if nothing else, it provides us with potential opportunities."

Running a hand through his mane, Kai considered the offer. While he had doubts in his ability to handle being a Margrave, he also knew Orelia was right. Plus, in a twisted sense he felt as though he at least owed Fusette a concession, considering their decision to step away from combat.

"Very well," he finally answered, "I'll do it."

The party burst into polite clapping. Fusette, on the other hand, looked ready to explode with happiness. "Oh that's wonderful to hear," she cried out.

"However," Kai continued, holding up a hand, "I'd like to have some say in which province I'll be taking over. I've been thinking about this retirement for a while, and I'd prefer it if we could base ourselves out of a town on the coast close enough to Galstein for Orelia to visit her family if need be. I've heard good things about Featherbrook, a tiny little port hamlet near the border."

"That sounds like a grand idea!" Orelia squealed, throwing her arms around Kai's neck and peppering him with kisses. "I know Mother and Father will be thrilled to hear the news."

"Permission granted," Fusette declared. "As I mentioned outside, I'll be working on restructuring the entire realm in the aftermath of the war. This likely includes redrawing the provincial borders. Thorncrest used to be the capital of the Stonecoast province, though with it being a decrepit ruin now, moving the province's operations to Featherbrook shouldn't prove too difficult. What do you plan to do after settling down?"

Glancing down at the two women on his arms, Kai's smile lit up the room.

"You should already know the answer to that, dear cousin."

Epilogue

F*ifteen Years Later...*

A loud yawn escaped Kai as he stood on the balcony. Gazing out the expansive grounds, he knew this house was much larger than those he remembered back in Havenfall, though nowhere near as grandiose as Fusette's original design.

He often wondered if his cousin's time as Grand Duchess skewed her sense of scale. Ever since her whirlwind romance and marriage to Rorik, Fusette had somehow become sassier than ever, to the point he received weekly correspondence from Saredi pleading for headache elixirs. Then again, that also might have been partially due to the Lord Chamberlain having to help the palace guards corral Fusette and Rorik's spirited young daughter, Hilda, who would be turning ten next moon.

At the same time, Fusette already knew he wasn't one for opulence, preferring the rustic and natural look of the forests he grew up around as opposed to the modern stone and stained glass found in Whistlevale. His manor's sturdy half-timbered construction and waves of ivy covering the outer walls were good examples of his most expensive architectural tastes. Still, Kai appreciated the extensive budget she provided as a late wedding gift to fund the construction. What hadn't gone into the building itself went towards the gardens and other projects in Featherbrook.

Once his family settled in the quaint seaside hamlet, it seemed as though a sizable number of folks wished to join them. The town was no longer as small as it used to be—in fifteen short years, Featherbrook's population swelled exponentially to over twenty thousand, transforming it into one of the largest cities in the duchy.

His eyes swept over the expansive gardens he had installed, including dozens of appleberry bushes scattered throughout as a gift to indulge his wife's tastes. Kai blushed, remembering the…exuberant way Maple rewarded him for *that* surprise. Still, they made her happy and provided his family with readily available snacks to nibble on in the early summer.

The sound of a child's voice clamoring outside the fence drew his gaze towards the gate. A deep chuckle rumbled in his chest.

"Now what is she up to?" he murmured, stretching out his back with a satisfying pop before leaping over the balcony railing to the cobblestone walkway below. He soon felt a small body slam into his chest, staggering him back.

"Papa!" a melodious voice rang out from around his waist. Kai couldn't hold back a grin as he knelt down and took in his daughter's disheveled appearance.

"Veldandi, what have I told you about playing in the dirt?" he scolded. She did her best to look admonished, but Kai could see the tiny smirk hidden there.

At thirteen, Veldandi was a perfect mix of Maple and himself, though she certainly inherited her mother's spark of life. Her hair, ebony with streaks of Maple's bright blonde mixed in, was cropped short with two chin-length bangs framing her face. She preferred having it short, claiming to despise the trouble of maintaining long hair. A pair of ears like his own sat atop her head, while two dorsal feathers jutted from her temple. Her wings were still small and covered with black feathers near the top but brightening to Maple's lemon shade at the tips. A scruffy mane was beginning to form on her upper chest, black with streaks of gold mixed in. Lastly, her two tails coiled around Kai's leg as she hugged him.

Wrapping her arms around her father, Veldandi buried her face in his chest. "I know, but one of the merchants visiting for the festival brought a family and they're not very nice. His son called Rowan and I freaks before pushing me over."

Kai frowned. The annual festival celebrating the Spring Equinox brought in all types, yet he hoped people had outgrown such nonsense. Then again, some refused to change with the times.

"I see. And what did you do, young lady?"

"I *may* have shoved him back, but you have to admit I didn't start it this time."

Chuckling, Kai sat in a nearby chair before setting Veldandi in his lap. "That might be true, sweetheart, but you know better than to fight. What kind of example are you setting for your siblings? You *are* the oldest, after all."

"But didn't you also tell me to stand up for our family?"

"Aye, that I did. Tell you what, let's go down to the market square and see if we can clear this up. Where is your brother, anyway?"

Veldandi rolled her eyes. "He ran to Mama's shop the first chance he could."

Kai exploded into a deep belly laugh. "That sounds like Rowan, alright. Come along, then."

Jumping from her father's lap, Veldandi shrieked when Kai plucked her off the ground once more and settled her on his shoulders. "Papa, cut it out! I'm not a little kid anymore," she exclaimed, thumping Kai on the forehead.

"Hush you. It wouldn't matter a whit if you were ten, twenty, or fifty years old; you'll always be my little princess, Veldi."

A thoughtful silence passed between them as Kai strolled down the road leading into the town proper. The apothecary smiled when he felt his daughter's fingers thread through his hair. "I guess that makes sense," she murmured, "but please don't embarrass me in front of my friends."

"Veldi, I'm your father. The tome of rules they gave me when you were born said embarrassing you was my primary job, even more important than being an apothecary."

She delivered another thump to his forehead. "You're just making that up!"

Kai snickered. "Perhaps, but you still love me, just as I love you."

Veldandi emitted a soft sigh, and Kai could visualize her looking at the ground with a hint of red in her cheeks. "I love you too, Papa," she whispered.

The market square was among the oldest areas in Featherbrook, though it had more than quadrupled in size to accommodate the booming population since Kai's family settled there. The plaza centerpiece was a brass statue of Morgan, cast and painted to a stunning likeness of the man standing tall with chest puffed out and his signature falchion leaning on one shoulder as he gazed skyward. While a local sculptor had done the casting, Kai had provided Tuvi her first commission as a crest-certified artisan to do the statue's planning sketches as well as painting the final product. The apothecary had been moved to tears by how realistic it looked once completed.

It was like having his brother back, watching over his new home from Finyt.

People from all walks of life bustled about the square, their faces bright and cheerful. Lines of push carts filled with material rolled in from the nearby train station. Steam trains were a technological marvel Kai still couldn't wrap his head around. The massive machines used much larger and heavier steam engines than what he was used to on river boats, yet they were capable of speeds that made travel across the realm quick and efficient to a level he never could have imagined as a younger man.

Across the plaza, merchants were prepping their stalls for the festivities to occur later that evening. Brilliant signs advertising their wares popped with color, each more eye-catching than the one before. Hordes of volunteers were assisting with the setup, some working on stalls with the merchants or helping out with those preparing food. The bulk, however, were amassed at the square's far end where they were constructing a massive stage. Fifteen yards tall at its apex and twenty across, it was an impressive structure.

It had to be, considering their intention to conduct a full song and dance performance on it as the highlight of the festival at moonrise.

Kai trudged along the street, offering passersby a jovial greeting with Veldandi waving from her perch atop his shoulders. Once they reached the plaza center, he set his daughter on the ground and ruffled her hair while sporting an affectionate grin.

"You want to go grab your mother and siblings while—"

A snide, drawling voice cut Kai off, decidedly male yet too high pitched to be an adult, "Looks like the little freak came back."

Eyes narrowed, Kai craned his neck backwards and set his gaze on a heavily muscled Soltauri boy about Veldi's age dressed in a soiled tunic and thick cotton trousers. His horns jutted forward from his temple, curving up at the tips, with a cocky sneer crossing his face while eyeing Veldi up and down.

"Now son," an older Soltauri grumbled behind the boy. His horns were identical to his child's, though he was of leaner build and dressed in a fine tan suit that contrasted against his darker skin. "You really shouldn't be so callous. After all, it's not entirely her fault she's an abomination—that falls on her parents."

Hand tightening into a fist, Kai threaded his fingers through Veldi's hair while pressing a single nail against her scalp. She stilled against him, clearly understanding the silent warning to not respond to their taunts.

"Judging by your accent," Kai growled, "You must be from Galstein. I'll admit it takes a lot of nerve to walk into an allied realm and hurl insults at people who haven't done a thing to wrong you. Especially when the one you're insulting is my daughter."

"On the contrary," the older Soltauri replied, "that wench assaulted my son. You can clearly see the dirt and mud covering him. I did not come to this backwater city to sell my wares just to see my heir trod upon by some mixblood trollop."

Despite a deep desire to roll his eyes, Kai suppressed the urge. His smile broadened when a familiar lilting voice trilled behind him.

"What seems to be the trouble, love?" Maple inquired. "Rowan came running into the store saying some boy was picking a fight." She was covered from dorsal feathers to talons in a thin layer of dust, the door of the general store she owned open just a few yards back. Her loose sleeveless tunic and bison-hair skirt fluttered in the breeze. Most importantly, her eyes, still bright and full of life, were pinched together in a tilted frown.

Behind her, a small head poked out drawing a kind smile from Kai. His younger son, nine-year-old Rowan, definitely took after his own looks more than his sister, with predominately ebony fur and feathers interspersed with minuscule streaks of blonde, as well as his trademark grey eyes. He was also one of the gentlest souls Kai had ever seen.

"So you're the mother of these...creatures," the Soltauri continued in his haughty tone. "It seems there's no accounting for taste among you Livorians."

Kai inched back a step, seeing his wife's eyes contracting into violet pinpricks. Even though he could be aggressive in defending his family, he had enough self-awareness to know he didn't hold a candle to his partners. Kai was grateful when, before Maple could smear the man across the cobblestones, another voice snapped from behind the surly visitor.

"What in the sacred winds is *that* supposed to mean?" Orelia intoned, her voice flat and lips set in a thin line. Behind her stood a congregation of small children of various tribes and ages. Several of them giggled under their breath, seeing Orelia brandishing her staff threateningly towards the Soltauri. "No self-respecting Galstan would treat a Livorian with such contempt."

One of the children piped up, "You tell him, headmistress!"

The visiting merchant's nostrils flared. "I suggest you keep your nose out of other's business, woman," he warned, "and take those brats with you."

Two small bodies pushed their way around Orelia, the front one shouting in challenge, "Don't you speak to my mother like that, you barrel-headed dipwit!"

Kai burst into laughter. Of all his children, Tyrhelm had a temper to match his mother Orelia's while only being younger than Veldi by a year, yet it was surprisingly balanced by a determination to defend those in trouble. Behind him stood the youngest of the triad's children, Cordelia. A shy, gentle girl of only five, she peeked out from behind her brother, her cyan eyes peering up at Orelia with a nervous expression.

His and Orelia's children paired their mother's dusky skin with Kai's angular features and dense muscles. Both sported a set of Vesikoi gills under their ribs, though Tyrhelm was noticeably stocky in build, a trait Guri once mentioned likely came from Kai's paternal grandfather. Tyrhelm's ears were long and thin like Orelia's, though covered in vermillion fur, where Cordelia's were an exact copy for her mother's. Both had a pair of red-furred tails swaying behind, with Tyrhelm's being shorter and thicker compared to his sister's.

The merchant's gaze swiveled between Orelia and Kai in disgust. By now, much of the crowd had halted their preparations for the festival, preferring to gather around the confrontation in keen interest. Kai's eyes darted back and forth, wondering the best way to diffuse the situation without causing an incident.

The Soltauri boy flashed a rude gesture towards Tyrhelm. "You're just as much of a freak as the other two, especially that ugly, vicious thing," he shouted, pointing a finger at Veldi.

It was no surprise when Tyrhelm's ears wiggled, his fur standing on end. "You wanna insult my sister again?" he warned while cracking his knuckles.

"Tyr!" Kai barked.

He was pleased to see his son grit his teeth and step back. "Sorry, Dad," he murmured. Orelia tugged him into a one-armed hug, a face-splitting grin stretched across her lips.

"Oi! What the piss is all the commotion over here?" a heavy baritone voice called out. Kai's smirk widened.

Veldi let out a happy gasp and launched herself at the trio ambling through the crowd behind them.

"Uncle Teos!" she squealed, slamming against the former smuggler's waist and nearly knocking him over. Her eyes grew brighter seeing the rest of her father's friends step in line behind Teos. "Auntie Io! Auntie Lu!"

Ione picked Veldi up and cradled her in a smothering embrace. "By the winds, young lady, you get bigger every time I come to visit," the former tavern maid exclaimed.

"Yeppers!" Veldi replied. "Mama says I'll probably be taller than her before I turn seventeen. How are Larina and the meadhouse?"

"Oh, they're doing well. Larina's proving to be almost as good a cook as your father, so I think it'll be just fine when she takes over if I ever decide to retire."

Veldi giggled. "Auntie Io, the only way you'll retire is if Papa or Auntie Fu march into Grantide and make you."

"She has you there, Ione," Lucretia piped up with a broad grin. "You love that meadhouse almost as much as I love my tomes. Granted, even I will admit I could not handle the workload of that place as well as you. I shall take my Highmistress duties at the Citadel any day."

"I've had enough of this nonsense," the merchant growled. "I demand the city guard be brought here at once to deal with that...child! I happen to be a good friend of the Margrave here, so you'd best start treating me with some respect."

Kai's eyebrows flew into his hairline. He shared an amused glance with his friends and family. Sweeping his gaze across the crowd, it was easy to see the majority struggling to contain their mirth. The head of the local carpenter's guild, a kindly older man who lived just down the street from the manor, was bent over with a fist jammed in his mouth.

It was Teos who cupped both hands to his lips and bellowed, "Oi, Kai, when did this happen? I've never seen this asshole before in my life! Are we not good enough for you anymore?"

That proved more than enough to send the entire plaza into con-vulsions of laughter. Men, women, and children alike fought to remain standing while wheezing in glee. More than half were pointing at the blushing merchant, whose face twisted into a mixture of shame and anger.

"How dare you!" the man finally screamed. His son looked equally angry yet seemed aware enough to hold his tongue. "What is that bastard even talking about? Why would I ever be friends with a winds-be-damned *peltneck*?"

The moment the words left his lips, the crowd's jovial mood shifted. At once, the laughter and hilarity transformed into outraged jeers and insults. His anger melted away, leaving a growing sense of fear as his eyes swept over the mass of people who looked ready to swarm him.

Kai's eye twitched, his hands resting at once on Maple's shoulder before the Aerivolk could begin advancing towards the man. "I'm giving the ben-efit of the doubt and assuming you haven't been to Livoria since the War," he stated, "but these days, tribal slurs such as that are considered Class 2 hate crimes, punishable by a two-week stint in the gaol, *at minimum*, plus a hundred mark fine."

The merchant's eyes narrowed. "Who in the blazes came up with a law like that?" he demanded.

Kai's lips curved into a smirk, his fangs glinting in the sunlight. "That would be my cousin, Fusette. You might know her better by her title of Grand Duchess, however." The man's eyes bulged. "Perhaps I should properly introduce myself: Kai Travaldi, chief apothecary of Feather-brook and, for reasons I still cannot fathom, Margrave of the province Stonecoast."

The merchant's eyes further swelled to a hilarious size, his breath catching. His head swiveled about, as if expecting the crowd to burst into laughter again due to Kai's statement being nothing but a joke. Instead, the angry stares remained. If anything, they now looked even more fu-rious, with several men cracking their knuckles and leering at him with dangerous expressions.

"Now then," Kai continued, "I'll give you two options. The first is you take accountability for breaking a law, even if you may not have been aware of it—ignorance is not innocence, after all. That means paying your fine and, if you're on good behavior, I can let you out of the gaol in a week rather than the required two."

The Soltauri frowned. "Why would you be so lenient?"

"To put it simply, I've heard that slur more often than I'd ever care to," Kai answered. "If bending the rules a little will let me get you out of this realm, and my fur, faster, I'm all for it. That's actually why I'd prefer you to take the second option."

"Which would be...?"

"Easy. You pack up your carriage and your family and start marching your tail back across that border, because if I still see your mug here when the festival starts in three hours, I might be tempted to leave your punishment up to my lovely wives. And trust me, they're *nowhere* near as lenient as I am."

The merchant's gaze swung between Maple and Orelia, both of whom wore haughty grins that promised an unpleasant experience if he tested their patience. Kai's ears twitched as he heard the man grumbling under his breath. Eventually, he gave a defeated nod and promised to leave. The boy stared at his father in shock.

"But Father-"

"Silence, Eldro! Now come. We must find your mother and prepare to leave. It is clear we're not wanted here." The man turned a stormy glare towards Kai. "Be aware, though, that I will be bringing this matter of your disrespect to the attention of the Galstan court and Her Majesty."

Rather than respond, Kai simply tilted his head towards the main road leading out of the city, a blank expression on his face. The man scuttled off with his son, loading the boy into a nearby carriage near the plaza entrance. Within minutes, he had also ushered a woman who could only be his wife into the carriage, climbed into the driver's box, and sent the two wirochs hitched to it into a rushing trot.

Maple slung her arms around Kai's neck and nuzzled her cheek against his mane. "Why'd you have to let him off so easy, love? I know how much you hate that word."

"I know. Think about it, though. What do you think Isolde and Ottoten will do if he's enough of a dipwit to go through with that threat? Especially considering I see Orelia over there penning what I assume is a letter to her father."

The crowd's eavesdropping was made clear when every head in the plaza spun to the priestess-turned-teacher, who was scratching a quill over parchment fast enough Kai could have sworn he saw smoke rising from it.

"I take it back," Maple quipped, "anything I can come up with will be a love tap compared to what Ottoten will do. Wish I could be a fly on the wall for *that*."

A young Norzen woman wearing a pristine uniform and armored breastplate over her strawberry blonde fur, with a partizan spear leaning over one shoulder, cast an affectionate glare at Kai. "With all due respect, milord, you just took away one of the rare chances for me or any of the other city guard to actually have some excitement on the job."

Kai shared a mischievous grin with his partners. "You know, Sigrid, I'm glad Guri recommended to have you finish out your guard apprenticeship here. You've done a wonderful job. However, if you're that desperate for excitement, I could always task you with keeping up with my rambunctious sprouts."

The young woman's eyes widened, drifting to Veldi and Tyr, both of whom rubbed their palms in a conspiratorial manner.

"I think I'll pass, sir. I love your children as if they were my own siblings, but I can already tell those two in particular will do everything they can to turn my fur as grey as my eyes before I even turn twenty."

Waves of snickers rose from the crowd.

"I think Lord Kai had the right of it," a grizzled Wasini man commented from where he was helping set up the stage, a large hammer in his hand as he wiped his brow. "Best to send him on his way back to where he came from and let *them* decide what to do with him. We didn't go through all that trouble in the War just to sit back and let bigots like him spout off. If he wants to say things like that, he can do it back home where he'll still have to face the consequences of running his mouth without thinking."

Kai let out a grunt when Veldi climbed up the back of his robes and perched herself on his shoulders again. "At least he's leaving now," she said. "But let's hurry and finished setting up for the festival. I want to watch the show!"

Everyone erupted into peals of renewed laughter.

"You heard the little lady," Kai declared, raising a fist into the air, "let's get this stage built so we have plenty of time to have some real fun!"

Cheers reverberated through the plaza. The crowd dispersed into a flurry of movement with everyone returning to their previous tasks. Kai and his family were joined by their friends as they approached the budding stage, each of the adults grabbing their own hammers and getting to work. Kneeling between a smiling middle-aged man and a burly Vesikoi woman, Kai's face bloomed into a smile seeing his children gather around to watch everyone working together, followed soon by the horde Orelia brought from the schoolhouse.

Memories of the past fifteen years of peace flashed through his mind, causing his grin to stretch from ear to ear. Things weren't perfect and there were still those with hateful views across Alezon. His confrontation with the Galstan merchant proved that. Still, it warmed his heart seeing the townsfolk get so outraged on his behalf. Such a thing would've been unheard of before the War. It may have been the roughest year of his life, filled with loss and worry, but Kai knew he wouldn't change it for anything. After all, it gave him the one thing he desired more than anything, the first taste of which he was blessed with on the day Gaspard and Verona Travaldi found him on the banks of the Great Ardei River.

Family—one forged not by blood, but by the bonds they made on their journey.

GLOSSARY

Abyssal – The traditional Norzen pantheon's equivalent to Nulyma. Said to be a dreary place filled with forests of dead trees tended by the souls of those who died committing more heinous selfish acts than selfless.

Aerian – The native language of the Aerivolk tribe.

Aerivolk – A bird-like faumen tribe able to take running glides at high speeds. They have the strongest eyesight and are considered the most peaceful of the tribes. They are most famous for their artistry with fabrics.

Alezon (pronounced Al-a-zon) – The southern continent of Nixtral. Consists of five realms and is infamous as the origin point of the faumen tribes.

Ashers – Conjurers able to channel the element of Dust, associated with stone and dirt.

Ausrina the Wanderer – One of the Wind Saints. An Aerivolk traveler who joined the Wind Saints during the Desolation Wars. Not much is known about her. Known as the Saint of Honesty.

Ballad's End – A range of rocky, cliff-ridden hills surrounding the plains outside Whistlevale. They earned their name from bards who could see Whistlevale from the hilltops, declaring it to be the beginning of the end of their long journey.

Belomas Highlands – An ancient Alezonian realm known as the birthplace of the faumen. They are led by a Chiefs Council, currently headed by Chief Velibor.

Berelmir – A warlord who conquered several Galstein provinces until meeting his end at the hands of the Wind Saints.

Blitzers – Conjurers able to channel the element of Spark, associated with lightning and magnetism.

Cacovis the Shadow – Co-leader of the Wind Saints alongside Galen. A Norzen carpenter and village leader who became infamous for bringing about the Desolation to free the lands that would become Livoria. Also known as the Fallen Saint or the Saint of Pride.

Centric – The primary trading language of Nixtral.

The Citadel – Livoria's foremost learning academy. Located in Runegard, it was once the fortress of the warlord Berelmir and now consists of four scholar divisions that work together to accumulate and advance knowledge within Livoria.

Conjurers – Individuals able to harness the magic of Origin. As of now, only those of faumen descent are believed to be capable of being born with the ability.

Corlati Federation – The most technologically advanced of the five Alezonian realms. Human superiority is preached as gospel, faumen are often kept as slaves, and most inhabitants follow the teachings of the warrior monk Cadell, known collectively as Cadism. Led by President Gideon Harmod.

Cuballa – The Norzen pantheon's equivalent to Finyt. A paradisaical land where the righteous go after death.

The Desolation – A massive explosion caused by Cacovis via triggering a massive lekrite vein, which wiped out a swath of land between Livoria, Galstein, and Corlati.

Dolmaru the Quillblade – One of the Wind Saints. A Wasini warrior scholar who joined the Wind Saints during the Desolation Wars. He was responsible for opening the Citadel and served as its first Highmaster. Known as the Saint of Courage.

Drifters – Conjurers able to harness the element of Breeze, associated with the wind.

Edeval the Bandit Lord – One of the Wind Saints. An Aerivolk thieving band leader and former nobleman who joined the Wind Saints during the Desolation Wars. Known as the Saint of Loyalty.

Exarch Knights – The most prestigious order of Livoria. Known as the duchy's most skilled protectors, they are a special class of noble given a unique epithet by the Grand Duke or Duchess called a Brand.

Faumen – Demi-humans with animal characteristics that *mostly* originated from the Belomas Highlands. There are six currently known tribes in Alezon with their own unique strengths. However, there are other tribes located throughout Nixtral's three other continents.

Feswili (pronounced Fez-wi-lee) – The northern continent of Nixtral. Not much is known about this place other than being much colder than the other continents and is the ancestral homeland of two faumen tribes: The Risbado and the Norzen.

Finyt (pronounced Feh-neet) – The land of paradise, according to Windbringer doctrine. It is said to be full of gardens and rivers where no war or conflict exists.

Fullblood – A faumen of pure lineage with no intermixing among humans or other tribes.

Galen the Sage – Co-leader of the Wind Saints. A human warrior monk who led the resistance against the warlord Berelmir. He was known for his wisdom and sense of fairness. Known as the Saint of Justice.

Grand Duchy of Livoria – The youngest of the Alezonian realms. It was once a series of Galstan provinces conquered by Berelmir, but gained independence following the Desolation Wars. Led by the Grand Duchess, Fusette Ardei.

High Norzen – The native language of the Norzen.

Holy Queendom of Galstein – A peaceful realm located in southeastern Alezon. Galstein is the historical ally of Livoria, ruled by a matriarchal royal family and famous for the potency of its medicinal herbs. Led by Queen Isolde Graffeld.

Igniters – Conjurers able to harness the element of Heat, associated with fire.

Kingdom of Hilderic – A predominently Norzen realm on the south-central coast of Feswili. It is the ancient homeland of the Norzen tribe.

Lekrite – A purple, energy-dense mineral found in scattered pockets throughout Nixtral. It is highly reactive to shock and will explode if mishandled. Cacovis used it in order to bring about the Desolation.

Luopari the Oracle – One of the Wind Saints. A Vesikoi soothsayer who joined the Wind Saints during the Desolation Wars. She is among the most popular of the Saints. Known as the Saint of Faith.

Mariners – Conjurers able to harness the element of Mist, associated with water.

Mixblood – A faumen of mixed heritage, usually with one faumen and one human parent. Mixbloods of two tribes are possible, but exceedingly rare and considered taboo.

Nixtral – The planet upon which the story takes place. It encompasses four major continents, one at each cardinal direction.

Norzen – A cat-like faumen tribe known for their two tails and sensitive ears. Now known to be originally from the southern reaches of Feswili. They are ostracized for their association with Cacovis, the one who caused the Desolation. However, they are also famous for their skills in engineering and scouting.

Nulyma (pronounced Nu-lee-ma) – According to Windbringer doctrine, a hellish void made of five levels where the damned go to suffer for their sins.

Order of the Windbringers – The primary church within Livoria and Galstein that reveres the Wind Saints as heroes and protectors.

Origin – The natural magic energy of Nixtral. The faumen tribes were originally able to manipulate it to achieve great magical feats. Now, Conjurers are able to harness it through six primary elements, each historically associated with a different tribe.

Risbado – A fox-like faumen tribe native to the northern continent, Feswili. They have thick, bushy tails and pelts of fur covering their arms and torso. Many Risbado are short and stocky compared to the Norzen, their taller, leaner historical rivals.

Rodekan Empire – The oldest of the Alezonian realms, the Rodekans were considered the premier slave traders of Nixtral for centuries until several of its provinces declared independence and formed the Corlati Federation. Currently led by Emperor Kabuji Aduleji.

Seeders – Conjurers able to harness the element of Timber, associated with plants and wood.

Soltauri – A bovine-like faumen tribe who typically have hooves for feet and two horns atop their heads. The tallest and strongest of the tribes, they are commonly seen as guards and soldiers. Historically nomadic, they are known for their skill in farming.

Soltish – The native language of the Soltauri.

Tapimor the Lifeweaver – One of the Wind Saints. A human apothecary who joined the Wind Saints during the Desolation Wars. Now considered a patron of the healing arts and the harvest. Known as the Saint of Compassion.

Vadako the Maiden – One of the Wind Saints. A Soltauri priestess who joined the Wind Saints during the Desolation Wars. A popular Saint among young women, she was famous for her kindness and willingness to help others. Known as the Saint of Generosity.

Vesikoi – A fish-like faumen tribe noted for their mottled skin, usually pale in the front with darker shades on the back. They are primarily water-based and famous for their craftsmanship with shells and gemstones.

Voidlands – The uninhabitable wasteland where the Desolation occurred. Once a thriving forest, it was reduced to a barren desert where nothing can grow by Cacovis' use of lekrite.

Wasini – A faumen tribe who have snake-like tails covered in armored scales for their lower bodies. They are the heaviest of the faumen and historically known as both great warriors and blacksmiths.

Wasjek – The native language of the Wasini.

Wind Saints – A group of eight heroes jointly led by Galen the Sage and Cacovis the Shadow who saved the lands that would become Livoria from the warlord Berelmir.

About the Author

Cyrus Whelchel grew up in Converse, Texas, where both his local and school libraries were his home away from home. His favorite book growing up was *The Thief Lord* by Cornelia Funke.

After hopping between various jobs in early adulthood, Cyrus re-discovered his love of books and dedicated himself to being a Children's Librarian, where he now shares his passion for stories with the next generation.

An avid reader of fantasy and mystery, Cyrus loves the challenge of anticipating the end of a good story. Inspired by the historical challenges faced by his father's Jewish ancestors, *The Faumen War Chronicles* shows the importance of accepting each other's differences, being true to oneself, and standing strong against discrimination, no matter where you may find it.